Face to Face

John Odd

Cover created by Clare Brayshaw

Set in Lucida Bright 10 pt

Prepared by:

York Publishing Services Ltd
64 Hallfield Road
Layerthorpe
York YO31 7ZQ
Tel: 01904 431213
Website: www.yps-publishing.co.uk

Dedication

The Author would like to dedicate this seven-year work to the following individuals:

John James Odd & Mildred Odd – for giving the form through which he works;

John Vince & John Paternoster – for giving initial editing and marketing systems.

Cathi Poole & Duncan Beal for the design & printing of this work.

---oOo---

The Author would like to dedicate this seven-year work to the following collectives:

The Rosicrucian Order of Freemasons;

All Patriarchal Orders & All Matriarchal Covens;

All Divine Faiths whose Diverse Spokes 'link' the Rim to the Hub;

To 'Man' & to God.

To Les
Good Luck with *Your* Book!

Jeff Odd

Foreword

This work was written over a seven-year period and represents an exhaustive 'download' of experiences gleaned from academic and illuministic theory & practice.

This work is of a highly occult nature. It has been written and arranged in a particular style so as to cause the conscious aspect of the reader's mind to gradually receive the 'hidden' illuminating intelligence via subliminal programming that is the birthright of all humanity – despite the protestations of the State.

Because of its nature and purpose, this work appears to contradict the intentions of all the governments of the world. The intentions of all 'elite' bureaucracies are to either manipulate (1st World tactic) or to intimidate (3rd World tactic) humanity in order to exploit, profiteer and control. The 'elite' are forced into this 'way of life' because of an in-built pathological fear of loss and death. This fear of death spreads systemically eventually corrupting all officials and corroding all pillars of authority. One may then reasonably ask why this work should exist since all know that "evil turns upon itself."

This work was created to release society from the bondage of a lie. The lie that "life is finite! This is it! Accept our rule or you'll pay a higher or even the ultimate price!"

Life is *infinite*. It is an *evolution* – a series of incarnations interspersed with periods of 'anti-stasis' where the individual temporarily becomes connected to a collective for a 'downloading' of experiences – and receives an 'upgrading' of awareness as a reward.

Via the 'medium' of a gentle 'fictional' story, this work will cause you to *remember*.

Through the eyes of the main character, David Thorne, the reader is brought into contact with all the 'thorny' issues that constitute a continuous 'plague' on humanity

All areas of contention are addressed via a synthesis of exoteric (Academic) subjects including:

> Theology/Theosophy/Philosophy/Psychology/
> Sociology/Anthropology/Etymology/Economics/
> Ecology/ History.

Together with a synthesis of 'reflective' esoteric (Illuministic) subjects including:

> Occultism/Mysticism/Psychism/Rosicruciansim/
> Cabalism/Paganism/Witchcraft/Alchemy.

All of the above are synthesised into one holistic principle from which this work was created for your entertainment and your enlightenment.

Chapter 1

High above the city skyline, the sun beat down mercilessly on the morning mist that had moved inland from the coast. As always, the sun would eventually triumph and those below who scuttled to work would actually curse yet another warm day.

Legions of industrial grade air-con units were already humming at full capacity anticipating another heavy day of commerce in this former temperate country.

Landlocked within an 'ocean' of corporate buildings, one non-descript building was already humming with activity. On the ground floor – behind the sterility of the reception foyer, a great beast continually roared and vomited up mountains of trivia for the consumption of its masters. One floor above, numerous figures were bent in supplication over altars of terminal input desperately trying to create new revelations to replace the old. If they ran out of revelations – if they actually failed to feed the beast on time, they were consigned to hell!

Compared to the shop floor, the general office was almost silent – but that was merely an appearance. It quietly hissed with controlled activity. Many minds were working at fever pitch disgorging nourishment into hydra mouths that were forever hungry.

One bright young mind that was housed in a prematurely ageing body was in the midst of creating another 'revelation' when his phone rang. He jumped nervously as he knew that direct phone calls meant trouble. He picked up the receiver aware that his colleagues were watching him. The disembodied voice was brief but clear.

"My office, please." The line went dead.

Putting down the receiver in as casual a manner as possible, the junior reporter tried to exit the general office without being noticed. He quietly closed the door behind him and walked a few paces down the corridor to stand before a similar door entitled: Assistant Editor (Special Projects).

Waiting in the corridor, the junior reporter winced as the choral hum of "Chestnuts Roasting On An Open Fire" floated from the general office door and down the corridor to where he was standing. He jumped and looked back to the general office as its door opened and a colleague poked his head around grinning and saying, "Yours are on a plate mate!"

The junior reporter hesitated outside the assistant editor's door, took a breath, knocked and waited.

"Enter." came a toneless voice.

He entered, closed the door and stood quietly in front of the desk.

David Thorne, Assistant Editor (Special Projects) was gazing at a small greying flower that was pressed behind glass in a small picture frame on his desk.

Silence descended.

"He's trying to make me sweat and it's working." the reporter thought.

That was his second mistake of the day.

The assistant editor sighed and let his gaze go to the young man and raised his eyebrows questioningly. "Well?"

"I'm sorry, it won't happen again."

"You're sorry it won't happen again? That smacks of anarchy!"

The reporter was momentarily thrown.

"You're sorry, *and* it won't happen again."

The reporter's face cleared. "Yes sir."

"What did you do?"

"I made an assumption and reported out of context."

"Yes, you did. It may be old fashioned and initially sells fewer newspapers but I believe in the principle of *reporting* news not *creating* it. It helps avoid wars by *informing* the public not *inflaming* them. Since you know what you've done, you will correct it before it goes to print. Good day, sir!"

The reporter nodded, relief evident on his face and left the office thinking that on balance it might be a good day after all.

Thorne watched him go and shook his head. Checking his desk diary and noting that today was the retirement party for the editor-in-chief, his thoughts turned once again to the flower and its significance.

---oOo---

Years before, he had been a senior reporter for the Tribune and had been sent abroad to report on a court case that had involved the death of a man who, because of his long list of convictions was likely to be mourned by few. The man's death was unusual in that he had been on the receiving end of a pike. What made it even more unusual was that the corpse was found inside the border of some obscure country that was adjacent to the one he was currently in, and that the perpetrator was one of its border guards who said that he was merely doing his duty.

In the court he had listened to the usual war of ideologies between Human Rights, Natural Justice and Diplomacy, or the Indignant, the Indifferent and the Incredible – as he regarded them – and had a fair idea who would win.

It was the usual format. The loudest were the Indignant trumpeting Human Rights, Civil Liberties, Penal Reform, Trauma Counselling and Compensation for the criminals who were actually the *victims* of society. As usual, the victims of the criminal were conveniently forgotten – the Indignant weren't so indignant about *them*.

The Indifferent, however, were all smiling quietly since they realised that because this case involved an *international* situation, the Incredible would probably win the day.

Sitting in the press gallery, Thorne was doing his job noting the impartial facts of the case, whilst another part of his mind was trying to judge the public mood, in order to slant the context prior to print in order to maximise sales. He was busy taking notes and starting to settle into his routine when something made him focus on the visiting ambassador speaking in court.

For a diplomat, the man's words made perfect sense, but his body language did not.

Thorne's nose for the unusual took over.

The representative seemed uncomfortable in his suit as though he was unused to such apparel, and this seemed to fly in the face of his obvious ability as an ambassadorial lawyer. The conclusion to the hearing was never in doubt; diplomacy had already won despite the vocal minorities in the house. Thorne had lost interest in the vanquished, but had gained considerable interest in the victor and was determined to learn more.

As the court was clearing, Thorne descended the stairs from the gallery and watched for the ambassador to emerge. Eventually he spotted him and followed him outside expecting him to get into a waiting car or at least hail a cab, but he did neither. The ambassador walked along the street for some distance, hesitated awkwardly at the curb, crossed the road in obvious unease, turned down a side street and walked halfway down arriving at a large but old hotel where he checked into the foyer. Watching from outside the entrance Thorne heard the ambassador ask for his key to room 420, which was on the top floor.

The ambassador, although fitter than average was well past middle years and Thorne, expecting him to take the elevator was quite surprised to see him use the foyer stairs. "Maybe he's a fitness fanatic!" he said to himself, but his instinct told him otherwise.

With plenty of time on his hands, Thorne surveyed the public lounge which was adjacent to the foyer stairs and, noting its air of faded glory decided to blend in with the scenery to see if the ambassador would return for any refreshment. He decided against ordering alcohol as it would dull his senses and necessitate his sitting at the bar. Instead, he ordered a pot of tea which would be more appropriate to sitting in the lounge near the flow of residents, plus it would allow him much more 'idle time' thus improving his chances of success.

As he was into his second cup, the ambassador walked in and sat down at the table next to his. Thorne gave him a friendly nod and raised his cup. The ambassador returned his nod and called over the waitress. He ordered a pot of hot water and she disappeared behind an ornate screen into the kitchen. When she returned and put down the tray, the ambassador removed a small bag from his pocket and tapped out a measure of its contents into the pot of hot water. Giving one brief stir he poured out a cup using the strainer, and looking in Thorne's direction he raised it and said, "Good health sir!"

Thorne raised his cup again. "And you sir, but is that tea?"

"Mint." replied the ambassador. "It cleanses the body and polishes the mind."

"I must try that sometime." said Thorne.

"I will be returning home tomorrow, so why not try some now?"

"Well..... thank you Mr.....?"

"Just call me Chevral." smiled the ambassador.

Thorne offered his hand. "And my name is David Thorne."

"Pleased to meet you Mr Thorne, I'll ask the waitress for a fresh cup for you." Chevral studied Thorne's outstretched hand and then, looking him directly in the face said, "I mean no offence but the customs of my people do not include contact between strangers."

Thorne lowered his hand and said, "Strangers are friends you have yet to meet."

"The words of a diplomat!" Chevral beckoned the waitress for another cup.

Thorne laughed. "I'm no diplomat."

"What are you then?"

"A journalist by trade."

"One of the report and distort brigade?"

"For someone who means no offence, you do a pretty good job offending!"

"If you felt offended, you wouldn't be a journalist – ahh, here's the cup!"

Chevral poured a cup of mint and offered it saying, "- Kills all known journalists!"

Thorne realising the social 'ice' had been broken started laughing and was joined by the other.

Post-glacial melt, and after several sips of mint; the atmosphere had eased and both felt it was time to level with the other.

"What do you *really* want Mr Thorne?"

"You spoke of the customs of your people, and I'd like to learn more."

Chevral paused for a few seconds and looked thoughtful.

"Is there a problem with that request?" asked Thorne.

"I presume you attended court today?" said Chevral.

"In gainful employment." said Thorne.

"I don't suppose you'd go away if I asked you?"

"I don't suppose I would."

"Hmm..... You have chosen the ideal time to strike, Mr Thorne, since my country cannot afford another scandal so soon after this one. The cards of Self Determination and Diplomatic Immunity can only be played sparingly if they are to remain effective."

Thorne was elated. *Now* was the time to push. "Unlimited access?"

"Agreed." came the mild reply.

Chapter 2

They had agreed to meet outside Chevral's hotel the following day at 09-00. On returning to his own hotel, Thorne had rung his editor that evening and got special permission for an indefinite stay on an 'exclusive' and packed his bags in advance. The following morning, foregoing breakfast, he rose particularly early and arrived at the hotel a good ninety minutes ahead of schedule, and waited below the stairs just in case Chevral decided to 'do a bunk.'

After ninety minutes of fighting feelings of guilt in case he was wrong, anger in case he was right and hunger because of his empty stomach he was rewarded with the sight of Chevral descending the stairs and Thorne's stomach let out a gurgle of anticipation.

"Good day Mr Thorne, shall we get started?"

Thorne hoped he meant breakfast but Chevral's words soon dashed that.

"I have booked a coach to arrive any moment and then I can honour my word."

Thorne smiled professionally. "Good." he said publicly. "Shit." he thought privately.

The cab duly arrived and, after stowing their bags they were soon speeding out of the city along a major route into the countryside. Thorne had briefly wondered why Chevral had referred to it as a 'coach' but was too busy trying to subdue his stomach whose gurgles were evolving into growls.

"Mint?" offered Chevral.

"Missed breakfast." confessed Thorne.

"Well you would, arriving when you did." Chevral sighed and shook his head. "Mr Thorne, I can understand your lack of trust due to the nature of *your* culture, but once you have understood the nature of *my* culture, you may be able to find from us that which you have lost from your own."

"A utopian civilisation? How come the rest of the world doesn't know?"

Chevral smiled. "A journalist equipped with unlimited access - *you* find out!"

"That sounds like a challenge!"

"Your problem, not mine."

Thorne spent the rest of the journey in silent contemplation.

The cab travelled for another half-hour before Chevral told the driver to stop. "Here we are."

Thorne looked around and saw open fields and little else. "Where?"

"Pay the driver would you, this is *your* assignment after all."

Thorne gave the driver his fare and was rewarded with his luggage.

"Am I being stitched up Mr Ambassador?"

"Not at all Mr Thorne." The cab left a cloud of dust behind. "Now we walk!"

"Which way?"

"Follow me!" said Chevral giving a wink. He pulled two straps from the sides of his bag and, pulling it over his shoulders, began to walk confidently down a track between fields towards some hills in the distance. Thorne trudged behind carrying his luggage, his stomach worse than ever.

After two hours of solid walking covering some five miles, Chevral looked around and announced, "Here we rest." He dropped his customised backpack and fished inside bringing out two bottles of spring water and a pack of biscuits. "Your culture has its benefits and you look as though you need them right now." He handed a bottle and the pack of biscuits to Thorne, "Just going behind that bush to get out of these awful clothes!"

Thorne hadn't lost his professional irony. "Headline news; Ambassador a Naturist!"

A chuckle came from behind the bush, "I don't think my *natural* costume would make any headline news, but perhaps my *national* costume might." Eventually, he emerged wearing clothing that was in the style of the mid/late Georgian period. He wore top- boots, dark brown riding breeches with matching frock coat, white shirt with cravat and a garish waistcoat in orange with gold leaves. Seeing Thorne's look of amazement he said, "Better than naturism eh?"

"Where's the wig and tricorn hat?"

"Never popular, too dated!"

Chevral drained his own bottle, packed it and hoisted up his backpack, "Time to go."

They started to climb the deceptively boring hills towards the forest above.

Thorne had always regarded himself as being fairly fit in comparison to the general populace of his own country. On his numerous jaunts along the streets he had lost count of the number of people who were – to him – Blobs. This attitude of smugness had contributed greatly to his own sense of superiority and thus to his confidence which often bordered on arrogance. However, finding himself two-thirds up this bloody hill, and having to ask for another rest – his *third* so far, he was faced with the awful realisation that he was unfit and overweight.

Strangely enough, Chevral had made no comment and had acceded to his requests each time. He would wait quietly for Thorne to dictate the pace of the ascent – leading Thorne to conclude that he was either sympathetic or patronising – he wasn't sure which.

Finally, they made it to the crest of the hill and stood facing a dense forest, which stretched as far as the eye could see; its deciduous trees casting a cool gloom. Both sighed in unison; one in spiritual relief, the other in physical relief.

Chevral's brisk manner was gone. "Now we enter the forest!" he said in a reverential tone.

"Where?" asked Thorne, uneasily.

"Over here." said Chevral leading the way.

They entered the forest between two particularly large oaks and emerged onto a narrow trail, which led into the soft green twilight. "Only another mile!" said Chevral as if he had read the other's mind.

The trail was firm underfoot and allowed easy passage. Thorne's breathing had eased since they were now walking on level ground and gradually his ears became attuned to the echo of birdsong. It wasn't the usual harsh chatter found in all 'modern' forests, but rather soft and thoughtful – as though the birds themselves felt the stillness of this ancient place and revered it. Exhaustion had given way to a serenity Thorne had never experienced before, and he was content to follow the other with no thought for any particular destination until he rounded a small bend and saw, stretching across the trail, a striped pole; one end fixed to a hut which was in the middle of a small clearing.

As they approached, the door opened, and two men armed with wicked looking pikes emerged and nodded respectfully when they saw Chevral.

Thorne's new-found serenity gave way to growing unease as he remembered the court case involving the death of the convict from the country he had just left. He found himself gazing at one of the pikes with its serrated edges and its crescent base and his mind filled in the blanks – he'd never seen pikes like these – and was that rust or dried blood? His mind became surreally detached from his body and he was only vaguely aware of Chevral explaining the difference between the various long-handled weapons carried by guards of the medieval period. "As you are probably aware, the term 'pike' has been applied generically to many forms of shafted weapons but this is erroneous. What you are admiring is a *partizan* and these, along with halberds and glaives have been in use in Europe from medieval times, through to the Tudor and Jacobean ages of your own country. The *halberd* is basically a 'pike' with the addition of a large axe blade which is used for chopping. The *glaive* has a long 'swordlike' blade at the end of its shaft and is used mainly for stabbing and the *linstock* is a 'pike' with two tines each holding a slowmatch to ignite cannon."

"Yeah....." said Thorne, warily.

"You're probably tired from the journey!" said Chevral. "I suggest you spend a few days here to acclimatise!"

Knowing that a live coward has more chance than a dead hero - plus, he was in no condition to resist, Thorne nodded in acquiescence.

"In here." said Chevral, and guided Thorne into the hut through one room at the front into a room at the back. He pointed out the room's features. "Bed here, en-suite there." he said pointing to another door. "One you'll know, the other you'll get to know!" he smiled. "Good night, Mr Thorne."

"Uh....."

Thorne was only dimly aware of bolts being pushed home, but right now all he wanted to do was sleep. Any panic could keep for tomorrow.

---oOo---

Thorne had slept like the dead - something he had not done since his teen years. He awoke in darkness and held his wristwatch up to see the luminous dial. He had estimated that he had crashed out about 15-00 and was amazed to see the hands read 03-00! He had slept for twelve hours solid and wondered what today would bring.

He needed to use the toilet and got up from the bed - still fully clothed - and groped his way towards the door of the en-suite bathroom trying to find a light switch.

He found the door, but no light switch. "Bugger!" he muttered, and groped his way forward trying to find the cool comfort of porcelain paradise. Instead, he found the warm comfort of a wooden box with an earthy smell. "Oh shit!" he said in exasperation - and, having no other option, did what came naturally. Alone in the darkness, an awful realisation had dawned and he prayed out loud. "*God, please let there be toilet paper!*"

Chapter 3

It was 06-00. The birds were singing their thoughtful songs and a shaft of soft green light was bathing the room where Thorne was still sitting, feeling utterly wretched when he heard the now *welcoming* sound of boot-steps. "Hello?" he shouted.

"Hello sir!" said a cheerful voice.

"I need help!" shouted Thorne.

"How's that sir?"

"There isn't any toilet paper!"

"Sorry sir, be right back!" promised the guard.

He was as good as his word. Within a minute, there was the sound of bolts being drawn back, some boot-steps towards the 'en-suite' door and a polite knock.

"I can't move!" said Thorne, icily.

"I'll be discreet sir." apologised the guard.

The door opened a fraction and a new toilet roll rolled politely towards him.

Following a great deal of heavy-duty paperwork, Thorne

turned his attention to the other luxurious items of 'en-suite' furniture and got the general picture. A niche in the wooden wall held a *real* bar of soap that was above a small wooden barrel half-full of cold water. He obligingly washed his hands murmuring sarcastically, "Wow, *soap!*" and wiped his hands on the large cloth that was hanging from a wooden peg. He now needed the other two 'S's,' a shower and a shave. The first presented no real problem, as the final item of 'furniture' was a large cooper's barrel sawn in half and also half-full of cold water. Thorne looked at the 'bath' and shivered, "Bloody primitive!" he muttered to himself. "I don't suppose you have any hot water for a bath do you?" he inquired out loud.

"Just heating some now!" came the friendly reply.

Five minutes later, there was the sound of boot-steps and another knock on his door. "Bucket of hot water to add to the cold!"

"Thank you!" said Thorne – and he meant it.

Once Thorne had got the knack of climbing into the half-barrel he had to admit that he actually enjoyed the experience, "Just novelty!" he said – but he found himself smiling anyway, and began to hum as he splashed around.

He was starting to feel quite at home in *his* barrel when his reverie was broken by those delicious words, "Breakfast in ten minutes!" – the guard wasn't so bad after all!

He emerged carefully from the barrel and dried himself down with the large cloth provided. After paddling across the floor to his clothes and putting them on with some regret, he nipped into his bedroom, opened his suitcase and plastered a good deal of deodorant under his arms to sweeten himself as much as possible. After combing his hair, he looked around for a power point for his razor and instantly realised what an idiot he was.

Feeling somewhat self-conscious, he emerged from his bedroom into the guardroom at the front of which one of the guards was bent over a stove.

"Good day sir, I hope you're hungry?"

"I'm bloody starving!" thought Thorne. "Indeed I am." he said, politely.

"We can start you off with some porridge. Do you take honey on it?"

"Right now, I'll take anything!" – the words were out of his mouth before he realised it.

The guard laughed. "An honest answer – there's hope for you yet!" He dished up a good portion of porridge into a bowl and poured plenty of honey on top. Offering it to Thorne he began to say, "Try thi....." when the porridge was intercepted and Thorne was wolfing it down.

Two bowls later, Thorne was in a position to feel civilised enough to thank the guard for his excellent cuisine.

"It's nice to be appreciated." said the guard.

"Don't you get many thanks?" asked Thorne, wiping his mouth with the back of his hand.

"Certainly not from my last guest." admitted the guard, sadly.

The penny dropped. "You weren't the one who.....?"

"I'm afraid so." said the guard quietly, pain showing on his face.

Thorne had heard of prisoners identifying with their captors but that took months, and he was with his guard for less than twenty-four hours – so he felt it was safe enough to feel some genuine sympathy for him. "What *really* happened?" Thorne asked, gently.

"Didn't you read the papers?"

"Yes, but the papers dis....." he stopped himself.

"*Distort* the truth?"

"What *really* happened?" pressed Thorne.

"He was being tracked by police dogs. He attacked me, and I ran him through in self-defence as much as doing my duty. You see, no-one is allowed to enter our country without express permission from the Duke."

"What would have happened if you hadn't defended yourself?"

"He would have killed me to get across the border and tried to enter my country and probably kill some of *my* people – but he wouldn't have succeeded in that."

"Why not?"

"I'm here for ceremonial/psychological purposes only – to deter the *civilised* mind – I cannot deter the *criminal* mind. Our true defence lies another mile down that track as you emerge from the forest to enter the meadows – he would have died there."

"What's down there?" asked Thorne.

"With respect, I'll leave that for Chevral to show you."

"Fair enough." said Thorne, knowing that he *had* gained admission. Seeing the guard's distress he decided to change the subject. "I notice that you are dressed identically to Chevral except for your waistcoat which is plain fawn, is there any reason for this?"

The guard visibly brightened at this change of topic, and Thorne felt somewhat guilty.

"Yes sir. All who are involved in the security of my country wear identical garb with the exception of the waistcoat, which indicates one's level of responsibility. Chevral wears orange with gold leaves and we wear plain fawn." he said proudly.

Thorne, expecting a longer list of bureaucracy was caught off-balance. "Oh." he said.

Trying to maintain the flow of conversation, Thorne asked where the other guard was.

"There's normally just one on duty; the only time there are two is at shift-change, but we share a few cups of mint and listen to the birdsong before one goes home."

"Ahh….. shift-work – the bane of civilisation!" said Thorne.

"Not really." said the guard.

"What? Six till two, two till ten and ten till six?"

The guard frowned in thought. "We don't work nights." he said, finally.

"Okay then. Six till two and two till ten?"

"Depends on the season."

"What do you mean?"

"Well….." said the guard, "We follow the Sun."

Thorne chuckled. "A golden rise and a scarlet fall – eh?"

"Poetic *and* true!" said the guard, admiringly.

"Doesn't that make life confusing? Not knowing *what* to do, or *where*, or *when*?"

The guard smiled gently, "We know sir – just look around. Can't you *feel* it?"

With a sinking heart, Thorne had to admit that he couldn't.

---oOo---

The guard seemed to understand. "Why not go for a quiet walk to find yourself."

"Aren't you supposed to guard me in case I go anywhere I shouldn't?"

"No sir, you're here to be acclimatised before you are admitted into our country."

Thorne looked around and saw trees, trees and more trees. There was nowhere for him *to* go. He was used to being alone in his own country - he could be surrounded by people and *still* be alone - that was normal for him. Here, he was surrounded by trees, which silently reflected his thoughts and feelings right back at him - making him painfully aware of his true nature - and that was *not* a comfortable feeling at all!

"I don't suppose you'd fancy a walk?" Thorne asked, feeling shame.

"I can't leave my post sir." apologised the guard.

"Of course not, sorry!"

A silence descending between the two was made amiable by the birdsong.

"What's your name anyway?"

"Tyler, sir."

"Just Tyler?"

The guard smiled, "One person, one name - it makes sense to us. Why make life complicated? Complicated is not civilised - complicated is stupid!"

Thorne wouldn't argue with the first part of that statement and couldn't argue with the second part. '*Complicated is not civilised, complicated is stupid.*' There was a simple logic to Tyler's words which couldn't be refuted. He decided to go for a walk after all, to consider what Tyler had said; and told him so.

"When you return, I'll get a brew going and I've brought some fruit from the groves."

Thorne acknowledged with a wave of his hand and went for a stroll.

Walking through the forest, Thorne soon realised that he didn't need to walk at all. He stopped – realising that his journey was a spiritual one, not a physical one. If the time was right – no – *when* the time was right, he would begin his journey – and it could be anywhere – it didn't matter. It was the *state* that counted – not the place. The place *without* was only important as far as it was a catalyst for the state *within*. The rest would take care of itself!

Shocked by this personal revelation, Thorne sat down in a hurry before he fell down.

Where the hell had *that* come from? He looked with his eyes and just saw trees – but something else – he didn't know what, made him shiver from within. He was aware of everything around him – aware of Change – and then his rational mind took over and he felt stupid and started to curse his naivety. Nothing had changed; the bloody trees were still here, and over there was Tyler at his post, drinking his cup of mint.

He wanted to stay where he was until he had regained his composure, but he leaped to his feet with a yelp and was dancing around beating his backside. Tyler heard the commotion and was running towards him with a look of concern on his face.

By the time he had arrived, Tyler had started to laugh, as he knew what was happening.

Thorne – cursing like a trooper – had whipped off his trousers and was shaking them violently.

"You've sat on an ants' nest haven't you!" – it was a statement, not a question.

"B*****d, b*****d, b*****d!"

"I'll take that as a 'yes' then!" said Tyler, solemnly, and he returned to finish his mint.

Ashamed of his language, it was some time before Thorne returned to the hut. Tyler said nothing, and gave him a fresh brew and some fruit to eat. Thorne nodded his thanks and spent the next few hours in silent contemplation. The second guard arrived and he and Tyler sat together over a few more brews. Thorne excused himself from their company – not feeling particularly sociable or hungry – and turned in just before the sun went down.

After spending a week in the forest on a diet of porridge with honey and fruit, Thorne's body had begun to lose weight, his mind was becoming calmer and his state was evolving some grace.

Paradox: Sometimes you need to lose something in order to gain something.

---oOo---

With plenty of valuable time on his hands, no trivial distractions and a correct attitude of mind, Thorne had learned how to get water from the stream some yards away from the hut; how to use the stove in order to prepare his bath and cook his porridge; how to clean up afterwards, *and* how to change the night-soil in his earth closet! He had begun to see that routine can be reassuring, rewarding and satisfying – something that his modern world had lost.

One morning, Tyler caught sight of Thorne up to his arms in manure, laughing and shouting, "It may be shit to you, but it's bread and butter to me!"

Tyler smiled quietly to himself, but said nothing.

That afternoon, when the other guard arrived to take over the shift, Tyler returned home to tell Chevral the good news that Thorne had acclimatised and was now ready.

Chevral smiled his appreciation and raised his eyebrows. "Earth closet?"

Tyler gave a gentle smile.

"Works every time!"

Chapter 4

The next morning, Chevral arrived outside the hut carrying a set of traditional clothing which he presented to Thorne – who by now, resembled something that had escaped from a laboratory – but who had developed an aspect of inner peace completely at variance with his wild appearance. Chevral noted the difference and smiled inwardly. "Good morning Mr Thorne, the day for your admission has finally arrived. When you are ready, we will begin our journey to my country and you will be staying every night at our inn as our guest. You'll find the surroundings and service much more appealing than here."

Thorne accepted the new clothing with gratitude and said, "I think I'm beginning to understand the significance of my isolation in the forest, and I have to admit that I was starting to find it almost enjoyable!" He rubbed his week's growth of beard and smiled ruefully. "Once I get cleaned up properly – I'm told your culture uses hand razors – I'd like to buy Tyler several drinks, and I could use a few myself!"

As Thorne went into the hut to get changed, Chevral leaned against the outside wall and raised his voice. "We are happy to accommodate your stay free of charge - as far as your bed, food and clothing are concerned - but any social events will have to be paid for. Is this acceptable?"

"Got traveller's cheques!" came the reply.

"Thank you, but your currency is not recognised here. If you need money to socialise, you'll need to get a job to earn some."

There was a noticeable pause from the hut as the grunts of Thorne changing had temporarily ceased.

"Don't worry, Mr Thorne, there are plenty of jobs to do - most of them simple and *all* of them useful - it's a good way to meet our people and understand our culture."

"I don't suppose you have a newspaper I could work for?"

"Apart from our quarterly broadsheet - no!"

"Didn't think so!"

The grunts resumed.

---oOo---

A few minutes later, Thorne emerged from the hut with a look of pleasant surprise on his furry face.

"What do you think?" he said, and gave a twirl.

Chevral studied the apparition before him and smiled inwardly. "Very good Mr Thorne, how does it feel?"

"Surprisingly comfortable. I like the fawn breeches, they contrast nicely with the brown coat, but the boots are a bit tight."

"Top-boots take time to break in, but we'll stop at the boot makers and check your foot size just to be sure. A gentleman will normally break in his new boots alongside his old for a while so his feet don't suffer unduly."

"You haven't got an old pair I can borrow – have you?"

"I'll get the boot maker to recondition an old pair in your size as well."

"Thank you!" beamed Thorne. "Don't I get a waistcoat too?" he added, with a cheeky grin.

"You're dressed casually, since your breeches contrast with your coat. This equates to wearing slacks and a blazer in your own country. Matching breeches and coat equates to formal dress, which would be accompanied by a waistcoat. This equates to wearing a morning suit in your own country." Chevral stated evenly.

"That's me told!" thought Thorne, and decided to change the subject.

---oOo---

"What is your currency?" he asked Chevral.

"Like all things here, a very simple one. We use stamped coins only, as they last a lot longer than paper money. Small denomination are Groats of 1, 5, 10 and 50 – they all have a centre hole. Large denomination are Crones of 1, 5 and 10 – they're solid."

"Crones?" asked Thorne visualising little old ladies.

Chevral laughed. "Our crones are like your crowns – when you *had* crowns!"

"So you have no foreign exchange system?" said Thorne, thinking of his useless wallet.

"Tourism as you understand the concept is forbidden, so we have no need of complex systems of exchange other than for import/export."

"Import/export?"

"Oh, yes. We *import* a few essentials – soap, razors, perfumes, toilet rolls, fabrics, medical items etc. – anything we can't fabricate. We *export* wine, honey and mead." Chevral continued. "Now that you are dressed like one of us; '*Thorne*,' it's time to pack your bag for the 'Long Walk' into our country!"

Thorne nipped inside and quickly sealed up his luggage to mask the heady aroma of its contents and emerged outside again. "I'd like to thank Tyler for his companionship and hold to my word concerning several large drinks." He went over to Tyler to thank him personally – remembering just in time *not* to shake his hand – and returned to Chevral to find the other with a look of amusement on his face. "Any problem?" he asked.

"No problem!" answered Chevral, indicating the way forward.

Together, they set off down the track into the country."

---oOo---

The walk was pleasant. On their journey, they broke through numerous shafts of soft green light, and listened to the sound of birdsong echoing through the trees. Thorne felt instantly at ease, sensing that something wonderful awaited him; but he was also aware of Tyler's words concerning the real defence of the country and wondered what form it would take.

Eventually, they had walked the other mile and were just emerging from the forest into the meadow when Thorne saw two figures dressed from head to toe in white shrouds barring their way. Visions of a Ku Klux Klan nation sprang to mind, and he tried to shake off the notion of burning crosses. "The overactive imagination of the press!" he thought to himself, and was surprised at his own reaction.

One of the two figures stepped forward and sprayed Chevral from a large syringe, the other 'decontaminated' Thorne. Recollections of "The Andromeda Strain" and "The Satan Bug" occurred to Thorne, and he began to worry about the 'defence system' that Tyler had mentioned. With thoughts of Anthrax, Sarin, Ricin and other 'bio-agents' floating through his mind, he was only *half*-relieved when Chevral told him that it was now safe to proceed. "I am my own problem!" he began to realise.

They walked some distance along the track between two huge areas of wild meadow, the grasses very tall and untouched and Thorne was amazed to see so many wild flowers of different shapes and hues. There was the sound of skylarks singing and the humming of many bees as they darted into and out of the blossoms.

"Walk gently, breath gently, keep your mouth closed." advised Chevral.

Thorne, sensing the other's seriousness, obeyed. Together they crested a small hill, and looked down into the valley below, and Thorne saw what the 'defence system' was.

There were scores of beehives, and the track they were on led down, right through the middle of them. Thorne marvelled at the perfect defence. *Security*; intruders would be stung to death within minutes if they hadn't been 'decontaminated' first. *Export*; honey sold or added to wine for mead. *Lighting*; beeswax used for candles. *Surplus*; wax made into polish for preservation and proofing – and so on!

He found himself looking down at his own highly polished boots.

"For those too!" said Chevral, apparently reading his thoughts.

Thorne's sarcasm and cynicism for the modern world – *his* world – had no place here, and he knew it. Profound admiration for this 'funny little country' was starting to evolve.

"Any reason why we walk and talk quietly?" Thorne muttered.

"Bees hate vibration, sudden movement and animal breath." was the muted reply.

"Fair enough." thought Thorne.

They strolled down into the little valley, passing shrouded keepers who were gently removing the frames of comb and harvesting the honey. Every so often the keepers would spray smoke to keep the bees quiescent. Everything was a slow and deliberate act – akin to raising the Eucharist in Mass or Holy Communion.

Thorne and Chevral continued their stroll up the other side of the 'bowl' to the opposite ridge. In the distance, a coach and horses patiently waited.

"Our transport." said Chevral, indicating a four seat Landau, parked where the track became a country lane.

As they approached the coach it rocked violently, and a giant in a dark red frock coat swung from the seat and crashed to the ground, "GOOD DAY, SIRS!" it boomed.

"Good day, Mycroft." replied Chevral.

Mycroft beamed at Thorne who – with bees in mind – replied with an awkward "Hiya!"

"HIYA TO YOU SIR!" roared Mycroft, "ALLOW ME TO ASSIST!" He loaded Thorne's luggage onto the rack at the back of the coach and returned to help Thorne into the coach. Between grunts, Thorne made it inside and sat down, followed by a graceful entrance from Chevral. Mycroft lumbered back up into his seat; took rein, and clicked the horses into a gentle walk.

Chevral leaned over to Thorne, "Sit back and enjoy the ride, I'll show you the sights as we progress."

Thorne was all too happy to be pampered, and decided to make the most of his stay.

---oOo---

The next three miles were a continuation of wild meadow where the bees were still merrily bouncing from one blossom to another and Thorne was just beginning to get a little bored when Chevral leaned over again and said, "Now the cultivation begins." Thorne peered ahead, and sure enough, fields started to appear along their journey.

"Over to your right are the fields of Upper North which holds two farms, and over to your left are the fields of Lower North which holds three farms. In a couple of miles, we will cross the bridge which lies exactly in the centre of our country."

Thorne looked at the lie of the land and was puzzled, "I can't see why it's called upper on the right and lower on the left, it looks the same to me!"

Chevral laughed and said, "You judge upper and lower by the lie of the land, but in ancient times, upper and lower was judged by the reach of the river!"

Thorne was still puzzled, and said so.

Chevral continued. "The reach of the river flows from right to left. It first reaches the land to your right. This is the upper reach. From there it flows under the bridge at mid-point and – flowing *down*-stream following gravity – it finally reaches the lower reach. If you look at the ancient maps of your *own* country, you can find what you would think to be anomalies - such as upper 'whatever' being on a lower land level than lower 'whatever.' It's all to do with the reach of the river, not the lie of the land."

"Pass!" said Thorne, raising his hands in surrender.

Within a mile, they crossed a bisecting lane that gave access to the farms of upper and lower north, and Chevral pointed out a lane on the left branching off from lower north to the river. "That branch lane leads to North Mill which processes all northern grain into flour."

A mile later, they came to the bridge and crossed over the river to the other half of the country.

Pointing to the right, Chevral said, "Over there, is South Mill which processes all southern grain into flour, and as you can see, its branch lane leads to another cross lane farther on holding the farms of....."

".....Upper and Lower South!" interjected Thorne.

"Very good!" said Chevral.

Thorne had noticed that on *this* side of the river were orchards along either side of the lane they were on, separating the fields mirroring the north, and he asked what they were for.

"Ahh, the Groves!" said Chevral wistfully.

"Yes....." prompted Thorne gently.

"The Groves give *love for the new*; they supply grapes, olives, apples, garlic, mint and herbs." He smiled, looking thoughtful. "The Groves also give *rest for the old*; all our dead rest here!"

"Christ!" thought Thorne, feeling a sudden chill despite the warmth of the day.

A mile later, they crossed the other bisecting lane that gave access to the farms of upper and lower south - three and two respectively. From then on, the lane and the Groves rose steadily and the air became cooler as they rode the last three miles up to the capital.

---oOo---

The capital was a typical stone-built medieval market town within high stone walls. They slowly approached the open archway and halted in front of two guards. Both were armed and dressed like Tyler.

"Whom have you there?" inquired one of the guards - earplugs firmly in place.

"A GUEST OF THE DUKE, NAMED THORNE!" roared Mycroft.

"Who will vouch for Thorne?"

"I will." answered Chevral.

"Enter!" said the guard.

The coach trundled on.

Thorne looked at Chevral with a questioning glance.

"Guests are very rare, so we make a production out of it. The guards *love* it - look!"

Thorne looked at the beaming guards, and beamed back at them feeling very silly but strangely happy.

Travelling slowly, Thorne was able to read the signposts in order to familiarise himself with the town. They were going down 'Main Street,' which had shops along both sides and

Thorne was busy viewing the populace. Chevral was right, nearly all of them were 'civilians' who wore fawn breeches contrasting with their frock-coats of dark brown like his own, dark red or dark green - no waistcoats were worn. Thorne *did* notice one 'official' who wore breeches matching his frock coat, and pointed him out to Chevral. "Who's dressed in black with a light grey waistcoat with silver leaves?"

"That's Straker, our senior deacon, and the lady by his side in the dark red dress and black shawl is Victoria, our senior doctor."

"She looks fierce!"

"She *is* fierce to those who malinger; but to those who are *truly* ill, she's an angel!"

"An Angel of Death!" thought Thorne - his cynicism briefly returning.

"She is the second of three sisters." Chevral was saying. "The first is Virginia - our senior keeper of bees, and the third is Veronica - you'll meet her as she assists the patrons of the inn where you will be staying." Chevral leaned out of the window and raised his voice. "Hold here Mycroft!"

"YES SIR!" boomed the reply.

Chevral leaned over, opened Thorne's door and motioned him to exit onto the street. After a clumsy exit, Chevral joined him. "Bradley our boot maker will check your size and recondition an old pair as you requested."

They both entered a shop whose sign simply read: 'Bradley - Boot maker.'

Bradley, a tall lean man wearing a leather apron emerged from behind the counter.

"Good day, sirs." he said, peering over his spectacles. "Can I assist?"

"Would you mind checking this gentleman's foot size and reconditioning an old pair for him?"

Bradley smiled knowingly and addressed Thorne. "Please be seated and remove your boots, sir."

Thorne plonked himself down, and, assisted by Bradley in the time honoured way, prised off his shiny new boots.

Bradley looked at the boots and looked at Thorne's feet and said, "New boots, old feet, I recommend an old pair to break-in against."

"My thoughts exactly." said Chevral. "Would you do the necessary reconditioning?"

"Tomorrow noon?"

"Tomorrow noon."

After refitting his new boots, they re-entered the coach and were soon on their way.

---oOo---

After a while, the coach halted at the end of 'Main Street' and there was a violent lurch followed by a loud crunch as Mycroft dismounted. Seconds later, the door opened followed by a stentorian blast of, "MARKET SQUARE SIRS!"

Thorne gingerly exited the coach and found he was standing near an empty horse trough in the centre of town next to a signpost, which read 'Market Square', and was joined by Chevral.

"Mycroft will show you to the inn – I will be joining you later for supper. Good day for now!" Chevral gave a courteous nod and withdrew.

"THIS WAY TO THE INN SIR!"

Thorne meekly followed the giant down the street praying that no one would stare.

The walk was mercifully brief, the inn being halfway down 'Market Square' and Mycroft stomped through the open door into the parlour with Thorne's luggage in one meaty hand and bashed on the oak bar-top with the other. "GUEST ARRIVED!"

There was a patter of footsteps and a wisp of a man poked his head around the side of the bar wall. "Good day, sir. You are the gentleman called Thorne?" he inquired.

Thorne smiled – instantly liking the little man. "Good day.....?"

".....Forgive me sir, my name is Giles. My friend Clive and I are the patrons of this establishment. We have so few visitors, so it really is quite wonderful to introduce someone else into our society. You shall have the best room on the first floor which overlooks the square, and we shall do all we can to assist your induction. *Thank you* Mycroft!" he said, taking Thorne's luggage, and, nearly falling over; managed to gasp out, "Would sir please follow me?"

"GOOD DAY, GILES!" roared Mycroft affably, and stomped outside.

"I *do* wish he'd have the courage to see the doctor about his hearing!" sighed Giles as he staggered upstairs with Thorne's luggage.

"Does he always shout like that?" asked Thorne.

"Yes. He's nearly deaf from shouting, and he shouts even louder to hear himself."

"A vicious circle!" agreed Thorne.

Giles could only nod in assent.

They had arrived at the door to Thorne's room, and Giles had put Thorne's luggage on the floor to catch his breath. "Are you all right?" asked Thorne.

"Clive and I are not as young as we used to be." smiled Giles between gasps, "But we have the assistance of Veronica who keeps house on the upper floors whilst we keep house on the lower floor. Clive cooks and I serve."

At the mention of food, Thorne realised that several hours had elapsed since his porridge and honey breakfast. "What time do you serve food?" he asked.

"Whenever you're hungry, sir."

"Well, I could use something about now – if that's convenient – it's been a long trip!"

"Hot or cold, sir?"

"Erm....."

"Potato, leek and onion soup with granary bread and butter?"

"Ohh....."

"Cold boar pie with apple and new potatoes?"

"Ooo....."

"Jug of wine or mead?"

"Ahh....."

"Or all of them?"

"Yes, yes, yes.....please that is!"

"It's *so* nice to have guests again!" beamed Giles, disappearing downstairs to see Clive.

---oOo---

Thorne picked up his luggage and opened the door to his room. He walked inside and surveyed the facilities. He saw a pitcher of water in a bowl, along with soap and razors on a chest at the foot of his bed. A portable candle holder with candle and matches on a bedside table and a large oak wardrobe. When he opened its doors, he found another two sets of clothing on hangers plus three sets of underclothes and two towels, all neatly folded. He had to admit that he was impressed with the generosity, but was curious as to how his measurements had been obtained regarding his clothes.

Aware of the *significance* of his stay in the forest, he did not expect to find en-suite facilities but guessed that any such facilities were probably downstairs outside. After sluicing his face and applying soap, he set about the careful task of shaving off a week's growth of beard using one of the hand-razors supplied. On completion, he wiped his face on the smaller of the two towels and decided to go downstairs and ask where such facilities were. Walking down the oak stairs, he returned to the parlour and, sitting down in one of the two settles that flanked a large stone fireplace, surveyed the room whilst waiting for Giles to return.

The floor was made of large flags of stone, and the walls were also stone but faced with polished oak panelling. On the walls hung four beautiful oils: A forest scene in spring with boar and deer; a meadow scene in summer with flowers and bees; a field scene in autumn with people harvesting corn and a town scene in winter with people and coaches in the street. All four oils were obviously done by the same artist with great sensitivity and an incredible eye for detail and were housed in elaborately carved frames. After tearing his eyes away from the oils, he saw that the ceiling was quite high and had huge oak beams supporting the rooms above. Turning his gaze towards the furniture; apart from the two matching oak settles, all other items were benches and tables - also in oak.

Giles emerged from the kitchen and had gone back behind the counter. Upon seeing Thorne, he smiled and said, "The food won't be long, sir – will you take wine or mead?"

"I'll try the mead!" said Thorne.

"Very popular with our customers." said Giles. He took a jug from a huge sideboard and put it under one of the barrels that sat on top and opened the spigot. Thorne watched in gleeful anticipation as the sweet golden liquid sloshed into the jug. He hadn't had a 'proper' drink for over a week and had grown tired of drinking mint. He watched as Giles closed the spigot and brought the jug and a mug over to Thorne's table.

"Good health, sir." said Giles, setting them down and returning to the kitchen.

"Good health to *you*, sir." said Thorne happily immersing himself in their culture.

He poured himself a draught, sat back and took a cautious sip. "Oh yes!" he said reverently, and took a long draught and felt the full effect. "Oh wow!" he said, and hoped that dinner would arrive soon, before he slid into oblivion.

Fortunately, Giles returned within a couple of minutes with a large bowl of soup, roll and butter which Thorne attacked with great enthusiasm. After his soup and a few more draughts, the boar pie with apple and potatoes arrived, and Thorne was starting to realise that his time in the forest had made his capacity smaller than his appetite. Nevertheless, he was determined to do justice to *this* meal anyway, and go easy for the remainder of his stay.

After finally finishing his pie and having a few more draughts, Thorne decided that wisdom and kindness were called for. He figured it was *selfishly wise* to stop drinking, and it looked *selflessly kind* to invite Giles to finish off the remaining mead in the jug. After complimenting Giles on the food, Thorne invited him over to partake of refreshment.

"Most kind, sir – may I take the liberty of inviting Clive to join us as he is the one who really deserves your compliments."

"My pleasure," said Thorne.

Giles disappeared into the kitchen and returned with Clive – and two *small* mugs.

Thorne poured out most of the remaining mead into their mugs and nodded politely to Clive, "My compliments for an excellent meal."

"Your health, sir," said Clive, and he and Giles raised their mugs and carefully sipped their mead.

"Like two peas in a pod!" thought Thorne, and then he remembered to ask Giles where the facilities were.

"Of course, sir – do you wish me to show you?"

"Directions are fine!" said Thorne.

"Certainly. Go past the stairs, out through the back door into the courtyard. Before you get to the stables there are two out-houses, the first is gents privy and bathing, the second is ladies privy and bathing – both doors are clearly marked."

"Thank you." said Thorne, and made his wobbly way outside – the mead taking effect.

Arriving at the 'gents' and expecting to encounter another earth closet, he was pleased to find a wooden top on a stone box and the sound of running water many feet below. His vigilance for the obvious was rewarded this time and his happiness increased. Afterwards, he took a peep at the bathing room

expecting to find a barrel, but was delighted to find a bath
– of sorts – made from blocks of stone, their joints caulked for
proofing. Pegs for clothing were on the opposite wall, and a
niche for soap and a peg for a towel were within easy reach of
the bather. Thorne had noticed that the thickness and height of
the stone made it relatively easy to bathe, even for those who
were infirm. "Credit where credit is due!" he said, marvelling
at their ingenuity, and returned to the parlour.

Giles and Clive were still sitting together and looked up when
he re-entered. "Everything to your satisfaction, sir?" inquired
Giles.

"Everything's fine, thank you." replied Thorne with such
genuine approval that it opened up his conscience, and he
added, "I know that I'm a guest here, but I'd like to find some
work to pay towards my stay in your country."

"Chevral will arrive later to discuss agreeable terms, and to
answer any questions you may have concerning what we
are about to give you." Giles got up from the table and went
behind the counter. He returned with a large piece of paper in
his hand and gave it to Thorne. "This, sir, is *your* copy of our
cultural broadsheet, please study it well."

"Cultural broadsheet?"

"On arrival, a new guest or intending resident is given a copy
of our cultural broadsheet to assist with their induction. As
you will see, it tells you pretty much all you need to know.
Having this amount of information should make your stay
easier and also save you from having to take copious notes for
your report back home!"

Thorne had to smile at the last remark. "Thank you!" he said.

"My pleasure, sir." beamed Giles.

Thorne settled himself back and began to read:

CULTURAL BROADSHEET
(Information for all Guests and Residents)

Country

Population	About 1,000 people – minimal variation.
Open Land	60 sq miles (12 miles north/south – 05 miles east/west).
Border Forest	84 sq miles (02 miles deep surrounding the country).

Industries

Farming (Arable)	Wheat, Oats, Potatoes, Onions, Beans, Leeks, Carrots, Cabbages, Turnips.
Farming (Stock)	Horses, Goats, Chickens, Boar, Deer.
Orchard (Grove)	Grapes, Olives, Apples, Garlic, Mint, General Herbs.
Keeping (Bees)	Honey, Beeswax.
Logging (Wood)	For turning into buildings, furniture, coaches and fuel.
Working (Stone)	For corsing into buildings and lanes.
Other Work	Milling, Seaming, Tanning, Turning, Carving, Corsing, Forging, Trading, General Work, Domestic Work.

Imports

Cloth	For seaming into clothing and drapes.
Metal	For forging into tools and tack.
Supplies	For industrial/domestic/medical use.

Exports

Material	Wine, Mead, Honey, Polish, Candles.
Spiritual	Retreat for the *select*, who wish to live a simple life close to nature, and are *appropriate* to our culture.

Structure	Feudal Autocracy in origin and external appearance.
	Social Democracy in internal practice and principle.
	Nationals have exclusive rights to vote on *all* issues.
	All national laws are passed by national referendum.
	Residents are forbidden from voting on *any* issue.
Religion	Florian – a quiet form of Mystical Paganism. We follow seasonal cycles – lunar and solar.
Economy	Highly stable – unchanged by world progress and market forces. We are beneath world interest and wish to *remain* so.

---oOo---

After reading it several times to get the gist of it, and noting in particular the sentences behind spiritual export, structure and economy, Thorne decided to go outside for a walk in the fresh air to sharpen his wits and excused himself from Giles and Clive.

He went outside into the square and wandered around taking in the sights. Looking at the square, he allowed himself a slight smile, as it was clear to anyone that it was a rectangle approximately three hundred feet long and one hundred feet wide. Being in the centre of town, it was surrounded by houses on all sides. In the square down the long sides were horse troughs – six each side – some empty and some full. In the centre, standing some twenty feet tall was an obelisk, which was surrounded by markings within a circle, and Thorne realised that these people did indeed follow the sun. On either side of the obelisk was a set of stocks that were designed to hold a criminal's legs to prevent him from escaping. It seemed a very *public* form of incarceration. His feet were starting to ache, so he decided to return to the inn and remove his boots.

On returning to the inn, Thorne saw that Giles and Clive had been joined by an attractive lady in a dark green dress and black shawl who had looked up at his approach. "Good day, madam." he said.

"Good day, Mr Thorne. My name is Veronica – I hope everything is to your liking?"

"Everything is fine – although my boots are a little tight!"

"How long have you had them on?"

"Since dawn."

"If those are new, they need to come off right now. You'd better sit down."

Thorne sat down.

"Raise your left foot level."

Thorne complied. She hitched up her dress, put one leg over his and grabbed his left foot. "Now, push hard with your right foot!" she said, with her back to him.

Thorne had done this previously with Bradley, but to put his other foot squarely on a lady's backside and shove hard seemed most out of place.

She sensed his hesitance. "Come on, we haven't got all day – just shove!"

Thorne shoved hard.

"Other one!"

Thorne obliged again.

She turned around holding his boots. "Better now?"

"Much better - thank you madam!" he said flushing with embarrassment.

"Your pleasure *more* than mine - I think!" said Veronica laughing. "I suggest you rest here until Chevral arrives. You'll have a few questions for him concerning *that*!" - she nodded at Thorne's cultural broadsheet.

"Just a few." he smiled, taking a bit of a shine to her.

Giles and Clive excused themselves and had returned to their tasks leaving Thorne alone with Veronica.

"I understand you help Giles and Clive run this place?"

"Yes, bless them!" said Veronica. "They're now too frail to run it on their own, and the stairs are really too much for them, so they live and work on the ground floor and I do the rest."

"It seems a lot for you to do on your own!" said Thorne thinking of the rooms.

"Not really, the rooms are only in use for guests and they are few indeed, so it's just a case of dusting, wiping and mopping once per week and making up one or two rooms per year - I think I can *just* about manage that!" she said with a little smile.

"Do you do any other work?"

"Oh, yes! Nearly all of us have several jobs during the year. Depending on the season, most of us will move from one job to another."

"That seems a *lot* of work!" said Thorne.

Veronica shook her head. "Not really; the few people who specialise stay in one job for life which carries a lot of responsibility - such as my sisters - but most of us are lucky enough to generalise and have simple jobs which vary through the year so we seldom get bored and we keep both feet firmly on the ground. In spring, summer and winter, I work here and at the castle. In autumn, I go *groving* - I help to harvest the grapes and apples."

"It sounds fun!" said Thorne.

"It *is* fun!" agreed Veronica.

"If you don't mind me asking, how much does a simple job pay?" asked Thorne.

"All jobs pay the same - 100 crones per week - that's about 250 of your pounds"

"*All* jobs?"

"All jobs sanctioned by the Duke are regarded as equally important, regardless of complexity - doctor or worker - it's all the same."

"So the doctor will earn the *same* as a worker?"

"Yes. Everyone has the opportunity to live equally, and are paid the same to enable them to do so if they *wish*! How they *choose* to spend their money is up to them. It's not how much you earn that counts, it's how much you *spend*!"

"Isn't the doctor a bit peeved?"

"No. We teach that people are judged on who they are - not what they do - unless its illegal, and then our laws take over."

"Feudal Socialism? Isn't that a contradiction in terms?"

"Only if you've never experienced it. The doctor is provided with the necessary tools to do her job – as is the worker. She is given medical equipment, medicines, herbs and a Brougham."

"A *broom* – is she a witch?"

A half-smile crossed Veronica's face. "Some might say!" She looked directly at him. "No, Thorne, a Brougham is a two seat coach which she uses in times of emergency for any patient in the country. In *her* job, time can be critical. A worker like myself is *also* given whatever tools they require. At the end of the day, the doctor becomes Victoria, and the worker becomes Veronica!"

"Speaking of the doctor, when will a certain gentleman be having his ears syringed?"

"Ahh, you've *met* Mycroft!"

"Oh, yes!" said Thorne, holding his hands to his ears. "*Very* memorable!"

"Well..... Now we have a *guest*, we could use your prescence to lure him here and grab hold of him whilst Victoria sees to his ears – that'll sort him!"

Thorne had a nasty vision of having to face a rabid giant and trying to pin him to the ground whilst a slip of a woman was worming out his ears, and was not at all happy with the prospect.

"Don't worry." said Veronica rising to leave, "I'll handle it – good day, for now."

"Good day." mumbled Thorne – his mind suddenly on personal survival rather than political sport with Chevral. "Nature has a way of prioritising things!" he thought.

About twenty minutes later, there was the sound of boot steps and Thorne looked up to see Chevral enter the parlour.

"I'll just order supper and I'll be right with you." said Chevral.

Thorne watched him order soup and a roll and a *small* mug of mead. He paid Giles with a couple of coins – each with a hole in the centre – and walked over to Thorne's table.

"Settling in?"

"Fine, thank you." replied Thorne.

"I see you've had chance to study our broadsheet – do you have any questions?"

"I'm fine with most of it, but I am a bit curious with some parts – is it okay if I take notes?"

"Certainly." said Chevral.

Fishing out the tools of his trade, Thorne said. "Under 'spiritual export' it mentions retreat for the *select* who wish to lead a simple life close to nature and are *appropriate* to our culture. Could you elaborate?"

"Yes. There are some occasions when guests wish to become residents in our country, and – being a *true* democracy, the decision to accept or reject is decided by national referendum. All intending residents are given a six month probation period where they work all over the country as labourers and in the course of so doing, they get to know us, and we get to know them. If they can happily accept us and we can happily accept them, then they are given residency, renewable at the end of each year on the clear understanding that they pay an annual fee of residency and that they *fully* embrace all our laws, culture and customs *above* their own, and that they sign an oath of loyalty."

They were gently interrupted by Giles, who arrived with Chevral's supper.

"Thank you, Giles - please continue, Thorne," he said between spoonfuls of soup.

"Why *select* and *appropriate*?"

"In *any* relationship, it is important that both parties have a clear understanding of each other's needs and that both can fulfil the other for mutual harmony and social order."

Thorne jotted down the reply. "How can social democracy come from feudal autocracy? Isn't that impossible?"

"Ask yourself the same question in six month's time."

Thorne made a note to do just that. "Under 'structure,' it says *nationals* have exclusive rights to vote on *all* issues - why not *residents* too?"

"Everyone here is happy with our culture - ask them. They are morally *and* legally entitled to keep what they have - if they want to. A *true* democracy *empowers* its nationals to decide their destiny via national referendum - unlike a *parliamentary* democracy, which *disempowers* its nationals within a bureaucratic system. As to your question concerning the exemption of *residents* from voting, the answer is simple - we want to protect our culture from the erosion of foreign influences. We like what we have and we want to keep it."

"Could that not be construed as *racist*?"

"It is more accurately described as *nationalist*!"

"What is the difference?"

"*All* nations have the right to preserve what has been created from their national evolution. If the nationals within become *unhappy*, they have the right to vote for change - assuming their nation has evolved a *democratic* culture."

"Okay so far." said Thorne.

"But those rights only apply within their national borders – and not beyond, otherwise nationalism becomes *imperialism*."

"Still happy." said Thorne.

"By reason; all nations have the right to be nationalist to preserve national harmony."

"Yes....." said Thorne warily.

"It follows that when nationals of country (a) wish to become residents in country (b), it is vital that *both* parties know how compatible they are with each other – if harmony is to be preserved."

"Agreed."

"How can *both know* if they are compatible with each other?"

"Clear communication."

"Exactly. It is vital that each *truly knows* what is expected of the other in order for an accurate decision to be made in the best interests of *both* parties."

"Agreed."

"Where does bureaucracy fit in?" asked Chevral.

"It doesn't." said Thorne.

"Why not?"

"Those in power must be *wise and bold*; then their decisions will be *clear* and their implementations *clean*. Bureaucracy erodes clarity of communication and confidence. It permits the growth of ignorance, indecision and moral cowardice. Bureaucracy is *evil*. If a country is *losing* its national identity, it is getting precisely what it deserves!"

"I couldn't agree more!" smiled Chevral. "Shall we now discuss racism?"

"Yes!" said Thorne, warming to the game.

"What is racism?" asked Chevral.

There was a few moments pause while Thorne was considering his definition carefully.

"The selective discrimination and persecution of those *present*." he said finally.

"Based on?"

"Erm..... age, size, infirmity, education, colour, gender, orientation or religion."

"All those are excuses for *discrimination*. Racism is *anti-culturalism* against migrants present within your own country – a *perceived* incompatibility between different cultures within the same nation."

"Okay, I'll concede that!" said Thorne.

"But the true cause of racism is *not* the migrants, it is the difference of perception between the leaders of the nation and the nationals themselves – between politician and citizen. In a *true* democracy, the politician serves the citizen and broadcasts *clearly* the national culture internationally. In a *parliamentary* democracy, the politician becomes insulated from the citizen and broadcasts an *unclear interpretation* of the national culture internationally – a recipe for disaster! This is why we practise the principles of national referendum – the *best* leaders are those who serve the nation; the *worst* leaders are those who serve themselves!"

"I'll certainly agree with *that*!" said Thorne.

"In all relationships – personal, social, communal, national or international – it is vital that there is – quoting yourself – 'clarity of communication and confidence' leading to the growth of harmony and happiness. What *you* have quoted, Thorne, helps to fulfil our *national* prime ethic of *continuity* and our *social* prime ethic of *compatibility*."

"Okay, if your nation is so wonderful, how come you all still live in the dark ages?"

"Do we?"

Thorne, sensing a trap answered with another question. "Don't you?"

"Your stay in the forest has taught you that everything is *relative*."

"I'll concede that!" smiled Thorne.

"We *appear* as we are for a good reason. The enlightened see a spiritual life whereas the ignorant see a primitive life. Thus we attract the *civilised* migrant and repel the *economic* migrant!"

---oOo---

Thorne had to laugh. "You win *this* time Mr Ambassador!"

"I'll look forward to another discussion in the near future." said Chevral.

"Can we now discuss my induction – in terms of employment?"

"Certainly. All work is paid 20 crones per day – that's 100 crones per week."

"What are the hours of work?"

"Depends on the season of the year and the nature of the job."

Thorne made a face. "You're not making this very easy are you?"

Chevral laughed. "Work until your conscience cuts in, or your body cuts out!"

"You're very trusting – aren't you?"

"Don't you consider yourself *worthy* of trust?"

"What sort of a question is that?"

"An honest one!"

"Well..... yes, I *am* worthy of trust – in most things; perhaps in one or two areas....."

"If you learn to *enjoy* the work, you'll learn the *value* of service, and you'll learn the *value* of the server!"

Thorne was surprised at the wisdom of those words. "The words of a diplomat?"

"The words of our deacon – you'll meet him and others as you move around."

"Where should I begin?"

"It's the warm season so why not work outside for now until it gets cooler and then you can work inside."

"Fair enough." said Thorne, pleasantly surprised.

"We can start you off with general work, doing things like digging and carting – it's steady and will break you in gently. You'll lose quite a bit of weight and will tone up and breath easier – but build up *gently* – a dead journalist could ruin our international reputation!" said Chevral with a twinkle in his eye.

"Oh, *thanks!*" said Thorne. "I feel *so* much better for you caring like that!"

---oOo---

They had agreed that Thorne should do nothing for the next two days other than wait for Bradley to drop by with a pair of reconditioned old boots for him to wear, and then he could go for a wander around town and get to know the place and its people. After that he would be 'working his passage' all around the country doing simple jobs and meeting anyone he chose. He was particularly happy when Chevral re-affirmed his earlier promise of unlimited access to people and places. "Just observe courtesy and decency and there should be no problem. If you receive a refusal, a reason will be given. If you are *not* satisfied with the reason – see me!"

With those assurances, Thorne bade good night and retired to bed a happy man.

Chapter 5

The next morning, Thorne rose from a comfortable night's sleep, sluiced his face and ears, brushed his teeth, shaved and ambled downstairs to see Giles about heating some water for his bath.

"There's some on the way, sir!" replied Giles.

Thorne trotted outside to use the privy. When he was done he returned inside and took the bucket of hot water back outside to the gentleman's bathing room and poured it into the stone bath. He then went out into the courtyard with the bucket and drew cold water from the well. Returning to his bath he poured in the cold to make the temperature pleasing. After all this, he felt he deserved his bath and revelled in the reward it brought. He knew taps were more efficient and labour saving, but without the labour, the reward was somehow lacking as well. After bathing, he pulled the wooden 'paddle' in the *end* of his bath and with some glee, sat watching the water as it gurgled loudly out of his bath along a gully and disappeared down into the sewer where it gurgled again. "Two for the price of one!" he chuckled to himself. He then got up rather quickly as the stone was already becoming cold on his bottom, and drying himself off, he dressed for the day.

Arriving for breakfast, Thorne was given the traditional porridge with honey and was also offered bacon and eggs – which he politely declined, opting instead for a cup of mint to wash out his mouth. Knowing that Bradley wouldn't arrive until noon, Thorne wondered what to do to kill time. "I don't suppose you have a map of the country?" he asked Giles.

"Certainly, sir." said Giles, disappearing behind his counter. He returned with another large piece of paper in his hand. "This is a copy of our geographical broadsheet showing our entire country to scale. When you start working outside the capital, you will need this for reference." he said, handing it to Thorne.

"Thank you." said Thorne.

He was about to start studying the map when he heard a commotion outside. He looked at Giles to find him just as surprised as he was, and together they went out into the square.

A small crowd of ladies were surrounding a very confused Mycroft, who – although towering above them and trying to look intimidating, was failing miserably. Thorne recognised Veronica and Victoria and heard the latter yell in a very un-ladylike manner, "Grab him and throw him in the trough!" All the ladies eagerly assisted. Mycroft was pushed by the crowd and literally fell into one of the horse troughs where he was wedged tightly between the sides. "Sit on him!" ordered Victoria, which three of the younger ladies happily did.

"He's in for it now!" a deep, husky voice – a *woman's* voice said in Thorne's ear.

Startled by that voice, he turned and saw a tall striking woman standing at his side who bore an uncanny resemblance to Veronica and Victoria. There, the resemblance ended. There was nothing ladylike in her manner of dress. She wore a black frock coat over matching breeches with top-boots, a white shirt with cravat but *no* waistcoat! She indicated the young lady who was sitting on Mycroft's chest nearest his face. "I see Drusilla has finally got her man!" she said with a croaking laugh. "Watch now!"

Victoria had opened her doctor's bag and had an evil looking syringe in her hand. She grabbed Mycroft's head and turned it so one of his ears was lined up. In went the syringe and down went the plunger. Mycroft froze and his eyes went wide.

"Ooo..... it's fizzing inside my head!" he exclaimed. Absorbed with this new sensation, he wasn't really aware when his head was twisted the other way and his other ear received the same treatment. All he could say was "Ooo....." at which the ladies shrieked with laughter and the doctor gave an evil smile of triumph.

"Fun's over ladies, you can let him go." said Victoria, and the ladies sighed and walked back to their waiting husbands who had been wisely keeping out of the way. As the crowd dispersed, one remaining lady slowly got off Mycroft's chest, and with a gentle smile on her face; helped him to his feet. She took his hand and led him quietly away.

"Ahh..... young love!" croaked the woman in the black frock coat. She looked at Thorne. "I'm Virginia, and I'm guessing you're Thorne."

"That's me!" replied Thorne, looking at the woman in fascination.

She sensed his interest, and gave a lop-sided grin. "Wasted on *me* friend!"

"I beg your pardon? Oh! I beg your *pardon!*"

"Relax, I'm not offended." she looked genuinely amused. "At least my charms have been verified – albeit by the wrong party!"

Thorne was too embarrassed to speak, but the colour of his face spoke volumes.

A look of compassion came into her eyes. "We'll meet again, good day." She turned in a swirl of black and was gone down the street.

Thorne stood for several seconds in a kind of shock, trying to come to terms with the fact that he – a confirmed bachelor with only two relationships to his credit – had received a rude awakening that the embers he thought were dead had suddenly flared up again, and was most annoyed at the intrusion. He drowned the embers in a cold wash of logic. He had been betrayed by the women in both his past relationships and had written off *all* women in the romantic sense. But he found himself becoming open to the possibility of a strictly platonic friendship with this fascinating woman.

The more he thought of it the happier he became – *this* was the perfect solution. There would be no misunderstandings – he wasn't interested in romance with anyone, and she was only interested in other women. There were no expectations, no assumptions and therefore no pressure – it was great! "An attractive and intelligent *friend* to be with and listen to – that's all I need!" He caught himself speaking aloud as he re-entered the inn and wondered if Giles had overheard him. If he had he gave no sign. "Fascinating lady." Thorne said out loud.

Giles nodded wisely. "Virginia is very independent and forthright."

"I admire those traits in a woman – there's less chance of deceit!"

"Traits to be respected from a distance, but not embraced closely, sir."

Thorne smiled at Giles' discretion. "I understand, but I value *only* friendship!"

Giles smiled at Thorne's discretion. "She *also* likes you as a potential friend."

Thorne was surprised. "How do you know?"

"She has given her sign of approval, sir."

"What sign of approval?"

"*We'll meet again!*" quoted Giles.

"I hope so!" sighed Thorne.

"She will see to that, sir."

Thorne nodded, and decided to study his map with great intensity.

GEOGRAPHICAL BROADSHEET
(Information for all Guests and Residents)

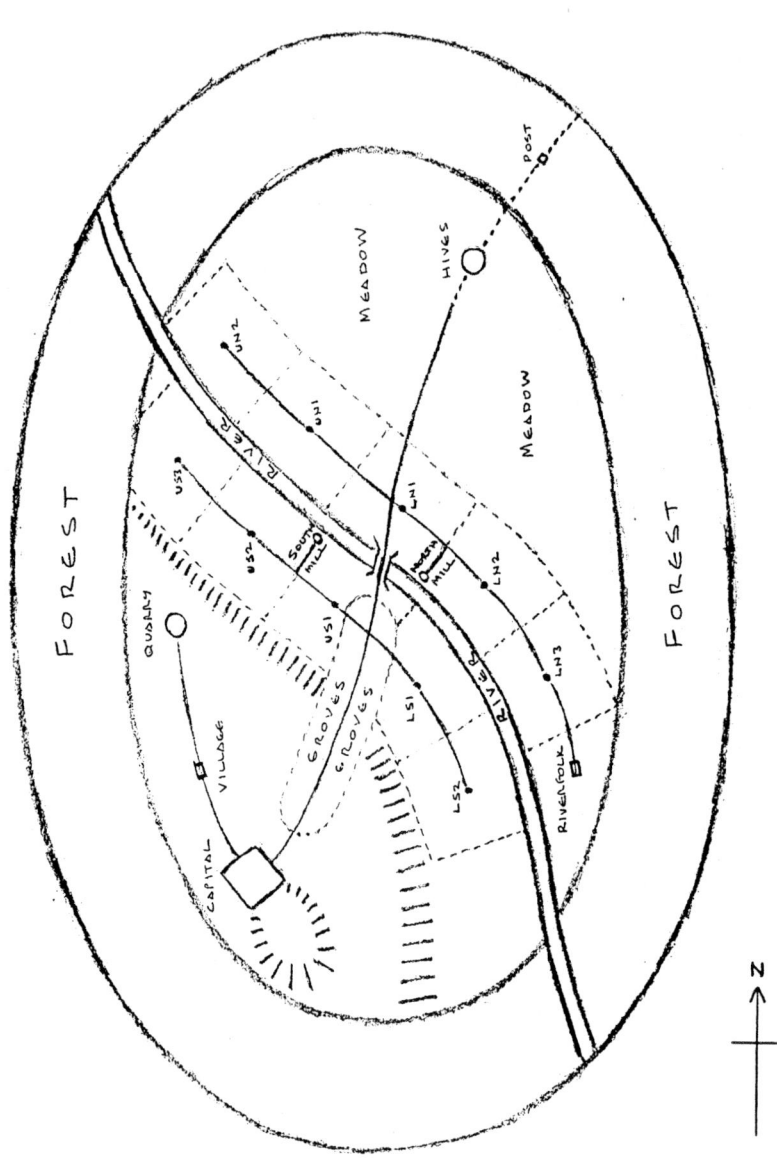

After studying his map for longer than he realised, he heard a polite cough and looked up to see Bradley standing in the doorway peering at him over his glasses and holding his new 'old' boots.

"I think you will find these are more suitable for you right now." said Bradley.

"Thank you." said Thorne, gratefully removing his old 'new' boots with the customary assistance from Bradley. He carefully put the old pair on and took a little walk around the parlour and beamed at Bradley. "Oh..... happy, happy feet!"

"Glad to be of service." said Bradley, taking his leave. "Good day, sir."

"Good day, indeed!" said Thorne cheerfully twinkling his toes inside his boots. He turned to Giles. "I think a spot of touring is in order now!"

"Perhaps a spot of dinner first. It *is* nearly noon, sir!"

"Dinner? Well..... just a little something – you see I've decided to go on a diet!"

"Indeed, sir?"

"Yes..... discipline, exercise, diet – a healthy lifestyle!"

"Very commendable, sir."

"Soup and a roll is not really fattening is it?"

"Not really, sir."

"Good – I'll have that please and a mug of mead!"

"Just a *mug*, sir?"

"Just a *mug*, Giles!"

"Very good, sir."

Thorne sat back in his favourite settle, warming to his new way of life – good food, good drink, good people, simple life and honest work – oh yes! He was *very* much at peace with the world.

Following his 'dietary' dinner, he was ready to get 'out and about' and, after thanking Giles, he went outside to explore the capital – he'd explore the country later. He was in 'Market Square' and had four choices. From there he could go north up 'Main Street' which was the way he had arrived, but he had no money at present so exploring the trading area which constituted 'Main Street' was futile for now. He could go east along 'Temple Street' – *this time*, or south down 'Castle Street' – *next time*, or west along 'Quarry Street' – *some time*.

Decision made, he strolled east hoping to see around the temple and maybe have a talk to Straker or one of his assistants. As he left the square, the houses closed in along both sides of the street and continued for several hundred feet until they parted to reveal another square – a *square* square, measuring one hundred feet. Behind him and to his left and right were more houses, but in front at the east end was a stone pillared portico fronting a large round temple. It was three stories high and had a domed roof.

"Unlimited access." he reminded himself, and tiptoed inside the portico. A cool gloom washed over him reminding him of his stay in the forest. He arrived at a pair of large oak doors and listened in case he was interrupting anything. On hearing nothing, he lifted the latch of the right door, pulled it open and stepped inside.

There was nobody around, so he closed the door and – feeling a little guilty, walked into the temple. The first thing that caught his eye was the altar. It was a large round stone in the centre of the floor and it had several items arranged in geometric precision on its top. As he had entered from the west the nearest object was an empty chalice. Walking clockwise, the next object situated north was a disc with a pentagram on it. In the east stood a thurible for burning incense and in the south was a dagger. In the centre of the stone was a large candle unlit. He shivered – suddenly feeling very alone in this alien place, and yet when he used his rational mind, there was *nothing* to indicate any sinister practices. As his focus left the altar he noticed there were four stained glass windows high in the walls. He looked east and saw a white sun in a golden sky with brown clouds – *dawn*. He looked south and saw golden sun in a light-blue sky with white clouds – *noon*. Looking west he saw an orange sun in a red sky with grey clouds – *dusk*. Looking north he saw a full moon in a dark-blue sky with black clouds – *night*.

Thorne was deciding whether to follow *selfless duty* and stick around to ask questions or to follow *selfish fear* and get the hell out asking *no* questions. As he was about to leave, the door opened and Veronica walked in carrying a feather duster.

"Well, good day to *you*!" she said.

"Good day, Veronica – I was just leaving."

"Not on *my* account, I hope?"

"There was no-one to talk to!" he said truthfully.

"Stay and talk to me whilst I'm cleaning – I can answer *most* questions for you."

"Ohh..... thank you!"

"I can clean and we can talk at the same time." she said, and began to dust the altar and its symbolic objects. "Phew – look at the dust!"

Thorne had to agree. "It looks as though those objects haven't been used for a while!"

"They're only used as symbols to aid contemplation, so they seldom get touched."

"So you don't have any ceremonies?"

"Gracious, no! We have *deacons* not priests – there's no formality." She paused, sneezed and carried on dusting.

"So people just wander in any time; turn on, tune in and chill out?"

"If I understand your words correctly, the answer is probably *yes*."

"So if there's no *preaching* there must be *teaching*?"

"Oh, yes! Straker teaches morality to the children and spirituality to the adults."

"So he prepares the children for a peaceful *life*, and the adults for a peaceful *death*?"

"Well put!" she said admiringly.

Thorne was being sarcastic and it had backfired on him beautifully. He smiled weakly.

"Why do you have those objects?"

"Historically speaking, they had their origins in medieval times. The chalice was used to hold wine or mead for drinking. The disc or pentacle was the trencher or platter for the meat. The dagger was used to stab pieces of meat to eat off the trencher – you are familiar with the phrase '*trenching away at your dinner.*' The thurible was used to burn incense to sweeten the air and the candles provided light."

Thorne was impressed and noted all this down.

Veronica waited him to finish before continuing. "Symbolically speaking, each of these objects relate to their corresponding counterparts which are reflected in each window." She directed Thorne's gaze upward where each window was deeply recessed – leaving the ceiling of the dome in complete darkness. "Let's start with each of the windows. The east represents Golden Dawn, the south represents Blazing Noon, the west represents Scarlet Dusk and the north represents Freezing Night."

Thorne felt a 'freezing night' creep in as he remembered blurting out a 'golden rise and a scarlet fall' to Tyler during his stay in the forest.

"Are you all right?" asked Veronica.

"..... Yes – please continue!" said Thorne.

"The east also represents spring, Light and Inspiration. The south represents summer, Life and Conviction. The west represents autumn, Love and Submission. The north represents winter, Law and Observation. The objects lying on the altar represent the elemental manifestations of the spiritual principles in the windows. East is Air, South is Fire, West is Water, North is Earth. The Centre is Ether, the fifth element and the balancing element, which unites and harmonises the other four. It is symbolised by the candle, representing Radiation and Revelation. All five elements must be in balance for personal revelation and are shown as the pentagram on the symbol of earth. This represents Perfection Manifest in the World of Form."

Thorne was scribing away furiously.

"I'm going to start mopping the floor now – I won't be long." She walked outside leaving the door open, and, picking up her mop and bucket, which were standing outside, she walked to the centre of the square and drew water from a well. A few minutes later she returned and started mopping the floor. "This temple is called the 'Solstice Temple' because it is oriented to catch the path of the sun around the midsummer solstice. At dawn, the sun's rays pass through the east window and cast a shaft of light that strikes the thurible. At noon the rays pass through the south window and strike the dagger, and at dusk they pass through the west window and strike the chalice." She paused to dunk and squeeze her mop before sloshing it around again. "Do you have any questions?"

"Yes - how on *earth* do you know so much?"

"Sorry! I forgot to mention that I sometimes assist Straker. I'm a Junior Deacon."

Thorne shook his head in disbelief.

She looked at him. "*I am - honestly!*"

"I'm just kicking myself!" he said.

The sloshing continued onto the next section. "Any more questions?"

"The north window - what happens there?"

"Different *laws* apply there!" she remarked cryptically.

He sensed he was about to tread on 'thin ice' - but remembered Chevral's advice about courtesy and decency - she could always decline to comment. "Would you prefer me not to inquire any further?" he asked.

She stopped mopping and looked at him. "Being 'solar' the 'solstice temple' is open to all during the day, but on certain nights it is closed to all except women who meditate on the *meaning* of the north window."

"Understood. I'll take up no more of your time. Thank you *very* much for your help."

Veronica smiled warmly. "Thank *you*, for your *discretion.*"

"Good day, Veronica." he said gently.

"Good day." she replied softly.

Emerging from the portico into the sunshine, Thorne decided to return to his room at the inn to begin sorting and storing his notes into certain cultural categories. Namely: Psychological, Political, Spiritual, Social, Judicial, Medical, Historic and Economic.

It was still the afternoon, and Thorne was wondering what to do next. He thought about walking down 'Castle Street' today – rather than tomorrow, but if he did that, what would he do tomorrow? 'Quarry Street' didn't sound very inspiring and he was starting to feel bored. "I could do to start work tomorrow rather than the day after!" he said to himself.

Heaving a sigh, he shrugged his shoulders and began to walk back the way he had come. He hated return trips – they smacked of futility – of *failure.* Thorne detested failure. The Japanese had a word for failure – a word they both hated and feared: "Shi-paii!"

No Japanese wanted to be associated with that word – and neither did Thorne.

Eventually, he re-emerged into the main square and just stood looking at the people passing by. He was experiencing the same feeling that he had in the forest. He felt totally out of place. How could he connect?

Self-consciously, he walked along the street and returned to the inn. As he entered the parlour, Giles looked up from polishing the bar top and smiled at him. Thorne gave a nod and went upstairs – not noticing the twinkle of amusement in Giles' eyes.

Lying on his bed, he sighed and stared at the ceiling. "I guess that's why people enjoy work so much – without it, they would die prematurely of boredom!" He recalled what his mother used to say when he was having one of his teenage tantrums venting his frustration. "Don't plan, plans always change; take each day as it comes." And his father's fictitious biblical quotation. "Blessed is he that expecteth nothing, for he shall not be disappointed!" He smiled at the memory of his parents – and then remembered that they had been dead for some years and his humour turned to pain at their loss. He wept silently, thinking of the happy people in the street.

---oOo---

When he had gathered himself together and sluiced his face, he realised that he needed to be alone – but not in his room – it felt like a prison right now. He needed solitude and freedom, so he did the opposite of reason and – emerging into the square – walked west along 'Quarry Street' without any plan in mind other than just needing to walk.

As before, as soon as he left the square, the houses closed in along both sides of the street and continued for several hundred feet until in the distance, he saw an archway under the town walls identical to the one he had entered when he was with Chevral. The huge gates were open and unguarded, so he passed under the walls and out of the town, and found himself standing at the beginning of 'Quarry Lane' which stretched for a good three miles – according to his map.

He felt more relaxed being in the open countryside, and started to stroll along the lane. Being over one thousand feet higher than the rest of the country, and outside the protection of the

town's walls, a fresh breeze cooled the air despite the warm sun and Thorne realised the wisdom of the national costume. Worn open, the frock coat would be fairly cool in the summer; worn closed, it would be fairly warm in the winter. The top-boots were also more than just fashion items – they were essential for walking and working in dirty or wet conditions. Being polished leather, they would be waterproof yet allow the feet to breath naturally – true 'Wellington' boots with the addition of the turned-down tops showing the fawn lining behind the blacked leather. Thorne realised that everything and everyone in this country had a purpose, and he must follow suit!

As he walked along the lane, he saw more wild meadow on both sides and stopped to look at the wildflowers that inundated the tall grasses. Colours of white, yellow, pink, lilac and blue danced above a wafting sea of green. Thorne stood still and listened to the sounds of birds singing, bees humming and crickets buzzing. As he started to walk again, his insecurities vanished and he began to realise the value of nature. Florianism made sense as a faith that *everyone* could relate to – whatever their former religion. As he was strolling along he saw a tabby cat sitting in the lane. As he approached, the cat gave a little miaow and walked towards him. Instinctively he bent down to stroke it and was surprised when it jumped onto his shoulders and made itself comfortable. He slowly straightened and continued down the lane with his new furry friend purring in his ear. After all, cats choose you – you don't choose them!

After a mile of walking with his friend constantly licking his earlobe with his rasp-like tongue, Thorne arrived at the outskirts of a small village where several people were sitting outside in the sunshine and children were picking flowers. As he passed by, the adults smiled and one of them said, "I see you've found Harold – or has he found you?"

"The latter, I think!" said Thorne. "Is he yours?"

"No-one owns him, but he's everyone's friend, as is Gerald, his brother."

"Well, I'll put him down anyway, my ear is soggy and sore!"

Everyone burst out laughing as Thorne disengaged Harold from his ear and put him on the ground. The man who had spoken offered Thorne a cloth saying, "It's clean, use it for your ear and collar – he's dribbled again!"

"Thank you!" said Thorne giving his ear a cautious dab and his collar a vigorous rub.

"We haven't seen you before, are you new here?"

"Yes, I arrived the other day."

"Do you plan on staying?"

"I love the place and its people, but I'm a guest for now. Thank you for the cloth!"

"You're welcome. Please be highly discreet about the culture of these people – they don't want to be swamped and lose what they have – nor do we!"

"*Nor do we?*" repeated Thorne.

"This village mostly comprises residents rather than nationals. We have retired from a high standard of living outside to embrace a high quality of life inside. I am a retired stockbroker, next to me is a retired industrialist, the two ladies sitting on the next bench are retired corporate lawyers and the man standing smoking his pipe is a retired underwriter. This village has got more 'top brass' in it than any village outside this country!"

"And you've all given up the high life to live here?"

"Damn right! This culture is the nearest thing to utopia and we see to it that it stays that way!"

"You see to it?"

"It's symbiosis. They have the soul, which we appreciate, and we have the mind, which they appreciate. They give us the culture and we give them the means to maintain it. Everyone is happy. You look surprised!"

"One of many, but I'm getting used to them." admitted Thorne.

"Here's Gerald!" shouted one of the ladies sitting on the bench farther down the lane. Everyone stopped to watch as a ginger cat swaggered up to greet Harold who was by now asleep under the gentlemen's bench. Gerald arrived and greeted the gentlemen politely. He then paused and looked down at Harold and gently poked him in the ear. Harold yawned and opened one eye. Gerald flopped down over Harold and then they both went to sleep.

"Even the cats love this country!" said the stockbroker.

Thorne looked at the cats; he looked at the residents, and he thought of the nationals and he had to agree. "Yeah." he said.

"It's a nice day boys!" shouted the other lady. "Shall we bring some chilled mint tea?"

"Splendid!" chorused the 'boys.'

Both the ladies disappeared inside one of the cottages and moments later emerged with a large jug and several mugs.

Thorne graciously accepted a mug and took a large draught and instantly knew that it wasn't just mint and water. "Wow, what's in *there*?" he asked

The first lady smiled. "Mint, water and potato mash."

"Potato mash?"

"As opposed to mashed potatoes."

There was a chorus of sniggers.

"You mean *Poitín*?"

"Technically no, Poitín is potato spirit distilled from potato mash. We haven't mastered that technique – yet! This is potato wine!" said the first lady.

"Ferment the wine! Distil the spirit!" said the second lady.

"Do I detect an Irish accent there?" asked Thorne.

"You do. Dublin's finest corporate lawyers (retired) – though we hail from Kerry!"

Both the ladies – who wore black dresses and white shawls, rose and gave a curtsey.

The stockbroker introduced them. "Meet Harriet and Geraldine O'Hara – from whom the cats are named although they are both neutered males!"

"As *all* males should be!" said one of the lawyers.

"And that from a Catholic!" said the stockbroker in mock surprise.

"We're all Florians now!" replied the other lawyer, "Even Isaac – aren't you Ike?"

The man smokng his pipe nodded, and blew a cloud of sweet aromatic smoke into the air saying, "No-one could accuse me of being Orthodox anyway!"

The O'Hara's giggled. "Ike brings home the bacon, and we cook it – literally!"

"Well!" said Thorne, "Between the cats and your good selves you have certainly brightened up *my* day!"

"Give it time son, give it time." said the stockbroker. "Have another drink!"

Thorne happily complied.

After a second round, they all agreed that they should have something to eat and so they decided to do what they called a 'put up and shut up' which amounted to the stockbroker putting up some potatoes, the industrialist putting up some onions, the underwriter putting up some bacon (after first knocking out his pipe) and the two corporate lawyers being shut up in the kitchen.

"The girls don't mind being in the kitchen - it reminds them of home when they were young. In fact being silly keeps us all young!"

"I think that's what's missing in my life!" said Thorne.

"You're still young enough to change. My advice is to make what you can - legally, and then spend your later years having fun. If you do it *that* way around, you'll be able to have fun with a clear conscience having paid off any loans!"

"It makes sense!" agreed Thorne.

"Dinner won't be ready for a while, so why don't we all go for a walk to the quarry and back?"

"Sounds great!"

It was agreed that the 'boys' and Thorne would go for a walk and keep out of the way of the 'girls' in the kitchen; but out of respect, they would ask 'Harry' and 'Gerry' if it was convenient for them to go.

"Sure, it'll be ready when it's ready, and if it's not it won't!" was the reply.

So Mick the stockbroker, Dick the industrialist, Ike the underwriter and Thorne wandered forth to look at a hole two miles away and then come home for dinner.

---oOo---

As the four of them were walking along, Thorne pointed out the children and asked whose they were.

"All the children come from families of nationals. Residents are discouraged from bringing any children into this country since they would be used to the outside world and would miss all modern conveniences including play stations and mobile phones. It would be relative hell for them and this would affect the general community and alter the culture of the country. Also working adults would find the culture ill-suited to their commercial aspirations. It makes perfect sense to admit only retired adults."

"What about medical problems as you get older?"

"We made a choice and accept the inevitable. We believe in *quality* of life over quantity of life or longevity of time – besides Victoria imports certain drugs to kill pain and make life pleasant. She also grows her own special herbs."

"What – like Cannabis?" asked Thorne jokingly.

"For those who suffer from glaucoma and multiple sclerosis – yes!"

"But 'waccy baccy' is more carcinogenic than 'kosher baccy' – or so I've heard!"

"Possibly, but a shorter life without pain is better than a longer life with pain. Don't forget – we emphasise *quality* here, not quantity. Pain is to be avoided but death is to be accepted!"

"You accept *death*?"

"Yes, but don't make the mistake of confusing death with *dying*!"

"What's the difference?"

"Dying can be frightening as the mind fights against the loss of the senses and then the soul fights against the loss of the mind. It's *loss* that frightens us - loss and pain. But we are taught that death is release from loss and pain. Death is release from dying!"

"And from the moment of birth, we've *all* been dying!" said Thorne.

"Exactly - that's why people's lives are so full of loss and pain!"

Thorne nodded, absorbing the concept. "Florianism?"

"Part of the teaching - yes!"

They walked on - one in green, one in red and two in brown.

After a while, Thorne asked them what they did in their retirement.

"We take each day as it comes. If it's warm weather, we will sit outside and drink mint and potato wine and cook for each other. If it's cool weather, we will sit inside and do the same."

"Nothing else?" asked Thorne.

"We paint, carve, sew tapestries, play backgammon - and the O'Haras' ferment hooch!"

Thorne laughed. "How do they keep it chilled?"

"North facing pantries with stone floors and stone shelves - who needs fridges?"

At the mention of 'north' Thorne asked if they knew why the women meditated on the north window – the only window representing the moon.

The men laughed, and told him that it had nothing to do with pantries.

"What then?" persisted Thorne.

"It's the only window that relates to the moon. In a closed community, women's cycles tend to occur together in a kind of unified rhythm. Beyond statistical average, women tend to ovulate during the new moon and menstruate during the full moon. Since it is vital that the population is kept steady at around 1,000 people, and it is the women who are in covert charge of society, they enter the temple on certain nights to meditate on the cycles of the moon and of their bodies. They consult the elders on when and when not to get pregnant. They are actually shown how to practise contraception!"

"Ahh..... *Now* I understand!" said Thorne.

"If ever you have any questions of a delicate nature concerning the nationals, feel free to ask any long-term resident – any of us will be happy to oblige!"

"Thank you." said Thorne. "They are lovely people but ..... "

"..... Xenophobic?" prompted Mick.

"Reserved." said Thorne.

"Reserved!" said Dick. He gave Mick a meaningful look.

"Here we are boys!" said Ike, pointing with the stem of his pipe to the large hole below them. "King Solomon would have been proud!" He filled his pipe and lit it, puffing great clouds into the air.

"Is that waccy or kosher?" asked Thorne.

"It's waccy – I have glaucoma!" replied Ike.

Thorne smiled in sympathy. He then looked at the overgrown quarry. "They must have moved tens of thousands of tons over the years."

"Easily. After blasting, it's shovelled by hand and carted by horse!" said Ike.

"Do they do much work in the quarry these days?"

"A bit of extraction for maintaining homes and lanes – that's all."

"That explains why it's so overgrown."

"Yes. Nature soon takes over again."

They all stood in silence for a while, listening to the song of a skylark and feeling the breeze on their faces. Thorne looked beyond the far side of the quarry and saw a mile of wild meadow with the dark forest beyond that. "I bet there's some wild game in those forests!"

"Plenty of boar and deer – so we never go hungry."

"Plenty of bee colonies too!" said Mick.

"Hive colonies *and* forest colonies?" asked Thorne.

"Centuries of hives plus annual migration of new queens – the forests are full!"

"Isolation guaranteed." said Dick with a chuckle.

"It says on the broadsheet that wood is used for fuel – you must get through a lot!"

"There's plenty of wood to go around, but demand is kept to a minimum since there is a limit on the number of houses that can be built and this has a knock-on effect on the population." said Ike.

"Hence the emphasis on Birth Control?"

"Hence the emphasis on Birth Control. This land could easily support twice the number of people, but Florianism teaches everyone to be responsible citizens and not to be greedy with what nature offers. Result: Everyone has plenty and nature is respected."

"Not like the outside world?"

"The outside world encourages humanity to breed, consume and spread like a virus. It rewards people with crèches, child allowances and priority housing over other people who try to live responsibly. Always remember: *You get what you reward!*"

"Crime too?"

"Crime too. Prisons *should* be miserable places and worse than the lowest living conditions. What *signals* are you sending to the community when all the prisons are full and new ones are constantly being built? *You get what you reward!*"

"I've seen the stocks outside in the square." said Thorne.

"They're never used because the thought of being locked outside in all weather and having to defecate in public fills everyone with horror! Public shame is a highly effective deterrent. What *signals* are you sending out when the welfare of the criminal has priority over the welfare of the citizen *You get what you reward!*"

"Capital punishment?"

"It exists here as the ultimate punishment for ultimate crimes. Citizens pay their leaders via taxes to protect them and what they have. Responsible leaders know their social duty and do not evade it by using weasel words to cover their moral cowardice. The goatherd must protect his herd from the wild beasts otherwise he will lose his goats *and lose his job.* It is no use approaching the wild beasts and trying to reason with them offering platitudes and comfortable living conditions. The nature of wild beasts is to kill defenceless animals – pure and simple!"

"Moral relativism?"

"Precisely! *That* is the corrosive influence that clouds the judgement of politicians and judiciary. Being of the 'liberal elite,' they live in locations of a more salubrious nature and avoid direct contact with the real world. Perhaps if *they* were to personally experience what the general public has to experience, they would change their minds – even if it was only for selfish and not social reasons."

"Justice?" inquired Thorne.

"Justice!" laughed Ike. He smiled at Thorne. "Everything is supposed to revolve around the core philosophy 'justice must be *seen* to be done' – but increasingly, it seldom is."

"How so?"

"The outside world now has the technology to determine who is innocent and who is guilty, but it is not being used because if it was, then the lawyers would no longer have the *power* to prolong trials and cash in on the excessive hours they generated. In effect, they would be on a vastly reduced income, and that would – in their mind – negate the value of their years of study for their degree and being called to the Bar!"

"They would be out of a job?" inquired Thorne.

"They would regard that profession as being economically unattractive!"

"How do you know this – after all, you're not lawyers!"

"True, but 'Harry' and 'Gerry' were, and they told us of the 'legal' stunts that were pulled to keep power within the judiciary as they forsaw a time when there would be an ongoing private war of power politics between the judiciary and the politicians."

"Politics?" prompted Thorne.

"Politics!" snorted Ike. He looked at Thorne. "The 'developed' world has many parties that *purport* to embrace variants of socialism, capitalism or liberalism, but few realise that socialism relies on social *fusion*, but liberalism relies on social *fission*!"

"How so?" inquired Thorne.

"It's simple. Take the collective and the individual. If the welfare of the collective is placed above the welfare of the individual, then you have social fusion and policies of socialism (with economic policy prevailing from social order). If the welfare of the individual is placed above the welfare of the collective, then you have social fission and policies of liberalism (with diplomatic policy prevailing from social chaos)."

Thorne smiled. "In the former; stability. In the latter; instability."

Ike nodded. "Exactly!"

Thorne paused in thought. "You have explained socialism verses liberalism, but what about capitalism?"

All three men chuckled, but it was Ike who spoke again. "Capitalism exploits *both* socialism and liberalism in that socialism gives it a slow but stable growth, whereas liberalism gives it a fast but unstable growth – followed by economic meltdown!"

Mick agreed. "Low risk/low yield versus high risk/high yield. These days investors tend to be of the *latter* category and eventually *that* kind of economy will crash!"

Thorne frowned. "The investors *drive* the economy, whilst the bankers *guide* it?"

"Yes. A quick killing, and get out before you burn out – or before the meltdown!"

Dick nodded. "Post meltdown, the politicians create a temporary culture of national socialism to occupy the people. Investments switch to a slower growth rate, until an economic boom triggers another liberalist spending trend – and off we go again!"

Thorne looked at Dick in silence.

Dick continued. "Politicians are just glorified salesmen. Salesmen in charge of a huge corporation called 'the nation.' They sell *concepts* to the public – not products, and they make damn sure they vote themselves huge pay rises – well above inflation. They are only interested in lining their own pockets – despite the political colour they purport to embrace! *Professional* companies have a Chief Executive who is either a production or a finance man – but never a salesman – its financial suicide! But there are *teams* of salesmen running most countries – salesmen or tyrants – *some choice*!"

Ike was looking into the middle distance. "You have several power-bases continually vying for more control; the judiciary, the politicians – and the *Church* of course!"

All three men chuckled. "The Church – the oldest swingers in town!"

Thorne smiled in mock innocence. "The Church seems harmless enough!"

All three men laughed. "*That* is the secret of its success!"

How so?"

Dick chuckled. "Can you think of any other company that promises so *much*, gives so *little*, yet millions of people are happy to embrace poverty - or martyrdom for it?"

Thorne shook his head and grinned. "*It's one hell of a sales pitch!*"

"Exactly! It controls its subjects in order to capitalise on them." said Dick

"Church, politicians or judiciary - different names, identical aims!" said Mick.

"The state always seeks control of its people - be it religious, political, judicial or economical - such as investors and bankers." said Ike.

"You realise that I'll be writing *all* this down for publication!" warned Thorne.

"We're retired and secure - so we can *afford* to be truthful!" said Ike, sadly.

They stood around looking at their little world, but seeing far beyond it.

"God help the outside world!"

"Amen to that!"

And then Thorne's stomach growled.

"Well..... *someone's* starving." said Ike.

"Home!" said Mick and Dick in unison.

With that, all four of them retraced their steps along the two miles back to the village.

---oOo---

By the time they had arrived back in the village and had entered the O'Haras' house, the dinner was keeping warm in the oven and 'Harry' and 'Gerry' were half-way through another mug of mint and potato wine and were blinking owlishly at each other.

"Hullo boys – you're back then?"

"Just in time by the look of it." said Mick.

"Would you dish up Mick – we're done in!"

Mick sighed and shook his head. He got six plates, six forks and a large spoon and proceeded to dish up the dinner. It looked and smelled gorgeous. A thick layer of bacon strips was topped by a layer of sliced onions which in turn was topped by a layer of sliced potatoes covered in melted goats cheese.

"We've served the garlic cream sauce separately in case the young gentleman doesn't care for garlic!" said Harry.

"Ohh..... the young gentleman *loves* garlic cream sauce!" said a *very* happy Thorne.

They all ate well. Afterwards, there was sufficient bacon left over to put into two wooden cat bowls outside for Harold and Gerald who came running after being called over by Mick. By the time the 'boys' had washed up, both Harriet and Geraldine were sound asleep. The 'boys' motioned Thorne outside to leave the 'girls' to sleep and the cats to scoff. "After a meal, we all retire to our homes for a spot of siesta. The girls will sleep for hours and the cats retire to a front porch!" said Ike indicating a series of porches that fronted each cottage.

"It's time I was retiring to my room as well!" said Thorne. "I wonder why the inn has so few customers?"

"It doesn't normally!" said Ike. "When a new guest arrives, everyone stays away for a week to allow the guest to acclimatise - after that it's business as usual."

"That's very considerate of them!" said Thorne.

"Well, it would be regarded as very tactless if everyone was buying drinks in front of a stranger who had no money of his own!"

"Ohh..... *of course!*" said Thorne.

"Good night for now, and drop by any time - you're always welcome." said Ike.

"Good night to you all - kiss 'Harry' and 'Gerry' for me!"

The 'boys' all burst out laughing. "The girls or the cats?"

"You decide!" smiled Thorne, and he waved good night

Cries of, "*The cats! The cats!*" came floating after him.

---oOo---

Walking back to the capital, Thorne was surprised that another day had gone well. It was so easy to mix business with pleasure in this country - in fact, he had difficulty in finding where one ended and the other began. He came in sight of the town walls and passed under them leaving the rural 'Quarry Lane' for 'Quarry Street' and its urban environs. Once again, the houses closed in along both sides of the street for hundreds of feet until he was at the west end of 'Market Square' and from there, it was a matter of a hundred and fifty feet to the inn at its centre. He had originally estimated that the town was smaller than it actually was. Experience gained in walking a measured map distance outside the town had led him to conclude that the town itself must be nearly one mile east/west and probably the same north/south. In these comfortable boots it was easy to walk a thousand feet believing it to be only a few hundred. To be sure of his facts he made a note to ask Chevral for information. He could always ask Giles if there was a map of the capital – after all, he seemed to have everything else!

As he entered the parlour, Giles and Clive were sitting facing each other, one in each settle like a pair of matching book ends each holding a small mug of mead. At his approach, Giles rose to serve him but Thorne bade him remain seated. "I'll be retiring early to write up some more notes."

"Is there anything you require, sir?"

"Do you have a map of the town itself?"

Giles rose again and Thorne quickly stopped him with a wave of his hand. "Tomorrow will be fine. Good night, gentlemen."

"Good night, sir." said Giles and Clive in unison.

Thorne ambled upstairs to his room.

Once he had removed his boots and clothing, Thorne sat on his bed writing, sorting and storing more notes that he had made that day. Certain categories were filling up quickly whilst others needed to be started; but on the whole, things were developing remarkably well. At this rate, he would have all his categories full within two weeks and his Editor had given him extended discretional leave amounting to months!

He decided to get his journalism done within a fortnight and spend the rest of his time working around – but still refining his notes according to personal experience to make sure that all his work was read and appreciated in its *true context relative to the whole* and not just certain pieces extracted and magnified out of all proportion to suit the personal whims of the individual. *Beware the people who just see what they want to see* – he reminded himself as he settled down to write. And his words took on a tone of sincerity and his journalism became authorship.

Chapter 6

The following morning, Thorne awoke to hear the sounds of wagon wheels trundling along the square. After taking several deep breaths to send more oxygen to his brain, he got up and peered through the window and saw that an outdoor market was being set up and that each stall was a flatbed cart pulled by a horse. As he watched, a stall holder detached his horse and it sank its nose into one of the now-*full* horse troughs.

"Market Square..... *of course*!" Thorne muttered, preparing himself for the day.

After due preparation and breakfast, Thorne received a copy of the town plan from Giles and strode out into the square which was gradually filling up with traders and public. He looked at each of the 'stalls' to see what they sold and noticed that members of the public were bringing items to the traders, smiling and walking away. As time went on, the trader's carts were filling up - instead of emptying, and Thorne started to smile as he realised what was happening. The shop keepers were supplying the traders with surplus stock and some of the public were also giving away what they no longer wanted; the traders would then sell to the general public and what money was made was split between the shop keepers and the traders

– a 'car boot' sale without the car! Thorne burst out laughing at the irony and several people looked at him with amused surprise as they passed by.

Looking at the quality of the merchandise, Thorne wished he had money so he could buy some of the goods but realised that labour must come before reward otherwise he would be sitting in the square with only a bucket for a friend!

He particularly had his eye on a circular pendant with a pentagram engraved on it. The pendant was particularly unusual in that it had a 'pool effect' on the metal, which told Thorne that it had been machined on a lathe whose revs were not in synch with the traverse of the cutter. A machine would run *contrary* to the culture he was in. It must have been *bought-in* and that would be costly. It was suspended from a good thick chain – a *man's* chain. It reminded him of the object in the temple and he felt drawn to it in a special way. He decided to ask the trader how much it would cost and if it could be saved for him until he had earned a week's wages to pay for it.

"You must be Thorne." the trader smiled.

"Does *everyone* know?" asked Thorne incredulously.

"We're a small country – *everyone* knows; that's part of our security."

"In a week's time, I'll have earned a hundred pou..... *crones*. How much would you charge me for the pendant and chain?"

The trader looked at the pendant and then at Thorne. "This clearly has some meaning for you – which is strange considering you have just arrived." He paused for a second and then came to a decision. "Take it now and *wear* it. When you are paid, seek me out and give me five crones for it."

Thorne did a quick mental calculation and realised it was only £12. 50. "It's worth at least twice that!" he said to the trader.

"Possibly, but when someone is drawn to something *beyond* mere curiosity, different laws apply!"

"Different *laws* apply?" said Thorne, thinking of what Veronica had said in the temple.

"This pendant must be intended for *you* – and no other, so it's price must be *lawful*!"

With that, the trader pressed the pendant into Thorne's hand. "Wear it *now*, sir!"

Thorne nodded, and fastened the pendant around his neck and tucked it under his shirt. "When I get paid, I will pay you *double*!"

"As you wish, sir." said the trader.

"Good day." said Thorne vaguely.

"Good day, sir." said the trader.

Thorne slowly wandered off feeling a bit weird.

---oOo---

Still feeling weird, Thorne looked around for somewhere to sit down and could only find one of the horse troughs whose water level was lower than 'soggy-bum' factor. Ignoring the presence of a friendly equine face, Thorne sat on the edge and wondered if his senses were the same. His face or *something* must have spoken volumes, because another trader approached him with a mug of mead. "With Giles' compliments, sir."

"Ohh..... thank you!" said Thorne, and started sipping before wondering how people were able to sense his needs before he did. He decided to find out and asked the trader who had brought his mead.

"We don't trade for profit, we trade for people!" was the reply.

"I don't understand!" said Thorne.

"Money is a mode of exchange - not a means of profit."

"I *still* don't understand!"

"We all live equally, so there is no need to make profit. We trade in order to help people find meaning in life - such as yourself!"

Thorne became aware of the weight of the pentacle around his neck and understood what the trader was telling him - social principle *before* capital practice.

"I really am looking forward to earning my wages so that I can return the compliment to everyone!"

The trader just smiled.

Suddenly, it had become very important to Thorne that he was working for others rather than earning for himself. Dedication for profit didn't matter. Dedication for people *did* - because this would reflect on himself and his value as a person. He began to see the depth of the culture of this little country and the scope of its potential in the outside world - *now* he knew why the residents were so protective of the nationals.

"Spiritual Symbiosis." he thought - and the 'Meaning of Life' was no longer a cliché.

He sat quietly in the sunshine, letting the atmosphere soak into him - discerning purpose within the human form.

As he sat, he saw three people walk into the square carrying stringed instruments. The first - a woman, carried a short-necked instrument resembling a mandolin. A man followed carrying a long-necked instrument resembling a mandola. Another man brought on an instrument which had a huge neck and resembled a medieval citterone or Indian sitar – he also brought a little stool to sit on.

By now, the square was full of people and Thorne realised that the 'market' was far more than just a place for commerce. He felt a light touch on his shoulder and looked around to see Veronica standing at his side.

"May I sit with you?"

"Yes, please do."

Veronica indicated the musicians. "Those people are part of the 'River-folk.' They sailed up the river generations ago and asked to stay. Later, we established fortified barriers at both ends of the river so only those with whom we trade can enter our country by that route. The 'River-folk' happily embraced our culture and have always entertained us with their music – they *voice* our thoughts. The small instrument they call a Barda, the middle one they call a Sanga, and the large one they call a Salka."

"Where were they from – originally?"

"Eastern Europe – I'm not sure which country."

The trader who had kindly brought Thorne a mug of mead was weaving his way through the crowd with three more mugs, which he gave to the players. They each smiled their thanks and took a hearty draught before settling down to play.

The crowd – which was fairly quiet, became absolutely silent as the music began. The songs sung by the woman were hauntingly beautiful as earnest notes came from her barda accompanied by rich mellowness from the sanga, and dark cold tones from the salka. Collectively the music embraced all the sweetness, richness and darkness of human life and love. Words were sung but they were a carrier for something else.

Thorne was mesmerised – sensing the connection, and words came into his mind from nowhere – "*All is One! The whole is greater than the sum of its parts! Gestalt!*"

He felt a light touch on his shoulder. "They've finished now!"

"…..What?"

"They've *finished* now!"

"They've just *started*!"

Veronica's look of amazement told him otherwise. "*So deep, so soon!*"

"I'm sorry?"

"*Don't be!*"

She squeezed his hand and got up and joined the crowd who were putting coins into a large jug, which someone had thoughtfully provided. When she arrived at the jug, she put in several large coins and said something to the players who all looked in Thorne's direction. She returned with a forced air of calm. "Let's have a spot of dinner!"

"It can't be noon already – I've just had breakfast!"

"Look at the obelisk."

Thorne looked at the shadow cast on the circle. It spoke volumes.

"You'd better finish *that* first!" she said pointing to his mead, which was nearly full.

Thorne silently picked up his drink and wondered if it had been spiked.

As they entered the inn, they were met by a questioning glance from Giles. "Is all in order madam?"

"It will be, Giles!" replied Veronica uncertainly. "What is available for dinner?"

"The River-folk have kindly brought some watercress with them, so Clive is making some cream of watercress soup – thickened with potato and flavoured with onion, followed by twenty clove garlic chicken wrapped in bacon, roast potatoes with onion and puréed carrots in butter."

"Sounds delicious, Giles." said Veronica.

"Sounds garlicky, Giles." said Thorne.

"Don't worry, sir. When garlic is roasted, fried or marinated in virgin olive oil, it loses its fire – it's the same with curry powder; when it's fried in butter it loses its fire and becomes sweet and mellow – trust us!"

"I trust you Giles, I trust you!" said Thorne.

Veronica gave a nervous giggle, which belied her calm appearance.

"Would *you* like a drink?" asked Thorne.

"A large mug of wine would be *much* appreciated!" said Veronica, sincerely.

Giles fished out a large mug and proceeded to fill it with wine from another barrel that sat on top of the sideboard and brought it across to Veronica.

"Thank you, Giles." said Veronica, taking a large draught.

Thorne's eyes widened as he watched her drain half the mug, but wisely kept silent.

"Dinner will be about twenty minutes!" informed Giles. "Will that be convenient?"

"Fine, thank you!" said Veronica.

Determined to put her at ease, Thorne decided to keep her mind occupied with trivia and asked her why 'dinner' was at noon rather than 'lunch.'

"Ohh..... that derives from medieval times – 'breakfast' in the morning, 'dinner' at noon, 'supper' in the evening and 'livery' at night. Later, we dispensed with 'livery' since it was just too much!"

"I see." said Thorne. "Why do your coins have a hole in the middle?"

Veronica fished inside the leather purse that was fastened to her belt and spread a series of coins out on the table, arranging them sequentially. "All groats have a centre hole because they are used more than crones and the public can identify them size for size against crones even if they are blind. As you can *see*, the diameter of the one groat is small and unique but the five groat matches the one crone, the ten groat matches the five crone, and the fifty groat matches the ten crone – so the only way to tell them apart with a casual glance or if you're blind is to see or feel the centre hole."

"Very practical, but there's also a circle in the centre of the crones." said Thorne.

"There's also a spiritual reason too." said Veronica, avoiding his comment.

Thorne compared groat and crone allowing intuition to surface. "..... *New* moon and *Full* moon."

"..... *Yes!*..... *How?*..... *How can you know that?*" asked Veronica, totally thrown.

Aware that he'd frightened her, Thorne instinctively took her hand and held it tightly. "*Don't worry, I won't tell anyone!*"

Veronica's response amazed him – she buried her face in his chest, and he found himself holding a very attractive, very distressed young woman. "*God help me!*" he thought.

---oOo---

Fortunately, Giles was still in the kitchen with Clive, so Thorne was able to free one of his arms enough to grasp her mug of wine. "Here....." he started to say but Veronica was already downing the other half of its contents. "Calm down sweetheart, we'll have dinner and then we'll go for a walk in the fresh air – you'll feel much better then!" He held her in silence for a while, just stroking her hair until he felt her shaking ease and her body relax against his. "*What have I got into?*" he thought.

Veronica raised her face and gazed into his eyes. "You called me *sweetheart*! No-one has ever called me sweetheart before – except my father!"

"I'm sorry....." began Thorne, but Veronica shushed him, smiling.

"I like it..... It's nice!"

Thorne struggled to control a situation, which could deteriorate into something all too horribly familiar. "Sit up straight! Giles will be along soon with our dinner!"

"Yes, daddy!" she giggled, and looked coyly at him through all too beautiful eyes.

Thorne downed the contents of his own mug – not caring any more if it *was* spiked.

"Would you like another drink?" asked Veronica, sweetly.

Knowing it would get him away from her, he rose from the table.

"I'll have another one too!" she said waving her mug at him.

"I don't think....."

"But I *do*!"

"Only *one* more." said Thorne trying to avoid a scene. "If you behave. *Promise?*"

"Make it another large one – and I promise!"

Thorne went behind the counter to refill his mug – and hers, cursing silently.

"Thank you, daddy."

"I'm not your da..... *father*!"

"You *look* like my daddy."

Thorne barely made it back to the table in time before Giles pattered down the corridor carrying two bowls of soup.

"Sorry for the delay, sir and madam, but Clive had to blend the watercress, cream and potato to the correct thickness before he felt it was just right."

"Take as long as you want – there's no problem there!" said Thorne – smile in place.

Veronica was positively beaming as Giles returned to the kitchen.

"Eat your soup!"

"Yes, daddy."

---oOo---

The soup was delicious, although Thorne's mind was in no condition to appreciate it. Veronica kept her promise and behaved, although her face became pinker and her smile broader from the effects of the wine. The main course arrived and ample justice was done to its excellence; after which, both Thorne and Veronica sat back against the settle and blew out their cheeks. Luckily, the meal had stopped some of the effects.

"Fresh air! Time for that walk young lady!" said Thorne, rising.

"Help me up then!" mumbled Veronica.

Thorne took her hand and pulled hard.

"*Whee.....!*" she exclaimed, and hugged him tightly like a limpet.

Thorne looked around in panic, but Giles had wisely disappeared.

Trying to disengage Veronica from his chest was worse than trying to disengage Harold from his ear, but eventually he prised her off and half-dragged her outside. "*Walk!*" he hissed.

"Must we?"

"*Yes!*"

"Where shall we go then?" she asked, holding his hand - in public.

"Let's go down 'Castle Street' - I haven't been there yet."

"*No! Not there!*"

"Why not?"

"Let's go up 'Main Street' and leave the capital - there's a *lovely* view of the country!"

Thorne was all too glad to get her away from public view so he happily agreed, and together they walked up 'Main Street' pretending to admire the shops along the way. They passed many shops along both sides of the street – including Butchers, Grocers, Drapers, Tailors, Bootmakers, Barbers, Printers, Saddlers, Furniture, Hardware, Opticians, Morticians, Occultists, Herbalists and Medical surgeries – the latter, they avoided!

Finally, they passed under the walls and emerged outside to a panoramic view of the entire countryside over a thousand feet below. Although the land descended gradually over a three-mile stretch, the view was still highly impressive. Thorne marvelled at the view and Veronica stood at his side. A sudden gust of wind chilled her and she shivered. Thorne removed his coat and placed it gently over her shoulders and she snuggled up to him. "Thank you." she said.

Thorne sighed, defeated, and put a fatherly arm around her shoulders. "How about that walk then?"

She gazed up at him with deep sad eyes. "Would you like to see where the marsh phantoms play?"

"Go on then." said Thorne, trying to cheer her up.

"This way." she said, steering them right for a clockwise walk around the walls.

Together they slowly walked east along the foot of the north wall. Eventually, they arrived at the north-east tower and walked around its base until they were at the beginning of the east wall. To the east, the land was higher, but it was still two hundred feet down. However, the gradient leading to it wasn't a gentle 10% but a scary 30%. Veronica pointed. "The land below was excavated out into a huge crater. What appears to be the surface of the land is really the surface of the marshes and that's where the marsh phantoms play!"

"I can't see anything."

"They only come out at night when the air is still, and then you see blue-green flames moving over the surface of the marshes. It's quite spooky, especially when you are only a few feet away but you must never follow them otherwise the ground opens up and swallows your body and your soul rises and becomes like them, and then you smell just as bad as they do!"

"Do you still believe that?"

"When you're a child, your fears create your imagination, and then you grow up."

"I frightened you today – didn't I?"

"I'm twenty-eight, *and still a child*!"

"Oh..... Veronica, I'm so sorry!" said Thorne, and he kissed her forehead.

"*Are* you mystical?"

"No, I'm moronic!"

They stood huddled together for a while and then Veronica spoke. "I haven't been down there for years. Let's see our phantoms *together*!"

"It's a long way down!" said Thorne.

"There's a firm path – it's used by the town's sewer inspectors."

"Hence the smelly gaseous phantoms."

"As a child, so little means so much."

"True in every culture."

Together, they followed the tortuous path down the hill. Veronica took the lead saying that as she was familiar with the route, it made sense. Even so, Thorne was concerned for her safety and, more than once, shot out a hand to grab her when he thought she was about to slip. Aware of this, Veronica kept her face averted to conceal a mischevious smile.

Eventually, they emerged onto a broad landing which had twenty stone steps going down to the level of the marshes and they sat huddled together ten steps up from its surface. Fifty feet from them stood a large outlet, which emerged from the hill high up and ran down to extend over the marsh ten feet above the landing.

"It'll still be a while before the sun sets!" said Thorne.

"I know, but sometimes it's good to be alone - or with a friend."

Thorne was perplexed, but content to be in her company. "Wherever I go, I see happy people - yet you enjoy being alone."

Veronica smiled, "I love my people, but sometimes I need to be alone - I think it runs in the family!"

"I know the feeling." empathised Thorne.

Veronica looked into Thorne's eyes. "Tell me about your people."

Thorne blew out his cheeks. "Where do I begin?"

"Are your people like mine?" Veronica offered.

"I wish to God they were!" Thorne exclaimed.

Veronica smiled gently and waited patiently for Thorne to find *somewhere* to begin.

Eventually, he was able to look *within* to begin to describe his own culture - or was it his own *nature*?

"We are a very unhappy people because we have no reason to exist. We *do* exist but we don't know why."

"Is that important?"

"It is to us."

"Why?"

"We *must* have purpose and progress in life. To exist without purpose is torture!"

Veronica frowned. "Could you define 'purpose' and 'progress?'"

Thorne paused as he tried to define his own fears – and found that he couldn't.

Veronica smiled at him. "You're afraid, but you don't know why."

Thorne was silent for a while. Eventually he spoke. "We are driven by a combination of fear and guilt. Each generation is conditioned to 'improve' on the previous generation's creations in order to feel worthy of existence. Everyone competes with everyone else in a desperate attempt to feel superior and thus gain confidence. Success is measured in profit, therefore profit must *always* increase and we are continually upgrading our technology to facilitate this increase. Ironically, our 'enhanced' technology advances beyond our control leading to errors that increase in both frequency and magnitude. We are constantly restricted by our bureaucracy so we are incapable of taking any corrective measures. We hide our failures behind statistics and blame others in order to avoid responsibility when it all goes wrong. Nothing is simple anymore. Over time, we lose faith in ourselves and we dread our own future."

Veronica nodded thoughtfully. "So your cultural values are based on growth of profits and not growth of people – appearance and not substance?"

"Yes – standard of living over quality of life."

"Hmm..... a fearful culture that values expediency."

"The outside world regards expediency as *efficiency*!"

"Does *all* the outside world feel that way?"

"It is rapidly becoming so – even the 'third world' countries believe we have all the answers to all their problems – hence their desire to emulate or emigrate!"

"And you don't have the answers?"

"No. The 'third world' also values the 'first world' on 'appearance and not substance' – to quote your own words."

"So the 'third world' are following the 'first world' – that's sad!"

"It is for us, and it will be for them because we are taking them along the same path that we have trod. Each generation repeats the mistakes that previous generations have made. We are progressing technologically but we are regressing culturally. We have forgotten how to evolve *ourselves* – so how *dare* we try to evolve *them*? In the end, they will become like us – dependent on technology and devoid of spirituality."

"Perhaps *we* can help *you* to help *them*."

"I pray it's true!" said Thorne.

"So do we!" sighed Veronica. "We see so much – yet we can do so little! Your own culture threatens to snuff us out – that's why we have always been so reclusive!"

"I know. You are the 'missing link' – in an *evolutionary*, not an archaeological sense!"

"We are aware of this." said Veronica.

"It seems that intuition supplies the answers *before* intellect can ask the questions."

"Do you have the answers?" asked Veronica.

Thorne listened to silence, and then his face slowly cleared. "I think so."

"What are they?"

"I need time and space to write them down for publication." he said, feeling strange.

Veronica smiled. "It's a bit late for that just now, we'll be seeing our phantoms soon!"

---oOo---

They sat huddled together in the gathering gloom, and presently Veronica pointed out blue-green wisps that were flickering and vanishing in front of them as though trying to entice the unwary forward into certain death. Most of the wisps were small and came and went frequently, but occasionally a large one would appear and dance majestically for a while before slowly fading away. Veronica pointed to it as it appeared again. "That's the 'queen-o-the phantoms' – she is the one who manifests as a beautiful woman and leads young men down to the marshes where they join her forever! The small ones are the souls of all the men she has snared and encased in flame..... *Whoooo!*"

"..... *WHOOOO!*" repeated an owl behind them, making them jump.

"You'd better stop '*whoo-ing*,' in case that owl takes a fancy to you!" said Thorne.

"I don't get much chance to woo anyone - so I'm making the most of it!"

"Your very attractive and charismatic." said Thorne, gently. "But I'm twenty years older than you - besides after two failed relationships, I'm a confirmed bachelor. I'd prefer to take it slowly and have the love of a beautiful friend with no expectations rather than rush headlong into the lust of a beautiful partner with high expectations."

Veronica was silent for a while, and then sighed. "Yes, you're right. I also have duties that deny me any immediate chance of courtship, but it's nice to pretend. As *friends*, could we keep pretending for a while?"

Thorne smiled fondly and gave her a hug. "Woo all you want, sweetheart - I'm very happy to play along!"

"Thank you!" she whispered, and kissed him on the cheek.

"..... *Whoooo!*" said Thorne, rolling his eyes.

"..... *WHOOOO!*" repeated the owl.

---oOo---

After an hour spent huddled together watching the phantoms - both wrapped in their own thoughts, Thorne turned to Veronica. "We'd better be returning, since I have to be up early to meet Chevral so that he can show me where I'll be working."

"Help me up then." said Veronica.

Thorne took both of Veronica's hands and pulled gently. She stood facing him holding his hands. "Thank you for this very silly, but very special night."

Thorne smiled. "First date: romantic evening for two at the cess pit!"

"Well, there's plenty of scope for improvement later on!" laughed Veronica.

"Great!" joked Thorne. "We'll do the *graveyard* next time!"

Veronica smiled thoughtfully. "The graves in the groves – yes, we must do that!"

"Okay, *now* you're scaring me!" said Thorne.

"There's no need to be scared – it's a beautiful place and very restful. It gives added meaning to a special friendship – trust me!"

"*I do.*" said Thorne, looking at her with growing affection.

"Ohh..... those magic words! Come on..... beddy-byes – or Chevral will be cross!"

Together, hand in hand, they slowly ascended the path towards the town.

It took them a good hour to re-enter the town, at which point; Veronica bade Thorne good night and watched him return to the inn. After he had gone inside, she quietly made her way down 'Castle Street' to sleep off the effects of the wine.

Chapter 7

The following morning, Thorne awoke from a deep and relaxing sleep and prepared himself for the day. After breakfast, he waited patiently for Chevral to arrive and was wondering what the phrase 'digging and carting' meant. It didn't sound complicated, so he felt confident and optimistic and listened for the familiar sounds of boot-steps. Within a half-hour, Chevral entered the parlour carrying a long apron, which he presented to Thorne. "Good day, Thorne, are you ready to start?"

"Good day, Chevral, I certainly am!"

"Excellent!" beamed Chevral. "Wherever you go, simply remove your coat and cravat and wear this apron. As you can see, it is a quick and simple transformation from gentleman to labourer since boots and apron give effective protection for almost any task."

Thinking of Bradley, Thorne had to agree. He followed Chevral outside and together they walked down the street to a waiting four wheeled, flatbed cart which held seven smiling people - four men and three women - *all* attired as male labourers sitting on the edge of the cart with their feet dangling down.

As he sat with them and exchanged greetings, he looked at the women in their boots and breeches and was reminded of Virginia. He smiled in irony - *two women who approved of him - and both sisters!*

Meanwhile, Chevral had nodded to the driver. "Thank you Mycroft!"

"Very good, sir." said the giant softly, and clicked the horses into a walk up the street, past the shops and out of the town. Emerging outside the gates, they were all treated to the panoramic vista which lay before them, and they slowly descended the lane to the farms some miles away. It was slow progress under a sky that promised to be favourable. The birds were already singing, but it was still too early for the insects to be out and about. As they trundled along, they sang little songs to pass the time.

Travelling slowly in the open air, Thorne found it easier to view the Groves and saw that on each side at the back, farthest from the lane, ran scores of mausolea which were heavily veiled by orchard trees. It reminded Thorne of the Appian Way out of Rome - but on a smaller scale. Finally, the cart stopped at the southern cross lane holding the farms of Upper and Lower South and Mycroft turned and quietly addressed them.

"If you please, ladies and gentleman, four to Lower South One, and four to Lower South Two - thank you."

Everyone jumped off the cart and the group began to walk down the cross lane leading to those farms. As they were walking, Thorne asked if there was any preference as to which farm had which people.

"No, but it's customary that the ladies take the first farm and the gentlemen the second. That way, the ladies don't have so far to walk, and it frees up Mycroft so he can return immediately for more labourers for the other farms."

"Fair enough." said Thorne.

After a mile, the group arrived at Lower South One, and the three women and the oldest man peeled off and knocked on the farmhouse door whilst the three younger men and Thorne continued down the cross lane for another two miles.

Finally arriving at Lower South Two, the men knocked on the door of the farmhouse and were greeted by the farmer's wife who bade Thorne put his coat and cravat on a hook and led them down the passage, which went through the house to the kitchen. Arriving in the kitchen, they were greeted by the farmer and his two daughters. After Thorne had secured his apron, the farmer, his daughters and the four men went outside into the farmyard. He opened the door of a small shed and turned to the men. "Well, gentlemen, the season is summer and the product is potatoes – what do we do?"

"Earth up!" chorused all – bar Thorne.

"Tools?"

"Spades to cover!"

"Usual rules apply, when *one* gets tired; then *all* will rest!"

There were nods of assent from all those present.

The farmer handed out spades to all four men and two more to his daughters. He chose another for himself. "This way." he said, leading them down a track towards a five-acre field that was heavily framed with hedgerow.

Thorne looked at the size of the field and the density of its border and was reminded of the whole country and its border of dense forest. "Why are the fields this size and the hedgerow so dense?" he asked the farmer.

"Five acres is a good size to judge five day's work for five people, and the hedgerow is high and dense to protect the crops from excess wind, rain and frost. It also acts as a haven for all the wildlife!" The farmer turned to his team. "Right everyone, we're here nice and early, so if we work steadily, the job *will* be done and we *won't* be!"

Thorne looked at the field again praying that he would be able to keep up with them.

The team was organised to work three furrows at once. Each furrow had two workers raising the loose earth and packing it firm around the potatoes to protect them from the autumnal weather that would come later. The farmer would check the furrows to ensure that all was as it should be and would occasionally beat further any areas that were deemed suspect. As Thorne was new to physical work, it was agreed that the farmer would keep a friendly eye on his progress. Initially, Thorne was concerned that his work might be found at fault, but as time progressed, he started to relax as the farmer was good natured and not the least intimidating as he had initially feared.

Mercifully, they worked steadily, and Thorne was able to do justice to the team spirit that developed along the furrows so that when they eventually took a break, he felt it hadn't been because of him and his sense of personal achievement grew. They would work steadily for about two hours and then rest for about twenty minutes drinking cool water from a large jug that the farmer's wife would bring. The long summer days allowed plenty of daylight so the work was unhurried. At noon, they downed tools and returned to the farmhouse for dinner.

Wisely, they ate lightly, since physical work on a full stomach is bad for the worker and bad for the work and then they strolled gently back to the field to continue.

"Careful now!" said the farmer. "We've just had our dinner so let's build up slowly, that way the work is enjoyed and not endured!"

They built up gradually and Thorne's body was already on autopilot – his mind relaxed and his soul at peace. He was actually quite surprised when the farmer announced that they had done enough for one day and it was time for 'liquid' supper!

They strolled back to the farmhouse carrying their tools, and washed them down before putting them away in the shed. On entering the kitchen, the farmer's wife treated them to chicken pie, onions and creamed potatoes. When Thorne inquired how it was possible to eat potatoes now whilst others were still being earthed up, the farmer told him that potatoes were like apples – different varieties were grown and harvested at different times. "Although our seasons are fairly constant, we have different climates depending on the terrain. In the lowlands, the earth is relatively warm and wet due to protection by the forest and the underground streams that supply our wells. In the highlands, the earth is open to seasonal change from the climate and is dryer due to rainfall draining quickly towards the lowlands. Result: constant seasons but variable climate! As for seasonal produce, the French are aware of the similarity between apples and potatoes – you've heard of 'pommes' et 'pommes de terres' or 'apples' and 'apples of the earth'- haven't you?"

Thorne nodded with a smile as he saw the connection.

The farmer disappeared into the pantry and returned with a large jug of mead, which he placed on the table. He then went to a sideboard and brought several mugs, which he handed out to everyone, and began to pour a generous amount into each mug.

"Is this your own mead?" asked Thorne.

"No. Every month, all the farms receive a small barrel from the cellars of the Groves courtesy of Mycroft's or Garfield's cart as a reward from the Duke for providing food for the country."

Thorne smiled at the gesture and then started to frown as he had a vision of vast underground catacombs containing barrels of wine standing among caskets of corpses. "Don't the dead get in the way?" he asked half-jokingly.

Everyone burst out laughing and the farmer smiled at Thorne. "No. Although both are underground, the catacombs are separate from the cellars and are on a lower level – so there's no chance of contamination."

"That's a relief! That's also a lot of mead!"

"We always have a large surplus of wine and honey, so we make surplus quantities of mead and sell half at half price to the citizens and give the other half to the labourers. Everyone's very happy!"

"I can imagine!" laughed Thorne. "Cheers!"

They all raised their mugs – including the farmer's wife.

---oOo---

After finishing their mug of mead, it was agreed that they would finish the five-acre field on Fiveday evening, rest Sixday and Sevenday and return to 'earth up' the next five-acre field over the following Oneday to Fiveday.

"Thank you for your help!" said the farmer as they were led up the passage to the front door. Thorne removed his apron and put his coat back on leaving his cravat loose around his open shirt collar. The group bade good night to the farmer's wife and began the two-mile walk to the farm at Lower South One.

"In future, I'll leave my coat and cravat behind and just wear my apron - it's far easier!" said Thorne.

"Everyone does when they're labouring!" smiled one of the men.

They walked along in the cool of the evening, and Thorne - still warm from work, was reminded of the pentacle hidden beneath his shirt. It felt reassuringly cold and heavy.

---oOo---

By the time they arrived at Lower South One, the three women and the other man were waiting outside to meet them. They all exchanged greetings and walked the remaining mile to the main lane where Mycroft would be waiting for them. As they caught sight of the cart in the distance, Thorne asked them how many journeys each day did Mycroft have to make.

"There are two regular drivers. Mycroft covers all weekday transport between the capital and Upper and Lower South. He will make two or three return trips each day depending on the requirement. On Sevendays, he is also the coachman for any mail deliveries. The other driver is Garfield who covers all weekday transport between the capital and Upper and Lower North. He will also make two or three return trips each day depending on the requirement. He is also the coachman for the Duke's Landau and the Doctor's Brougham."

"I arrived in a Landau - is that the Duke's?" asked Thorne.

"The Duke owns all the coaches. He has one special Landau with a solid roof and extra windows, two general Landaus with folding roofs and two Broughams."

"That seems a lot for just one man!"

"Only the special Landau is reserved for the Duke, the general Landaus are for public transport on Sixdays. Danvers and Gilmore run services between capital and country."

"Danvers and Gilmore?"

"Danvers is the third driver. On weekdays he takes the keepers to the hives and the loggers to the forest, and Gilmore fills in for all three of them giving each a good two days rest. They often work each other's routes just for a bit of a change!"

"That explains why it was Mycroft who brought me from the hives!" said Thorne.

Finally, they all arrived at Mycroft's cart and greeted him as they jumped up onto the flatbed. After they were all safely aboard, Mycroft clicked the horses into a gentle walk home and Thorne stretched his body as his muscles were starting to ache.

"Before you retire, you would be wise to have a long hot soak in a bath, and then you will sleep well and be fine for the next day!" suggested one of his companions.

"I certainly will, but I'm afraid that Giles or Clive will have difficulty with the large boiling kettle!"

"I think you'll find that Veronica has taken care of that – at least for the first week – so make the most of it!"

Thorne smiled in contentment as his companions started to sing their little songs on the journey home.

Eventually, they arrived back in the capital and the cart pulled into the square. They all jumped down, and, after bidding good night to Mycroft, they retired. Thorne walked to the inn and entered the parlour. Giles was giving his counter a little dust and smiled as he saw him. "Good evening, sir, is there anything you require?"

"I'm advised that a hot soak is in order each night before I retire - is that convenient?"

"We have anticipated your needs. Might I suggest a small mead to accompany it?"

"By all means, Giles - and thank you!"

"You're welcome, sir." said Giles - pouring a rather *large* 'small' mead.

Thorne spent the next hour in comparative luxury lying in soapy state and steaming up the bath-house. Sipping his mead, he admired his clothing hanging majestically from one peg whilst his pentacle dangled merrily from another. He surveyed his life through the bottom of his mug. "I don't want to go home!" he said simply.

An hour later, snug in his bed, Thorne was blissfully asleep.

---oOo---

The next four days were more of the same - except that the supper on Twoday was roast boar with apples, onions, and carrots and a mug of mead; Threeday was boar casserole with brown beans and onions topped with suet crust dumplings - and a mug of mead; Fourday was roast goat with mint sauce, onions and potatoes - and mead. Fiveday was *pay-day* and they were treated to goatherd pie with brown beans and onions - mead - and one hundred crones each!

That evening, on the cart back to the capital, Thorne felt huge satisfaction with life. He had worked well and enjoyed both the work and the company of his friends. He had his first wages and was determined to seek out the market trader and pay him *ten* crones for the pendant that he constantly wore beneath his shirt. He knew that much of *this* week's wages would be spent entertaining all those who had befriended him - including the lovely Veronica and the long-suffering Tyler! After his initial gesture of genuine appreciation, he could always be more prudent in the future. But right now, let's have some *fun*!

After breakfasting on Sixday morning, Thorne thanked Giles for showing discretion concerning clientele until he had earned his first wages. Giles just gave a little smile and said nothing, but that day, the parlour started to fill with customers and Thorne realised just how much everyone had considered his feelings and he felt very moved. He asked Giles for advice on how best to show appreciation to all those who had worked to make his induction easier.

"Our surplus wine and mead is sold at half-price to all the citizens. If you were to donate an appropriate sum, I will ensure that all involved will be rewarded."

"Excellent, Giles – but how much would be considered appropriate?"

"A large mug of wine or mead costs forty groats – that's about one pound sterling."

"So if I left, erm..... forty crones – would that be appropriate?"

Giles' eyes widened. "That's about one hundred pounds, sir. Are you sure?"

"Not enough, Giles?"

"Too much, sir. That will supply fifty people with two rounds of large drinks!"

"I think I know about twenty people right now."

Giles recalculated. "Five large rounds per person – they'd be flat on their backs!"

Thorne grinned. "A day to *remember*, eh?"

Giles cringed. "A day to *forget*, sir!"

"Just this once, Giles, and I promise to be good in the future."

Giles sighed as he took Thorne's coins. "I can guess who those people will be."

"Make sure you and Clive are among them."

"Thank you, sir."

Thorne pondered. "A hundred less ten less forty still leaves fifty – God I'm rich!"

"As a *guest*, yes – relatively speaking." said Giles.

"But not as a *resident*?" asked Thorne.

"Please bear in mind that residents have to buy their own food, drink, clothes, supplies and pay an annual residency fee!"

"Okay, so how much would it cost per year to remain a resident?"

"Typically, *guests* would work for six months and have all food, clothes and lodging for free – so they should be able to save at least two thousand crones. If they became *residents*, then the annual cost of food and drink would be about one thousand crones; existing clothing should last at least five years – so if we add that potential to the cost of supplies both should not exceed five hundred crones – plus an annual residency fee of four thousand crones. Total cost is about five thousand five hundred crones."

"Working fifty weeks a year, I'd only earn five thousand crones at best!"

"Correct. You would have to use some of your own money that you saved back home ensuring that you enter this country as a committed *giver*, not a committed *taker*!"

"Very shrewd!" said Thorne. "Like the policy of the former European Union?"

Giles smiled. "Redistribution of Wealth is a noble policy – to all who are *givers*, but if any are *takers*, then *they* end up with all the wealth and we would have elitism again with reversed cultural values. First World and Third World would just change places."

Thorne laughed. "You sound just like Chevral!"

Giles was solemn. "We are *all* of one accord."

"*True* Socialism!" said Thorne respectfully.

"That's what we aspire to. Anyway, as a resident, you could live where you wanted and since like tends to attract like, you would probably live among others who share your nature."

Thorne smiled. "You mean the *ghetto* of 'Quarry Lane' Village?"

Giles nodded. "A cruel word, but true."

"Human nature – like *all* nature, follows the path of least resistance. Nature is *lazy*!"

"Like lightning." said Giles.

"Lazy lightning!" smiled Thorne. "I would live in the capital – among the nationals."

Giles looked quizzically at Thorne. "Why?"

"It's important to have something to aspire to – and not just retire and fade away."

Giles nodded. "That's why Clive and I decided to live here and not in the village."

"So you are both aspiring after the ideal?"

"We are both artists – in different ways."

"How so?"

"Clive is the artist in catering, and I am the artist on canvas." Giles indicated the four beautiful oils hanging in the parlour. "Those were part of my final series."

Thorne looked at the paintings and back to the frail little man in his apron and slippers. "With quality like that, you could make a fortune outside this country!"

"I did, and that's half the reason why Clive and I retired here. We were tired of being judged on the grounds of material wealth. We wanted to be accepted for who we *are* not what we *had*!"

"What was the other half of the reason?" asked Thorne – without thinking.

Giles smiled sadly. "Political Correctness has done more harm than good to people such as Clive and myself. It has made public all relationships that should remain private and sacred. In *this* country, there are no public displays of affection – either heterosexual or homosexual – since heterosexuals find homosexual display distasteful, and homosexuals find heterosexual display equally distasteful. Public display either way is offensive to the other. Outside this country, everything is – to quote an American phrase – 'In Your Face' and *everyone* suffers! Truly civilised people are aware of the feelings of others and restrict all intimate practices to the bedroom. It is vital that neither side offends the other. That way, *everyone* can be happy together; and gay in the *true* sense of the word!"

Thorne was amazed. "May I write this down as part of my report?"

"With our blessing, sir." said Giles. "I know Clive will approve."

---oOo---

Thorne left Giles to serve the customers and wandered upstairs to his room with a mug of mead in his hand and a jug of thoughts in his head. After taking and storing more of his notes, he decided to finish his drink and go for a walk down the hill to the Groves. As he returned to the parlour and handed over his mug, Giles informed him that all his shirts, socks and unders would be brought to his room that day - together with fresh linen.

"Thank you, Giles. I'm just off for a walk to the Groves. I'll be back after noon."

"Very good, sir. It's roast venison with gravy, cabbage and croquette potatoes."

"*I'll be back!*" said Thorne, giving his best Terminator impression.

Giles gave a giggle and waved him off with his bar cloth.

---oOo---

Arriving outside the town gates and viewing the sky over the north end of the country, Thorne felt that it would probably rain later. Well..... he'd had two weeks of sunshine so it would be churlish to moan over a little rain! He walked confidently down the lane that led to the Groves whistling the tune to one of the songs that his friends had sung on their journeys to and from the fields on Mycroft's cart.

Eventually, he came to the beginning of the Groves, which lay either side of the lane and wondered which side to explore first. "Spoilt for choice!" he said to himself, and decided to go down the left and come up the right. Like everywhere else, the Groves were designed in a very efficient and aesthetically pleasing way. Nearest the road ran high dense hedgerows to protect all produce from the excesses of the weather. Going between a gap in the hedgerow and down a track used by the grovers, he entered long rows of olive trees and saw that these would probably be ready in several weeks time. Moving in farther he encountered long rows of apple trees whose fruit was still fairly small and green. It would be a few months before this variety would be ready for groving! Moving in deeper, he finally encountered the long row of mausolea and was surprised to see equally long rows of garlic separating him from the grey stone buildings. "Vampires have it tough here!" he muttered to himself.

Keeping to the track, Thorne made his way between the furrows of garlic. He took a peep inside the open archway of the first tomb, and saw a broad flight of stone steps descending into the earth. He looked at the back wall expecting to see some family names, but all he saw was a niche, which held a lamp and a box of matches. Thorne was pleased with what he saw, but puzzled with what he didn't see. He exited the tomb and peeped into the next tomb. Aha!..... Here were the names and two sets of dates, birth and death. He peeped into the third which was like the second, and the fourth was the same. He went back to the first tomb, and realised it was used by the mortuary attendants who carried the caskets down to the catacombs – hence the lamp and matches so thoughtfully provided for exploration!

Feeling like Indiana Jones or Van Helsing, Thorne took the lamp, which was ready for use and lit a match. When the flame on the wick was steady, he carefully closed its little glass door, and – taking a deep breath, he descended into the flickering gloom.

Descending the steps was easy since daylight shone past him illuminating his path all the way down to the bottom. However, once he arrived on the floor of the catacombs some twenty feet down, darkness enfolded his senses like some cool dry blanket and he was forced to rely on his fragile looking lantern, which cast a pale half-hearted glow around him. "Okay." he said to himself. "Where technology ends, spirituality begins!" Patting his pendant for good luck, he set off north down the corridor.

He'd only gone some ten feet when he arrived in the space under the second tomb and saw that he stood between two walls of stone – each containing three levels of niches, and each containing three bodies wrapped in shrouds – *but no caskets*! These corpses were mummified in a preserve, which included large quantities of salt and mint! Thorne felt uneasy, as – once again – he was made aware of the cultural differences between 'his' people and these people. His rational mind knew that salt dries and preserves the body, and that mint sweetens the air – so their culture made sense in minimising the use of wood, which was used to benefit the living, and not wasted on the dead.

Out of respect, he did not touch the corpses, but continued down the corridor finding more of the same. He had walked the length of nine tombs when he was aware of daylight ahead and he realised that every tenth tomb was another entrance for the mortuary attendants. Realising this, it made sense that a corpse didn't have to be carried for a mile or so underground to its resting place but could be carried on a cart and taken down the entrance nearest to its family vault.

Emerging into the daylight, Thorne blew out the lantern and – feeling stupid – walked back to the first tomb to replace the lamp in its niche. "*Now* I get the picture!" he said, and walked back along the tombs at ground level occasionally peering into a family vault. Under each family vault the catacombs held eighteen bodies and Thorne was wondering what happened when the capacity exceeded that number. Was there a kind of rotation system where number nineteen replaced number one, and number one being nicely dry was cremated? It would certainly explain why all the shelves were full and no new tombs were being built. It would also explain why there were far more names with dates carved into the walls of the tombs than the capacity of eighteen underneath!

Becoming bored, Thorne decided to walk as far as the centre tomb and then return to the capital. He arrived at the main tomb far sooner than he thought and realised that although the Groves stretched for several miles on both sides of the lane, the line of mausolea ran for less than a mile each side, and the other buildings were storehouses.

Walking into the main tomb, Thorne saw that it belonged to the Ducal family. He ran his eye down the list of names with dates and noted with surprise that nearly all the men's names showed Saxon heritage - though one or two seemed Danish. There were: Osberts, Oswulds, Oswulfs, Osmunds, Guthrums, Leofrums, Wulfreds and Wulfrums. There were many women's names, which evolved through the generations - although the men's did not. "Feminist Psychologists would have a field day with that one!" observed Thorne, dryly. He noticed that from the 1700's women's names became a lot more graceful such as: Miranda, Sabrina, Demelza, Ophelia, Arabella, Callista, Claudina, Georgina. There was also a Clarissa, who had died fifteen years ago aged only 40! Even the Ducal family were not immune to tragedy!

By now the sky was darkening, and Thorne - hearing a rumble of thunder, decided to head for home. He made it just beyond the first tomb and then the skies opened and he had to dash back and sit inside in the dry whilst the rain pelted down. An hour later, he was still sat there cursing his curiosity and wanting his dinner but the rain had other plans. Two hours later, he was thinking of making a serious dash for it and *sod* his frock coat – he had two more to go at – when a tall figure in boots and a hooded cloak entered the tomb, and looked down at him sitting on the floor. Hands on hips, it shook its head.

"Residents giving you a hard time?" it croaked.

"Yeah! They won't talk, but I'll dig deeper!"

"I'll get you a shovel. In the meantime, put this on – Giles is sick with worry!" So saying, the figure removed its cloak to reveal Virginia. She handed it to Thorne.

"What about you?" he asked.

"I'll just sit and wait for the storm to pass – besides, I've eaten!"

Feeling rather un-gallant, Thorne meekly put it on. "Thank you..... I'll just....."

"Yeah – whatever!" she shrugged her shoulders and stared blankly into the rain.

Thorne left her standing in the tomb and felt lower than a dog.

---oOo---

By the time Thorne had arrived, it was after noon – *well* after noon, and Giles looked up with such concern on his face that Thorne felt a pain in his stomach – and it wasn't from hunger.

"Oh..... Divine! We've been so worried – are you all right?"

"I'm fine, Giles, I just got caught out in the rain and spent a few hours in a tomb!"

The parlour fell silent and everyone including Giles stared blankly at him.

Thorne tried to joke his way out. "Big mistake, eh?"

Giles found his voice. "Yes, sir. Big mistake."

"I'm sorry, *really* sorry. I'll go to my room."

"I'll bring some food up!" said Giles, trying to smooth things over.

Thorne smiled weakly. "If you did, I probably *would* right now!"

David Thorne spent all the evening and all the night sitting on his bed feeling like a dog. In the morning, he also looked like one.

Chapter 8

When it was light, Thorne heard a patter of footsteps followed by boot-steps and expected to see Giles followed by Chevral. Sure enough, it was Giles who knocked politely on the door, but when Thorne mumbled "Enter," Giles opened the door and a figure in black with a grey waistcoat trimmed with silver leaves entered the room.

Thorne looked up in surprise.

"May I sit?" asked the man, whom Thorne knew to be Straker.

"Yes." said Thorne emptily.

"Thank you." said Straker.

Silence cloaked the room.

Eventually, Thorne sighed. "I was wrong, *very* wrong. But I don't know *how* to be right!"

"Why do you seek answers among the dead, and not the living?"

Thorne paused. Finally he looked at Straker. "Because I have no faith in the living!"

"Your people, or *my* people?"

Thorne sighed. "*My* people – I guess."

"Understandable, but you are applying *your* values to *my* people."

"I know, and I'm *truly* sorry – I can't help the way I am!"

"Believe it or not, but you have made great progress since you have been here."

Thorne snorted in disbelief.

"*Truly*, you have. If you could compare yourself as you *are* against as you *were* two weeks ago – you would be amazed!"

"I have offended everyone – and I wasn't even aware of it!" said Thorne heavily.

"Why do you think you have offended everyone?"

"I was playing at being Indiana Jones!"

Straker paused in thought. "Tomb Raider?"

Thorne looked at Straker with bitter amusement. "That was Lara Croft!"

"I'm sorry." apologised Straker, somewhat confused.

"No, Straker, *I'm* sorry. My culture loves to escape from reality because it can't stand the reality of it's *own* culture!"

"Ahh.....!" said Straker, smiling. "Hence the value of entertainment and illusion."

"Dreams are all we *have!*"

"Very sad, but potentially instructive – have you ever studied Rosicrucian Cabalism?"

"I've heard of it!" admitted Thorne.

"Do you feel *Sorrow for the Past*, or do you seek *Change for the Future?*"

Thorne looked blank.

"Study and compare Hermetic Magister with Orphic Magus."

"..... You've lost me."

"For now, perhaps!"

Thorne was silent, just staring out of his window at the people in the street as they set up their market stalls for Sevenday trading. Finally, he said. "There are no locked doors – or even *doors* – to the tombs or the catacombs!"

"It's a sad culture that requires physical barriers for social enforcement."

"I am *part* of that sad culture – and I *don't* want to infect yours!" said Thorne. He took out ten crones from his pocket and gave it to Straker. "There's a trader by that horse trough. I owe him ten crones for a purchase I made last week. Would you please give this to him?"

"I will – on one condition."

"What's that?"

"Prepare yourself for the day – and come fishing with me!"

"Fishing?"

"Fishing."

Somewhat thrown, Thorne agreed to be ready within two hours and Straker left the room to give the trader the ten crones that Thorne had promised, and to return to the inn with his fishing tackle.

"What will the public think when they see me with you?" asked Thorne apprehensively.

Straker paused at the doorway and smiled. "They'll understand - don't worry."

---oOo---

Following a lonely preparation and breakfast, Thorne sat silently, huddled tightly against the wall wrapped in his own thoughts. He looked up at the sound of approaching boot-steps to see Straker standing in the parlour with a fishing rod in one hand and a bait box in the other.

"All set?" Straker inquired - handing his rod and box to Thorne.

"I guess so!" replied Thorne - looking at what he held with uncertainty

Giles emerged from the kitchen carrying a basket. "As you requested, sir - four rounds of egg sandwiches, four rounds of chicken sandwiches, two large slices of boar pie, two apples and two bottles of mead." he gasped.

"Thank you, Giles - I'll take that!" said Straker, quickly removing it from the little man before he fell over. He walked outside and secured it to a rack that sat over the rear wheels of a two seat Brougham parked in the square and turned to receive the rod and box from Thorne. Opening the door, Straker put the tackle on the floor and closed it before Thorne could enter the coach. "Up there!" said Straker, pointing to the driver's seat.

Thorne wisely said nothing, but his face spoke volumes.

"Do what I do, and you'll be fine!" said Straker, climbing up into the seat.

Gingerly, Thorne did the same, and managed the ascent without too much trouble. He sat down next to Straker feeling very much on public display and grabbed the seat rail as they lurched forward into a gentle trot along the street.

Emerging from the capital into the countryside, Thorne let out a mental sigh of relief, as he felt free of the imagined gaze of the citizens and then grabbed the seat rail in reflex to the gentle three-mile gradient down through the Groves to the river. Straker looked at him in amusement. "It's a spectacular view from the driver's seat!"

Thorne managed a nervous smile but remained quiet.

"Don't worry, we have good brakes!"

Passing through the Groves, Straker pointed out the other buildings that followed the mausolea. "Those buildings are for pressing, bottling and storing our wine, mead and olive oil. We also pack and store our apples and garlic and dry out our mint to make mint tea. Where those buildings end, there are vineyards as far as the eye can see!"

Thorne finally found his voice. "What about the honey from the hives?"

"Drained into jugs and transferred here by flatbed cart where it's bottled and stored."

"I didn't realise you had a bottling plant."

"We import bottles from companies outside who distribute our produce. We receive them sterilised and unseal them prior to filling. After that they are stored ready for dispatch across the border."

"Quality checks?"

"A registered official from each company follows the import, supervises the filling and storing, and follows the export out of the country. The lady or gentleman concerned will stay at the inn for the duration and blend in accordingly."

"Historically speaking, how long have you been trading?"

"From Georgian times at least – hence our national costume! But things *really* evolved when we were registered under the former European Union's Third World Initiative!"

Thorne burst out laughing. "*Third World – that's rich!*"

"Everything is relative." smiled Straker.

"And on your terms!" thought Thorne.

---oOo---

They finally arrived at the southern cross lane holding the farms of upper and lower south. They turned left and followed the lane leading to the farms of Upper South One, Two and Three. They travelled for about two miles and turned right at a point between Upper South One and Two and descended the mile-long branch lane to South Mill.

Halting the Brougham in the courtyard of the water mill, Straker motioned Thorne to dismount and did the same himself on the other side of the coach. He called out to Thorne to grab the tackle and lean it against the wall of the mill whilst he unstrapped the picnic basket. When this was done, Straker put the basket with the tackle and, detaching the horse, led it to a water trough where it gratefully sank its nose. Thorne was invited to see around the mill – but first, they would ask the miller if it was convenient.

They walked to the front of the water mill and Straker pointed out the fact that the wheel was turning in its channel since the sluice gate was open to the river. "It looks like Dusty's working right now!" he said to Thorne, and opened the door to a chorus of clanks and rumbles. "Dusty?" he shouted.

Nothing

"DUSTY?" he yelled.

"What?" came a muffled response from above.

"ARE YOU FREE FOR A WHILE?"

"Be right down."

The clanking ceased as a set of gears were disengaged but the rumbles continued along with the swishing of the water wheel. They heard the thumps of boot-steps across the ceiling and the clumps as they descended the stairs and a man in boots, breeches and an open-necked shirt greeted them.

"Good day, Straker." he beamed from under several layers of flour – or possibly the worst case of galloping dandruff that Thorne had ever seen. "Good day, Dusty – it *is* you under there?" asked Straker, peering at him.

The miller proved the worth of his nickname as he clouted himself several times and it snowed in summer. "Good for the complexion!" he grinned as both Straker and Thorne hurriedly stepped back to preserve their clothing.

"Being Sevenday, I wasn't sure if you would be working!" said Straker.

"I like to keep the stock topped up all the time. Let me guess; touring and fishing?"

"Is that convenient – seeing that you're working?"

"No problem – as long as you remove all loose clothing. I don't want you being caught and dragged through the gears." 'Dusty' looked at Thorne. "This is one of the few jobs where an apron is *not* recommended!"

Straker and Thorne were all too pleased to remove their coats and cravats and 'Dusty' told them to go next door into the cottage and hang them from the pegs in the entrance hall – which they duly did. On their return, they were given a tour of the mill.

'Dusty' guided them both outside to the water wheel. "As in all industries, let's start at the source. Once the sluice gate is opened, part of the river flows down the channel and hits the paddles on the wheel. Because it is a slow moving river rather than a fast moving mountain stream, we use the 'undershot' principle with paddles, rather than the 'overshot' principle with buckets and we gear the querns accordingly."

Thorne raised a hesitant hand – like an errant pupil in class. "Erm..... why do you have *two* sluice gates close together?"

'Dusty' beamed. "Because we work on the principle of an 'heir and a spare.' As you see, we only use the *inner* gate for regular working, but after several months, we need to check the condition of the gate and so we raise the inner and drop the *outer* gate to stem the flow so we can maintain the inner – and the channel if necessary. We monitor the inner gate every few months and the outer gate every year. Now, let's go inside."

Straker and Thorne followed 'Dusty' inside.

"The wheel turns the horizontal shaft and the bevel gear on the shaft meshes with the bevel on the main vertical shaft and it turns within the heart of the mill. Above the main bevel is the main gear which meshes with the two quern gears each side and the shafts from the quern gears turn the upper querns against the lowers which grinds the grain into flour – but you'll need to go upstairs to the first floor to see that!"

Obediently, they trooped upstairs.

"Over there, are two troughs each fed by a chute from the grain vat above us on the second floor. Down here, grain is shovelled from a trough into the centre of the quern stone, which crushes the grain into wholemeal flour and it drops below into sacks downstairs. Two chutes and two querns simply double the yield. If whitemeal flour is required, then I go downstairs and lock a sack of wholemeal onto the pulley and jack up the sack to the second floor where I tip it into a second vat which feeds a chute down to the flour grader over here where wholemeal is graded into whitemeal!" he said pointing to a wooden box fed by a pulley from which a shaking sound was heard.

"Whitemeal flour from the grader drops into sacks below and both whitemeal and wholemeal are stored next door for the flatbed carts to take up to the capital to sell. Remaining husk or bran is raked out of the grader and can be added to some of the wholemeal flour to create wheatbran flour - for those with horse's teeth!" he added with a smile, and led them upstairs to the second floor.

"Here, we have two vats. The farther receives sacks of grain which feeds two chutes and two querns downstairs that crush the grain into wholemeal, and the nearer for receiving sacks of wholemeal which feeds one chute downstairs through the grader to become whitemeal. Overhead, is the pulley system which jacks the sacks from the ground floor up through trap-doors to the second floor for use - and that concludes your tour, good sirs!"

Straker smiled his thanks. "We have a basket of food and mead which will certainly feed three - would you care to join us before we fish?"

"I'm not this shape for nothing!" grinned 'Dusty' - patting his stomach and creating a small avalanche. "I'll bring out our fishing stools from the cottage!"

They all descended and 'Dusty' went to his cottage to get the stools whilst Straker and Thorne got the hamper and tackle and went down to the riverbank. They set up the stools and Straker took the rod and – propping it upright using a forked stick – left the line to dangle limply in the river.

Thorne frowned. "No bait?"

Straker opened his 'bait' box to reveal a pipe, matches, cleaners, tamper/reamer and a good measure of sweet, rich, dark tobacco. "The fish don't bother me – so I don't bother them! Pass a bottle – would you?"

Thorne opened the hamper and passed a large bottle of mead to Straker who opened it and asked for three mugs. Thorne obliged and soon they were all feeling distinctly cheerful – and hungry. Ever thoughtful, Giles and Clive had added a pot of mayonnaise with a note saying 'it makes the sandwiches more interesting' and when added to all eight rounds – it certainly did. The 'two' slices of boar pie could feed *four*, and a knife had been kindly provided in anticipation of a guest.

After they had finished, 'Dusty' excused himself saying he'd better get back to work, and that they would find a sack of wholemeal from his surplus stock sitting in the cab of the Brougham for Giles and Clive. Straker thanked him and said that when he came to fish next Sevenday, he would bring some fresh loaves from G & C.

Left together, Straker and Thorne settled down with two apples and another large bottle of mead. After finishing his apple, Straker took a draught and put his mug on the vacated stool. "Time for a little cremation!" he said, looking at Thorne with a smile and started filling his pipe. A rich aroma of apples and prunes filled the air from the bait box and hung around even after the lid was closed. Straker struck up and puffed gently and the fruit salad floated into the trees.

Being aware that he was in the presence of a 'man of the cloth,' Thorne phrased his next question carefully. "What sort of tobacco is that?"

"Black Cavendish." said Straker. "I used to smoke a very special brand which we imported from an island near Denmark. Unfortunately, they decided to add Light Virginia Leaf, which made smoking hot, dry and rough in the throat. They tried to mask the effect with vanilla – but it was never the same. After that, I just smoked ordinary black."

"The pressures of commercialism!" said Thorne.

"Virginia for cigarettes, Havana for cigars, Cavendish for pipes!" said Straker.

"Being a non-smoker, I'll accept your opinion."

"Opinions are only relative anyway – how's the line doing?"

Thorne looked at the bateless line dangling in vain hope. "Dreadfully!"

"Good. I can't stand fish!"

"A man of God who hates fish?"

"A Christian might have a problem with that – but not a Florian. Through Florianism, a Jew or a Muslim can eat Pork, and a Buddhist can eat Meat – in fact it is a myth that all Buddhists are vegetarians or vegans anyway. In the mountains of Nepal, some groups feast on Yak!"

"And yet you can't stand fish?"

"It makes my waistcoat smell."

"You're not supposed to put them in your pocket!"

Straker started coughing and nearly bit the end off his pipe.

"Sorry." said Thorne. "I couldn't resist that!"

"And that's your problem." said Straker, wiping his eyes.

"That I'm curious?"

"That you don't know *when* to be curious, and *when* not to."

"I lack wisdom in judging proportional values?"

Straker was silent, gently puffing on his pipe.

"I lack wisdom in judging proportional values!"

"I'd make a note of that!" advised Straker.

Thorne nodded and sat in silence for ten whole minutes before he spoke again. "Is *now* a good time to ask about your funeral customs?"

"I'm not dead yet!" said Straker, looking out of the corner of his eye.

"I deserved that!" agreed Thorne, raising his hands in surrender.

"You wish to know about the funeral customs of my people?"

"Is that okay?"

"I view the body and issue a death certificate. The body is put in a casket and moved to the mortuary. It is removed from the casket and embalmed in a chemical and salt preserve, which dries all internal fluids. It is wrapped in linen bandages containing more preserve and sealed in a thick shroud. It is put back in the casket and moved by cart to its family vault where it is removed from the casket and placed in the niche of a previous body in order to dry-cure in the circulating air of the catacombs - hence the open vaults. Dried mint leaves are sprinkled over the body to sweeten the air. The body that was previously interred is put in the casket and taken from the catacombs and moved by cart to a special location, which has a circular stone altar in the centre of a large stone circle. It is removed from the casket and placed on the altar and wood is piled all around it. Finally, *it is burned to ashes on the centre!*"

Thorne blew out his cheeks. "Phew!"

"Any questions?" asked Straker.

Thorne hesitated, and then spoke. "I have a few questions to ask – if that's okay?"

"If I satisfy your curiosity, you should have fewer reasons to be indiscreet."

Thorne nodded. "Why do *you* examine the body – and not the doctor?"

"The doctor heals the living physically and the deacon heals the living spiritually – but I also attend the dead to ensure that the spirit has left the body and will not return."

"So you have no interest in *why* someone died?"

"Why should I? There's no crime here, thus no morbid curiosity for autopsies."

"Do you at least *honour* the dead?"

"We honour the *living* where it can be appreciated – the dead are beyond everything."

"It doesn't seem very....."

"..... Christian?"

"Well..... yes!"

"We're Florians. We venerate the Infinite Divine by preparing everyone for a peaceful life and a peaceful death."

"Do you sanction Cannabis?"

"To *alleviate suffering* thus granting a peaceful life – yes!"

"Do you sanction Euthanasia?"

"To *alleviate suffering* thus granting a peaceful death – yes!"

"Why?"

"To know Peace is to know God. Florians put world affirming *before* world denying."

"What is our purpose on this world?"

"To learn the lesson of incarnation."

"Which is?"

"To accept Temporal Loss and evolve beyond Sorrow. In life, so much is taken away from us – possessions when we're younger, and people when we're older. In death, we are taken away from whatever remains. It is clear that all worldly attachments are to be transcended. 'Fixed' *Being* is part of the Rosicrucian grade of Magister. The process is internalising, the principle is assimilation or tendency to fusion."

"Sic transit gloria mundi!" said Thorne. He looked at Straker. "And then?"

"To embrace Eternal Love and evolve beyond Change. To submit to the Divine Plan, and to identify one's nature with that of God and not of Man. The passions are gone, the compassion is also gone. The personality is no more. The individuality is all that remains. 'Mutable' *Becoming* is part of the Rosicrucian grade of Magus. The process is externalising, the principle is transformation or tendency to fission."

"And then?"

"To recognise (re-cognise) the Infinite Divine without *as* the Infinite Divine within. To dispassionately return to source.

This state of pre-existence is beyond everything actual and anything potential. It pre-exists all space everywhere and all time anywhen. 'Cardinal' *Not-being* is part of the Rosicrucian grade of Ipsissimus. The *state* is abstraction, the principle is regeneration or anti-stasis."

"Where does Christianity fit in?"

"Christianity as a *Religion* encourages dependence on bureaucracy and politics. It is a form of state control over the minds of the people – as are all religions. All religions are spiritually *false*. Man submits to the rule of *Man – giving pain.*"

Thorne digested this. "What about Christianity as a Faith?"

"Christianity as a *Faith* is personal to the believer – as are all faiths. All faiths are spiritually *true*. Man submits to the rule of *God – giving peace.*"

"And faith came before religion?"

"Yes. All true teachers were people of peace and wisdom. Jesus guided his disciples in *faith* to leave behind all attachments to worldly possessions and follow him. But his message was distorted by ignorant zealots in *religion* to mean giving away all worldly possessions and value the virtue of poverty. There's no sin in having possessions as long as you see them as transient. Mohammed guided his followers in 'jihad' which in *faith* means a holy war against one's own passions. Like the teaching of Jesus, it is a system of self-purification, an *internal spiritual* war. But his message was distorted by ignorant zealots in *religion* to mean an *external physical* war against all who were not followers of Islam. Christianity and Islam are closely related, and are like two brothers who fight over the same woman!"

Thorne nodded. "What about Buddhism?"

"Although classed as a 'religion,' Buddhism is actually a *ritualised philosophy* based on the teachings of Sidhartha Gautama, an Indian Prince – who became the Buddha. Some say that Buddhism is the only religion without a God as the Buddha was an enlightened man. Christians, Muslims and Jews regard enlightened men as prophets."

"Was Jesus a prophet?" asked Thorne.

Straker smiled. "This is one of the root causes of argument which separates Christians from Muslims and Jews. Christians regard Jesus as the messiah – in other words, they see him as God incarnate who took a personal interest in humanity and came to earth to save them. Muslims regard Jesus as the prophet of the Christians, and Abraham as one of the prophets of the Jews. They regard Mohammed as the prophet of Islam and the senior prophet. Muslims argue that in stating that God showed a *personal* interest in humanity, the Christians were limiting the greatness of God to human emotions. They argue that this insults God, who is supreme and without limit – *God is God*! He needs no help in ruling the universe. His greatness inspires all men. The greatest of whom are recognised as prophets."

"So the Muslims venerate *all* prophets – through *faith*?"

"Yes."

"But chiefly Mohammed – through *religion*?"

"Yes."

"Through *faith*, could Christians, Muslims and Jews unite as One under God?"

"Yes."

"Through *religion*, could the Three become One?"

"No."

"*God help humanity!*" said Thorne.

"*Religion won't allow that!*" smiled Straker.

They both sat in silence watching time flowing by carrying the river.

---oOo---

"How do you know so much about other religions?" asked Thorne.

"Everyone uses the Duke's library for research and reference. All junior deacons must become specialists in Florianism as they are the foundation of our culture. Our first priority is to know ourselves. We have three deacons who are available to guide those who need help in Internal Florianism. They cover the theosophical and philosophical aspects of our faith. Veronica is particularly good with children and she often sits with them in the library. The Senior Deacon must be able to integrate the former work with the psychological and sociological aspects of Florianism and also become a generalist in external state religions. Our second priority is to know outsiders. I synthesise the entire work into External Florianism showing comparisons between ourselves and outsiders, and have added my volume to the volumes of previous deacons."

"It sounds very complex!" said Thorne.

"In content – yes. In essence – no."

"What is your idea of *essence*?"

Straker paused to re-fill his pipe. "Compare the cabala with the university."

"*Is* there a comparison? One is esoteric and the other is exoteric!"

"You spoke of *essence*." reminded Straker.

"Go on then." said Thorne, warily.

"The structure of the cabala and the structure of the university are identical, since they are both reflections of the *civilised* mind. The left side of the brain is systematic and intellectual – it favours a deductive scientific approach. The right side of the brain is automatic and intuitional – it favours a conceptive artistic approach. When both sides are balanced, deductive and conceptive take their rightful places in the centre, with the former leading up, and the latter leading down. This relates to the Aristotelian aspect of deductive empiricism leading up and the Platonistic aspect of conceptive rationalism leading down."

"So you have the Sciences, the Arts and the Philosophies?"

"Yes, and there are three levels which reflect the personal, the social and the spiritual."

"Would these equate to the degrees of Bachelor, Master and Doctor?"

"Yes, they would."

Thorne looked at Straker. "Come on, you can't seriously believe that – can you?"

"Why not?"

"It's too far-fetched!"

"Most people would say the same, but sit quietly and work it out for yourself."

"So you *are* serious?"

"It makes sense to me." replied Straker.

---oOo---

Thorne sat quietly in thought for a while, listening to the sounds of a song thrush nearby. Finally, he looked at Straker. "You've said so much about other religions, but so little about your own faith – why is that?"

Straker smiled gently. "You wish to know the *essence* of our faith?"

"Yes! Why are your people so happy?"

"We know that the terrestrial world is merely a place to learn and to leave. Our true home is the celestial realm. Our home is full of love. In the end we all go home."

"So you're like sailors on long-term shore leave?"

Straker laughed. "We're in a land-locked country – so I can't answer that question!"

"Okay. How would you describe yourselves to the outside world?"

"We know how to pleasantly kill time until time kills us."

"And you've never had a war – or even civil unrest?"

"We have no need to fight for any cause – be it geographical, theological or political."

"So wars are about territory, religion and politics – not spiritual faith?"

"Correct."

"..... and Florianism is a religion based on faith?"

"Yes – we have deacons to guide and enhance."

"..... and other religions are based on politics?"

"Yes – they have priests to guard and enforce."

"Democracy and autocracy!" muttered Thorne.

"Democracy and theocracy!" smiled Straker.

Their gaze returned to the river.

After a while, Thorne looked at Straker. "I haven't seen any mint in the Groves!"

"Were you so absorbed with the tombs, that you didn't look *behind* them?"

"I guess so!" admitted Thorne.

"Do you make a habit of seeking the dead and missing the living?"

"What do you mean?"

"Look at the *living* world, you'll learn so much!"

Thorne looked at Straker with troubled eyes as the cleric continued.

"You have good intellect and great intuition, but your culture has blinded you. Your potential to do real good is being stifled by your social conditioning. *All* of us can see that you are a good soul trapped in the body of a fool. That's why we make certain allowances for your behaviour. It's not the *result* that matters, as you quoted earlier: 'sic transit gloria mundi' – 'the glories of this world are transient.' Nothing matters 'here' except the *intent*, and we all believe that you will be instrumental in some higher purpose – hence our *faith* in you as part of something significant!"

Thorne shook his head. "I don't see myself as an agent of God."

"*Down here, true agents never do!*"

Thorne began to feel uncomfortable. "I'll just try to be normal!" he said.

"Good." said Straker. "You'll fail!"

---oOo---

The rest of the day was spent sitting in the sunshine. They talked about the earlier religions ruling through *fear* and the later religions ruling through *guilt*. They talked about the spiritual death of the outside world, which had led to global fear of physical death. The paranoid need to reproduce humans by any means and at any cost, through the bureaucratic arrogance of 'human rights' and the technological ignorance of 'sperm banks' – that disregarded reasons of economy, ecology and ethics. Any female 'queen' could become an asexual incubator and – once the banks were full – most of the male 'drones' would be surplus to requirement. The 'miracle' of the virgin birth wasn't a miracle any more. Using parthenogenesis, any 'queen' could become a 'Virgin Mary.' Matriarchy had 'de-cloaked' to become *overt*. The feminine had become the feminist.

In the evening, as they returned home, Thorne realised that he and Straker had much in common.

Once again, Straker had caught no fish – but he bore his loss with clerical dignity.

Chapter 9

Determined to adapt, Thorne rose early for work the following day remembering to leave his coat and cravat behind. After preparation and breakfast, he donned his apron and nodded his thanks to Giles before walking purposefully outside to the waiting cart. As before, his colleagues were sitting waiting and nodded to him as he arrived. One of the women smiled at him as he hopped up onto the flatbed and Mycroft clicked the horses into a gentle walk. As they trundled down the hill and past the Groves, Thorne was worried that someone might mention his 'transgression' but was considerably relieved when no one did. After a while, he found himself humming the tune to one of their songs and felt a warm glow in his heart as – one by one – they all joined in with him.

Once again, they split into two teams and Thorne's team returned to the farm at Lower South Two and spent the week 'earthing up' the potatoes in the second field. Each day his happiness increased and the week's work went well.

On Fiveday, after receiving their wages, they were told that they would be required for the next two weeks to work in two five acre fields that were lying fallow. They would be reaping and binding the wildgrass, and carting it to the air-barn where it would be dried into hay for winter food for the animals. The farmer apologised since he and his daughters would not be with them for those two weeks as the wheat was now ready for harvesting, and he would need his daughters and more labourers for that task.

"Couldn't we help you with that too?" volunteered Thorne.

The farmer smiled knowingly. "Thank you, but it's very labour intensive. First, the wheat has to be reaped with a scythe. Second, it has to be thrashed with a flail to separate the grain from the heads. Third, the grain is shovelled into sacks for milling. Fourth, the stalks go through binding and carting to the other air-barn and are left to dry into straw for winter bedding for the animals. Fifth, the field has to be ploughed and left to grass over."

Thorne digested all of this. "Why do you leave some fields to grass over?"

"We use crop rotation on a yearly cycle. The fields are in groups of four. Each year, each group receives early or late cereal, early or late roots – and one field is always allowed to grass over and rest completely for a year – so as not to exhaust the nutrients in the soil. This allows us to feed not only ourselves but also our animals right through the winter – otherwise we would have to slaughter them in the autumn because there would be no food for them. *All* fauna would then die out!"

"I presume wheat and oats are cereals, whilst potatoes, onions and carrots are roots?"

"Yes, but we grow turnips as the root food for animals."

"So people don't eat turnips in this country?"

"Sometimes we mash them with carrots."

"But they're not very popular?"

"Only medically, not socially!"

As the room erupted into mead-induced hysterics, Thorne realised the meaning of the farmer's remark and ended up with his face on the table unable to move. As sobriety slowly returned, everyone was very careful not to look each other in the eye. They all murmured their appreciation to the farmer's wife and Thorne and his three companions departed.

As they were leaving, Thorne said. "I thought we were the only labourers here?"

"We are general labourers and work full-time. On average there are four of us to each farm. However, when harvesting is required, special labourers are requested to boost the workforce. Depending on the type of work, there's usually four to eight of them working part-time, plus the four of us."

"When do the harvests occur?"

"Depends on the season, but cereal crops are harvested in mid/late summer and root crops are harvested in the autumn - along with the fruit from the Groves. There are some varieties of cereal, root and fruit that are planted and harvested early - but these are not the main crops. We eat spring produce *wisely* all through the summer, and eat autumn produce *boldly* all through the winter."

"What sort of weather do you get in each of the seasons?"

"Spring is cool and dry since the earth has absorbed all the rain and it is a good time to work in the fields. The weather is fresh and bright and so are the people. Summer is warm and dry with the occasional heavy storm as we had a few days ago. Even so, it is still good to work in the fields although it can sometimes be too warm. The weather is calm and relaxing and the people follow suit. Autumn is cool and wet since gentle showers of rain are frequent but brief, and the earth quickly absorbs it. Even so, we wear hooded cloaks over our shirts to keep us dry, and it is a time when the people are quiet and reflective - particularly when the mists come heralding winter. Winter is cold and wet and our country is completely shrouded in mist for months. We have a saying which goes like this: 'spring for our children, summer for our friends, autumn for our parents, winter for ourselves,' and it reflects our feelings for our seasons."

Thorne considered this deeply. "What about gales or snow?" he finally asked.

"Our forest holds out the gales, but holds in the mists. As for the snow, we seldom have any. What little falls in the mists, turns to water - and is absorbed by the earth."

"So you've never had a white Christmas?" asked Thorne.

"We've had many a grey Yule!" they all laughed.

"My mistake!" smiled Thorne, warming to life.

Trundling back to the capital, one clear sentence kept coming into his mind:

"*This is my home, and these are my people!*"

Chapter 10

The next morning was Sixday - the weekend had arrived again! Thorne prepared and breakfasted and returned to his room to spend a quiet morning updating his journals and watching the stalls being set up in the square. After sorting and storing more notes, he decided to explore the north/south aspects of the town as he'd done the east/west areas the previous weekend.

Aware that he had earned another 100 crones - plus his fifty from the previous week, he felt it wouldn't hurt to explore the shops to see what they sold and he toyed with the idea of buying a little something for Veronica!

Turning right outside the door and gently threading his way through the growing crowds in the square, he turned right and started to stroll north up 'Main Street' taking a close look at the merchandise on display behind the windows.

Having all his food supplied at the inn, Thorne wasn't interested in the Butchers or the Grocers and walked past to pause at the window of a clothing shop whose sign read: 'Stedman & Spelman - Gentlewear.' Peering through the window, Thorne saw coats and breeches hanging on pegs down one side of the room, and shirts and cravats down the other. Noticing an absence of *blue* frock coats, he decided to go inside and ask if blue was a forbidden colour. As he entered, one of the fitters looked up. "Good day, sir – can I help you?"

"Good day." replied Thorne. "Forgive me for being curious, but since I arrived here I've seen clothing in several dark shades, but none in blue. Is blue forbidden?"

The fitter smiled. "Blue is generally regarded as a cool colour and contrasts too sharply with the warm colour of fawn breeches – unlike the warm colours of brown, red and green. If you wish, we can take your measurements and create a blue frock coat according to your taste."

Thorne raised his hands in negation. "Thank you but that's not necessary, I was just curious as to why blue is not used."

"We feel close to the earth and favour earth colours rather than sky colours which are rather cool and detached – we affirm this world *before* the next world!"

"Ahh..... I see!" said Thorne – remembering what Straker had said.

"There *is* one among us who favours unusual garb!" said the other fitter.

Thinking of Virginia, Thorne raised his eyebrows in question.

"Our Duke has very bold taste!"

"Really?"

"Oh yes! He loves to wear a purple frock coat over magenta breeches – and his favourite waistcoat is bright blue with gold leaves!"

"Wow!" said Thorne, somewhat stunned.

"Indeed, sir – it is *most* impressive!"

"He must have a very cheerful nature!" remarked Thorne.

Stedman and Spelman smiled thoughtfully. "He does it more for his people than for himself. Since the death of his first wife, he was determined to maintain continuity for all concerned – regardless of his personal feelings."

Thorne, acquiring a degree of sensitivity, decided to change the conversation and asked how his measurements had been obtained whilst he had been in the forest.

"When he is not on guard duty, Tyler is our sizer and cutter. Every so often, he needs to rest his eyes from close work indoors and does guard duty in the forest – the soft green light and fresh air actually helps restore his eyesight. All he has to do is look at someone and he knows the measurements. The open style of the frock coat allows for a degree of variance and the breeches waistline can be adjusted discretely from the back – we leave nothing to chance!"

Thorne smiled at their talents. "Well, gentlemen, thank you very much for your time. At the moment my wardrobe has ample clothing so I'm afraid I won't be buying much for a while!"

"Not even a bright blue waistcoat with gold leaves?" ventured one of the fitters.

Thorne laughed. "I wouldn't dare offend the Duke by trying to copy him!"

Both fitters smiled. "Very commendable, sir!"

Thorne nodded in appreciation – noting the sincerity of their words. He knew that in any other country, such comments would be regarded as mere tokens of politeness. In *his* world, so much was said, so little was meant. He bade them good day and left the shop to continue his tour of the high street.

Walking on, he arrived at the Barbers, and observed a customer being shorn. Everything was pretty standard; the hair was back combed and any 'fluffy bits' that stood proud were neatly trimmed with a pair of scissors. The style was simple yet dignified. It was quite proper for a gentleman beyond the age of twenty to have his hair styled back to show a premature 'widows peak' – suggesting that twenty years might be the 'coming of age' for men and possibly women. After completion, the barber took a little bottle from his shelf and sprayed the customer's hair. A whiff of mint floated out of the door and up Thorne's nose. "Mint for everything!" he observed with a smile. The barber removed his cape from the customer who rose and thanked him as he was being dusted down. He put on his frock coat and paid with two fifty- groat coins. "Two pounds fifty – cheap at the price!" muttered Thorne. Feeling a bit 'fluffy' himself, he decided to risk a trim and surprise Veronica.

After greeting the barber and removing his coat, Thorne settled back in the chair and was enrobed in the cape. Fortunately, his hair was long and soft enough to be back combed and styled accordingly. Had his hair been springy, he would have resembled a hedgehog. After trimming, he was asked if he wanted any mint balm to condition his hair and scalp. Thorne gave his assent and was very pleased with the smell and cool freshness of the balm. On this warm day, his head felt as if it had emerged from a north-facing pantry and he told the barber so.

"Very popular with the gentlemen *and* the ladies!" said the barber with a smile.

After admiring his 'new look' in the mirror and being struck by a certain resemblance to Sherlock Holmes, he thanked the barber and paid him with a one-crone coin.

Stepping outside and feeling slightly self-conscious, Thorne continued his stroll up the street and quickly stopped at the next shop whose sign read: 'Queller – Printer.' Feeling a little glow of pride for someone who was *also* involved in the media – even if only distantly related, Thorne *had* to go into the shop to meet its owner. When he entered, a reassuring aroma of polished leather embraced his senses and he felt as if he were entering a sacred library. There was no-one behind the counter, so he wandered around the shop admiring hundreds of leather-bound books sitting on oak shelves.

The books were divided into two colours – claret leather and green leather, and two sizes – hand size and arm size. He picked one of the hand sized claret-bound books and read its gold-printed title: 'Wuthering Heights – Emily Bronte.' Feeling slightly surprised, he put it back on the shelf and removed its companion whose title read: 'Jane Eyre – Charlotte Bronte.' Replacing this, he picked out three claret-bound books one shelf down and read: 'Republic – Plato,' 'Politics – Aristotle,' 'Ethics – Aristotle.' "All imported classics!" he exclaimed out loud.

A polite cough made him turn around.

"If you wish to see some of our own publications, they are bound in green leather."

"Oh..... thank you!" exclaimed Thorne. "You must be Queller?"

"Indeed I am – please forgive me, I was in the back room printing 'Whisky Galore' by Compton Mackenzie for the O'Hara sisters!"

Trying to keep a straight face, Thorne asked, "Isn't copying other works illegal?"

"Commercially, yes. But I only print ten copies – one for public entertainment which is available on loan, and one for public education which is kept in the castle library."

"What about the other eight?"

"Sealed for archival storage for future generations - the original is destroyed."

"So there's no mass sales and distribution?"

Queller shook his head. "This is a library - not a shop."

"So I could walk out with any book I wanted?"

"Feel free to browse. When you have chosen your book, simply write your name and the title of the book in the register on the table by the door."

"Is there any time limit on returning a book?"

Queller shrugged his shoulders. "A season for a book, a year for a volume."

"So there's no real urgency?"

Queller smiled. "Not in this country."

Thorne nodded.

"If you will excuse me, I shall return to my work. Sergeant Odd is about to assist the villagers in hiding the cases of whisky - which has just reminded me why I came out here in the first place. I was going to stop for a mug of mead. Would you care to join me?"

"I'd be delighted!" beamed Thorne.

Indicating a chair in the corner of the room, Queller disappeared into the back room and returned with a large jug and two mugs. "Inspirational purposes only!" he said as he poured a generous amount into Thorne's mug and drew up a stool. "Good health!"

"Good health to you, sir." said Thorne raising his mug.

As they settled down, Thorne asked Queller if the library was financed by the Duke.

"Yes. The Duke believes in educational, spiritual and physical welfare. I am paid to provide a service here and at the castle, as is the deacon and the doctor."

"The Duke is a generous man!" observed Thorne.

"He is, but he receives a percentage of the profits of all international trade plus rent from all the residents and there is always a large surplus of food and drink."

"Is this because the country is under-populated and the people are not greedy – they respect nature, they work well and they consider each other?"

Queller nodded cheerfully, and had another draught.

---oOo---

Thorne leaned back in the chair and had a large draught and looked at Queller's ink stained fingers. "Why do you go to all the trouble of copying imported works on a press – surely it would be far easier and quicker to *buy* ten copies?"

"Yes, it would. But like all things, we judge *quality* on internal content and not on external appearance. I first read the work to determine the quality and significance of the content, and then print it on top quality paper for durability. I then bind the copies in leather to improve preservation."

Thorne nodded. "The original import is destroyed because.....?"

"..... Being on inferior quality paper its lifespan is limited. Its modern cover might also distract the reader from its content.

A leather-bound copy will last at least *three* times longer than the original – it's the same with our clothing."

Thorne smiled, knowing this to be true. "Yes, *everything* here speaks of quality!"

"Thank you." said Queller. "By the way, were you looking for a specific book – or were you just curious?"

"Being in journalism, I was more than a little curious about your trade."

"Aha!..... A kindred spirit!" exclaimed Queller. Rising from his stool, he beckoned his new friend to follow him saying, "My printing press is through here!"

Thorne followed Queller through the door and couldn't resist a smile of nostalgia when he saw what sat in the middle of the room.

---oOo---

Beautifully carved in solid oak and polished to a shine with beeswax, sat a hand press that could have been owned by Caxton. Thorne's smile grew broader as he compared this 'antique' to what was used back home. "Can I watch you at work?" he asked with a dopey grin on his face.

Queller took another draught and set his mug on a window ledge. "I've nearly finished setting the type for this page." he said selecting some more letters from a box that were marked in sets of upper and lower case. Expertly, he slid the 'keys' in place, making sure that each word was correctly spelled from right to left. Finally, he finished the last word of that page and locked the final line of 'keys' in place to stop them from moving. He then took a sheet of heavy-duty paper and laid carefully on the lower of two joined plates which he called a tympan. Next, he folded over the higher of the two joined plates which he called a frisket to mate with its twin. He took a wooden maul, which was faced with several layers of linen and rolled it around in the ink tray. Carefully, he sponged the entire typeface with the maul working it around in sections until the whole area was evenly covered – in a similar fashion to the way Veronica had mopped the temple floor. Asiding the inking maul, he folded both plates over the typeface and the entire assembly was slid into place under the press and locked in place. Looking at Thorne and giving a little smile, he raised his hands to the crank handle and lowered the press plate until it was just above the typeface. Looking at Thorne with a twinkle in his eye, he turned the crank once and made contact with the face. He then gave it an extra tweak and immediately raised the plate from the face. Unlocking the assembly, he slid it towards him and unfolded it carefully to reveal the printed paper. Checking to see that all was well, he finally asided the printed paper to a bench to dry and looked at Thorne. "All I do now is print nine more sheets and then soak the keys and return them to their correct places in the rack, and then we start all over again."

"So much re-prep and de-prep for such a short cycle!" said Thorne.

"Totally inefficient – I agree, but so rewarding – considering the *purpose!*"

Thorne smiled and shook his head – everything was crazy, but everyone was happy! Knowing that cleaning all those keys would take time – even though there were two complete sets (one soaking and one in use), Thorne drained his mug and thanked Queller for his hospitality.

"Feel free to browse, and register a book you like." said Queller, happily immersing himself in his work. As Thorne returned to the front room and started to eye all the books on the shelves, he heard Queller chuckle to himself. "Captain Wagget and the Customs Officers are *not* going to be happy tonight!"

Deciding to get a better feel of the culture, Thorne chose various imported books at random before turning to the green-bound domestic works. Other claret-bound names appeared such as: 'The Wind in the Willows – Kenneth Grahame,' 'The Chronicles of Narnia – C S Lewis,' 'The Tales of Beatrix Potter' – Thorne got the general picture. In the spiritually healthy environs of this culture, children were actually *born* to have a childhood – unlike the 'civilised' world where children were *bred* and discarded to make their own entertainment through sex, drugs, alcohol and technology.

---oOo---

Returning the last claret-bound book to its slot, Thorne turned his attention to the green-bound books, which were fewer in number. A set of 'Your World – My World' by various authors was arranged in chronological order from 1700 onwards, and Thorne saw that the name printed on the most recent book was Straker's. These books were the collective works of the various Deacons from the time when this country began trading with the outside world. Should he read it? Thorne's hand hesitated, and then he decided to return it to its slot. "Your Work – My Work!" he said quietly – knowing that his journals should be based entirely on his *own* experiences and not plagiarised from someone else! Reaching up to the top shelf and wondering if he would find any naughty material, he picked out 'Herb Lore – Cordelia,' and had a quick look at some of the pages. He was amazed at the uses of so many herbs and had to admit that nature seemed to have a cure for virtually everything. Depending on the herb, it could be used to speed up or slow down metabolism, cure ailments, kill pain or end life! If anything, this material was more 'top shelf' than top shelf material! "Definitely for adults only!" he mused, and realised how pathetically shallow his own people were.

Also on the shelf, he found a set of books entitled 'Physical Diagnoses – Drusilla' and another set entitled 'Surgical Techniques – Drusilla.' Thinking of the sweet young girl who had held Mycroft's paw in one slender hand, Thorne imagined her with a scalpel in the other. "Lamb to the slaughter – poor Mycroft!" he said, and had a fit of mead induced giggles despite knowing that *this* Drusilla was not *that* Drusilla!

After finally being able to replace a book that would have warmed Freddy Krueger's heart (had he had one), Thorne had to conclude that books such as these were placed on the top shelf because they were to be used only in the direst of emergencies by trained professionals. Everyone else would ignore them – in the same way that they would ignore an open door if they hadn't been invited to enter. The famous quotation, which said that 'to the innocent, all things are pure' – could have been coined by someone who had lived with these people. "Bless them all!" he whispered gently, and turned his gaze two shelves down. Along this shelf, he found numerous children's stories. He then took a sample of books from each shelf to get the distribution and the priority of the culture. After returning all books to their proper places, he deduced that seventy-percent of books were oriented towards morality/ fiction, twenty-percent covered cultural/history and ten-percent were medical/science. Clearly, emphasis was placed on the formative years creating character that was optimistic, inquisitive and sensitive to everything and everyone it encountered – mutual reverberation would do the rest. Barring the medical/science books, Thorne noticed that there were no books covering any practical work and realised that theory is *not* practice. No matter how high anyone's academic grades are; apprenticeships are far more valuable. In the outside world, apprenticeships had been replaced with 'on the job' training and this would virtually guarantee numerous and costly errors which could never be corrected in time because time was *money*! 'Firefighting' had become the cultural norm. Errors were given a paperwork 'snow job' making bureaucrats the 'cretin's friend.' Small wonder self-esteem was at rock bottom. This resulted in lucrative jobs for personal psychiatrists, motivational managers and management consultants. If all *this* failed, then everyone could sue everyone and the lawyers would have a field day!

In this 'third world' country, people invested in people by passing down their skills.

Thorne noted down all these thoughts for future reference. He had read no books but he had seen enough to write a volume of his own. Strangely sober, he quietly left the library and returned outside to the street.

---oOo---

Strolling along the pavement, Thorne halted briefly to observe a pair of horses drawing a four-seat Landau whose driver wore a dark green coat. He also had a pair of spectacles perched on his nose. Garfield or Gilmore? Thorne wasn't sure; but those within were a family out shopping for the day. As the coach eventually came to a halt in the square, the driver dismounted and opened the passenger door nearest the pavement. Sure enough, a man exited and assisted his wife onto the pavement followed by two smartly dressed (and well behaved) children – a boy and a girl.

Watching the husband pay and thank the driver, Thorne's face broke into a huge smile as he watched the family walk down the street, the boy holding his father's hand and the girl her mother's. Thorne tried to recall a similar scene in his own country and was saddened to find that he couldn't. Making a quick note of such subtleties of behaviour, he continued his walk.

He passed by the Saddlers shop and peeped into the window of the Furniture store. Since browsing over a mug of mead seemed normal and there was no pressure to buy, Thorne decided to wander inside – but would politely refuse any further inebriation!

As he entered, the familiar smell of polished wood teased his nostrils, and his eyes widened in appreciation of the furniture on display. Despite the Georgian style of clothing, the furniture reflected the earlier period of the Jacobean age. All furniture was made of solid oak with a simple yet tasteful carving that would look well inside a Christian church or a Gothic castle. There was a single, a double and a treble 'pew' style seat which looked good for one's back but numb for one's bum – cushions were probably an optional extra! There was an imposing lectern-desk with an angled face, which was designed to safely support a large volume at chest height thus freeing both hands to turn the pages. There was a large study-desk with a magnificent chair behind it. A large refectory table was placed near a wall with two dining benches each seating three people. A chest for storing blankets stood next to a bedside table, and there was a two and a three-unit sideboard. Due to the amount of space that was taken up, the wall that separated the front and back rooms had been removed and a graceful arch supported the floor above.

Seeing that no one was present in either room, Thorne wasn't sure whether to leave the shop or go right through and out into the back yard. To kill a little time in the hope that the shopkeeper would emerge, he decided to test out some of the seats for comfort. Plonking himself down on the 'pew' seats, he knew that they did indeed require cushions. Casting his eye around he found one and after placing it on one of the seats, he tried again and was pleased with the results. The bench seats were for dining use only and he knew that people would be too busy enjoying the pleasures of *anterior* comfort to care about posterior comfort. Eyeing the glorious chair behind the study-desk, he knew he just *had* to try that out for size. Easing himself down, he let out a huge sigh of relief as the seat was beautifully padded with black leather – the first hint of Georgian style he had seen – barring the seats in the Landaus and Broughams!

As he sat in the chair, he heard the sound of hammering coming from the back yard and rose to investigate. As he opened the back door to the yard, he realised that it led into a huge workshop. The front third of the workshop was devoted to the production of domestic furniture, but it was the back two-thirds that interested Thorne the most.

---oOo---

A Brougham was up on blocks and two men in shirts and aprons were holding a wheel whilst a third – a giant of a man who bore a resemblance to Mycroft – was hammering out the locking pin. Thorne was amazed that so many people seemed happy to work on a weekend. As they caught sight of him, one of the men left the group and walked towards him. "Good day, sir. I'm sorry I wasn't in the shop – may I be of service?"

"Good day." replied Thorne. "I was just browsing and I heard the hammering – I'm not intruding am I?"

"Not at all. We are just changing the wheels of this Brougham – you're welcome to stay and help if you wish."

"I'm afraid I have no experience in coach building – so I'd probably get in your way."

"Just hand us any tools we ask for – that's *always* useful. Besides, there's a pasty and a mug of mead in it if you do!"

"Okay!" beamed Thorne.

Happily cancelling his earlier vow of abstinence, Thorne eagerly removed his coat and cravat and, hanging them up with the others, he quickly returned to the site.

"Maxwell will lend you his apron and hammer whilst he goes off to get the pasties and the mead!"

Thorne found himself wearing Maxwell's apron and had a lump hammer the size of Mjollnir thrust into his hand. "He won't be long – will he?"

"By the time he returns, we'll have all four wheels off – he's already freed up the first."

As the two remaining men held the wheel firm, Thorne gave the pin a cautious tap, but nothing happened. "I thought you said it was freed up?"

"It is. The sound of the metal changes tone when it starts to free up, but it still needs a good clout to remove it."

"Okay." said Thorne, and clobbered the pin loose. As the men removed and asided the wheel, Thorne retrieved the locking pin and put it on the bench. He looked at the men with a twinkle in his eye. "One down, three to go!" and moved onto the second wheel. After checking that the men had the wheel firm, Thorne gave the pin all hell, and after six good smacks he heard the note change from a dead sound to a ringing sound. Two clouts and the pin fell to the floor. Away went the wheel and the second pin joined its friend on the bench. Wheels three and four were also removed in similar fashion. As they all stopped for a breather and to await the return of Maxwell, one of the men looked at Thorne. "You were really enjoying yourself there, weren't you?"

"Yes!" beamed Thorne, and realised that the expression on his face matched those of the guards he had seen from the Landau when he had first arrived at the capital. "Is there anything else I can do?" he asked – waggling 'Mjollnir' with new confidence.

"We'll pause for refreshment, and then we'll check the suspension, brakes, axles and swivel bolt before fitting new wheels."

"Okay." said Thorne, brimming with optimism.

Five minutes later, Maxwell returned with four large pasties and a large jug of mead. He opened a cupboard door above the nearest bench and fished out four mugs. As he began to pour, the others drew up stools and sat down. Thorne was handed a very handsome pasty and a mug of mead – his second drink in half an hour! Deciding to eat first in order to mop up the effects of the alcohol, he attacked the pasty with great gusto. As the rich aroma of wild boar with onions filled the room, Thorne realised that good food and good drink *has* to be accompanied by good physical work in order to keep from getting fat. Working the body also rested the mind – doubly beneficial!

After they had finished their dinner, the men cleared up and began to examine the four suspension bows for any wear. Upon satisfactory inspection, they coated all the bows with a thick grease to prevent the metal from rusting and turned their attention to the brakes. Both brake blocks – which halted the rear wheels – were slightly worn but still very safe and one of the men clambered up to the driver's seat and tested the action. The lever joints were oiled and it was tested again for good measure. Both the axles were in excellent condition and were thoroughly greased. Finally, the swivel-bolt – which allowed the front axle to steer the coach, was thoroughly inspected and given a good plastering from the grease pot.

"Follow us to the Wheelwright's forge, and we can all bring a new wheel." said one of the men to Thorne.

They all trooped outside and walked some distance to a building which stood well away from all other buildings. When Thorne remarked on this, he was told that all forges were placed well away from everything to avoid the risk of fire spreading.

Thinking of London in 1666, he could understand why.

"There's a smell of singed wood!" said Thorne, sniffing the air.

"Don't worry. The wheelwright heats the metal rims to expand them prior to fitting over the wheels. Once they're snug, he pours water over the metal to cool and shrink them ensuring a very tight fit - that's what you're smelling!" said Maxwell.

They each took a wheel, and began to slowly roll them back to the coachworks. On arrival, each wheel boss was greased and the wheel slid over its axle stub. Thorne was given the honour of homing them secure with four new locking pins and Maxwell finished Thorne's work with a couple of good smacks apiece - just to make sure.

Job completed, they all sat down to finish the jug of mead and then tidied away all the tools and binned the old pins.

"What happens to the old pins?" asked Thorne, looking at them in the scrap bin.

"All scrap metal is returned and re-forged - nothing is wasted."

"I should have guessed!" smiled Thorne.

Finished for the week, they all changed and bade each other good day, and walked from the workshop through the shop and onto the street. As the other two men left, Thorne asked the shopkeeper what would happen if any customers had been and gone.

"If I've missed a customer, they leave a note and I deliver the item requested."

"Oh!" said Thorne, surprised at such a simple system.

"Good day, and thank you for your help." smiled the shopkeeper.

"Good day, and thank you for your hospitality." beamed Thorne.

As the shopkeeper returned to his shop, Thorne looked around the high street and wondered where to go next. There weren't many shops left to see on his side of the street and the city walls were quite close, so he crossed over the road and began to walk down the pavement on the other side.

---oOo---

On this side of the street, Thorne peeped into the window of a shop whose sign above read 'Cordelia - Herbs & Spices' - and wondered if he should try his luck in a woman's domain - bearing in mind that *this* woman would be a medical expert! Armed with the courage of two large meads, he opened the door and ambled inside.

He had to smile as his eyes surveyed the layout of the room. It was an old-fashioned apothecary's shop. Behind the front service counter was a preparation counter that stretched along the back wall of the room. Along this counter were arranged several measuring cups of different sizes together with several mortar & pestles used for the preparation of various compounds. Completing the equipment was a set of polished brass scales. Above the preparation counter was a large oak cabinet that was divided into numerous compartments. All manner of medicinal herbs and spices – *drugs* – were displayed to the public. Thorne's eyes went wide as he realised that such an open display of drugs was unheard of in his own country – it was druggie heaven!

An attractive young woman dressed in black with a white shawl and gold spectacles was arranging bottles on a shelf. As she caught sight of him, she hurriedly removed her 'specs' and placed them on the counter. Walking slowly towards him, she blinked myopically and beamed at him. "Can I help you..... *is it Mr Thorne?*"

"Just, *Thorne.*" smiled Thorne, totally used to being known by complete strangers.

"That's nice!" she said, staring into his eyes and making him start to feel a little uneasy.

"I noticed your name on your shop – it matches one on a book I saw at the printers."

"My grandmother wrote 'Herb Lore' a long time ago!" said the young woman.

"It's..... erm..... nice that you keep her name on your shop." said Thorne.

"Cordelia is *my* name also – most children are given the name of a grandparent."

"That's..... *nice.*" said Thorne – aware that everything had suddenly become '*nice.*'

"It's practical!" said Cordelia.

"How so?"

"We keep things simple in this country and use only a single name. As a result, certain names tend to run in certain families.

Since it can be confusing when the child has the same name as the parent, we tend to be named after our grandparents so names skip a generation – two names are used alternately."

"I see. So Mycroft's girlfriend is named after her grandmother?"

Cordelia nodded. "Drusilla's grandmother was a leading authority in surgical techniques – but she was considered rather radical and somewhat of an outsider."

"An outsider?" asked Thorne.

"It was felt that she was excessively influenced by the outside world."

"Is that bad?"

"Too much medical interference alters the cultural emphasis from quality of life to longevity of life. Consider the ultimate ramifications of your Hippocratic oath."

"How do you mean?"

"Life at any cost means *longevity* of life, not *quality* of life. Outside this country, most people live in accordance with the laws of humanity – they seek to prolong life because they are afraid of death. They are motivated by fear not love. Inside this country, we live our lives in accordance with the laws of divinity. A dignified life *and* a dignified death is an example to all and – we believe – the mark of a civilised culture."

Thorne recalled Chevral's words. "The value of service and the value of the server?"

Cordelia smiled. "Value in living *and* in serving." She paused. "May I be of service?"

Thorne looked slightly uncertain. "Well..... I was thinking of buying a small gift."

"..... For a lady or a gentleman?"

Thorne coughed in embarrassment at the question. "A lady."

"Something small and personal that can be carried easily?"

Thorne's face brightened with relief as she rescued him. "Yes..... please!"

"Tokens are often exchanged between close friends."

"Tokens?" asked Thorne.

Cordelia replaced her spectacles on her nose and indicated a row of velvet drawstring bags that were on display. "Different colours indicate different intentions - as do the scents of different herbs and spices." Noting the vacant look on his face - a look common to most men in this predicament, Cordelia hid her amusement and smoothly continued. "Cooler colours indicate calmer feelings and warmer colours indicate deeper feelings."

Thorne was impressed. "What a great way to communicate without speaking!"

"It has always been more popular than fan language."

"Fan language?"

"In Georgian times when couples met socially, a lady always carried a fan to silently indicate her responses to different situations. For example, held closed in the right hand and waved in front of the face like a stick indicated a reprimand. If it was held closed in the right hand with the tip resting on the left shoulder, it indicated intention to converse. A half-open fan held against the left cheek indicated a negative response. A fully open fan held to the left of the head was a declaration of love. A fully open fan held in the right hand in front of the face was a signal for the gentleman to follow her and a closed fan held in the right hand with the handle held to the lips was an invitation to be kissed – despite the demure looks on her face!"

Thorne blew out his cheeks. "Phew! That's complex!"

"The ladies were taught the exercise of the fan and the gentlemen were taught how to interpret the signals – but in separate classes, and on separate evenings."

"The ladies seemed to have called all the shots!" remarked Thorne.

Cordelia frowned. "I beg your pardon – *called all the shots?*"

"My apologies. To be in *control.*"

Cordelia looked at the floor. "Societies are always more stable when controlled covertly by matriarchy. But it all goes wrong when we lose confidence and are no longer subtle. All covert control is lost. We become brutal, seeking *overt* control."

Thorne nodded. "Gentlemen appreciate the feminine, but not the *feminist.* In the outside world, men and women have forgotten their places in society and have invaded each other's areas of exclusivity."

"In Georgian times, boys and girls were educated separately and each received sound instruction as to their separate and conjoined roles. Discipline was fundamental to an orderly society."

Thorne smiled in irony. "In my world of 'enlightened liberalism,' discipline and duty are considered barbaric – since they were used in association with forging an empire."

Cordelia nodded. "Imperialism is wrong, but you still need discipline and duty to maintain social order even in a democracy. Don't your people have a phrase about not throwing babies out of their baths?"

"Something like that!" laughed Thorne.

Cordelia smiled shyly and went pink – just like Veronica.

---oOo---

Being reminded of Veronica – and trying to save her embarrassment, Thorne changed the subject and guided her thoughts back to the business in hand. "You mentioned that different colours indicated different intentions?"

Recovering her composure, Cordelia smiled and pointed to each of the bags. "White symbolises affection between parent and child. Lilac represents affection with no expectations. Pink indicates fondness with emotional support. Red is for couples who share deep commitment."

"Does this system cover all types of relationships?"

Cordelia nodded. "*All* types!"

"No exceptions?"

Cordelia smiled. "With every introduction the favour is always returned and the giver receives either lilac or pink. Established couples exchange red tokens like anyone else."

"It seems very simple!"

"It is. There's little chance of signals being misunderstood – unlike flirting or dating."

"It makes good sense!"

"We think so. All ladies dress in a specific colour to indicate their social state."

"Social state?"

Cordelia smiled shyly and looked at her boots. "If the lady wears green, then she has no commitments and is free for friendships to evolve into relationships. If she wears red, then she has other commitments and is not free for relationships. If she wears black, then she is either married, widowed or uncomfortable with anything beyond friendship."

"So the colour of the dress determines the colour of the token?"

"If the gentleman is sensitive – yes. To be rushed into a relationship is frightening!"

"It's frightening for the gentleman as well!" admitted Thorne.

"I wondered if it was." said Cordelia. Sighing, she gave a little smile and looked at Thorne. "May I ask what colour your friend's dress is?"

"Green." said Thorne, unsure as to whether this fact was good – or bad for him.

Cordelia brightened. "Then you have the greatest potential available. May I suggest a pink token, then the lady feels truly honoured and is free to accept *this* level at least?"

"Oh..... Er..... Yes!" said Thorne whose face complemented the colour of the token.

Cordelia picked up a pink drawstring bag from the shelf and turned to the cabinet above. Opening a jar, she took a teaspoon and scooped two spoons of powder into the bag. Sealing the jar and replacing it in the cabinet, she then opened a drawer under the counter and took a little bottle from an inner rack and removed its stopper. A strong aroma of roses wafted up Thorne's nose making him sneeze. "Bless you!" laughed Cordelia. Allowing a few drops of liquid to soak into the contents of the bag, she replaced the stopper and returned the bottle to its place. She then pulled the drawstring tight and knotted it twice saying "Once for luck, and once for love!"

After holding it for a few seconds, she handed it to Thorne. "Do you require anything else?"

Noting Cordelia's black dress, Thorne asked. "Could I have a lilac token as well?"

Masking her surprise, Cordelia took a lilac bag and – taking another teaspoon, scooped two spoons of another power into the bag. Opening another bottle she repeated the procedure and a strong scent of lavender floated through the air. Knotting it twice and repeating her charm on it, she handed it to Thorne. "That will be four crones please." As he paid her, Thorne had to admit that it was exceptional value considering its social implications. After putting the pink token in his pocket, he gave Cordelia a gentle smile of thanks and placed the lilac token in her hands.

As he left the shop, he didn't see the blank look on her face transform into a smile as warm as the summer sun.

---oOo---

Pink token in his pocket, Thorne wandered down the street wondering what would hit him next. He had never felt quite the same since he had sat and listened to the music in the square and was vaguely aware that part of him was in eternal stasis under review whilst the temporal remains were left to pleasantly kill time until time killed *it*.

The next shop he saw was the occultists, which was owned by a lady named Lucinda. Upon entering, he was greeted by a lady dressed in black with silver-grey hair and fathomless brown eyes whose age could have been thirty or fifty.

The atmosphere felt different, and Thorne instantly knew it was wiser to study the jewellery and tools on display rather than engage in casual banter with this lady.

Feeling self-conscious, he decided to wander around the shop and take his time as if browsing. Sensing that her eyes were on the back of his neck, he fought to remain casual and deliberately took his time. Looking at the merchandise, he saw that it fell into two categories. At the front of the shop, it was small and designed solely to be worn around the neck. At the back of the shop were sets of occult tools that were intended for spiritual use within the home. Knowing it would be wiser to keep his distance, Thorne 'browsed' the occult tools that were farthest from the front counter. As each group of tools was labelled and designated, Thorne was able to read the use of each group of tools and he soon became quite engrossed and forgot about the 'wyrd shopkeeper.' Sitting on a golden cloth were several thuribles that were designed to burn incense. The label read:

> Thurible (Element of Air). The thurible or incense burner is placed in the east and burns incense appropriate to the nature of the mage. Incenses such as sandalwood, cedarwood, opium and musk are the most popular – although personal choice is always the final arbiter. The function of the Thurible is to act as a **tuner/amplifier**.

Moving along, he saw a scarlet cloth with several daggers arranged precisely in line and began to study its label:

> Athame (Element of Fire). The athame (Lunar Matriarchal Coven) or ceremonial knife (Solar Patriarchal Order) is placed in the south. It represents the will of the mage and is used to project that will for any purpose that strictly conforms to the divine plan/ magnum opus. The function of the Athame is to act as a **transmitter**.

Further along, he saw an aqua cloth with several chalices grouped together and began to read the following:

> Chalice (Element of Water) The chalice is traditionally placed in the west. It represents the soul of the mage in his/her divine quest. All souls are drawn towards union with the divine and this union is the ultimate sacrifice. In making one *sacred* - one becomes divine. The function of the chalice is to act as a **receiver**.

Finally, Thorne arrived at a black cloth with several pentacles arranged neatly on top and read the label:

> Pentacle (Element of Earth). The pentacle is traditionally placed in the north. It represents the body of the mage and is meant to remind him/her that despite all aspirations, the mage is limited to operating on the terrestrial world and not integrating with the celestial realm. The function of the pentacle is to act as an **earth safety system**.

Thorne felt the hairs on the back of his neck stand up as he experienced a realisation that occult tools each had a function that mirrored the principle of electricity. Even the altar doubled as a control console in an electricity generating station. Thorne gasped out loud. "*A power house!*" He then stopped himself as he remembered the presence of Lucinda. Conscious of the woman's penetrating gaze, Thorne smiled weakly at her. As his brief tour was finished, he found himself facing her. Sensing his obvious unease, she raised her eyebrows questiongly.

Once again, he felt an abyss opening beneath him and was completely lost for words.

Lucinda pointed to the display counter in front of her. "The four circular pendants you see before you each contain a different design incorporating four lines. The first containing four *straight* horizontal lines represents earth, the second containing four *wavy* horizontal lines represents water, the third with four *broken* horizontal lines is air and the fourth with four wavy *vertical* lines is fire. Each person feels an affinity with one particular element which is *usually* determined by the date of birth and wears the appropriate pendant."

"….. Just like an Astrological birth-sign?" ventured Thorne.

Lucinda shook her head. "Not really. As usual, those in the outside world made a simple system complicated. We don't have twelve individual signs but four triennial signs and we don't predict specific events but *character responses* to specific events! Like religion; astrology was created for the purpose of social engineering, and social engineering is the occult aim of politics – note all absences of national referenda to affairs that would demand national referenda in a truly democratic society!"

"*So that's why there is a periodic purge of all free-thinking people by the State?*"

"Yes. Those in the '*power house*' hate to be second-guessed by those they deem inferior – hence the periodic persecution of Witches, Illuminists, Freemasons, etc!" Lucinda watched in amusement as Thorne had whipped out his notebook and was busy scribing away. She raised her eyebrows. "I thought this was common knowledge in your world?"

"It will be!" muttered Thorne.

---oOo---

After pocketing his notebook and pen, Thorne looked up to find Lucinda watching him closely. "Does *everything* you stock have a specific meaning?"

"Yes. For example, this amber and jet necklace represents the interaction of masculine and feminine energies. It is however, worn only by women in authority. Over here, is a pentacle worn by those who are seeking balance. The pentacle is a universal symbol and is popular with those who wish to create harmony within and without – regardless of religious persuasion or persecution. It is always worn with one point uppermost to signify the dominance of celestial spirit over the four lower terrestrial elements – *are you feeling unwell?*"

Aware that his hand was on his chest over the pentacle under his shirt, Thorne gave a weak smile. "I'm fine – thank you."

"You don't look it. Sit down in that chair whilst I go next door for some herbs."

Before he had chance to protest, Lucinda had gone next door to see Cordelia.

Looking around the shop, Thorne noted how small it was and realised that like the herb & spice shop, all its merchandise had a specific function. There was no room for the trivial – neither within nor without. "Clarity of purpose!" he murmured to himself and jumped as the two 'women in black' entered the shop and descended upon him like a pair of ravens.

"I'm really fine – honestly I..... arrgh!" Thorne began and abruptly stopped as Lucinda expertly dabbed a pressure point in his face and his jaw obligingly dropped open.

"Keep this opiate under your tongue and you'll calm down!" she advised, and Thorne felt his tongue being rolled back like a carpet and something small was shoved in his mouth.

Whimpering in protest was not part of Thorne's normal psychological makeup - but here *nothing* was normal, so he was free to whimper all he wanted. As he was about to give vent to his fear he felt all traces of terror wash away and his eyes glazed over.

"Let's get him back to his room at the inn and then we can examine him!" said Lucinda.

Together the women lifted a vacant-looking Thorne to his feet and half-carried him back to the inn.

---oOo---

Stepping inside propping their cargo between them, the women made for the stairs and were followed by the glances of several curious customers and one horrified look from Giles.

"What's happened? What's happened?" pleaded the little man as he watched the women drag a gently smiling Thorne upstairs.

"He didn't look well – so I knocked him out until I could examine him further!"

"Should I call the Doctor?"

Lucinda paused to look at Giles. "Between myself and Cordelia, there's plenty of medical experience to look after him – don't forget who *taught* Victoria her trade!"

Watching Thorne disappear from view, Giles slowly returned to his counter and sighed as he poured himself a small mead. "He's away with the fairies now!" he murmured.

---oOo---

Mr Thorne was certainly 'away with the fairies,' and enjoying every minute of it. He knew absolutely nothing and cared even less. As Lucinda was busy opening his shirt to give him her version of a 'medical scan,' Cordelia was radiating so much concern that Lucinda stopped and turned to face her. "You have deep feelings for *this* one. Why?"

Cordelia's face went scarlet in reply.

Lucinda's face softened at her student's reaction. "Your intuition serves you well!"

Cordelia looked at teacher. "You sense it too?"

Lucinda nodded and turned back to a comatose Thorne and opened his shirt to reveal the pendant around his neck. Smiling in satisfaction, Lucinda drew back from Thorne to let Cordelia see the pendant for herself.

Cordelia's eyes widened. *"He's one of us!"*

"But doesn't know it – *yet!*"

"What shall we do?"

"Absolutely nothing. I recognise that pentacle. See the metal around the pentagram and note the concentric ripples emanating from its centre. I know what it symbolises and who owned it before our friend acquired it."

Cordelia's face showed confusion.

Satisfied, Lucinda buttoned up Thorne's shirt and motioned to Cordelia. "He *must* be allowed to follow his destiny – but one of us must watch over him wherever he goes."

"Oh yes!" breathed Cordelia, and the eyes behind the spectacles shone brightly.

Chapter 11

The evening and the night of Sixday came and went and Thorne was completely unaware of it. As the sun climbed well into Sevenday morning, he returned to his body and awoke to the familiar sounds of the market.

Propping himself up on one elbow, he peered through the window at the obelisk and guessed that he had been out for about sixteen hours. Recalling the previous day, he remembered with clarity the moment when he was knocked out.

"The bloody witch drugged me!" he exclaimed in anger and leaped from his bed and onto his feet before realising that he had never been able to do *that* since he was a teenager.

Amazement replacing anger, he re-assessed his current condition and had to admit that at that moment, he felt better than he had for the last thirty years. "Even so, she should be sued for assault and malpractice!" he muttered to himself – trying to salvage some moral indignation – after all, it was his *human right* to be miserable if he chose!

Realising the utter stupidity of his last thought, Thorne started to laugh at such juvenile behaviour and saw that it was precisely *this* kind of attitude that alienated people from each other and could – on a national basis – lead to social paranoia and even warfare.

How easily 'human rights' became human wrongs!

To his professional credit, Thorne noted this down in his journals before preparing himself for what remained of the day.

---oOo---

Stepping outside into the sunshine, Thorne decided to explore the south end of the capital and – threading his way through the customers in the market – he walked down 'Castle Street' towards the Duke's residence.

The street itself was unremarkable. Houses on both sides ran its length until the street opened up to reveal the turreted castle at its terminus. Towering over him stood the gatehouse, which loomed over a portcullis whose teeth had definitely seen better days. Fortunately for him it was raised and, taking a deep breath, Thorne tiptoed underneath to encounter a beautifully kept garden, which fronted the castle itself.

As there was no one around except an ancient lady in a wheelchair, Thorne walked towards her to inquire if he was permitted to enter. As he drew nearer, he observed that she was dressed in the usual 'widows black,' but his face broke into a smile when he saw her raise a long-stemmed pipe to her mouth and gently blow smoke rings into the air. By now, his nose had become accustomed to the smell of 'waccy baccy,' and he correctly guessed that she was suffering from multiple sclerosis.

On hearing his approach, the old lady lowered her 'churchwarden' and peered at him over a pair of elegant gold-rimmed 'pince-nez' spectacles. "Good day, young man!"

"Good day, madam." Thorne replied. "Am I intruding, or may I visit the castle?"

"If you have to ask *that* question, you must be new to this country!"

"I arrived recently and am in the process of immersing myself in your culture."

She gave a gentle smile. "Immerse yourself dear boy, immerse yourself!"

Sensing a directness that was beyond the norm – even for *this* country, Thorne decided to get a senior citizen's perspective on life in order to obtain a more balanced report. "Since my arrival, you are the first senior citizen I have encountered."

"Most people don't live beyond sixty-five – but I am eighty-two!"

"Sixty-five years is a short lifespan!"

"Maybe, but it is sixty-five *good* years – *and all our corpses are healthy!*"

Thorne did a mental double-take at the apparent contradiction in terms.

She continued wistfully. "Prolonged ill-health is soul-destroying – both for the sufferer and for those who have to sit by and watch." She pointed to a compartment in the arm of the wheelchair with the stem of her pipe. "That's why I keep *this* handy!"

"What's in there?"

"Dignity. The freedom to choose when enough *is* enough!"

Thorne was slightly shocked. "They chose to *give* you euthanasia?"

"No! I chose to *take* euthanasia – and I will use it on *my terms*! Your reaction betrays your conditioning by an 'Iron Hand in a Velvet Glove.' People must be free to evolve and not be manipulated into depending on the State – however inviting it seems!"

Thorne nodded. "Big Brother masquerading as Nanny State."

"Exactly. Be a dear and pass me some more 'baccy' – my pipe's just gone out!"

Thorne reached over and passed her some more weed from the leather pouch, which sat in her lap. She paused and looked at him expectantly. "Would you tap out and refill my pipe – my coordination is not so good."

Groaning inwardly, David Thorne found himself fixing a 'spliff' for a little old lady.

"Thank you. A match, please?"

Thorne obligingly struck up for her and she puffed away contentedly. She eyed him over the clouds of smoke and gave a little smile. "On *my* terms!"

---oOo---

Settling back in her wheelchair, the old lady sighed, relaxed her body and looked at her pipe. "My friend gives comfort by keeping muscle spasm to a minimum. As long as it works, I am content to live another day. If it ever loses its effect, then I am free to end the pain forever and slip away peacefully." She looked up at Thorne and smiled at the concern on his face. "You seem a nice young man – would you take me for a stroll around the garden?"

Thorne went behind the wheelchair to take the handles and guided her gently along the path that surrounded the lawn and listened to her commentary on the various flowers that were in the borders below the surrounding wall.

"I have always preferred wildflowers – 'weeds' – to most people, since they are natural and grow as they please – as should we. I love to see the snowdrops that herald the spring, and the bluebells, periwinkles and summer foxgloves but dear 'Woolley' is particularly fond of flowers that he can pair up in his favourite colours of purple and magenta – he keeps those exclusively in the conservatory!"

"Woolley?" asked Thorne.

The old lady laughed. "Wulfrum is my nephew and the current Duke. I am Agatha."

"Whoops!" thought Mr Thorne to himself.

Agatha continued with her commentary. "I find that wildflowers tend to have much greater significance in our lives. For example, I keep an eye on the garden to make sure that a certain yellow flower does not appear anywhere. The aconite, or its Latin name of *aconitum vulparia* – known as 'wolfs-bane' is truly a bane on our family. Whenever it appears, it heralds a premature death. In the distant past, sons who were named Wulfrum or Wulfred, tended to carry the curse and our family gave them such titles as 'Reckless,' 'Luckless' or 'Clueless' – to *warn* future sons who carried that name to take care when alone. Generations later, we realised that our family was too inbred which resulted in a predominance of idiots being born. Following a revelation, we deliberately married outside our small family and into the larger community – hence the change from Feudal Autocracy to Social Democracy."

Agatha sighed and puffed at her pipe thoughtfully. "For years, everything was fine until the premature death of my husband – the Duke's uncle – by drowning, and the premature death of Clarissa – the Duke's first wife – and then I discovered an aconite growing in the flower bed. In time, the Duke remarried and his young wife gave birth to two sons who were named Wulfrum and Wulfred – according to tradition." She paused to blow another smoke ring into the air. "If the curse *has* returned, we wonder if it will take the Duke's young sons leaving only the daughters from his first wife!"

Thorne shook his head. "Coincidences often lead to superstition."

"True, but at what point *beyond* statistical average does 'coincidence' evaporate?"

"All opinions are subjective – it's *vital* to maintain objectivity for clarity."

Agatha was silent, and another smoke ring floated into the air.

---oOo---

Thorne continued around the garden with Agatha, and it was sometime before he spoke again and with some difficulty. "..... I..... er..... met a lady whom I admire, and I would like to be her friend, but I don't know how to be a friend to a woman without her getting the impression – the *wrong* impression – that I expect more!"

Another smoke ring floated away. "You need *love*, not lust." – it was a statement.

Thorne sighed. "Yes."

"Does the lady know how you feel about her?"

"She thinks I *like* her."

"But you *love* her?"

"I want to help her find happiness – even if it is with someone else."

"You *do* love her – in the noblest way possible!" said Agatha admiringly.

"I guess I do."

"I will see 'Woolley,' and ask if he can arrange convenient meetings through her family!"

"That's most kind – but is it *wise*?"

"Nonsense, dear boy! What is the lucky girl's name?"

"Veronica!" said Thorne.

There was a noticeable pause from Agatha. "*Really!*" she finally managed.

"Is..... Is there a problem?"

"*Not at all!*" chuckled the old lady.

Thorne's face brightened with relief, and they continued their tour around the garden.

On the approach to the castle, the door opened and a familiar figure in a dark green dress walked outside and stopped when it saw them. It then decided to walk quickly towards them and Thorne's face lit up when he saw that it was Veronica. As she arrived, she nodded respectfully to the old lady in black and then looked at Thorne.

"G..... Good day, I didn't expect to see you so soon!"

"Good day, Veronica, I nearly didn't arrive at all. I went shopping yesterday to get you a little token of my appreciation and I encountered Lucinda and Cordelia."

Veronica's face showed confusion "You went shopping *yesterday* – but you nearly didn't arrive *today* – because you met Lucinda and Cordelia?"

"They drugged me on the pretext that I was unwell – but I'm fine and I'd like you to accept *this* token of my appreciation." said Thorne giving her the pink token. As Veronica received it with some surprise, doubt crept into Thorne's mind and he started to smell a rat. "You said you didn't expect to see me so *soon* – what do you mean by that?"

She shrugged her shoulders. "Just that. I'm often here and it's always a surprise when anyone calls – especially when they bring me one of *these*!"

With a sinking heart, Thorne realised that an attractive and charismatic woman like her would have several if not many admirers – she didn't need his friendship at all – but he obviously needed hers! Disgusted at his weakness and ignorance, he pulled together what dignity he could find, and politely withdrew. They watched him vanish under the gatehouse. Veronica looked at the little pink token in her hands and her eyes filled up.

"I just said I was surprised; aunt Aggie!"

"But that's not what he *heard*, my dear."

---oOo---

Back in his room at the inn, Thorne had given up on women once again. It always started well but always ended badly. It had been a 'miracle' that he had been in two relationships at all! All he wanted now was friendship, but friendship with a woman was a lot harder than leaping into bed with one – and he couldn't face *that* anymore! "The good ones don't need me, and I don't need the bad ones!" he muttered to himself.

Deciding to do what all disillusioned men do at such times, he went downstairs to the parlour and paid for a *full jug* of mead and sat silently in the settle, staring at nothing. He was well into his second mug when a figure in black sat down opposite him and poured itself a mug from Thorne's jug.

"It's tough being heterosexual – isn't it?"

Thorne slowly raised his eyes to meet those belonging to Virginia. "Yes!"

"You're fond of her, you're fond of me – is there anyone you're *not* fond of?"

"If I told you to sod off, would you go away?"

"If you answer my question, I will."

Thorne wearily closed his eyes and spoke from the heart. "I care about *humanity* and it scares me – it's bloody unnatural, and I hate myself because I've been betrayed by all those I've cared about. *I need someone who is a friend first and a woman second!*"

The room became quiet. Eventually, he had the courage to open his eyes.

Virginia had kept her promise.

After knocking back a *third* mug of mead, Thorne had enough common sense to mop most of it up with a meal and he retired early to bed determined to lose himself in his work on the farm.

---oOo---

On Oneday morning, somewhat hung-over, he rode down on the flatbed and spent the day helping to reap, bind and stack the wildgrass – prior to it being carted into the farmyard for off-loading into the second air-barn. As the farmer and his two daughters were away harvesting, Thorne and his three colleagues were left to work the fallow five-acre field on their own.

Although the job was simpler and lighter than earthing up potatoes, the team consisted of four instead of seven and had to be divided into two reapers and two binders. Thorne was given the opportunity to swing a scythe, but after an hour his shoulders and sides ached so much that he opted for the 'easier' task of binding which involved gathering up the grass into large bundles, tying each with string and cutting off the string from the roll which was in the pocket of his apron. Even this job became painful as his back ached with having to bend down.

When the farmer's wife arrived with a large jug of cold water, Thorne gratefully poured out a mug full and downed it in one go. The fresh air had made him lose his hangover, and he was grateful that he was occupied with something useful and did not have to dwell on the previous day. Dinner came and went and they worked steadily through the evening. When they finally returned to the shed to put away their tools, Thorne's back was hurting and he was looking forward to a long hot soak.

Arriving back in the capital, Thorne walked stiffly to the inn and went into the parlour to ask for his customary mead and bath. He got the former, but not the latter.

"Miss Veronica offers her apologies, but she will be detained every evening!"

"So there's no hot water?"

"Only in the morning, sir."

Unwilling to risk his back preparing and carrying buckets of hot water, Thorne nodded his thanks to Giles and took his drink upstairs hoping that a good night's sleep would sort things out. Unfortunately for him - it didn't.

Twoday morning, he awoke with a stiff back and had to spend some time cautiously stretching his body before getting out of bed. Other than that he prepared and travelled in the usual way. Whilst working in the field, the warmth of the summer sun eased his back, but in the cool of the evening the aches returned - to haunt him more than before.

Threeday was worse, and on Fourday, he only just finished before realising that he was in serious trouble!

He managed the walk back to Mycroft's cart but had to lay full length on the flatbed and each time it went over a bump, he prayed for Lucinda and Cordelia to appear and knock him out with their magic pill. By the time they arrived in the capital, Thorne's back had seized up and he couldn't move so Mycroft dismounted with his customary crunch and - picking up Thorne in a fireman's lift, proceeded to carry him back to the inn amid a chorus of screams that would shame a banshee.

A whimpering Thorne was carried through the inn, up the stairs and plonked on his bed - which elicited another scream. Mycroft frowned at him. "Do you *have* to make so much noise?"

"*That's bloody rich, coming from YOOOOOO!*" he yelled, as Mycroft proceeded to remove Thorne's clothing - including his pendant - and put it all neatly away in the wardrobe, leaving Thorne horizontal in his unders.

"Once you're tucked up in bed, I'll send for the doctor."

"*Oh no! Oh no! NOOOOOO!*" he yelled as he was lovingly tucked up.

"Hush! You'll wake the dead!" said Mycroft, winkling his ears in disbelief. He turned to go and smiled kindly. "Be patient sir, she won't be long!"

"*That's what I'm bloody afraid of!*" said Thorne staring rigidly at the ceiling.

That night, few in the capital got any sleep as – amid the demented shrieks – Victoria practised her black art of osteopathy on Thorne's defenceless body.

---oOo---

Fiveday morning arrived, and Thorne was still awake and feeling horribly mangled from the vicious ministrations of Victoria. He wondered with some guilt if this was in retaliation for the way he had mishandled his friendship with Veronica. He sighed to himself. "Women always stick together – especially if they are sisters!"

Since he had plenty of time to prepare himself, he decided to slowly get ready and see if he could finish the week's work and salvage *some* self-respect. With this in mind, he cautiously moved his body and was surprised to feel no pain. He moved the covers aside and slid his body out of bed – and promptly fell flat on the floor.

Lying face down on the floor, Thorne had to admit that the muscles in his back had been so effectively loosened that he had little control of them now. It was whilst lying in this position unable to move, that he heard frantic footsteps running up the stairs and knew that they didn't belong to Giles.

The door was flung open and it caught Thorne smack in the face knocking him out cold. When he eventually came around, he found that he was back in bed with a cool wet cloth over his forehead and nursing one hell of a headache. Cautiously, he opened one eye and saw a very familiar and very concerned face looking down at him.

"Oh..... Thorne, I am *so sorry* for knocking you out. I heard you fall and I ran upstairs to see if you were all right!" Veronica held Thorne's face in her hands – which elicited a loud squawk from her patient. She jumped back and cringed, holding her hands over her face. "I'm sorry, I shouldn't have done that either. Victoria *told* me to be gentle with you!"

"Victoria..... *Gentle*?"

"Yes. She was very concerned. She spent a long time with you last night."

Thorne looked at her incredulously. "I know..... *I was there*!"

Veronica smiled. "Of course – silly of me!" She giggled nervously. "How are you?"

"*Oh..... I'm bloody marvellous*!" exclaimed Thorne.

Veronica promptly burst into tears. "..... *I always end up hurting those I love*!"

"Just like Victoria!" said Thorne sarcastically. He did a double-take. "*You love me*?"

"Yes..... just like Victoria!" sobbed Veronica sitting down heavily on Thorne's bed and making him feel sick. She reached around for a handkerchief and could only find the cloth across Thorne's forehead. Without thinking, she took it and blew her nose loudly on it and then realised what she'd done. Gingerly, she replaced a now *very* soggy cloth over Thorne's forehead and – seeing the look of incredulity on his face – quickly backed out of the room and slammed the door which made him wince.

Alone in his bed, Thorne was silent for several seconds and then he slowly let out a quiet sigh of exasperation. "Oh..... shit!"

The rest of the day and all the night was spent slowly recovering. In the appropriately named 'wee hours,' he managed to get up and – dreading a long trip downstairs – hoped that there was a chamber-pot under his bed, otherwise he would be forced to open his bedroom window and sprinkle the street below.

Fortunately for all concerned – there was.

---oOo---

Sixday came and went. Thorne wasn't taking any chances – he stayed put!

Sevenday arrived, and nature rather than desire forced Thorne to prepare for the day. Wisely, he took his time and when he arrived in the parlour, he found Veronica sitting in his favourite settle fidgeting nervously. She looked up at him with concern on her face as he approached. "Are you are feeling better?"

Thorne smiled wearily as he sat down beside her. "I'll live."

Veronica cleared her throat. "I..... I have been told to watch over you – in case you have concussion – but I was wondering if you would like to go out for some fresh air?"

The invitation was so clear – even a man like Thorne couldn't miss it.

Admiring her simple sincerity, new confidence flooded into Thorne's soul and he looked into her face with great compassion. "*I'd love to – but please be gentle!*"

Veronica's eyes shone. "I'd like to take you to the Groves – it's very restful!"

Thorne's eyes widened but he was happy to follow this weird custom. Gallantly, he helped her to her feet, and together they left the capital and descended the three-mile slope towards the highly romantic mausolea. As they were descending, Thorne gently asked her why the Groves attracted the living.

Veronica looked around to make sure that they were alone and then took his hand in hers and looked into his face. "*Eternal love – in life and in death.* We affirm our closest friendships in the presence of those who have gone beyond. It is our custom to present our special friends to our dead family *before* we present them to our living family. *The eternal take precedence over the temporal.*"

Thorne was acutely aware of the gravity of this gesture and said so.

Veronica's eyes radiated peace. "I've chosen well!" she said quietly. Together, they walked along the lane until they arrived at a track, which led directly to the ducal family tomb. Veronica confidently walked forward expecting Thorne to follow. When he stopped, she paused and looked back at him. "What's the matter?"

"We can't go there, that's the Duke's family tomb!"

She looked at him with deep affection. "Yes..... We can!" So saying, she gently pulled him forward and they soon arrived under the portico.

She sat down halfway up the steps and patted a place for him beside her. After a moment's hesitation, Thorne reluctantly sat down wondering what would happen next.

Veronica sat silently with her hands folded in her lap and her eyes became unfocused. Copying her, Thorne tried to do the same, but kept looking sideways at her to make sure she was still there. After some time had elapsed, he began to get worried, as he was feeling light-headed from his trauma and from not eating for thirty-six hours. He let out a sigh, which brought Veronica out of her trance-like state and she realised how fragile he still was. Her maternal instincts took over and she gently pulled him towards her and stroked his hair. All resistance gone, he accepted her kind offer of solace. As he drifted off into a delicious sleep, his awareness made the connection and he knew who her family were.

---oOo---

The sun was setting when Thorne eventually awoke to find Veronica had snuggled up against him – emitting a purr-like snore – which reminded him of Harold the cat. He'd got another special friend – one who probably didn't dribble quite so much – but he'd check his coat later on just to make sure!

He had to move before he seized up. In so doing, he heard a dreamy sigh as Veronica yawned and slowly sat up. They looked at each other in contented silence – as only *true* friends can do – and then Veronica stood up and helped Thorne to his feet. He staggered slightly and Veronica held him tightly and looked into his face.

"You're *still* not well – are you?"

"No – not really!" he finally had to admit.

"I'll ask the Duke if he will give a dispensation to allow you to recover fully."

"That's very kind, but I must continue my work on the farm."

"The Duke will allocate someone else to take your place. No production will be lost."

"The Duke – *your father* – is most kind, but I am a giver, not a taker."

"It's important to give, but it's equally important to be willing to receive – in *all* things."

"Even in relationships?"

"If they are to work – yes!"

Thorne looked thoughtful. "I guess I've never really learned how to receive. I've been so preoccupied with trying to make others happy that I've ignored their attempts to reciprocate."

Veronica smiled sadly. "It's important to be willing to receive from others, otherwise they will feel insignificant in their role."

Thorne saw the wise woman within the beautiful girl and he loved her deeply.

She looked at him strangely. "What do you see?"

Thorne laughed. "A *woman* within the twenty-eight year old child!"

So saying, he gently took her face in his hands and kissed her fully on the mouth and then drew back to watch her reaction.

Veronica stood wide-eyed and immobile for several seconds, and then she sat down heavily. "Oh!" She blinked several times absorbing this new sensation and finally drew a deep breath. "Ohhhhh!" She then looked at Thorne. "Could I have another please?"

Thorne smiled gently. "I think *one* is enough to be going on with – for now!"

"Are you sure?"

"I'm sure."

"Oh....."

Thorne helped her to her feet. He gave her a hug and kissed her on top of her head.

She gazed into his eyes. "What was that for?"

"To show you that I love you, and that I'll do all I can to help you find happiness!"

She melted in his arms and he held her for ages gently stroking her hair. Finally, he said, "Come on sweetheart, let's go home - I'm up early for work again."

She gently held his face. "No. You will take this week off - I'll speak to my father!"

"Is that wise?" he asked.

She grinned. "My father may be the Duke - but I and my sisters run the country!"

A thought struck him. "If your father is the Duke - do *you* have a title?"

She burst out laughing. "My sisters and I are all Countesses - but we never bother with our titles!"

Thorne closed his eyes in dismay as he recalled his words to Virginia. "I recently told a Countess to 'sod off!'"

Veronica laughed even harder. "Yes. Virginia told me about that!"

"*Oh God!*"

"Don't worry. She admires your honesty!"

Thorne didn't know where to put himself, so he just held on to a giggling Veronica.

---oOo---

After a time, Thorne became aware that darkness had fallen. He removed his coat and placed it gently over Veronica's shoulders. Holding hands, they retraced their steps to the capital walking most of the way in an easy silence that only comes when two souls are made for each other. As they walked under the gatehouse, they released contact and continued down the main street and paused in the square. Veronica turned to Thorne, with a look that brooked no contradiction. "*David*, I want you to rest all this week. I will take care of everything!"

Surprised at her use of his first name, Thorne meekly acquiesced. Returning his coat with a warm smile of gratitude, Veronica bade him good night.

Chapter 12

One day morning arrived, and Thorne was awake and feeling he should be getting ready for work on the farm. Hedging his bets in case Veronica's efforts with her father had been in vain, Thorne ambled downstairs to prepare for the day when Giles intercepted him in the parlour.

"Excuse me, sir, but Miss Veronica's instructions were very precise!"

"No work, huh?"

"No work, sir."

Thorne pursed his lips. "Could I at least prepare for the day?"

"Prepare for a week of leisure - indeed, sir!" said Giles brightly.

"What would happen if I tried to jump on the flatbed?"

Giles looked solemn. "My instructions are to summon Miss *Victoria*!"

"*Whoa, Giles - that's fine!*" said Thorne, raising his hands in surrender.

Following a *very* leisurely preparation and breakfast, Thorne was back in his room wondering what the hell to do for a whole week. He'd seen pretty much the whole town in all four quarters. He'd seen enough of the Groves, and had no need to return to the village in the lane to the quarry. Everywhere else was too far to walk – bearing in mind that he would have to allow for the return trip as well!

He was bored and felt depression set in. An all too familiar depression – that plagued so many in his own country. His own culture was constantly searching for new ways to entertain the terminally bored, the unemployed and the unemployable – but nothing could ever compensate for that feeling of utter worthlessness.

Feeling that he had been set a spiritual challenge, Thorne was wondering what to do when it occurred to him to be creative – rather than destructive. He began to realise that nearly all the content of newspapers is negative and deliberately slanted to cause maximum controversy in order to optimise sales. *Why did the public actually buy newspapers? Why were they willing to pay good money to feel miserable?*

Over the last few years, newspaper sales had diminished to such an extent that they were advertising free CD's with many Sunday issues. *Were the public finally getting sick of misery?*

Thorne sat on his bed and wondered what would happen if newspapers actually reported the news – both bad and good – in equal measure? What if there was a special column, which showed many of the *good* things that also happened in life?

He recalled a subtle difference between his culture, and the culture he saw in America.

During one of his assignments that had involved coastguard operations, he recalled the difference in philosophy, which involved the marker buoys – 'booeys' – in the channel.

In his country, the buoys were placed primarily to *guard* traffic from entering areas of danger – a *negative* emphasis! In America, the reverse seemed true. Their 'booeys' were placed primarily to *guide* traffic along secure routes – a *positive* emphasis!

It was a very subtle, but a very significant *cultural* difference.

Thorne sat in thought. *Could a jaded journalist become a social engineer?* Thinking how 'natural' it was to slant the truth to reflect the negative side of life, he saw that he was trapped within his own culture and wondered if he should change polarity in order to redress the balance.

It was the *balance* that had to be maintained.

His newspaper – *'The Tribune'* – was no different from any other newspaper. Thorne considered the possibility of creating a page devoted to publishing articles of a positive nature. He thought of calling it *'The Tribune Tribute'* – a corny title to be sure – but it might get the public's attention! If sales increased, it could catalyse *complete* change – and for the right reason! He smiled to himself when he recalled Straker's words.

It was the *intent* that counted.

He made a quick note in his journals and drew a circle around the core philosophy to remind him to consider working from this source of inspiration. Now what?

Feeling a need for further inspiration – a new perspective on life – he decided to return to the Solstice Temple and wait for something to happen. He wasn't bothered about shafts of light striking the objects on the altar, but he needed to absorb the atmosphere that permeated the fabric of the building. 'Stone Taping' came into his mind.

---oOo---

As he entered the temple and was walking towards the altar, he saw that nothing had changed in the physical sense. All was as before. The spiritual atmosphere was also the same. All was as before. *Everything was fixed.*

However, *he* was changing. *He was mutable.*

He no longer felt any repulsion to the atmosphere – on the contrary – he felt attraction. He had replaced fear with peace – *but not consciously.* The *other* part of him – the part that was in 'eternal stasis under review' had decided to take a temporary interest in his affairs and had given him a kick up his spiritual backside.

Experiencing this minor revelation, Thorne sat down near the altar and patiently waited for something else to happen. He waited for ages. No sunlight. No cleaner. Nothing.

He looked at the altar and the windows and knew that he was seeing the manifestations of religion. If he wanted to see faith, he would have to look *within* – not without.

"Okay, it now feels right – but I'm still no wiser!" he said to himself.

Words appeared: *Why do you seek answers among the dead, and not the living?*

Thorne jerked awake, thinking he must have fallen asleep. Needing to go somewhere but not knowing where, he left the temple and walked outside and propped himself against one of the pillars that supported the temple portico, and felt that he was back under the portico of the ducal tomb.

"The answers are among the *living*!" he said to himself.

He thought of all the people he had encountered and interviewed since his arrival. All had ranged in age from 20 to 60 – plus one in her 80's – *but no children*!

Thorne's heart sank when he realised he might have to interview children. He had to admit that he loathed children! *They exemplified society uncloaked*! In the outside world they were noisy, dirty, demanding, destructive, expensive and bloody irritating if one was in the process of dating their mother! This was why he had only dated women who were 45 plus - when the little buggers had flown the nest!

He looked up at the sky. "Don't do this to me - *please!*"

The sky apparently thought otherwise.

He thought of the handful of women he had dated, and of the two with whom he'd actually shared an intimate relationship. Each in their turn had been ten years older than him but he had felt safe - since he believed that at *that* age, they would have been content to have a peaceful and playful relationship - akin to faithful carthorses.

Once he had restored their confidence, each had unfortunately defaulted to type. In their turn, each had become dissatisfied with gentle love and had wanted to recapture their lusty youth - akin to faithless racehorses.

Even in his prime, Thorne's nature could *never* have been described as passionate, dynamic, gymnastic or explosive, but unfortunately for him this was just what his respective partners had wanted. In their turn, each had become bored with stability and had enjoyed the attentions of much younger men whilst Thorne had unwittingly been demoted to a 'sugar daddy' for older women.

After two years in each relationship, Thorne had been given the bullet and had given up after number two. He'd gained *some* satisfaction when he was reliably told that after number two (in her 50's) had claimed her new man (in his 30's), he had lost all interest and had dumped her for a girl in her 20's!

There was *some* justice!

More words appeared: *You are applying your values to my people.*

Looking at the people in the small square, Thorne doubted that anyone in this little haven was capable of deceit – he'd bet his life on it! The children also seemed well behaved. Thorne slowly nodded to himself. No pre-judging. No pre-slanting. He made a decision to ask Veronica if he could attend one of her classes for children.

He hoped that they would all be nice to him!

---oOo---

Faced with this awful prospect, Thorne did what any man would do. He returned to the inn and downed two mugs of mead before tackling a plate of roast boar in a honey and mustard sauce with carrots, onions and croquette potatoes. He then looked at Giles. "Could you pass on a message to Miss Veronica?"

"Certainly, sir!" beamed Giles.

"Would it be possible for me to attend one of her classes?"

"With the children, sir?"

Thorne nodded sourly. "Educational perspective!"

"Miss Veronica will be arriving – to prepare the *evening* water."

Thorne was up to speed with events again. "Thank you, Giles!"

"My pleasure, sir." smiled the little man.

Thorne wondered what he could do to kill time until Veronica arrived that evening. He finally decided to accept his enforced holiday and wandered slowly outside to 'imbibe the vibes' and watch the folk pass by. It was another lovely day, and Thorne's soul was definitely thawing out. His body sitting in the sunshine and his aura slowly tuning in to the gestalt, he became aware of an apparent paradox. How could he *love* humanity, but *loath* children? The answer gently arrived. He loved the ideal, but loathed the real – akin to a zealot!

Careful now!

Children exemplify humanity uncloaked – currently rough and unpolished – as when hewn from the quarries of nature. Humanity in its polished *noblest* state represents the return to Divinity. Humanity is *always* an extension of its children – hence its *current* condition of spiritual self-disgust – which *currently* manifests as terrestrial purgatory.

Children always mirror humanity's <u>current</u> condition!

Perhaps this explained why children were often chastised – 'made chaste' – made *pure*?

Was humanity continually punishing/purifying itself because of its fall from grace?

When humanity is Perfected, it will no longer need to create children to remind it of its imperfection – the mirror of reflection will be redundant. The nature and science of reproduction will also be redundant.

Humanity was not intended for terrestrial existence – hence 'The Fallen' connotation. Humanity had violated nature. Fruit only falls when ready, otherwise it arrives torn and bleeding – its nature bitter, its purpose useless. *How many people felt like that?*

Thorne was suddenly curious to see how the children of this little country behaved, as they would give a true representation of its people. *A litmus test indeed*!

---oOo---

Jotting down these notes for future reference, Thorne put away his notebook and watched the people and the traffic pass by. Everyone was relaxed and orderly and strolled through life. Over a period of an hour, he watched people and traffic pass before his eyes but his soul was seeing much more. Finally, his body returned to the inn and went upstairs to rest on its bed and digest what his soul had seen. Within its cocoon of flesh, Thorne's soul was 'away with the fairies' again – but, this time, *without* the assistance of an opiate!

---oOo---

He returned to his body when someone – probably Giles – was knocking on his door.

"Excuse me, sir – but Miss Veronica has just arrived!"

"Thank you, Giles." he heard himself say.

Thorne slowly got up and wandered towards the washing bowl. After a quick sluice, he donned his boots and ambled downstairs to make known his request.

Arriving in the parlour, Thorne was pleasantly surprised to see Veronica sitting in his favourite place under the inglenook fireplace wisely holding a *small* mug of mead! As he sat down beside her, she nodded in the direction of his empty drinking hand. "No mead?"

Thorne smiled. "I've learned to have only two at noon with a meal – it's far safer!"

Veronica looked at her drink and grimaced at the memory. "I'd forgotten just how strong it is – that's why I now follow the example set by Giles and Clive!"

Several seconds passed and then Thorne took a deep breath. "….. Would it be possible to attend one of your classes?"

Veronica looked quizzical. "*With the children?*"

Thorne swallowed hard. "Yes….. with the children."

She shrugged her shoulders. "Certainly – but why?"

"Educational perspective!"

Veronica sipped her mead slowly. "Most of the education takes place at home since all parents are highly conscious of their children's welfare. Parents teach their children reading and arithmetic and they show them how theory relates to practice within their own craft. I show how theory relates to practice in the wider sense, by taking them on tours to *all* the crafts to inspire *integral* interest. When we return to the library at the castle, I test their knowledge and correct any mistakes they may have made. I give each child a note of strengths and weaknesses to give to their parents, so that parents are fully informed as to their child's progress and can emphasise areas as required." Veronica paused to have another sip. "That covers their *technical* education!"

"What about their *cultural* education?"

Veronica smiled. "I read them another chapter of one of their favourite stories!"

"What happens when a child requires clarification within a *fictional* story?"

Veronica laughed. "*I tell the child to find out for themselves!*"

"Is that why they are taught *within the library?*"

She gazed at Thorne. "*Seek and you will find!*"

Thorne nodded slowly. Once again, he was aware of the woman within the child. He also realised the subtle but significant difference between technical practice and cultural principle. The former determined standard of living and the latter determined quality of life – in other words – the works of the scientist and the artist respectively. "Magister and Magus!" he murmured to himself.

"You've been fishing with Straker – haven't you?"

"Yes – but where does Ipsissimus fit in?"

"The scientist works from *fixed* principles, the artist works from *mutable* principles and the philosopher works from *cardinal* principles. Unfortunately for the *temporal* world, cardinal principles are *eternal* and cannot manifest here. When philosophers apply cardinal principles all they do is un-manifest all that is manifest."

Thorne frowned in thought. "They de-construct something to see how it works – but they can't re-construct it to improve on its original function?"

Veronica nodded. "Exactly! The operation is a success – but the patient dies."

Thorne looked at Veronica but had a vision of Victoria. He shuddered.

Veronica continued. "Philosophy ultimately attempts to manifest the un-manifest and is doomed to failure in the *temporal* world. This is why the grade of Ipsissimus is known as the 'Hidden' Intelligence!"

"Hidden?" inquired Thorne.

"Anything which manifests *without* the body and catalyses the mind via sensory perception/reason is regarded as 'real' by scientific philosophers following empiricism. Anything which manifests *within* the mind and catalyses the same via inspirational revelation/reason is regarded as 'real' by artistic philosophers following rationalism."

"*Hidden?*" repeated Thorne.

"Philosophical principles can only manifest in this world via another medium – such as economic politics (Conservative) or diplomatic politics (Liberal)." Veronica looked sad. "*Pure philosophy is un-manifest.* It can only be cognised via its works – which are imperfect expressions of its essence – like all human concepts of God!"

"Hidden!" admitted Thorne.

Veronica had another sip of her drink. She grew quiet and her face remained sad.

Sensing the change, he tried to cheer her up. "You know a lot about other cultures!"

"*To learn and to leave.*" said Veronica looking *through* him.

"Isn't that good?" asked Thorne somewhat confused.

"Not for those we leave behind!" she replied.

..... So *that* was the essence of their faith!

---oOo---

Thorne gazed at the young woman and marvelled at the scope of her crafts – cleaner and teacher – the former enhancing places and the latter enhancing people. Veronica exemplified the ethos of social order upon which their culture rested.

---oOo---

Referring to their conversation, Thorne asked jokingly. "I don't suppose you teach the children to *this* level?"

Veronica smiled gently. "The *essence* is the same at any level. I just help them to pull back the lens from the page of life – so that they can see the book."

"They must have access to an extensive library!"

"They also have many friends to interact with."

Thorne was silent, realising that in his world, creative interaction was being smothered under a blanket of drink, drugs and discos (with their attendant results). Liberal excess was to blame – regardless of the party in 'power' – and everyone wanted votes!

A gentle nudge from Veronica woke him from his musings and he smiled fondly at her.

"I was just thinking of the world outside this country."

"Are you feeling sick for home?" inquired Veronica.

"I'm feeling sick *of* home!" said Thorne.

"No-one should feel like that."

"True. No-one *should*!"

Patting his hand in affection, she finished her drink and rose from the settle. Thorne stood to let her pass and, as she was walking towards the kitchen, she turned briefly.

"The children and I will be waiting for you at the castle entrance. Please be prompt!"

"Yes, Miss Veronica!" replied Thorne meekly and gave a court bow.

He missed the smile on her face as she entered the kitchen.

Chapter 13

Twoday morning arose, and the dawn was gently heralded by the customary birdsong, which had permeated Thorne's psyche. As he slowly awoke to their soft melody he understood why no one needed alarm clocks. In harmony with nature, everyone's mind was used to silence and slept soundly through the night until called to labour by the soothing music of dawn's early light.

After preparation and breakfast, Thorne strolled outside and walked across the square and down 'Castle Street' towards the home of the woman whom he had started to regard as a special friend. He had no immature illusions concerning *physical* intimacy with all the attendant problems of an addiction, but he was genuinely relieved to be in a relationship of *spiritual* intimacy, which he knew could only enhance both their lives.

He encountered the jagged smile of the gatehouse and passed quickly under its canines to follow the path across the lawns towards the entrance. As he reached the huge oak doors, he heard the quiet murmuring of children's voices. Thorne politely swung on the brass ring that was attached to the mouth of a blazing sun and an explosive boom rang throughout the castle. Thorne leaped back in shock.

Veronica opened the door and looked at Thorne. She shook her head in resignation. "Most people just walk inside – as they do at the Solstice Temple!"

There was a chorus of nervous squeaks behind her and she turned around to face her class who were sitting inside the porch on two long benches. "Be quiet! He doesn't bite!"

The tension evaporated in a shower of giggles – which were ignored by Veronica. Master Thorne was instantly on his best behaviour – for *her* sake! "..... I'm sorry, Miss Veronica – I didn't realise the acoustics were so good."

"Now that you know differently – you won't repeat *that* mistake?"

"Not *that* one, Miss!" he said with a mischievous grin.

Veronica caught the inference and tried to keep a straight face. "Come inside and meet the children!" she said silkily.

Master Thorne shuffled inside and was met by twenty pairs of eyes.

"Children, this gentleman is called 'Thorne' and he will be with us *all day!*"

Thorne flinched when she had said "all day" but he nodded to the children politely.

"GOOD DAY, SIR!" they all yelled in unison, and the castle yelled back at him.

The little buggers were already exacting their revenge!

"Good day, everyone." murmured Thorne automatically siding with Veronica and instantly qualifying for 'Teacher's Pet' – in *his* eyes at least. He caught Veronica's expression of 'I told you so' on her face – *she was enjoying this!*

"Settle down everyone! Our guest has mentioned an interesting subject – *acoustics*." Veronica eyed the class. "Can anyone tell me what 'acoustics' means?"

"NOISE!" they all yelled, and Thorne's ears nearly dropped off from the reverberation.

"No!" said Veronica, simply.

There was confusion as the children (and Thorne) looked at each other and then finally back to Veronica in expectant silence. She had their attention.

"Acoustics is the science of sound and the study of its phenomena. A place can be built to reverberate or magnify sound – such as part of this castle or the temple. The *intention* creates the conditions, but sound is a *manifestation* of a physical action. The castle and the temple are primarily places of intention!" Veronica looked at Thorne. "Have you recovered from your..... accident?"

"My *accident*?..... Yes, I think so!" said Thorne raising a mental eyebrow.

"Good!" She addressed the class. "Remain seated, I shall return shortly."

Thorne was left in charge of the class as Veronica disappeared inside the castle. A few minutes later, she returned carrying a wooden box. "Everyone to the temple!"

Thorne groaned inwardly. Not the bloody temple again!

Holding hands (!) the children filed outside followed by Thorne and Veronica. As they began their journey, Thorne quietly asked Veronica why the children held hands when it was frowned on by their culture.

Veronica smiled gently. "Any physical contact between people indicates that they are seeking reassurance from each other. They are actually *un*happy and lack confidence. We understand that infants need comfort, but *mature* adults should have evolved beyond mutual dependence!"

Thorne snorted. "Who held *whose* hand when we went down to the Groves?"

Veronica nodded. "As I said before, I am twenty-eight and *still* a child."

"Are you saying that intimacy is an expression of *fear* and not of love?"

"Yes – 'children' beget more children – just as fear begets more fear!"

"Is that why there are so *few* children in this country?" he asked.

"Is that why there are so *many* 'children' in yours?" she replied.

---oOo---

They finally entered the small square and walked towards the temple. As they went under its portico, Veronica told them all to wait and opened the wooden box to reveal a golden bowl, which closely resembled one of the 'Singing Bowls' of Tibet. As she placed the bowl gently on the ground outside the temple, she took a rod and waited. "It is my *intention* to make a 'noise' under the conditions existing here!"

She glanced around the class, waited deliberately and then lightly struck the bowl and began to run the rod around its rim. A quiet hum came from the bowl and slowly increased to become a steady ringing sound. Thorne and the children were captivated. After several seconds, she stopped, picked up the bowl and walked inside the temple. "It is my intention to make a 'noise' under the conditions existing *here*!"

Everyone ran inside and Thorne was left behind. He quickly got the idea and also ran. Veronica walked to the centre of the temple where the altar stood and moved the large candle - which marked the focus of the dome overhead. She moved it just enough to centre the bowl in its place. Once again, she waited deliberately emphasising her intent and then repeated her action and again, the hum slowly changed into a ring - and then something else took over.

The dome - and then the walls of the temple, began to hum in harmony with the sound. Thorne and the children were transfixed. Thorne was able to identify several individual harmonics within the collective 'chorus' of sound - yet still hear the bowl. He looked at the children and saw that any fear had left them. They all stood with their hands at their sides and a look of rapture on their faces. One by one, each child began to hum the note that he or she could hear.

Thorne was standing at Veronica's side and murmured to himself. "*Far out!*"

Veronica smiled and whispered in his ear. "*Without the drugs..... Try it yourself!*"

There was something wonderfully alien about the event, and Thorne wished he could have recorded it on digicam. He felt completely relaxed, and found himself humming to a sound that he found particularly beautiful. The temple sang back to him and the reverberations increased until they entered his mind - and lifted him out of his body.

---oOo---

Frozen in a white light of celestial eternity, Thorne was aware of everything. Aeons ago, incarnate humans *were* discarnate 'angels.' Most 'angels' embraced collectivism and selflessly served their creator. Some 'angels' embraced individualism and selfishly served themselves. The 'socially' minded stayed in place and the 'liberally' minded fell from grace. The 'Fallen' were incarnated/incarcerated in physical forms so as to isolate them from the collective although *they* believed that their individual 'freedom' was being guaranteed. They elected to inhabit the terrestrial species that showed the greatest potential for evolutionary integration with the celestial realm.

They intended to return home to 'liberate heaven from divine oppression!'

Via numerous incarcerations, the 'Fallen' advanced but barely evolved. They would always fall out among themselves and repeat the same mistakes over and over again. As humans, they 'killed' each other countless times over *duality* in politics, theology, philosophy, psychology, sociology etc. etc. To 'kill' time, they deliberately created subjects to argue over in order to assess their personal worth and whilst so employed, they were actually going nowhere. As they had lost virtually all their spiritual links, they were operating at the inferior mental and astral levels with a 'personal' agenda.

There was still time to learn and to leave, but in the end there would be no-time left.

Thorne was aware that he was witnessing the gradual withdrawal of time leaving an expanding void of no-time. Thorne then returned to his body to fulfil his part in the Divine Plan. He stood in the now, silent temple and saw that he was surrounded by twenty small children – plus one wise 'child.'

"Well?" she asked in curiosity.

"Yes, thank you." he replied.

"What have you *seen?*" she persisted.

Thorne took a deep breath. "We were exiled to earth, and have been trying to return to heaven – in order to raise hell!"

Veronica nodded in confirmation.

Thorne looked *through* her. "It explains the 'guardian angel' mythology!"

"*Which is?*"

"A guardian to oversee the evolution of every criminal. In *time*, this will lead to Divine Judgement and *spiritual* resurrection for those who are to be re-admitted to heaven. But *time* is running out. If we don't change, there will be no resurrection for anyone. 'Angels' are immortal, but not eternal – *we can be un-created by our creator.*"

"*Un-created?*" asked Veronica.

"Destruction implies existence lost. The 'Chosen' are in stasis in the centre whilst universal time is reversed. The 'Fallen' are still subject to temporal laws and begin to un-create until time regresses past the point of creation – *and then they never existed!*"

"*Can that truly happen?*" whispered Veronica.

"Scientists are already postulating about universal expansion/ contraction but they are not *consciously* aware of the magnitude implied." Thorne's eyes came back into focus and he gazed down at the children. "Did *they* see what I saw?"

Veronica shook her head. "Our esoteric culture is mystical. Mystics see what they have to *be.*" She looked at Thorne with great tenderness. "Occultists see what they have to *do.*"

Thorne recalled Lucinda and understood. "United in principle, divided in practice."

Veronica nodded and changed the subject. "I think we have had plenty of *experience* for one day – so we should try to balance this with some *education*!" She put the golden bowl safely in its box and secured the lid. "Everyone to the main square!"

Obediently, they all trooped outside and made for the town centre.

---oOo---

Arriving in 'Market Square' with its stone obelisk and solid oak stocks, Thorne sensed intuitively that the former was intended to assist newcomers until they became attuned to the cultural gestalt, and the latter were to remind all of their social duty – *or else*!"

Veronica followed his gaze. "The stocks are a very *public* form of incarceration for good reason. If criminals are actually *hidden* from society, they are unable to *directly experience* society's disgust at their behaviour. By hiding criminals, a liberal society is actually sparing them from the social impact of their crimes. Small wonder that criminals feel no remorse at being hidden away. In psychological terms, criminals are being *assisted* in maintaining a contempt for that society which attempts to ignore them. Ergo: *A 'liberal' society is weak and hypocritical to the criminal mind*!"

Recalling his 'public display' atop the Brougham with Straker, Thorne had to agree. "Have they ever been used for public punishment?"

Veronica shook her head. "Not within my lifetime!"

"What about capital punishment?"

Veronica shivered. "Not within living memory!"

"Could you elaborate?"

Veronica looked haunted. "To be cast *unprepared* into the meadows to face Natural Justice via the hives, is not something anyone cares to contemplate!"

Thorne nodded and raised an eyebrow. "The perfect deterrent?"

"*The perfect deterrent..... Can we talk about something else?*"

Thorne was apologetic. "Yes – of course we can!"

Veronica forced a smile. "I was thinking of showing you the town's carving centre."

Thorne smiled at the thought of age-old skills that created works of art.

Veronica turned to the children. "Everyone to the carving centre!"

Everyone followed Veronica halfway down 'Quarry Street.' They turned north up a side street that ran parallel to 'Main Street' and halted in front of a large yard. She told them to wait whilst she spoke to the foreman and walked inside one of the workshops that fronted the yard. She returned in less than a minute and motioned them to follow her inside where they were introduced to the foreman. "Bentley has kindly agreed to show us around!"

Prematurely grey, his blue eyes twinkling behind his spectacles, Bentley gathered everyone around him. "As you know, we carve *two* materials here – can anyone tell me what they are?"

"Wood and stone!" the children said.

"Good! These days we mainly carve wood. Why is that?"

"Wood is weak so we need more of it. Stone is strong so we need less of it!"

"Very good! We have to be *very* careful when we use wood. Why is that?"

"We must not be greedy or we will run out of wood and then the world will see us!"

"What will happen to us if the world sees us?"

"We will change and lose everything!"

Bentley nodded and looked at Thorne who had to agree. Before he had arrived in this country, Thorne would have called such education 'indoctrination' but he had received enough vision that he easily saw the arrogance and ignorance of raising such an issue.

"What is the difference between *building* something and *carving* something?"

"Building is adding bits on. Carving is taking bits off!"

"Life is the same. You can add bits on for quantity or take bits off for quality!"

Thorne started to smile at the significance of the statement, as Bentley continued.

"What does Straker say in 'Your World – My World?'"

"Your world builds for *quantity*. My world carves for *quality!*"

"Let's see what they are carving today!" said Bentley, leading everyone inside.

---oOo---

The inside of the large workshop was a joy to behold. This workshop dealt purely with solid timber which was to be marked, sawn, turned, carved, sanded and waxed into rails, columns, mouldings etc. These would be secured to otherwise complete furniture such as desks, chairs, tables, settles, benches, sideboards and so on. They were taken to the first stage, which was the timber store and were shown the stacks.

"This is the first stage where all the oak timber is stored after the trunks have been sawn by two men using a bow saw and split several times using sledgehammers and wedges. Unlike most timber, it is far easier to work oak when it is still 'green' than when it has dried out. Most timber has to dry out before it is worked but oak is an exception. From here, the timber is taken into the workshop where it is roughly marked and sawn using a rip saw and planed down to the correct thickness. For fine sawing, tenon, jig, fret or piercing saws are used. For a rail, the timber is tenoned with a tenon saw. For a column, the timber is turned on a lathe and then mortised with a mallet and chisel - it can also be carved to add detail. Mouldings are the most intricate and are marked; fine sawn and carved using many different chisels - some fat and some thin, some flat and some curved. Spokes for wheels are shaped with a spoke shave and all finished work is sanded for smoothness and waxed for proofing and lustre!"

The next two hours were spent watching people at work and identifying which tool was being used on which job and why. Veronica whispered to Thorne that the children would be tested on what they had learned before they went home in the evening.

Thorne learned that the children would be taken to every craft several times in order to gain familiarity. Upon reaching the age of fifteen years, they would be sent out as labourers to one of the crafts in which they had showed the most interest and promise. As 'labourers,' they would be labouring until noon. After noon, they would be trained as apprentices. There was no social pressure for boys and girls to follow specific paths so there was opportunity for all. However, natural talent would emerge in some and not in others and labourers could – with their consent – be exchanged inter-craft within the five-year probation period until all felt comfortable. The naturally talented would be made 'apprentices' and would receive a further five years training before being made 'fellow-crafts' whilst any labourers would remain as such but could farm or grove as the season required. As all jobs were given equal pay, inter-craft exchange was viewed as personal preference rather than social stigma. Talent was admired but not rewarded. *One did not profiteer from a divine gift.*

Thorne saw the serenity on the faces of the fellow-crafts as their expert hands gently sculpted the wood and realised that their work was its own reward. Watching the wood being shaped had given him an idea. He motioned the foreman outside for a conspiratorial chat and felt Veronica's eyes following him. Ensuring that they were out of earshot, Thorne spoke quietly to Bentley. "Erm..... If I draw you a design, could you build or carve me a sailing ship?"

Bentley shrugged his shoulders. "A real one or a toy one?"

"A toy one..... I mean a *model* sailing ship!"

"If you design it – why not *create* it as well?"

Thorne blew out his cheeks. "I can't do what you do!"

Bentley laughed. "You don't have to. I'll show you how to create your..... *model!*"

"Thank you. I have all this week available – so I'd like to use my time *creatively!*"

"Very wise!" said Bentley approvingly. "Will I see you tomorrow?"

"Erm..... Yes." Thorne gazed at the workshop. "Will you promise me one thing?"

"If I can, I will." said Bentley

"*Don't tell Veronica!*"

---oOo---

The tour ended with everyone viewing the furniture that had been finished. It was in the final process of being waxed and buffed up to protect the wood and give it lustre. One of the apprentices was dipping a rag into a beeswax pot and rubbing the wax into the wood in small circular motions. She looked up at the group and gave a little smile.

"The wax helps to seal in the wood's natural moisture so as to preserve it from drying out too quickly and cracking. If wood is allowed to dry out completely it will slowly turn to dust. It is important to wax wood occasionally to keep a protective coat on the surface – besides it looks so much nicer!"

Everyone made noises of agreement.

"Is..... Is wax waterproof?" inquired Thorne.

"Against spillages – yes. Against immersion? No. Several coats of varnish are better!"

"Do you have any varnish on site?"

"For proofing external woodwork against the weather – yes."

"Just checking!" beamed Thorne, aware of Veronica's renewed interest. He looked at Veronica, and gave her a friendly wink.

Veronica's eyes narrowed. *He was up to something!*

The tour being concluded, Veronica thanked Bentley for his consideration in showing them around the workshop at relatively short notice. She instructed the children to thank the workforce for their kindness and to wait outside. As they left the building, Veronica guided the foreman to one side in order for him to check the accuracy of her notes prior to testing the class on their knowledge of the craft. Following confirmation of her notes, she looked Bentley straight in the eye. "I notice that Thorne is showing a particular interest in woodcraft!"

"Is *that* his name?" asked Bentley, carefully avoiding her question.

"It is - and he is." Veronica raised an eyebrow expectantly.

Bentley met her gaze with a look of innocence.

Veronica smiled sweetly. "What is he up to?"

Bentley shrugged his shoulders and smiled.

"Thank you Bentley - I'll remember this!"

Veronica walked outside to her class - who were waiting in the yard.

Bentley blew out his cheeks and raised his eyes in divine supplication.

---oOo---

Veronica greeted her class brightly. "It is nearly noon, so I propose that we all have some dinner before returning to the castle to answer ten questions on today's craft." She led them in line back the way they had come with Thorne trailing at the rear.

Master Thorne was having lurid visions of eating school dinner with Veronica standing over him. His grim thoughts happily vanished when everyone was led into the parlour of the inn and were told to sit down and behave. The gleeful smiles on the faces of the children told him that this was a special treat!

Thorne was becoming used to being left with the children – all of whom were polite and well behaved. He could actually *understand* the joys of parenthood, when a child was brought – *without its consent* – into a culture such as this. Despite the revelations in the temple, Thorne's face took on the expression of the children around him as he realised that children such as these were infectious in the nicest possible way!

Veronica brought two large plates heaped with boar & onion pasties and placed them on the table before returning to the kitchen. A chorus of "Ooohs!" were soon muffled as eager hands grabbed pasties and they all chomped blissfully away. Veronica came back and placed a tray of small mugs before them and then went behind the counter. Face full of pasty, Thorne could only watch as he saw her draw off two large jugs of liquid from the barrel and return to the table. She read the expression on his face. "I think they've earned it – don't you?"

Thorne was speechless as she poured out twenty-*two* small mugs of mead.

"Good health, children, but drink it *slowly*."

"Follow Miss Veronica's example!" chimed in a recovering Thorne.

Twenty small hands raised twenty small mugs. "*Good health, Miss Veronica, but drink it slowly!*"

Veronica cringed and looked daggers at him.

Thorne beamed at her, and raised his mug.

"*Don't you dare!*"

Thorne saw that he was undermining the authority of a good friend, whose purpose was to instil reason within the pliable minds of the next generation, thus preserving social order. He was suddenly aware of the consequences if his actions continued. Thorne was experiencing the Vision of Cause and Effect, and rose from his seat. "I'm sorry everyone, I'm behaving very badly. May I be excused?"

Veronica was surprised at the sudden change in his mood and wondered whether it was due to spiritual revelation or physical concussion. Feeling responsible for both events, she also rose and addressed her class. "Return to the castle, I shall escort David up to his room and will join you shortly."

"Thank you, but it's not necessary!" said Thorne, holding out his hands in negation. Veronica took Thorne's hands in hers and the atmosphere in the parlour was electric. Gently, she led him upstairs to his room in full view of patrons and children alike.

---oOo---

Sitting together on Thorne's bed, Veronica looked at him with genuine concern as Thorne was shivering violently.

"You're not well David – I'll send for the doctor!"

"No! This is something I must face myself!"

"Do you know what is happening?"

Thorne forced a smile. "*I'm being brought into alignment with my true nature!*"

Veronica understood. "Your personality is going through a metamorphosis."

"Does this happen to everyone who arrives here?"

"Only outsiders who are male."

"Why..... Why is this so?"

"Your scientists say that females are XX and males are XY."

"So what?" shivered Thorne.

"Straker says that females are fixed and males are mutable!"

Thorne frowned. "*Mutation is due to the Y chromosome?*"

Veronica sighed. "We don't know the reason. We *do* know the result!"

"*Bloody hell!*"

"It will pass."

Secure in the knowledge that Thorne was not suffering from any concussion, Veronica left him sitting on his bed and returned downstairs to the parlour. She met everyone's inquiring look with a relaxed smile. "He's just going through the change!" she said.

---oOo---

Alone in his room amidst a cold sweat, Thorne's now *overactive* mind was occupied with the cabalistic principles of fixed, mutable and cardinal and an abstract possibility of mutation via the Y chromosome. "So much for the bloody 'X' Men!" he muttered in irony.

Gradually becoming aware of the subtle forces that continually illumined life, Thorne wisely retired early to bed in order to fully assimilate and recover from the physical effects of his spiritual mutation. He also wanted to prepare himself for several days of crafting his model ship under the tutelage of Bentley. Thorne's transformation had reached the pivotal point.

Chapter 14

The following morning, Thorne arrived at the entrance to the yard feeling strangely rested. He walked into the workshop and saw that Bentley was in the process of sorting out some small pieces of timber, and placing them on the floor beside a foot operated wood lathe. Bentley nodded to Thorne and pointed out the timber.

"Good day, sir. As you can see, I have placed several sizes of timber for your perusal as I wasn't sure of your requirements concerning dimension!"

Thorne eyed the timber and pointed to a particularly large block, which should allow for many anticipated failures along the messy road to perfection. "Good day, Bentley – I'll take the big one please!"

Bentley smiled, aware of Thorne's fears. "Wise choice, sir. A fine model!"

"*You're optimistic!*"

Bentley laughed. "It's easier than you think! Did you bring your design?"

Thorne shook his head. "No. I'm afraid I had other issues to deal with."

"No matter. I'll show you what to do!"

So saying, Bentley took the block of wood which measured thirty inches long by six inches wide by six inches deep and measured both ends diagonally corner to corner. He marked the centre points with a pencil, and aligned one end against the pin of the drive wheel and slid the stock holding the free wheel with its pin to accurately mate with the other end of the timber. After operating the foot treadle to spin the timber, he locked down the stock and turned to Thorne. "I suggest you remove your coat and put on an apron. Take a fairly narrow flat chisel from the rack and sit behind the lathe."

Thorne removed an apron that was hanging on a peg and hung his coat in its place. He looked at the variety of chisels and chose one which seemed quite friendly. Sitting on the stool behind the lathe, he looked at Bentley expectantly.

"Spin the wood using the treadle to get the feel of the lathe. When you are happy, we will start to carve the body of the ship."

Gingerly, Thorne pressed down on the treadle and the timber started to spin on its axis. As he became more confident, the timber spun faster and a dopey grin slowly spread across his face. Bentley nodded to the chisel in Thorne's hand. "Place the chisel against the fence and slowly cut away the corners to turn the block into a column."

Keeping the wood spinning, Thorne carefully obeyed and felt an intermittent resistance as the blade encountered each corner of the block. Holding the chisel firmly, he slowly carved a channel into the wood, which eventually became continuous as the corners in that section were removed.

"Good. Repeat as required along the full length of the block."

Moving the chisel along the fence, Thorne repeated his work and – bit-by-bit – a column slowly appeared out of the block. When he had finished, he looked at Bentley.

"How do I get one end to become pointed?"

"As before – only cut each section slightly deeper towards the point. Because the cuts are gradual – you'll need a very narrow chisel for this!"

Thorne nodded and rose from the lathe. He returned the used chisel to its place in the rack and removed a very narrow one. Looking at Bentley, who nodded in approval, he sat down to carve the prow; and paused in thought. "How can I make the sides curve towards the point like an arch?"

"Unlike a pencil?"

"Unlike a pencil!"

Bentley nodded in understanding. "I'll carve this part for you whilst you direct me."

Thorne gratefully vacated his place and eased his back as Bentley sat down behind the lathe and handed Thorne a pencil. "Draw in two dimensions what you wish me to carve in three dimensions."

"On what?" asked Thorne, looking around for some paper.

"*On some wood!*" laughed Bentley.

Picking up a piece of wood, Thorne carefully drew the type of curved prow he wanted carving and gave it to Bentley. Giving the drawing a quick glance, Bentley nodded in satisfaction and spun the column on the lathe. Shavings poured off the wood onto the floor and Thorne wondered if there was going to be any ship left. Only minutes later, Bentley stopped and looked at Thorne. "Will this do?"

Thorne's eyes took in the beautifully carved prow and he nodded in admiration. "It's perfect! How do we carve the deck and the keel?"

"How *you* carve the deck and the keel is up to you. Please remember that we have little experience of ships due to our country's location!"

"Of course!" sighed Thorne shaking his head. "My apologies."

"No apology is necessary. *You have the will, we have the way* - make it happen!"

Something went 'click' inside Thorne as another piece of the puzzle fell into place. He looked around the workshop and made a decision. "At the moment, the ship looks more like a bullet from a large gun. Part of the top needs to be sliced off to reveal a deck!"

"Like slicing the top off a boiled egg?"

"Yes!" said Thorne, pleased with Bentley's analogy.

"Take it from the lathe and put it in a vice with fabric over the jaws to avoid marks."

Thorne carefully complied.

"Return the chisel to its place in the rack and obtain a medium sized plane."

Thorne obeyed.

Bentley took the plane from Thorne and adjusted the blade to a fine setting. He then handed it back. "Keep the plane flat to the wood and use long slow full passes."

Thorne looked at Bentley who nodded encouragingly and began to plane as instructed. After ten full passes, he stopped to check the result and realised that he needed to remove about one third of the cylinder just to make it resemble a dug-out log. With growing confidence, he carefully planed away the surface until it looked reasonable to his untrained eye and then looked at Bentley for advice. "The whole body needs to be tapered gradually towards the rear."

"Draw what you want on a piece of wood."

Thorne amended his sketch and handed to Bentley who glanced at it and grunted.

"It needs to go back in the lathe, give it to me and I'll taper it for you."

Thorne handed over his creation and watched as Bentley secured it in the lathe. He stood back as the master craftsman took a narrow chisel and the shavings poured off the wood once again. Thorne couldn't help wincing as he was already becoming fond of his creation, and was concerned that Bentley might hurt it.

He needn't have worried, the result was most gratifying and Thorne's face beamed with childlike delight.

"Better?" inquired Bentley.

"*Oooh..... Yes!*" said Thorne with such enthusiasm that all the craftsmen smiled.

"What next?"

"I think it needs a keel to keep it upright in the water!"

"Sketch please!" instructed Bentley.

Thorne eagerly complied and showed Bentley the result.

Bentley removed the model from the lathe and placed it upside-down on the bench. He carefully measured the centre point from one-third down the hull and two-thirds down the hull and marked each. He took a rule and drew a line joining the datum points and two other lines running parallel to the former – one each side of centre. "The outer lines allow for the width of the chisel as I cut the mortise slot." He then took a mallet and a very narrow chisel and started to chisel out a long narrow slot into which the keel would tenon.

Thorne looked on with admiration. "I'm glad you're doing that!"

Bentley chuckled. "So am I!"

Once the mortise was cut, Bentley turned to Thorne and gave him some sandpaper. "Whilst you are sanding the body smooth, I'll look around for some thin wood."

"Okay!" beamed Thorne, and happily sat down to smooth over his model. As he was sanding his model, Thorne looked at the prow and wondered what to do with the lathe pin mark. He smiled to himself in satisfaction when he realised that he could bore and glue a dowel partly into the front to act as a bowsprit for a jib sail. "Or a multi-coloured spanker!" he said out loud (confusing stem and stern sheets).

There were howls of laughter from all the craftsmen.

"*It's a type of sail!*" he said, with a smirk on his face.

Happily shaping the hull, Thorne decided that the jib should resemble a spinnaker in gaudy colour if not in shape or function. He decided that as it was *his* creation, he could dictate the rules of form. He had to admit to himself that alternate stripes of purple and magenta would look good to *his* eye and would blend the principle of *this* culture with the practice of his own. In deference to *tradition*, the mainsail would remain plain!

His gentle musings were momentarily diverted when Bentley returned, carrying a piece of wood, which was ideal for a keel to stabilise Thorne's creation. "Is this suitable?" Bentley inquired.

Thorne smiled as he realised the occult significance of the '*hidden* stabiliser that would balance his craft on the currents of the river.' He dimly heard Bentley's voice.

"From *your* plan, *I* will shape the keel and let *you* inspect its worth!"

Thorne just beamed.

"Aren't you hungry yet?" inquired Bentley gently.

"What?" blinked Thorne – returning to 'earth.'

"It's well past noon!"

Thorne looked around and realised that all the craftsmen were munching their pasties. He remembered his stomach and it remembered him.

"Oh..... yes! I'd better grab something to eat!"

As Thorne rose, Bentley caught his eye. "Rest now. Return tomorrow."

Thorne nodded his assent.

---oOo---

Entering the parlour of the inn, Thorne wandered to his favourite place and sat down. He emitted a huge sigh of satisfaction and stretched his toes comfortably inside his boots.

"Refreshment sir?"

Thorne smiled at the little man. "What's on the menu today, Giles?"

"Carrot and coriander soup followed by roast goat with mint and onion stuffing, cabbage and creamed potatoes."

For no apparent reason, Thorne's appetite evaporated.

"Could I just have soup and a roll?"

"Of course, sir. Would you like a drink?"

"A *small* mead, please!"

Giles smiled knowingly. "Indeed, sir."

--oOo---

Thorne retired early to his room and lay quietly on his bed. He had stopped taking notes for his journalism – it was no longer important. Instead he gently assimilated the significance of all his experiences and knew that he was all he needed to be and to do.

The garden of his soul was no longer dark and barren. He felt at one with the nature of the culture and sensed the growth of his own life. Thorne made a decision. When his body was ready for work and his model was ready for play, he would hang up his brown coat – and wear the green one!

Chapter 15

It was Fourday, and Thorne arose to the now familiar dawn chorus. He had a simple breakfast consisting of porridge with honey and washed it down with a cup of mint. As he strolled along the quiet street humming a little song to himself, he gazed at the horse troughs and it occurred to him to water-test his model to check for correct ballast and balance. It wouldn't do for a ship to float like a cork or a brick and it had to lie evenly in the currents of the river despite carrying a mast and two sails! With this in mind, he arrived at the workshop and – greeting everyone – he approached Bentley. "Would it be possible to test my model in a horse trough to see if it floats properly?"

"Good idea! To maintain secrecy, we'll do it now before the public are on the street!"

So saying, Bentley motioned his colleagues to follow him outside. All the men were eager, but the women just looked and grinned when Bentley swore them to secrecy. It was decided that Thorne would carry the model and the men would cluster around him and try to look as inconspicuous as possible!

Bentley peeped around the door to see if the coast was clear and nodded assent to the fellow-crafts. The morning silence was broken by the patter of many feet as the group of men – still wearing their aprons – shuffled along the street surrounding the bearer of a large wooden trophy. To the untrained eye, the scene resembled an eccentric order of phallic worshippers who had just come out of the closet!

Arriving at the nearest horse trough they were relieved to find it half-full. Thorne lowered the model into the water and everyone clustered around for a good view. To everyone's delight the model sat true in the water – although the stern needed a slight trim for cosmetic reasons to remove the other lathe pin mark. With a furtive glance, Thorne removed the model from the trough and they all scuttled back to the workshop to fit the mast, boom and bowsprit.

Whilst Bentley created the aforementioned, Thorne measured out the dimensions of the cloth required to make the sails. He politely excused himself explaining his intention to visit the tailor's in order to obtain their services.

Arriving at the tailor's – still clad in his apron, he opened the door and went inside to find Stedman and Spelman quietly at work. "Good day, gentlemen!" beamed Thorne.

"Good day, sir." they replied. "Can we be of service?"

Thorne cleared his throat. "Would it be possible for you to make me a couple of sails for a model ship that we are creating?"

"Certainly, sir – if you have a design we can work to!"

Thorne gave the shape and dimensions required and asked them if they could make the smaller sail in stripes of purple and magenta using some spare cloth – if they had any.

Both tailors smiled conspiratorially. "Indeed, sir!"

Thorne thanked them and returned to the workshop whistling the tune to one of the songs that the 'River-folk' sang. He figured three coats of varnish would probably suffice to proof his model.

Arriving back in the workshop, Thorne was pleasantly surprised to see all three scale miniatures of mast, boom and bowsprit were lying on the bench beside his model.

"How did you make all three so quickly?" he asked Bentley.

"I didn't!" laughed Bentley. "I made one and just cut it in three!"

Thorne shook his head in admiration. "Another trick of the trade?"

"One of many! We could produce thrice the furniture in the time we normally take!"

"Why don't you?" inquired Thorne.

"The quality of the workmanship and the care in which the products are treated by the public means our furniture will last several generations."

"No 'planned obsolescence' to create a demand for a continuous supply of products?"

"No. We create quality for the pleasure of creating quality."

"Why is there so much wood in such a large timber store?"

"Most of it is scrap – like your model."

"Okay. Why is there so much scrap?"

"Most scrap is from fallen trees. We use scrap to fuel our fires – including the pyres on which we place our dead."

"Oh....." said an appropriately *mortified* Thorne. Displaying unusual sensitivity for one in such a brutal profession, he gently asked if standing trees were ever felled.

"Only those that are coming to the end of their lives. It's *vital* that we preserve our forest - *for its sake and for ours*!"

---oOo---

Thorne spent the rest of Fourday morning drilling and gluing the mast and bowsprit. He secured the boom to the mast via a small strip of leather that was looped and riveted into a tiny collar by the owner of the Tack Shop. After his noonday pasty, he oiled the leather collar and waxed inside where it contacted the mast, and applied the first coat of varnish to the entire ship - masts and all!

Mr Thorne was becoming hooked on quality!

---oOo---

On Fiveday, all he had to do was apply the second coat of varnish and wait for it to dry. He asked Bentley if he could use the day creatively by sweeping the floor and tidying up for them to show his appreciation. Bentley smiled and told him that his assistance would be most welcome. As Thorne happily got to work, he started to whistle the same tune he had whistled the day before and was quite surprised when everyone sang along with him. When he caught Bentley's eye, he was told that they regarded it as their National Anthem. Thorne's instinct was to feel surprised, but his intuition told him otherwise. He merely smiled and then realised why *everyone* did!

He was aware what it was like to be psychically linked to them in mystical union with divinity. But as a nascent *occultist*, he knew what he had to *do* for humanity outside.

---oOo---

On Sixday, he applied the final coat of varnish and happily continued his labouring. At noon, he excused himself and wandered down the street eating his pasty, and entered the tailor's shop knowing that S & S would have finished his sails.

As he entered, Stedman looked up from his work and, greeting Thorne, disappeared behind the counter and presented the finished product. "More or less as you requested!" he said with a twinkle in his eye.

Thorne heard a snigger from behind the curtain that divided the front of the shop from the rear and Spelman poked his head around the corner. "If you please, we took a small liberty with your request, but be assured that we do not wish to charge you for this particular service!"

"What have you done?" inquired Thorne, with growing unease.

Stedman unwrapped their gift and Thorne saw their small 'liberty.'

True enough, the jib was beautifully sewn into stripes of purple and magenta – but the mainsail was certainly not plain! The brothers had used some scrap from the waistcoat material that belonged to the Duke. The result was a mainsail of bright blue with gold leaves!

---oOo---

Showing surprising grace, Thorne sincerely thanked them, as he realised that his model was largely created for him by the people of this country as a token of their affection. Be it ever so stupid, his heart had finally spoken and they wanted to help him realise his dream – even if their maritime skills were zero!

Smiling philosophically, Thorne returned to the workshop with his gift and showed it to Bentley – who nodded appreciatively – and then cocked his eye at the model. "The final coat of varnish will be dry by tomorrow. The sails can then be fitted."

Thorne nodded. "I'd like to have it ready for when I go fishing with Straker."

Bentley smiled knowingly. "I'll ask him to drop by here, tomorrow morning!"

"Thank you!" beamed Thorne – eagerly reaching for the sweeping brush.

---oOo---

On Sevenday morning, Thorne arrived at the workshop particularly early and fitted the sails. He stood back to admire the finished model and decided to give it a name. The sails clearly determined the name of the ship, and Thorne acknowledged the obvious. "*I name this ship the 'Woolley.' God help her and all who sink in her!*"

He stood to attention and saluted – giving a mock bugle rendition of the 'Last Post.' As he finished, a round of applause erupted from behind him and he turned to see all the fellow-crafts plus Bentley and Straker standing in the doorway grinning at him.

Thorne looked at them sourly. "How long have you all been there?"

"*Long enough!*" they all laughed.

Thorne sighed quietly to himself.

Straker smiled. "Let's go fishing!"

---oOo---

Sitting on their stools by the riverbank, both Straker and Thorne were 'not fishing' as usual. Straker was 'not fishing' with his pipe, and Thorne was 'not fishing' with his ship.

He had borrowed the cleric's fishing rod and had baited the line with his model. Each time the 'Woolley' would float down the river, and each time Thorne would reel it back. Because the line was attached to the bowsprit, he could reel it up-river pretending it was 'running' before the wind.

Once again, they had eaten well and were on the second bottle of mead when Thorne turned to Straker. "I'm looking forward to working in the fields again, but I'm concerned that I'm too old for such pursuits!"

Straker looked at Thorne, and looked at Thorne's model floating down the river.

"Okay – 'the boy & his toy' – but my *body* is too old for such pursuits!"

Straker just chuckled and blew some more fruit salad into the trees.

"You're my guide – *say something*!"

"I'm honoured!" said Straker.

Thorne sighed in exasperation. "*I need guidance!*"

Straker looked in the direction of the water mill and Thorne followed his gaze.

It made sense. All Thorne had to do was to load a sack of grain onto a sack-barrow and cart it from the grain store to the water mill. Once he had hooked it onto the jack and engaged the gears, it would be hauled by pulley up to the second floor. He would walk upstairs and wait for it to arrive. On arrival, he would unhook the sack and tip the grain into the appropriate vat and the mill would do the work. Ensuring there was always a fresh sack under each chute on the ground floor, he could confidently stroll downstairs whilst it was slowly being filled and release it onto the sack-barrow for carting to the flour store. Such tasks as unloading the sacks of grain from the farmers' flatbeds and carting them to the store, and carting the sacks of flour from the store and loading them onto the market flatbed would be undertaken twice or thrice per week at most. Thorne smiled confidently – yes, he could do that!

Noting Thorne's air of growing optimism, Straker told him that he would arrange for a labourers' flatbed to take him to and from the mill each weekday. When Thorne inquired if he was receiving special consideration, he was told that it was 'Dusty' who was receiving special consideration, as he needed a rest.

"You will run the mill!" said Straker.

"On my own?" faltered Thorne.

"After the first day – yes!"

"*Oh..... shit!*" murmured Thorne – almost to himself.

Straker grinned as his friend quickly reached for the bottle.

---oOo---

After several minutes of silence had passed, Straker decided to lighten the atmosphere by asking his friend how his ship was performing. Realising that he was going to work in precisely the place where he was free to float his model in his spare time, Thorne's face visibly lit up as he realised that – once again – his current life was being engineered to accommodate him.

Occupied with this happy thought, Thorne was suddenly aware that the 'Woolley' was far down the river and the line was running low. It would have to be quickly reeled in before it slipped the rod. Thorne started to reel it in and as the line tightened, the ship did a smart one-eighty (impossible for a real ship), and 'sailed' up-river.

"You nearly lost it that time!" observed Straker.

Thorne nodded. "I'll be more careful in future."

As the ship gently nuzzled the riverbank, Thorne sighed and looked at his new friend." I suppose Veronica will find out about my toy boat?"

"Does that bother you?" inquired Straker.

"Yes." admitted Thorne

"Why does it bother you?"

"How can she have any confidence in me – if she sees I am still a child at heart?"

"Have you considered that her thoughts might *reflect* yours?"

Thorne frowned as he recalled Veronica's words: '*twenty-eight and still a child*!'

Straker smiled at Thorne's reaction. "Veronica is highly empathic with strangers!"

"Empathic with *strangers*?"

"Initial contacts with a stranger are highly charged, but the magnitude diminishes in proportion to the frequency of those contacts."

Thorne looked at the 'Woolley' with its garish sails. "Familiarity breeds contempt?"

"An extreme analogy, but there is merit in that phrase."

"Are you saying that Veronica is not as vulnerable as she appears?"

"One who is a carer, a cleaner, an educator and a companion is hardly vulnerable."

Thorne pursed his lips. "What about *lonely*?"

Straker raised his eyebrows. "*Her or you*?"

"I don't understand the question!" evaded Thorne.

"*Why* is Veronica a carer, a cleaner, an educator and a companion?"

"..... Because she *chooses* to be?" ventured Thorne.

Straker nodded. "Exactly! She cares for those people who are 'waning' – so that they can look forward to a peaceful death. She cleans places that provide inspiration for those people who are 'waxing' – so that they can look forward to a peaceful life. She educates those children who are 'new' – so that they may evolve. She is a companion for those who are 'full' – so that they find fulfilment of purpose in life."

Straker paused to blow some more smoke into the trees and then continued speaking. "We *choose* to be strong or weak, clever or stupid, happy or sad – as we believe each occasion demands. Paradoxically, we are a Collective Individuality – *a Gestalt* – but we *choose* to project multifaceted personalities in response to perceived multifaceted states. The outside world has conditioned people to believe that they are their own projections – creating psychoses via feedback. They are then ensnared by the State to be controlled through *fear* if they are ignorant, or *guilt* if they are educated, or *debt* if they are arrogant. State control began as Theopolitical and became Psychopolitical."

"It's now Cyberpolitical!" murmured Thorne. He was aware of humanity's obsessive reliance on technology and that individual freedom had been replaced with collective thraldom.

Straker looked at Thorne's toy boat and smiled sadly. "*Who is truly vulnerable?*"

Thorne gazed at the gaudy symbol of his lost innocence – and knew the answer.

They both sat in silence for some time until Thorne frowned and looked at the cleric. "This may sound cynical, but Veronica seems ideally placed to encounter strangers!"

Straker nodded. "True."

"..... And to communicate her empathic impressions to those who rule the country?"

Straker smiled. "True."

"..... And from the moment of my arrival, I have been under observation?"

Straker grinned. "True."

"..... Bastards!"

Straker laughed. "False. You'll find no bastards among *my* people!"

---oOo---

Thorne sighed deeply and stared into nothing. "So, she was using me all the time!"

Straker shook his head. "No. Veronica really *cares* for you - somewhat clumsily!"

Thorne snorted. "*If she's an empath, she'll care for <u>everyone</u> - it's her nature!*"

The cleric stared straight ahead. "..... *And you don't?*"

Thorne was jerked out of his morose reverie. "..... *I'm an empath?*"

"When you were 'in your cups' you intimated as much to Virginia."

Thorne recalled his alcoholic episode when Virginia had asked him why he cared for so many people. On the condition that she would 'sod off' following his reply - he had dutifully answered - and she had dutifully complied.

He played out some of the line and gave the 'Woolley' a shove with the end of the rod and watched the ship float towards the centre of the river where it caught the current and began another voyage. Without taking his eyes off his model, he addressed Straker. "What is love?"

"Empathic giving between evolving souls."

"What is lust?"

"Vampiric taking between devolving souls."

"..... *That simple?*"

"*Life* is simple when we learn to see behind the appearance. Our culture *appears* to be retarded. Veronica *appears* to be vulnerable. Victoria *appears* to be vicious. Virginia *appears* to be masculine, and the Duke *appears* to be a fool. *Appearances*! Why do you think we never joined the former European Union, but merely accepted limited trade with selected countries? Like Switzerland, we control our own economy and are free from foreign influence. The only difference between our country and Switzerland is that we *appear* poor and they *appear* rich!"

"Why are you telling me all this?" inquired Thorne uneasily.

Straker laughed. "Don't worry! Our secrets remain safe. Who listens to fools?"

---oOo---

Thorne watched the 'Woolley' float serenely down the river and found himself thinking about Straker's remark concerning Virginia's 'appearance.' "Did you say Virginia appears to be *masculine*?" he asked cautiously.

Straker smiled knowingly. "Virginia's appearance and behaviour seem to indicate a lack of interest in men and those who meet her naturally assume she is interested in women."

"Really?" inquired Thorne neutrally – hoping to invite further comment.

"Indeed!" affirmed Straker – playing the same game.

Thorne focused on the 'Woolley' and watched it – and him – gradually run out of time. "Bugger!" he muttered, and started to reel it back up the river.

Straker concealed a smile. "Have you wondered why people *choose* an orientation?"

The ship wobbled in the water as it sailed up the river. "*Choose*?"

"Why do people choose to become heterosexual or homo/lesbian or bisexual?"

"Erm..... Medical Science has evidence that orientation is predetermined!"

Straker smiled. "*The human mind is far more powerful than society cares to admit.*"

"Are you saying that the experts are wrong – or even worse – that they are liars?"

"*The human mind as <u>currently</u> expressed allows all 'experts' some credence.*"

"..... But?" prompted Thorne.

"How many people have followed one path – only to choose another in later life?"

Thorne shrugged his shoulders in reply.

"Far more than is realised – think of the Iceberg Principle."

"Twenty percent visible, eighty percent hidden?"

"The twenty/eighty rule is the Pareto Principle, but you're close enough. Only a small percentage makes headline news and *credible* statistics have to be based on published findings only. However, humanity is far more 'mutable' than society can truly control. Few have bothered to look at the one factor that is common to all those mentioned."

Thorne frowned. "*Is* there a common factor between such social polarities?"

Straker laughed. "You have just answered your own question!"

Thorne pondered. "..... *Social* polarities..... The belief that one is incomplete and the desire to find those complimentary aspects within another for completion!"

"Precisely! *They all desire another for fulfilment, but that is <u>not</u> the Divine Plan!*"

Thorne frowned. "..... So we should all be asexual or non-sexual?"

Straker nodded. "Absolutely – and content so to be."

"So much for orientation – what about gender?"

"There is even less reason for gender."

"We become just like the angels?"

"Yes. The 'Fallen' must rise."

"Humanity will die out!"

"*To learn and to leave.*"

Thorne recalled his vision in the temple and understood the purpose of the immortals. In order for immortals to be taken into the next aeon of creation by the Eternal One, their incarnate souls had to join with their discarnate spirits to *become* immortal! Their union must be spiritual – and in the spiritual realm – *not* on the physical world. *That was the source of the concept of finding one's 'soul' mate.*

Thorne looked at Straker. "*Why do your people exist on this world?*"

"Not for *our* benefit – I assure you!" replied the cleric.

The final penny fell into place. These people existed to provide humanity with an orderly return to divinity – thus avoiding the vision that Thorne had experienced. He sighed in relief. No hell would be raised in heaven!

The little boat nuzzled the riverbank once again. Thorne watched it wobble in the currents – and felt himself do the same. "*We shouldn't be here – should we?*" he inquired.

Straker shook his head. "No. This world belongs to the animals. Observe how *naturally* they follow their patterns of life – both individually and collectively with their kind – and with other kinds." Straker paused and sighed. "Now look at humanity!"

"..... *We're unnatural*!" admitted Thorne.

"Our *bodies* are natural to this world, but *we* are unnatural to this world because we are misplaced. Because we are misplaced we are having to evolve cognisant reasoning to understand our condition – which in itself is unnatural to integration....."

"..... Because the gestalt is intuition – not intellect!" finished Thorne.

Straker smiled and blew another smoke ring. "*To learn and to leave!*"

Thorne frowned and scratched his head as he recognised that he had intuitively answered his own question before his intellect had even thought of asking it.

"Fleas?" inquired Straker mildly.

Thorne didn't reply. His mind was occupied with the realisation that the laws of Time & Space have little effect on the intuitive faculty but great effect on the intellect.... and what the hell *was* a gestalt anyway?

"*What is a gestalt?*" asked Thorne – feeling he had just put the cart before the horse.

Straker chuckled. "Intuitively you are aware of it. But *intellectually* speaking, a gestalt is defined as 'an organised whole that is greater than the sum of its parts.' This however, is only a convenient cover for its occult significance. Occultly speaking, a gestalt is a collective thought-force that has been generated by the sub-conscious minds of many people that have inhabited a place over a long period of time. Any building can posses a gestalt as it permeates the fabric and it can be detected and 'read' by the psychic art of 'Stone Taping.' This explains why 'holy' places feel special or that some buildings feel strange when entered. Latent gestalts can sometimes be activated accidentally by psychics, or deliberately by occultists for specific purposes."

In a brief psychic shock, Thorne felt himself separate from 'reality' as he realised that the cleric was answering all his 'visions' since he had arrived. Suddenly he felt very small.

"*Don't worry, it will pass!*"

Thorne finally found that he could submit to a wisdom that was far greater than he possessed, and was instantly rewarded with a sense of colossal relief. He looked at Straker who merely nodded and smiled.

The rest of the day was spent in relaxed silence watching time flow seamlessly by. In the evening before they trotted home,

Straker left a message inside the mill cottage telling 'Dusty' that his apprentice would be starting tomorrow.

Chapter 16

Thorne awoke from his slumber and slowly stretched his body to the fresh sound of birdsong. In any other country, the revelations he had received would have resulted in him being certified and sectioned, but in *this* country, it was everyone's birthright.

After a casual preparation and breakfast, he strolled to the flatbed waiting in the square and settled himself among his companions. He had left his coat, cravat *and* apron behind – the latter in accordance with the safety requirements of the job. Those aboard the flatbed nodded and smiled in approbation.

When they arrived at the southern cross lanes holding the farms of Upper and Lower South, Thorne bade them all good day and jumped down from the cart and confidently made his way along the lane leading to the farms of Upper South. Two miles later, he turned right down the branch lane that led to South Mill.

Arriving at the mill cottage, he politely knocked on the door and waited. After a couple of minutes had elapsed, he shook his head as he realised that 'Dusty' would be working in the mill as the wheel was turning in its sluice. Thorne walked across to the mill and, opening the door, he yelled at the top of his voice.

"Be right down." came the reply, and Thorne heard the familiar sounds of thumps from the room above and clumps down the steps as 'Dusty' arrived spreading his 'dandruff' far and wide. The miller beamed at him. "Good day, sir. I've taken the liberty of compiling a set of step-by-step instructions as to the process of obtaining, milling and storing the three different types of flour and also a map showing the three levels of the mill with all the attendant machinery and operating instructions."

Thorne's eyes widened in alarm. "Are you sure I can learn all this in one day?"

"Don't worry, it's highly repetitive with only slight variations for each type of flour!"

Thorne bent to look at the four sheets of paper and saw to his relief that it was actually quite simple. The first sheet told him exactly what to do in order to make wholemeal flour, the second sheet told him how to make whitemeal and the third sheet was for wheatbran. The fourth sheet was also infinitely reassuring as it gave complete floor diagrams of all relevant machinery and each machine was numbered and tied in with the work instructions. Thorne was *very* grateful for the 'idiot's guide' and said so.

'Dusty' laughed. "Simple instructions minimise errors and maximise confidence!"

Thorne relaxed and quickly absorbed the job as it was being demonstrated so that by noon of the first day, he was confident and competent to work the remainder of the day on his own. He was so happily immersed in his work that 'Dusty' had to remind him that the day was over and he should be walking back to the southern cross lane.

"What happens if I'm late for the cart?" asked Thorne – somewhat concerned.

"They'll wait – besides, there's always some mead under the driver's seat!"

Thorne strolled happily along the lanes and eventually arrived at the waiting cart. To his amusement – and delight – someone had indeed opened the mead barrel!

---oOo---

The working week passed quickly, and Thorne was wondering when 'Dusty' would be taking his well-earned rest.

The miller just smiled. "You're doing all the work!"

It was as simple as that.

On Fiveday, Thorne received one hundred crones wages. He also received the miller's compliments for a job well done and it was a mark of Thorne's evolving character that he took greater pleasure from the latter. He was offered the customary 'liquid supper' at the end of each day – but after some thought, he had politely declined saying that he felt it would be easier to 'find the cart *before* the mead!'

Before leaving for the evening cart, Thorne asked 'Dusty' if he could return to the mill on Sixday and Sevenday as the job was physically relaxing and spiritually refreshing.

'Dusty' grinned at his new apprentice. "You really *love* this job – don't you?"

"Yes I do. I'm also glad that I don't have to take a bath each night to recover!"

"Does Veronica know of your change in requirements?"

Thorne felt quite sad. He knew that he did not need her services anymore but he was unwilling to tell her because he had grown fond of her – despite her eccentricities – or possibly because of them.

The master looked at his apprentice and smiled gently. "*To learn.....*"

"*..... and to leave.*" finished Thorne.

Sitting on the cart wrapped in his own thoughts, he returned to the inn to see Giles.

"She knows." the little man said softly.

---oOo---

Thorne proved a worthy apprentice. He worked five full days and two half days per week with confidence and competence. He was able to suspend his conscious mind and work intuitively and automatically. As a result, his personality became calm and clear – allowing his individuality to function unimpeded. He also slept soundly.

The summer days came and went – most were fine but some were stormy. When the thunder rumbled and the lightning flashed, Thorne would smile gently to himself and continue working ignoring the monsoon that he knew would go as quickly as it came.

Over the weeks, he had received many crones and spent none. He knew that his work was enough for his needs and for the needs of the country. It was the service that had value – not the coinage. The money just sat in his bedroom and piled up.

---oOo---

One day in late summer when he was upstairs, there was a loud whistle from below.

"Be right down." he yelled.

As he walked across the floor and clumped down the steps, he had to pause to knock the flour dust out of his hair before opening his eyes to see twenty children and one young woman hurriedly step back from the avalanche.

"Good day, Thorne." said Veronica, smiling rather shyly.

"Good day, Miss Veronica." beamed Thorne, gazing at her with happy affection.

The children gazed up expectantly into his floury face.

"Good day, children." added Thorne, with almost equal affection.

The children beamed in delight.

Veronica cleared her throat. "I..... I was wondering if you would show the children around the mill..... for educational purposes?"

Thorne radiated warmth. "I'd love to!" he said, gazing into her face.

"..... Perhaps you could take them two at a time – for reasons of safety?"

"Of course. Those who are waiting may like to see my model boat which I often float along the river when time permits."

Veronica tried to conceal a smile. "I'm sure they would love to..... *Thank you.*"

It was agreed that Thorne would take the children in pairs around the mill whilst Veronica kept an eye on the rest of the group. It was noted that several were already showing an unusual interest in Thorne's model, which sat on a bench inside the door.

Each pair were given a comprehensive tour around the mill until everyone had returned to the main group. They were then asked to wait outside whilst Veronica and Thorne negotiated ten appropriate questions for the children to answer prior to going home.

After the questions had been determined, Veronica took Thorne's hands in hers and looked into his face. "*Thank you, David; for being so understanding!*"

"*And to you!*" said Thorne, and gave her a gentle kiss on the nose.

She smiled at him and returned to the group outside. As she was preoccupied with counting all those present, she didn't sense that all the children had the same thought:

'*Why has Miss got flour on her nose?*'

---oOo---

Thorne returned to his work happy in the knowledge that he had his place in life and Veronica had hers. He remembered Straker's words when the cleric had told him that everyone is self-fulfilling. In essence, mutual love is good but mutual lust is bad.

More weeks passed and more money accrued but Thorne didn't care. Of late, he had taken to wearing his new green frock coat and going for solitary walks along the bank of the river at mid-day. He would carry his 'bait box' which contained (at his request) two rounds of egg sandwiches, one pot of mayo, one boar & onion pasty and a bottle of cold mint tea - he had finally grown tired of mead!

A self-imposed regime of physical working, sensible eating and sensible drinking were improving his body as his experiences were improving his mind and spirit. Thorne had evolved from being a pathetic creature with a poisoned mind into becoming a civilised gentleman with a magnetic nature.

One weekend at noon, when he was sitting by the river slowly reeling in his model, he heard the sounds of several boot-steps and looked behind to see several boys from Veronica's class admiring the 'Woolley' as it returned to the bank. Thorne nodded to them pleasantly. "Good day, gentlemen."

"Good day, sir." they all replied - rather uncertainly.

Thorne sensed their dilemma. "Can I help you?"

"Begging your pardon, but we were all admiring your model!"

Thorne grunted to himself as he rose from the bank. "Have fun - *but don't fall in!*"

The faces of the boys broke into smiles of relief as Thorne returned to the mill.

As he resumed his work, Thorne decided to keep an eye on them - just in case.

As usual, he had already surpassed the weekly requirement of flour, so he could afford to take his time and keep regular checks on the safety of the boys playing outside. The next hour passed and he was just beginning to relax his guard when he heard a shout from outside and he rushed to the window to see that one of the boys had fallen into the river and was being swept away.

"Shit!" he exclaimed, and dropped the sack he was holding to race outside. He ran past the other boys who were all staring open mouthed. "Get the bloody doctor!" he yelled, and ran along the bank until he had overtaken the boy who was flailing desperately away trying to keep afloat. Knowing that he himself was a poor swimmer but a good floater, Thorne leaped into the river and made his way towards the lad – who was starting to go under. Thorne managed to grab hold of him and pushed him to the bank – where he clung on to the exposed root of a tree. Thorne, however, was swept away by the current.

Time was against him. He was becoming tired, and he had realised – too late – that his top boots were filling with water. He tried again and again to keep afloat, but the weight of water inside his boots was gradually pulling him under. His lungs started to fill up and he instinctively coughed the water out but he could not draw his breath as more water took its place. His mind screamed as it was torn from the world – and then he felt a strange peace as blackness overtook him.

---oOo---

As the boys had rushed off to sound the alarm, another figure had seen and heard the commotion and was running along the bank. Such social graces as modesty had been temporarily overridden as she was focusing on running and removing her dress at the same time. By the time Thorne had gone under, she was naked and had leaped into the river swimming strongly towards his last position. Instinctively, she dived under the surface – sensing his presence before actually seeing him – and had grabbed him round his chest. She broke surface and began to swim towards the bank dragging his body desperately behind her.

Mercifully, Thorne was not actually present in his body and was therefore unable to appreciate the benefits of a particularly brutal – but efficient – resuscitation technique. As soon as he was showing signs of recovery, he was turned over to throw up half the contents of the river whilst his saviour made a hasty exit to retrieve her dress – and her dignity.

Dazed and shaken by his ordeal, Thorne remained lying on the riverbank – too tired to move. Some time later, he vaguely heard the sound of approaching hooves and an all too horribly familiar red dress swept into view. Looking up at Victoria, Thorne braced himself for renewed torment, and closed his eyes in fear.

Curiously, her strong hands were surprisingly tender.

Victoria quickly checked him over and started to unbutton his shirt for further examination. As the pentacle around his neck was exposed to her view, her hands froze - her concentration evaporated - to be replaced by amazement.

"Wh..... where did you get *that*?" she asked - her eyes showing increasing alarm.

Thorne flinched when he saw her face. "I bought it at the market from a trader."

The doctor looked at the river, and then down at her hands - they were shaking badly.

Sensing her stress, Thorne began to empathise with her. "..... *What's wrong?*"

Victoria was going into some kind of shock as her whole body began to convulse. Thorne looked on in stunned disbelief as her cold hard face crumbled in front of him. She held her face in her hands and wept. Instinctively, he reached out to her and held her shoulders gently and she fell forward into his arms. Immediately, he was seized in an iron grip and deafened as she wept loudly into his ear. As the doctor gave vent to her emotions, her unfortunate patient was slowly being smothered.

Eventually, Victoria became aware that something was not quite right with Thorne and she released him just before he passed out. As his face fell forward onto her chest, she held him tenderly and began stroking his hair. A look of peace came into her eyes and she began to smile in almost maternal affection. "Everything's fine! Everything's fine!"

Her patient was in no condition to argue otherwise.

---oOo---

When Thorne came to his senses and realised that his face was buried in the doctor's bosom, he politely cleared his throat. "Thank you, Doctor - I feel much better now!"

Victoria gently held Thorne's face in her hands and gazed into his eyes with affection. "*You're coming home with me!*"

Thorne whimpered as he was lifted to his feet and marched to the doctor's Brougham. As he was shoved inside, he heard her address the coachman, who was still sat up top. "*Garfield. The castle please!*"

The driver nodded assent, and they sped quickly and smoothly towards the capital.

---oOo---

Passing under the portcullis, the coach travelled to the main entrance where it halted. Victoria exited the coach and helped Thorne do the same. She then held his arm and guided him gently but firmly to the door where she threw it open and pushed him inside. The door slammed behind her with a great boom and she seized his arm to prevent him from running away. "*You will be our guest for the rest of your stay!*"

"Is this a com*men*dation or a con*dem*nation of my behaviour?" he asked, uncertainly.

Victoria smiled warmly - which was unnerving in itself. "Rest now, worry later!" She led him across the great hall and up the stairs towards one of the guest rooms where she opened a large oak door and motioned him inside. Thorne's fears evaporated when he saw the room where he would be sleeping and his eyes grew wide in surprise. "All this – *for me?*"

"Bedroom here, en-suite there!" she said pointing across to another large oak door. Thorne smiled as he recalled those very words spoken by Chevral when he had been introduced to the facilities in the forest hut. "Erm..... I don't suppose....." he began.

"*Two* rolls." said the doctor, opening the door. She paused briefly and turned to face him. "I want you in bed before I return!"

As the door closed behind her, Thorne tiptoed across the floor and opened the door to the en-suite. He nodded in satisfaction and returned to undress. As he slipped beneath the sheets, a gentle smile crossed his face. "*Two rolls!*" he murmured, and fell asleep.

Chapter 17

The following day, Thorne awoke and slowly stretched himself before realising where he was. As he looked around, his gaze fell upon the doctor who was asleep in a chair in the corner of the room. Thorne frowned at such dedication from one so fierce! As she was asleep, he studied her face and was surprised to see that all traces of ferocity had vanished to be replaced by a countenance so gentle – he had to wipe back tears.

As he sniffed, she awoke and smiled at him with a weariness he had not expected from one so young. "Hello, David."

All he could do was to give her little a wave with his fingers, which peeped over the blanket.

Victoria gave a little laugh. "Do I frighten you *so* much?"

"You frighten *everyone* so much!" he replied, truthfully.

Years suddenly etched into her beautiful face. "*I'm truly sorry!*"

Thorne did the unthinkable; he patted the side of his bed. "Come here!"

Amazingly, she rose and slowly walked across the floor to sit beside him on his bed.

As she looked into his face, he took her hand and held it gently. "*Why are you sad?*"

She was silent for a while and then sighed. "When my mother died, I suddenly found purpose in my life. I *had* to become a doctor!" Victoria smiled at the memory. "I apprenticed myself to Lucinda and learned all that I could as I worked with her and with another of her apprentices."

"Cordelia?"

The doctor nodded. "Eventually, I was allowed to practice alone; but my first case involved trying to resuscitate a drowned man - *my uncle*"! Victoria's face grew tired. "I followed the standard medical procedure and opened his shirt - *and saw the pendant around his chest - the one he <u>always</u> wore!*" The doctor closed her eyes. "I knew he had left this world, but I *had* to resuscitate his body - *I couldn't fail my first patient!*" She was crying now. "I lost my mother and I lost my uncle. *I failed them both!*"

Thorne held her in his arms and began to weep with her as he stroked her hair. *Damn this bloody empathy and sod that trader!*

They remained locked together for ages.

---oOo---

As he felt her pain ease, Thorne spoke with such clarity that she was mesmerised. "*The Hippocratic oath is <u>not</u> about preserving life (impossible). The Hippocratic oath is <u>all</u> about postponing death (inevitable). Our test; is to <u>accept</u> the inevitable.*"

Thorne felt her slowly stir in his arms as she raised her tear-streaked face to meet his. "*What are you?*" she asked, gazing into his eyes.

"What do you mean?" asked Thorne - somewhat taken aback.

"The words you speak – where do they come from?"

Thorne blinked in confusion as he looked within and saw only a void. He shook his head. "I don't know, I see nothing."

The doctor held his face in her hands. "You see a void? An abyss?"

Thorne considered her words and then nodded in agreement. "Yes, an abyss."

Victoria nodded. "Knowledge comes from the Abyss and returns to it. Knowledge or *Gnosis* is held in trust for all incarnate souls who still require the ultimate library."

"You sound just like Veronica!"

Victoria smiled. "When one passes *beyond* the Abyss, all knowledge becomes 'void' as one moves from physical world to spiritual realm gaining Universal Awareness."

"You *really* sound like Veronica!"

The doctor shrugged her shoulders and smiled. "It runs in the family!"

At the mention of 'family,' Thorne remembered the boy who had fallen into the river. "How is the boy? Is he safe?"

Victoria closed her eyes and nodded. "Very safe and very sorry."

"Why sorry?"

"He feels guilty for the loss of your model – and worse still – *for nearly losing you!*"

"If he'd drowned trying to recover it, *I'd* feel guilty! It can be replaced – *he can't!*"

Victoria gazed at Thorne. "*You can't be replaced either.* The Duke is furious!"

Thorne frowned. "What's it got to do with the Duke?"

The doctor sighed. "The boy whose life you saved is Wulfred, the Duke's second son."

---oOo---

Thorne remembered his conversation with the pot-smoking granny in the wheelchair and recalled the family curse "Why is the Duke furious? I've broken the family curse. The boy doesn't have to be called 'Wulfred the Gormless' - or whatever!"

Victoria blinked in surprise. "I see Agatha has been having conversations with you!"

Thorne nodded. "Tell Agatha to talk to the Duke. He shouldn't be angry but happy that the curse is lifted."

The doctor remembered the death of her mother and her uncle and knew that Thorne was trying to be kind. She smiled at him and held his hand. "I'll talk to Agatha and ask her to persuade my father to calm down." She rose from Thorne's bed and walked towards the door where she paused and looked at her new patient. "I'll prepare some hot water for your bath. Once it's ready I'll call you - it's just down the corridor outside your room."

"Thank you!" said a somewhat bemused Thorne. As the door closed, his eyes started to take in the size of the room he was in. The furniture was carved in solid oak and the room measured some twenty by thirty feet. Initially, he felt he was living in opulence - until he gradually realised that the furniture was virtually identical to that which was in the bedroom of the inn. He got up and walked around his new room comparing all its furniture with that in his previous bedroom.

"Similar bed, similar chest, similar table, similar chair, similar wardrobe. The only real difference is that there is more space!" Thorne scratched his backside in deep thought. "*Bloody hell! Status is measured in space – not form!*" Holding that thought, he had to make a mad dash to reach the privy in time.

When he finally emerged – still contemplating the Value of Nothing, he heard a call from outside his room. Wrapping a towel around his waist, he wandered across to risk a quick peep around the bedroom door to see if it was safe for him to emerge. Seeing that the coast was clear, he paddled down the long corridor towards an open door that beckoned invitingly.

The next half-hour was spent in luxury and Thorne finally settled back in the bath to admire the lancet window in front of him. It admitted enough light for him to see that he was in one of the castle turrets whose walls measured ten feet thick – judging from the depth of the window ledge. "Simplicity is luxury!" he sighed in contentment.

---oOo---

After he had returned to his room to dress, Thorne took a deep breath and descended the stairs that led into the great hall.

Seeing that the hall was empty – barring a huge circular fire pit whose stone sides rose three feet high terminating in a flat rim suitable for seating, his gaze wandered across to the opposite side where another oak door was ajar. Feeling slightly self-conscious, he knocked on the door.

"Enter!" said a commanding voice – whom Thorne knew to be the doctor's.

As he entered the room, she rose from a high-backed chair and walked towards him. "Good day, Thorne." Victoria smiled. "I'd like you to meet my father."

Thorne's gaze was drawn away to a wide medieval fireplace whose flue was supported by two stout pillars. A large fire burned merrily within. Standing in front rubbing his backside with a look of intense pleasure on his face was the Duke. Barring the lurid colours of the Duke's apparel, the resemblance between host and guest was not lost on Thorne, and he recalled Veronica's drunken comments and understood her attraction to him. "A father-figure indeed!" he murmured out loud.

The Duke beamed. "Good of you to say so!" he turned to his daughter. "Take note!"

Thorne realised his gaffe and began to panic. "I'm sorry..... I didn't mean....."

"Nonsense, sir!" said the Duke. "*Don't ruin good honesty with false humility!*"

Thorne managed a weak smile and received a knowing look from Victoria.

The Duke continued. "A spot of breakfast followed by a tour of the castle." He eyed his guest with approval. "It's now time for *me* to get to know you – Mr *Throne!*"

Thorne opened his mouth to correct the Duke – and then realised the joke and smiled.

They sat down to breakfast and Thorne was surprised when Virginia appeared with bowls of porridge and indicated a large jar of honey. He instinctively rose from the table on her arrival but she bade him remain seated. Victoria leaned across explaining that, as *eldest* daughter, it was traditional for Virginia to cook and serve breakfast. "It's something our mother did!" she smiled sadly.

As Virginia joined them, Thorne was surprised that such a masculine woman should show such feminine skills. Looking at Virginia, his face must have shown something because she raised an eyebrow. "*I can cook!*" she croaked.

Thorne suddenly found great interest in his porridge and failed to notice the amused glances that appeared on the three faces that surrounded him.

"Not just porridge!" added the Duke. "Their mother was an excellent cook and Virginia was particularly adept in mastering these skills." he smiled fondly at her.

The eldest daughter acknowledged her father's compliments and gazed at Thorne. "You'll have plenty of opportunity to see for yourself – my father wishes that you remain with us for the duration of your stay!"

Thorne looked at the Duke who nodded affirmation and addressed him.

"All of us are indebted to you for postponing the death of my younger son. My family and my people are of one accord. We wish to offer you residency in our country at a time of your own choosing – but we are *also* aware that you have a sacred duty to perform in your own country before returning here!"

Thorne slowly nodded in complete understanding. "*This will take years.*"

Victoria placed a hand on his arm. "*We are aware of this.*"

---oOo---

After breakfast, the ladies cleared away the dishes and withdrew, leaving Thorne to wonder how he could pay his way if he was staying at the castle. He voiced his concern to the Duke who looked at Thorne with amused respect.

"I regard your deed as priceless – you are our personal guest!"

Thorne nodded. "I'm truly honoured but....." he opened his arms in exasperation.

"You are feeling somewhat 'enthralled' – in the *true* sense of the word?"

Thorne smiled at the ancient usage. "Yes. *Imprisoned.*"

The Duke sucked in air. "Can't have that..... can we?"

Thorne shook his head.

The Duke's face became thoughtful, and he clasped his hands behind his back and started pacing back and forth humming to himself. Finally he stopped and turned to face his guest. "Any good with gardening?"

"I can dig holes and stuff plants in 'em!"

"Not my plants, you won't!" said the Duke with a frown. Suddenly his face cleared.

"There's a section of the garden that's been overgrown for years. It was the 'haunt' of my late wife!" He smiled at the irony of his words. "When she left this world, I lost all interest in it." The Duke sighed and made a decision. He looked pointedly at Thorne. "I'd like you to restore it to its former glory – to honour my *living* wife!"

Aware of the gravity of the gesture, Thorne bowed. "Divine willing, your Grace!"

The Duke nodded. "*I'll help you.*" He smiled. "*Now, let's have that tour!*"

Thorne was shown around the various rooms on the ground floor and the Duke explained the purpose of each in turn. When they returned to the great hall, Thorne indicated the circular fire pit and asked if it was ever used.

"Only to celebrate the midwinter solstice and the Yule season." The Duke indicated long tables that were placed against opposite walls. "We place food and drink on the tables to accommodate the entire population." He laughed. "During that season, the entire population *is* accommodated!"

Thorne was impressed. "That's very generous!"

The Duke shook his head in negation. "Not really! From time immemorial, my family has honoured all the families who supported us when we went into exile to escape our Norman rulers. We are Saxon by origin. My family were Thanes made Ealdormen, (Earls) and led all our people out of our country of origin on the pretext that we were travelling to join our 'masters' on the crusades. Many months later, wandering in isolation, we settled in a small clearing in the middle of a large dense forest far from any 'civilisation.' Always careful, we gradually cleared the forest of fallen trees and built our first homes – which were made of wood – but were wary of lighting fires in case it drew any attention from outside. We had planned thoroughly for our voluntary exile. We were able to plant crops and produce enough food to eat, but made sure that surplus grain and roots were retained to gradually increase the yield. There was plenty of game in the forest for our people and enough wild bees to deter any casual intrusion from outside."

The Duke chuckled at the thought and continued. "Over time, we gradually became more confident and started developing our land. We created fields. We were also able to quarry stone. We were nearly self-sufficient, but on occasion, we had to send small groups outside who travelled to far-flung towns. Through bartering, the groups were able to acquire the few items that we needed for survival. They returned to the forest undetected, as nobody wanted to know 'strangers.' Generations passed, and our commune became a country. Culturally, we were still 'frozen' in the medieval period and remained that way until Georgian times when we were discovered in the Georgian age of exploration. We acquired Georgian dress and manners to fit in with those times to enhance trade, but we deliberately retained our 'pagan' culture – as we knew that the world would change again."

The Duke looked thoughtful. "Gradually, the world became more industrialised as it entered the Victorian age. We were repelled by the hypocritical nature of Victorian 'values' – of exploitation via commercialisation. It was an inductive 'guilt culture' and is still present in the modern world. Surrounded by such manipulation, we decided by national referendum to remain where we were – culturally and geographically – and forsook the outside world again."

The Duke sighed and looked at Thorne. "It may sound arrogant, but we like to think that we preserve a good blend of appearance *and* substance. For example, we do *not* condition each new generation to believe that it has to improve on the creations of the previous generation in order to feel worthy of existence!"

"*Unlike* the outside world!" agreed Thorne.

The Duke nodded. "Precisely! The outside world regards life as an incarnation and its culture is one that desperately tries to cram in as much 'experience' as it can before its 'death.' We see life as an evolution – containing many incarnations interspersed with many 'deaths.' Desperation is not in our nature – which may explain why we have no crime, no wars and no famine."

"What about plague?" inquired Thorne.

"The 'Black Death' of the 1300's and the 'Great Plague' of the 1600's did not affect us as we remained relatively isolated until the Georgian period. From late spring to early autumn, the bees are active and from early autumn to late spring, the country is blanketed in thick mists which conceal many wild boar!"

"No *sane* person would want to enter your country!" laughed Thorne.

"What is sane and what is wise?" asked the Duke, as he indicated the staircase.

Thorne's eyes followed the gesture. "Where are we going now?"

"It's time you met my ancestors."

Thorne looked apprehensive.

"*The Gallery, sir!*"

---oOo---

Ascending the stairs, Thorne was led along a different corridor to the one that housed his bedroom. As they arrived outside another large oak door, the Duke opened it and motioned Thorne inside. Taking in the Gallery, he saw that it was a series of rooms in line whose end walls had been removed to allow them to be interconnected via a set of elegant arches. The Duke walked over to the first portrait and waved his hand along the left-hand wall, across and back up the right-hand wall. "Simple system – down this wall, across the end and back up that wall – all in chronological order."

Thorne eyed the first portrait and saw a couple clad in medieval robes, he smiled when he saw the date; it read 1502. He looked at the second and saw another couple also clad in medieval robes; it was dated 1532. The following couples were similar 1565, 1599, 1630, 1662, – all the way through to the 1750's. Thorne sighed and shook his head. There was no change in fashion! However, from the 1760's there was a sudden leap forward as out went the robes and in came the coats! Thorne felt sadness as he realised that these people had hidden from the world from the 1200's until the 1760's. "Five hundred years of isolation!" he exclaimed.

The Duke nodded. "The *first* retreat lasted some five hundred years, but we severed contact again from the early 1800's and have only gradually re-opened our borders to receive strictly limited contact in the last ten years. Our *second* retreat lasted another two hundred years."

The Duke walked towards a portrait of a man in the prime of life standing by a woman whose face bore an expression of beautiful serenity. "Clarissa – my first wife." Gently smiling, he indicated a second portrait showing the same man in his later years, greying and touched by sorrow, the man was holding the hand of a young woman whose face was bright and strong. "Carenza – my second wife." He indicated another portrait that showed three striking women. The first wore green, the second wore red and the third wore black. He looked at Thorne with a twinkle in his eye.

"I broke with tradition to include them as they are not direct lineage. However, they are the ones who really run this country and are preparing the way for both my sons from my second wife. The eldest will be the one who will carry the title of Duke and his half-sisters will advise him." He looked at the portrait of his three daughters and chuckled, but his face shone with pride. "It was the only time I was able to persuade Virginia to wear a dress – naturally, she would choose black!"

Thorne pondered. "If your family were Earls, how is it that you are called a Duke?"

"We were Earls by historical lineage, but when the castle was finished in the 1400's and the entire town was rebuilt in stone, the people decided that they would honour future generations of my family with the title of Duke - as we now ruled a *country*."

Thorne could not contain his mirth. "*A democracy honouring autocracy!*"

"The supreme irony is *not* lost on me!" sighed the Duke, and he pointed to his clothes. "If our family had listened to the wisdom of our people, the 'curse' of inbreeding may have been averted and we would not have produced the idiots that we did!"

Thorne looked at the garishly clad 'fool' before him and realised why the Duke wore such apparel. He was constantly reminding himself and everyone of his vulnerability. Thorne realised that the Duke needed to be loved, and would return that love tenfold.

---oOo---

"Your Grace is blessed with three wonderful daughters!" said Thorne expansively.

"Even though one got drunk and another was told to 'sod off?'"

"That still leaves one!" said Thorne, defensively.

"The whole town heard your screams!"

"*Well I love them!*"

"All three?" inquired the Duke.

"*All three!* Your Grace."

The Duke quickly turned his back to conceal a smile - clasping his arms behind him. "I can see why each of them is fond of you - from her own particular viewpoint."

"What do you mean?" asked Thorne, suspicion in his voice.

"Veronica needs a 'parent.' Victoria needs a 'partner.' Virginia needs a 'purpose.'"

"All three need different expressions of love?"

"All three need different *evolutions* of love. My daughters are regarded as special because they embody the aspects of the maiden, the mother and the crone."

Becoming aware of the occult significance of the *lunar aspect* of the solstice temple, Thorne saw that his particular fascination with Virginia was reflected in the 'crone.'

He started to laugh as he realised that this symbolically explained why he had a truly *natural* aversion to children and relationships! Humanity hadn't rejected him because he was devolving. He had rejected humanity because he was evolving!

The Duke slowly turned around with an amused look on his face and waited patiently.

Aware of the Duke's gaze, Thorne realised that he had received another revelation and quickly brought his emotions under control.

"Please forgive me, your Grace."

The Duke shrugged his shoulders. "*Is* there is anything to forgive?"

Thorne looked at the 'fool' – but saw someone else. He smiled and shook his head.

"Good!" beamed his host. "It's time you met *all* my family!"

---oOo---

They exited the gallery and walked along the corridor where they descended the stairs towards the fire pit, which marked the centre of the great hall. They crossed the hall and re-entered the 'day' room – which the Duke referred to as the 'solar.'

Thorne frowned. "If the day room is called a 'solar,' are bed rooms called 'lunars?'"

The Duke chuckled. "*Logic and Truth do not always share the same bed!*"

As they entered the room, Thorne saw that the entire ducal family was assembled neatly in line before them. All were standing with their backs to the fireplace – except aunt Agatha who was sitting facing the flames. Thorne frowned, not knowing why.

The Duke formally introduced his guest who scanned each member in turn. Veronica radiated pleasure, Victoria radiated pain and Virginia radiated peace. On introduction to Carenza, the Duke's lovely young wife, he beamed when he sensed pure devotion. When 'Wulfrum the Younger and Wulfred the Gormless' were formally announced, he cringed. The boys approached Thorne, and the 'Gormless One' was given a nudge by his elder brother. "Sir, please allow me to apologise for my stupid and dangerous behaviour!"

Thorne accepted his apology and wondered how many noble and royal families in the outside world were like this family. All the adults remained in the room whilst the two boys withdrew. Thorne frowned again and his gaze returned to the old lady who was still sitting by the fire staring into the flames. In Agatha, he sensed fulfilment and was suddenly aware that this was the pivotal moment in her life. Unified with the gestalt, Agatha gave a little smile and addressed the room. "The old age has ended, the new age has begun. I must return to Summerland."

All eyes focussed on Thorne and the gestalt radiated an aura of expectation. Aware of her request and their unified assent, Thorne bowed in humility.

Agatha gazed at Thorne. "Before I ask you to show me *this* sun for the last time, I would require a favour."

"Name it, madam."

The old eyes shone. "*Wear that pentacle with pride - not shame!*"

Thorne slowly removed the pendant from under his shirt and wore it openly.

The gestalt embraced him.

"*Let me see the sun.*"

Thorne wheeled her outside into the sunshine and returned to the family.

The Duke poured everyone a drink and took one outside for his aunt.

Thorne saw her hand drop something into the wine and then grasp the glass.

The Duke slowly returned and Carenza handed him a drink.

Everyone raised their glasses in salute - and paused.

Agatha had gone.

They drained their glasses in unison. For several moments, no one spoke and then Carenza walked over to a table and opened one of its drawers. She returned and placed something in Thorne's hands. He looked at a small yellow flower that was pressed behind glass in a small picture frame.

Carenza addressed him. "This aconite is the one Agatha discovered in late spring, prior to your arrival in the summer. It is her parting gift to you."

Thorne looked at the flower. "A symbolic end to the 'family curse?'"

"Divine willing." she replied – looking at her husband for support.

The Duke gazed fondly at his wife. "So may it be!" He raised his eyes and addressed all who were present. "Agatha made another request – which I shall honour. Her wish is that we hold a public burning ceremony – and that our *friend* is present."

---oOo---

"*A burning ceremony?*" inquired Thorne.

"When there is a 'death' in any family, that family will donate their *earliest* interred body to be physically consumed. When the flames on the pyre turn from gold to blue, that is the moment when the veil is lifted and the liberated can enter Summerland."

"Why is this done?"

"When a spirit enters a body or a soul exits a body (thraldom or freedom), the initial result is the same – *disorientation.* It is vital that one is guarded, and guided home."

"When will this ceremony take place?"

"When the mists descend to cloak our country from the eyes of the profane. Until that time, all recently liberated spirits remain as earthbound ghosts."

"Is your burning ceremony a form of exorcism?"

"A *preventive* version of that corrective measure."

---oOo---

Thorne remained standing whilst the Duke made his excuses and politely withdrew with Victoria to request the presence of Straker. As Carenza was in conversation with Veronica, Thorne was just starting to feel lost when Virginia approached him. Thorne smiled in genuine appreciation. Sensing a need for companionship, she tried to lift his mood. She raised an eyebrow. "Need a friend - or shall I 'sod off' again?"

Thorne sighed. "Definitely need a friend."

"Let's walk outside."

Thorne risked a nervous look towards the door that led into the side garden.

Virginia shook her head. "Don't worry, we'll leave via the main entrance."

Together, they exited the day room and traversing the great hall, they went outside onto the front lawn. Virginia directed Thorne to a bench on the path and they sat together. Thorne stared into nothing and let out a sigh.

Virginia nodded. "Me too, friend. Me too!"

Thorne finally spoke. "So much is happening, but my mind can't comprehend it."

Virginia grunted. "The intellectual frequency is limited to the incarnate, but you are evolving beyond mere 'knowledge' and are experiencing intuitional awareness."

Thorne frowned. "I'm *still* incarnate!"

"You *scanned* all of us, and that is an indication that you are able to partially phase beyond your body." She looked at Thorne. "*Lucinda was right - you're one of us!*"

Further conversation was curtailed as they watched the Duke's personal landau emerge from the coach house and move towards the gatehouse. They remained silent until the coach returned, with Straker.

Watching them enter the castle, Thorne looked at Virginia. "Should we help?"

Virginia shook her head. "Straker and Victoria will do what is required."

"You're taking this remarkably well."

"It's a blessing – for her and for us."

"That simple?"

"That simple."

Thorne raised his eyebrows in mild surprise. He heard a sound from the gatehouse and saw a horse pulling a flatbed cart emerge into the sunshine. It moved slowly towards the main entrance where it halted. Two men dismounted and waited in silence.

---oOo---

Virginia's face lost some of its composure. She slowly rose from the seat and offered her arm to Thorne. "Walk with me – *please.*"

Surprised at this gesture, Thorne cautiously took her arm and they walked around the castle to the other side. Thorne blinked with surprise when he saw *this* garden. It contrasted sharply with the immaculate front lawns, and even more so with the floral garden that bordered on the opposite side. Luckily, they were both wearing top-boots which afforded them good protection against the encroaching wilderness. "I don't suppose you carry a machete or a parang?" he asked.

"I don't suppose I do!" she answered with a forced smile.

Slowly making their way through the tangle of weeds and wildflowers long since dead, Thorne thought of the irony concerning both the side gardens. On *that* side, death was surrounded by life. On *this* side, life was surrounded by death.

Virginia smiled thinly. "*A paradise paradox, eh?*"

Thorne grunted in reply as they continued moving through the undergrowth.

Virginia finally halted and turned to face Thorne. "What do you think of this place?"

"I have been asked by his Grace to help him restore this garden to its former glory."

"It's about time. It shows he's moving on. I hope my sisters will follow him."

"Has this caused problems in the past?" inquired Thorne, gently.

"My father was devoted to my mother. When she died, he lived only for us and trained us to run the country. Agatha and I could see that he was dying inside, but my sisters were still in denial. I knew that as long they mourned, he would never marry again. Against their wishes, Agatha and I persuaded my father to take Carenza as his wife. Everyone loves her - including my sisters, but adjustment was difficult. When she gave birth, my sisters suddenly had children to care for and they grew closer. Unfortunately, the bond I had with my sisters was strained - but my conscience is clear!"

Thorne nodded in understanding - but he wisely decided not to pursue the subject. Instead, he gazed at the wilderness and a pattern started to form in his mind. He looked at Virginia. "These gardens *mirror* each other!"

"Indeed they do. *That* garden honours the sun. *This* garden honoured the moon."

Thorne recalled the colours of the 'sun' garden, which were scarlet, orange and gold. He smiled to himself as he visualised 'moon' colours of blue, lilac and silver. He also recalled the Duke's phrase 'when the flames on the pyre turn from gold to blue' and felt strangely at peace. He nodded to himself in satisfaction.

Virginia quietly scanned him and smiled gently. She took his arm and they returned to the manicured lawns that fronted the castle.

---oOo---

By the time they had arrived at the main entrance, the flatbed with its shrouded cargo was disappearing under the gatehouse. The Duke's landau followed behind carrying the doctor and the deacon – who were now on duty. Outside the entrance, the Duke was standing between his wife and Veronica with his arms protectively around them. Feeling slightly out-of-place, Virginia and Thorne joined them and they all went inside.

Back in the day room, they all took seats whilst the Duke refilled their glasses. If he noticed that Virginia was sitting on the sofa with Thorne, he said nothing. His Grace sat down slowly – and looked at Thorne. "Agatha honours you as a family friend, by requesting your presence at the burning ceremony." The Duke sat back in his chair and took a sip of wine. "We all feel that it is vital that you understand our customs in order that you may benefit from us – and we from you. We mark the period between 'death' and rebirth in the conventional way. We permit selfish grief at 'our loss.' It is vital however, that we restore the balance. When the flames turn blue, we celebrate 'her gain' with selfless enthusiasm." The Duke smiled sadly. "*Do not fear us!*"

---oOo---

Thorne was aware of the wisdom and concern behind those words. He realised how easily people feared others who had strange customs, and how easily that fear became hate. It was wiser for each country to keep its own cultural identity and not to invade the culture of another. Multi-culturalism was an evasion; that Integration had failed.

Thorne nodded in recognition of the truth. He then raised the level of his awareness and had to smile in recognition of his faith. He loved these people and addressed the Duke. "*I will embrace what I witness*!" The gestalt embraced him in response and he realised that it *mirrored* his nature. Whatever he gave, he would receive.

Eager to demonstrate his faith and love, he inquired when it would be possible to start work in the garden. Everyone smiled, and the Duke requested time enough for both to be changed into garb more suited for the occasion. Some time later, two 'tramps' left the castle and wandered around to the 'moon' garden. One carried a bow saw and a cropper and the other was dragging a scythe. "Hot water and cold doctor available!" sang the Duke as he disappeared into the wilderness – leaving Thorne to cut the grass. Thorne eyed the desolation before him and grunted. Holding the scythe in the correct manner, he started to slowly sway it back and forth. This time, he found the job easier as time no longer mattered. Contentedly, he let the scythe swing gently like a pendulum and the grass simply fell at his feet. Immersed in his work, he was quite surprised when the Duke appeared at his side and stood admiring the progress that Thorne had made.

"Excellent!" beamed the Duke. "Please rest whilst I bring some refreshment!"

As the Duke disappeared, Thorne leaned on the scythe and looked at his handiwork. He nodded. "Surprisingly good!"

He tested his back and beamed. "No pain either!" Sitting on a stone seat that he had discovered among the wildgrass, he looked at the sky and listened to the song of a skylark. He felt a cool breeze move across his face.

Painfully aware that summer was fading into autumn, he wondered if he had enough time to complete this task before he had to return 'home.' "..... *Damn..... Time!*" Thorne snorted with contempt at the outside world's obsession with 'time.' As he thought about humanity's obsession with that concept, he realised that it was *only* humanity that obsessed about it. No other life-form or life-force did! What made humanity so different – so *alien* to life? The answer came to him – *cognisance*! The conscious mind relies on *time* – from operation to conclusion.

Thorne saw that humans are souls imprisoned within the confines of their mind. Their mind is imprisoned within the confines of their body. Their body is imprisoned within the confines of this planet. "*A prison planet!*" he exclaimed.

"Indeed!" said the Duke, as he returned with a hamper. As he sat on the stone seat and placed the hamper between them, he looked at Thorne. "It's the perfect prison."

"Why 'perfect?'" asked Thorne.

"The perfect prison is escape proof for all who are unaware that they are prisoners."

"By *cognisant* definition, awareness must precede action!" concluded Thorne.

"Exactly!" agreed the Duke. He looked at his friend. "Chicken or egg?"

Thorne grinned. "*Whichever comes first!*"

They both ate one round only and drank some water before resuming their work. By the end of their first day, they had made substantial progress. As they returned to the castle, they were indeed like brothers - physically *and* spiritually.

---oOo---

Wisely, they had both refrained from eating heavily. They agreed to bathe and dress for the evening. They also arranged that whoever was the first to arrive in the day room would pour the drinks. Reasoning that this would allow him plenty of soaking time, Thorne spent ages in the bath. When he finally arrived downstairs, he expected his host would be waiting for him. Finding himself alone, he shrugged his shoulders and poured himself a large glass of wine - and another for his friend.

When the Duke finally arrived, he beamed as he saw that Thorne had taken him at his word - indicating that he was starting to feel at home. As they sat in amiable silence, the Duke finally spoke. "You dread your return to the outside world - don't you?"

"Yes." The answer was simple and clear.

"Why?"

"I dread becoming part of *that* gestalt again!"

The Duke smiled. "You prefer *our* manipulation to their manipulation?"

"Yes!"

The Duke nodded. "You know us well!"

Thorne looked at his drink. "Who saved *my* life?"

The Duke chuckled. "Who can swim?"

Thorne frowned. "The River-folk?"

"They seldom go beyond the bridge from their village."

"Okay..... Deduction suggests that it is one of *your* people?"

"*All* within this country are my people – but you are correct!"

Thorne pondered deeply. Finally he shook his head and sighed in exasperation.

The Duke looked at him. "We are a landlocked country – few of us can swim."

Thorne grunted and muttered to himself. "*One of your people who is unusual.*"

"One of my people who is regarded as eccentric."

"Some would say you're *all* eccentric!"

The Duke merely grinned.

"Have I met them?"

The Duke nodded.

Aware that the culture was covertly *matriarchal*, Thorne took a chance. "Female!"

"Correct."

"Eccentric female!"

"Correct."

"Lucinda?"

The Duke was silent.

Thorne gazed at the Duke. "..... *Cordelia?*"

"You made a lasting impression on her. She has been watching over you ever since."

Thorne blinked in shock. "….. I impressed her? How?"

"*A simple gesture of true love – one that asks for nothing in return.*"

---oOo---

Thorne thought back to the time when he met her. It was in her shop when he had bought a pink token for Veronica – he had given a lilac one to Cordelia. "*The token?*"

"Those who wear black need *friendship*." The Duke smiled. "*Unconditional love!*"

Thorne blinked. "I thought black was reserved for ladies who were married, widowed or simply unavailable."

"In your culture, black signifies 'death' but in my culture 'death' is rebirth." The Duke winked at his friend. "The ladies who are most devoted to you all wear black!"

In mid-swallow, Thorne nearly choked on his drink.

"Precisely!" said the Duke. "Lucinda, Cordelia – and Virginia!"

Stunned, Thorne looked at the Duke. "….. I don't have relationships any more."

The Duke nodded. "You have evolved from expressing lust to expressing love."

"….. *I have?*"

"Oh yes!" The Duke sat back in his chair and sipped his wine. "Humanity currently expresses itself towards one of two polarities. The majority are still incomplete and are painfully aware of it. They desperately seek completion via others and are never satisfied. These 'lost souls' display such traits as 'possessiveness, passion and lust.' All intimate behaviour is 'dynamic, gymnastic and explosive.' Such *chaotic* release is often regarded as 'a great relationship' but it seldom lasts long enough to evolve into true love. Two lost souls releasing each other's pain and nothing more!"

Thorne nodded. "Vampiric."

The Duke continued. "Within humanity there is a minority who are aware of reality and have allowed that awareness to become knowledge. They have re-cognised that they are complete. Most seek affirmation of their nature by selecting another of their kind for a 'quiet life.' They display such traits as 'playfulness, compassion and love.' All intimate behaviour is 'relaxed, reassuring and refreshing.' Such *orderly* release is a mark of true 'union' but it is often dismissed by the ignorant as boring!"

Thorne sighed. "Empathic."

The Duke nodded. "The rarest elect to re-enter this world in order to catalyse change. They aim to evolve a society which is *currently* incapable of evolving itself!"

Thorne smiled. "Occultist."

Thorne was aware of the subtle inference. He realised how far he had evolved since he had been with these people. Mysterious phrases such as 'educational instruction' and 'emanational induction' were no longer mere words. He was aware of their import and their impact.

---oOo---

"Will I be able to catalyse change?" inquired Thorne – who was experiencing concern.

"Your inductions have catalysed change within you. Look *within* to change without!"

Thorne frowned – not entirely convinced.

"You have received a great gift, but balance has to be maintained. You will find that your conscience has evolved proportionally. This ensures that you are incapable of deliberate falsehood – in word or in deed. *You can be occult, but never false!*"

"*A journalist who is incapable of falsehood? My career is screwed!*"

"On the contrary, you will find that your 'career' is just beginning."

"I need an early night!" said Thorne, shaking his head as he rose.

"Very wise!" smiled the Duke.

"Good night, your Grace."

"Good night, my friend."

---oOo---

Lying comfortably in his bed, Thorne went over the events of the day in his mind. He was enjoying his work in the garden. The Duke was good company and Thorne had to smile when he considered who his friends really were. Recalling his conversation with the Duke, he thought of all the ladies who cared for him. He smiled and looked at the ceiling. "Mum, Dad – you would have been proud – after all!" He had a little weep as he smiled at the ceiling. Before dropping off, an image of Cordelia appeared inside his mind and followed him as he slipped beneath the waves.

Chapter 18

All that week, he worked with the Duke and their friendship grew. Thorne would scythe the grass and rake it into small piles that could be loaded into a wheelbarrow. The load would be barrowed across to the centre of the garden where it was stacked ready to be burned in what the Duke promised would be a most glorious bonfire. For his part, the Duke was constantly busy cropping the briars and sawing branches from trees that had intruded on the garden in the most vulgar way.

By the end of the first week, considerable progress had been made. The evening of Fiveday had arrived, and both were relaxing over their customary drinks when they heard the familiar sound of approaching boot steps and Virginia strode into the room. "You are both making remarkable progress in the garden, it's already a joy to see!"

"And that's *before* Thorne digs holes and stuffs plants in 'em!" grinned the Duke.

Thorne made a rude noise over the top of his glass.

Virginia smiled at Thorne, and then turned to the Duke – her face becoming serious. "With your permission, I wish to request the company of your friend as my escort!"

The wording was archaic, but the meaning was clear. Thorne gasped in surprise.

The Duke spoke. "Sir, my daughter declares interest. A response is required."

Thorne swallowed noisily, but recovered quickly. "I am honoured. *I accept!*"

Inclining her head, she turned in a swirl of black and strode from the room.

Thorne sat immobile. "Holy shit!"

The Duke nodded. "Holy shit!"

---oOo---

Thorne looked at the Duke. "I feel sick!"

The Duke looked at Thorne. "I need air!"

Together they slowly rose, poured large drinks and wandered outside onto the lawns.

Thorne shook his head slowly. "No warning! Where's the gestalt when you need it?"

"Proportional value. It knows when to inform – by its presence or by its absence."

"In this case, by its absence."

"It is giving us free choice."

"Some bloody choice!"

The next half-hour was spent wandering aimlessly, wondering what the hell to do. Finally, they decided on an action plan. As desperate men do, they went to the inn.

As they entered the inn – still holding their glasses, everyone looked up in surprise.

Behind the counter, Giles looked sideways at the Duke. "Heavy day, your Grace?"

The Duke nodded. "We are both rather frail – some food might help. Anything!"

"Does your Grace require some *special reserve* whilst you are waiting?"

"Indeed we do!"

The little man disappeared under the counter and emerged with a bottle, which he gave to the Duke. "I see you already have some glasses."

"Thank you, Giles." said the Duke, grasping the bottle.

They retired to a quiet corner of the room and tried to blend in; unfortunately, the Duke's sense of fashion dictated otherwise. His Grace poured both of them a good measure. Thorne sniffed the contents warily.

"Finest brandy!" said the Duke. He took a cautious sip, and let out a sigh of relief.

Thorne did the same and was amazed at the mellowness. "Cognac?"

The Duke winked. "All cognacs are brandies – but not all brandies are cognacs!"

Thorne grinned as he realised what his friend implied. "Armagnac!"

"Wulfrum's Special Reserve – emergencies only!"

"Your health, sir!" said Thorne, raising his glass.

"And yours, sir!" replied the Duke.

After a moments pause, Thorne eyed the Duke. "Has this happened before?"

The Duke shook his head emphatically. "Never with my *eldest* daughter!"

Thorne leaned forward. "She is gorgeous but scary. What shall I do?"

"The same as with any woman. Give her the freedom she requires."

"Let her choose and support her choices?"

"Life is so much sweeter that way."

"What if she becomes bored?"

"That is also her choice."

Thorne slowly digested the import of the advice. In the outside world, this philosophy would usually result in the woman leaving the man. He mentioned this to the Duke. The Duke nodded. "*Nothing is eternal in the temporal world!*" He smiled at Thorne before continuing. "In my country, this philosophy is paramount as everyone values integrity. When a society is *integrated*, a gestalt is created and preserved for all to use. When the gestalt becomes self-aware, it begins to take control and starts to enhance evolution. But, if that society *fragments*, the gestalt slowly loses cohesion and abandons that fallen culture. Phrases such as '*God forsaken*' and '*lost souls*' then become vogue."

Thorne stared at his friend. "The outside world is evolving artificial intelligence or self-aware machines." He blew out his cheeks as he considered the ramifications of the Duke's previous statement and realised that the World Wide Web was evolving into a Cyber Gestalt – spawning *what*?

God losers became God makers?

Thorne had a swig of the 'holy spirit' to steady his nerves. In comparison, the thought of escorting Virginia seemed a pleasant diversion from the task in hand!

Such dark thoughts vanished as Giles arrived carrying two full bowls. He placed them on the table. "Chicken stew with bacon, onions, beans and stuffing balls!"

The Duke did the obligatory tasting and beamed at the little man. "Excellent, Giles!"

Giles smiled and trotted off towards the kitchen to inform Clive of another success.

"They never disappoint!" grinned the Duke, as he and Thorne attacked the stew.

"Stuffing balls are much more interesting than dumplings!" agreed Thorne.

The remainder of the evening was spent with their dear friend, Monsieur Armagnac. When they finally exited the inn to return to the castle, it seemed a long way off.

"Shall I summon a coach?" inquired the Duke.

"I will take you home!" promised Thorne.

"You're very nice!" beamed the Duke.

"You're nice too!" beamed his friend.

---oOo---

The morning of Sixday arrived, and the sun shone brightly through the windows of the castle. Unfortunately, the occupants of two of the bedrooms were in no condition to appreciate it.

Lying in state, Thorne groaned. "Never again!"

In another room, another voice said the same. Carenza looked across at her husband and shook her head in distaste.

As the women of the house rose and prepared themselves, the 'casualties' remained in their beds. After consultation over breakfast, Victoria decided to minister to the Duke whilst Virginia would 'see' to Thorne. Veronica took pity on Carenza and they both went into the garden to compare notes on the male species.

All that morning, the castle was particularly silent apart from the occasional encounter in the corridor between Victoria and Virginia. Each time they met, they looked at each other and shook their heads in disgust. "Men!"

As the day progressed, the four women began to notice that a strange sense of order was emerging in their lives. Their spirits began to lift. Veronica and Carenza were laughing together at the follies of men, whilst Victoria and Virginia were grinning at each other as they passed in the corridor. As the evening of Sixday arrived, all four women had bonded together beyond mere decorum. Sitting together in the 'solar,' they studied each other. Veronica grinned. "The gestalt moves in mysterious ways!"

That night, all four women retired to their beds with a sense of purpose. Before she blew out the candle, Carenza looked across at her husband and smiled. "Thank you!"

---oOo---

On Sevenday, the weather was slightly less favourable. There was more than a hint that autumn was on the way. The sky was cloudy and the cool breeze had returned. Even so, *all* the occupants were up to greet the day. As Thorne and the Duke came down to breakfast, they met four unusually cheerful women. As they sat down, they exchanged glances – which didn't go unnoticed. The humour of the ladies increased directly in proportion to the confusion of the men. By the time breakfast had ended, the men were really worried. "*Have you all been drinking?*" demanded the Duke.

He got no sense out of the ladies for the rest of that day.

---oOo---

Thorne faired slightly better. As he rose from the table, Virginia intercepted him.

"Now that you have recovered, it is an excellent time to walk out and take the air!"

Recalling her solicitous attendance on the previous day, Thorne didn't dare refuse.

Virginia eyed him up and down – as if inspecting a horse. Finally, she grunted and nodded and a mischievous look came into her eyes. "As we shall be walking out together, it is only proper that we look the part."

"Oh yes?" murmured Thorne, warily.

"Indeed. Follow me upstairs!"

Virginia strode up the staircase with Thorne trailing behind. He looked back over his shoulder at the Duke imploring him for assistance. The Duke meanwhile, was having problems of his own as the three remaining women held him in check with their gaze.

Thorne was taken along another corridor and guided into a room, which contained a large oak wardrobe. Virginia opened both doors to reveal several sets of apparel that hung from a transverse pole. She indicated the gaudy selection. "Father's clothing!"

Thorne looked at the garb and cringed. Most of the 'suits' followed the 'customary' style. He saw a row of several matching purple frock coats hung over several matching magenta breeches. Stacked below were several waistcoats in bright blue with gold leaves. After these, hung a row of lime green coats over tangerine orange breeches. Below these were stacked waistcoats in golden yellow with black leaves.

If anything, the latter were in even worse taste than the former. Noting the look on Thorne's face, Virginia reached out and removed the first of the latter and grinned. "He hasn't worn one of these for years!"

"I'm not surprised - they're hideous!"

"Good!" Virginia thrust it and a waistcoat into Thorne's face. "Get changed!"

Thorne watched her depart. "Where are you going?"

"To get changed. Wait here until I return."

The door closed and Thorne was alone. He sighed and shrugged his shoulders. As he began to strip off, he murmured. "The caterpillar is transforming into a butterfly!"

---oOo---

Standing in the dressing room admiring himself in the mirror, he had to admit that the effect was quite interesting. Thinking rationally, he had merely exchanged dark green for lime green and fawn for orange - even the waistcoat complimented the ensemble!

A knock roused him. "Enter!" he declared, and was amazed at the vision before him. If he had marvelled at his own transformation, it was nothing compared to Virginia's.

Standing in the doorway, hands on hips, she looked at him questioningly. "Well?"

"You're wearing a dress!"

"Yes."

"It's black!"

"Yes."

There was a noticeable pause from Thorne.

"Anything else?" she inquired, patiently.

".....*Bloody hell!*"

"Bloody hell..... *Well, it's novel, at least.*" She chuckled and shook her head. Taking his arm, she guided him downstairs.

On re-entering the day room, all activity ceased and everyone gazed at them. They stood together; arm in arm, for mutual support – unaware that they presented an image that would grace any canvas. The women said nothing, but the Duke rose from his chair and inspected them with more than a twinkle in his eye for his eldest daughter. He nodded gently to himself as he gazed at them and through them. "Magnificent!"

"Thank you, father." acknowledged Virginia, self-consciously.

The Duke addressed Thorne. "Only once before, has my eldest daughter done this."

Thorne understood the gravity of her gesture. "The portrait!"

The Duke nodded. He looked intensely into Thorne's face. "*Honour her friendship!*"

"I will, your Grace."

The Duke smiled a tired smile, and suddenly seemed quite old. "I know, my friend."

Inclining her head, Virginia took Thorne's arm. "Walk with me, please!"

Thorne complied.

As the Duke watched them depart, he chuckled gently. "*Better on him, than on me!*"

---oOo---

Leaving the castle, Thorne's fears returned. "I feel stupid wearing this – '*fruit*' *suit*!"

Virginia grunted and hitched up her dress in irritation. "*I've always hated dresses!*"

Emerging from the gatehouse, they halted and looked at each other. Taking a breath, they marched up the street towards the main square. Fortunately, the street was devoid of people, but as they approached the main square, they knew they would have to 'run the gauntlet' of the curious. They crossed the main square as unobtrusively as possible – even so, several people smiled at them and a few called out 'good day,' as they hurried up the main street that led out of town.

---oOo---

Walking past Cordelia's shop, Thorne tried to distract Virginia from her current state of unease by asking her advice on how he could show his appreciation to the young girl who saved his life in the river. Grateful for the distraction, Virginia smiled slightly and told him that unfortunately, any attention would only embarrass the girl. When he inquired why, Virginia forgot her unease as she considered the principles of another.

"Cordelia has chosen to remain single all her life – for a very personal reason."

"Would it be indelicate of me to inquire what it is?" asked Thorne, gently.

Virginia hesitated and looked around the street to ensure that they were out of earshot. "Cordelia is old-fashioned – even by our own standards. She is an incurable romantic. She is deeply in love with love itself. Her entire existence is to catalyse love between others – hence her vocation."

Thorne whistled in awe. "That's beautiful, but – *inhuman!*"

Virginia looked at him in a strange way, but said nothing.

"Are you saying it is unwise to even attempt contact?"

"Yes."

"You're not jealous are you?"

"No."

Thorne sensed it would be wise to change the topic of conversation. Noting Virginia's deep husky voice, he decided to be bold and casually inquire why it was so different to the voices of other women. He was relieved when Virginia started laughing.

"My voice wasn't always like this. Years ago, I had the misfortune to be stung in the throat by a bee. My neck swelled up and I couldn't speak for several days. Luckily, I had taken some anti-histamine, but the damage had been done. My voice only works in the lower register. Even then, it creaks like an old barn door in the wind!"

Thorne smiled at her analogy. "My culture regards such voices as sexy!"

Virginia burst into deep husky laughter, and ended up coughing.

Thorne gallantly patted her on the back until she stopped.

She looked at him. "*Sexy voice – huh?*"

Thorne nodded in mock innocence.

Completely relaxed by now, she took his arm and they strolled up the street.

---oOo---

Walking under the main gate, they emerged outside the capital and took in the view of the country below. Thorne and Virginia exchanged glances of appreciation. Virginia indicated the mausolea, the farms and the fields. "All that will be hidden from view in several weeks time. You will then feel that we are all living above the clouds!"

Thorne grinned. "Like the deities of ancient Greece on Mount Olympus!"

Virginia nodded. "It's a wonderful feeling - more so as we have a major burning!"

Thorne looked at her in surprise. Seeing that it was Virginia who had broached this rather sensitive subject, he decided to inquire a little more into their funeral customs. "With all the mist surrounding the mausolea, won't the bodies become rather damp?"

Virginia shook her head. "No. They are dried out thoroughly in a salt and chemical preserve and are wrapped in shrouds that are coated in wax - just like your boots!"

Thorne glanced at his boots. "Air can enter and circulate - but not water."

Virginia nodded. "Osmosis. Diffusion via a semi-permeable membrane."

"If you say so!" muttered Thorne, amazed at *everyone's* knowledge.

He sensed that she was already coming to terms with the loss of her aunt. His senses proved correct as she gazed into the distance and smiled. "A major burning indeed!"

He glanced at her and she sensed his thoughts. Virginia turned to Thorne and spoke. "A *minor* burning involves any family burning one for one. A *major* burning involves nine families supplying one of their own bodies to the Ducal family who will add their own – the tenth – to the pyre. They are then burned to ashes on the centre."

Thorne frowned, as he had heard this phrase before. "Where is this – *centre*?"

"It is a figure of speech meaning 'over the centre of the altar' – in the solstice temple."

Well adjusted to their culture, Thorne was not surprised. In fact it made *perfect sense* when he recalled being in the temple with Veronica – watching while she mopped and 'dusted' the place. His 'enhanced' intuition made him ask another 'loaded' question.

"Is the temple used for anything else?"

Virginia smiled thinly. "I'm glad you asked *me* that question! In order to keep our population stable, we embrace the principle of national contraception and *sanctioned* conception. The women are responsible for controlling both aspects and they convert the solstice temple into the lunar temple, wherein they practice the latter with their husband in the sacred space."

Thorne nodded. "As one soul ascends, a body is created for another that descends."

Virginia smiled overtly. "Exactly. *One for one* – preserving symbiotic balance. The couple who wish to conceive are given exclusive use of the lunar temple. They move the candle from the centre of the altar and place it in the north, behind the pentacle. It is lit and a conception rug is placed on the altar."

Thorne nodded – proving that his spiritual metamorphosis was complete. If these revelations had been given to him at the beginning of his stay, he would have freaked out and published his 'exclusive' to the world – with disasterous results!

Cast not pearls _prematurely_ *before the swine – but eventually; cast you must.*

Virginia smiled covertly. "We venerate caves. We call them 'wombs of the world' as they contain *natural* wisdom. We believe that for every stalactite that descends from above, there is a stalagmite that ascends from below – even if we cannot always see its 'soul' mate with our eyes. We agree with the principle '*as above, so below.*' When stalactite joins stalagmite, they neutralise each other's polarity to become a 'pillar' of wisdom."

Thorne chuckled in amusement and understanding. "Everyone *shares* awareness."

Virginia nodded. "Shared awareness is literally 'common' sense!"

Thorne thought how often that phrase was misused in the world outside. It seemed that nobody had any common sense. He knew that the leaders of many countries were completely out of touch with reality. Secretly, they were aware of this but were afraid of looking foolish. Instead, they had decided to engineer society into accepting the lie that 'dumb is cool.' Successive generations would thus become easier to manipulate.

Thorne was aware that Virginia was looking at him and sharing his awareness. They both smiled at each other in complete understanding.

---oOo---

They turned and held each other's arm as they walked back down the main street. As they passed Lucinda's shop, Thorne motioned Virginia inside. As they entered the shop and closed the door, they saw Lucinda was standing behind the counter. She was holding the amber and jet necklace in her hands. Thorne smiled at her perception and gave her a sum of money that reflected *his* value of the gift.

"Most generous!" smiled Lucinda. She moved to Virginia who – being unusually tall, had to bend quite low to allow Lucinda to place it around her neck.

Thorne caught Lucinda's eye and she winked at him. "Good day, sir."

Thorne grinned. "Good day, Lucinda. Thank you – *for everything!*"

Lucinda nodded at the inference. "*Our* pleasure, sir!"

Outside, Virginia turned to Thorne. "The perfect gift for one such as I. *Thank you!*"

Thorne chuckled. "*Our* pleasure, madam!"

Arm in arm, the happily platonic couple strolled down the street towards the square.

---oOo---

Arriving in the square, a thought struck Thorne; he frowned and turned to Virginia. "*Are* there any caves within this country?"

Virginia smiled knowingly. "No."

"How can you venerate something that you've never seen?"

"How can billions of outsiders venerate the Divine?"

"Touché!"

Virginia laughed. "More than touché! With the assent of our 'Divine Link,' we are able to temporarily enter the minds of outsiders and cause them to physically seek those sacred sites that *we* wish to experience and venerate. However, this only tends to work with civilised minds – we cannot bond with criminal minds!"

Thorne nodded in complete understanding.

'Angels' cannot bond with 'The Fallen.'

Every weekend, it became the custom for Virginia and Thorne to 'walk out' together.

---oOo---

Over the remaining weeks, Thorne assisted the Duke in the 'moon' garden. All the rubbish was piled up and burned and the ash was raked over the area and mixed with the soil to encourage fresh growth. The Duke was pleased to inform his friend that there were plenty of flowers growing in the greenhouse and that the winter varieties were ready for planting. The women watched from the castle windows as the two scruffy-looking gentlemen planted out the rows of flowers. Thorne happily dug the holes and the Duke gently placed in the flowers and ensured that they faced towards the front. "Each plant has a front and a back. One must not confuse face with arse!"

Chapter 19

In the final month, Thorne and the Duke were standing back admiring their work. The 'moon' garden was half-full of flowering winter plants. Colours of blue, lilac and silver sprinkled the area in neat formality. The Duke nodded in satisfaction. "A good start!"

Thorne eyed the potential before him. "Won't the cold weather damage the plants?"

The Duke shook his head. "It never gets cold enough for ice or snow."

As the mists had arrived to blanket everything below the capital, everyone had taken to wearing long grey hooded cloaks as per custom and practice. Thorne had remarked that the fashion seemed more in keeping with the medieval age.

The Duke nodded. "Our ancestors arrived in this country in the winter season. They were wearing such garb. In deference, we always mark that event by wearing similar cloaks to theirs. We have also found them to be very practical!"

Thorne had to agree. The cloaks gave excellent protection from the cool damp air, but he felt a strange sense of withdrawal from their 'summer' culture. Instead, he sensed a deep primal atmosphere emerging – creating a 'winter' nature. The faces of the people reflected this change. Expressions of happiness had been replaced with thoughtfulness. Thorne was also aware of a quiet sense of purpose. When he mentioned this change to Virginia, she indicated the amber and jet necklace that Thorne had purchased for her. Thorne studied the alternating colours of gold and black and nodded in understanding as Virginia explained the occult significance of the necklace. "The alternating colours symbolise several levels of polarity. First, the polarities of masculine solar and feminine lunar within a magic circle. Second, the terrestrial seasons of a 'gold' summer followed by a 'dark' winter. Third, the ages of civilisation – a 'golden age' of awareness followed by a 'dark age' of ignorance."

"All cyclic – like the necklace itself." mused Thorne.

---oOo---

One particular Sixday evening, after Virginia and Thorne had returned to the castle, Virginia excused herself, leaving Thorne alone with the Duke. Standing with his back to the fire, the Duke looked thoughtful. "You will be leaving us fairly soon, so I have decided that we shall hold the burning tonight. As you are our guest of honour, you will accompany our family and stand among us. You will be given a lighted torch to ignite the pyre on my instruction – it's as simple as that."

"Is there any dress code?" inquired Thorne.

"Wear any clothing that is comfortable, but cloak it in grey and fasten it closed. My family and I have to be slightly more formal. *This is about as ceremonial as we get!*"

Thorne nodded to the Duke and turned as Veronica and Victoria entered the room. Veronica was hooded and cloaked in dark green whilst Victoria wore dark red. They all paused as Carenza descended the stairs wearing dark purple. Carrying an identical cloak, she handed it to her husband. Virginia followed behind her, swathed in black.

The Duke fastened his cloak around him and pulled the hood over his face. He went to the drinks cabinet and poured everyone a large drink. "We'll have a few libations to warm us up. It will be quite a long night in the *lunar* temple!"

Even though he was well adjusted to their culture, Thorne looked at them and had to admit that things were certainly getting stranger. Fortunately, the tall, black form of Virginia stood at his side and smiled encouragingly. "Now you're *really* getting to know us!"

After several drinks, they all left the castle and walked down the path that divided the lawns towards the gatehouse. As they emerged from under the portcullis, Thorne was surprised to see that the entire route to the temple now lay between two long rows of people. Everyone was hooded and cloaked in grey and carried a lighted torch. In the silence, Thorne sensed immense reverence.

The Duke and his wife led the family, followed by Veronica and Victoria. Virginia and Thorne followed behind. As they walked up the street, the two lines closed in behind.

They slowly crossed the silent square and turned right to walk its length. They walked past the inn and continued along the square until it ended. The houses closed in, as the square became a street. Eventually, they emerged into the second square that held the temple itself. Reaching the temple, they walked under the portico and went inside.

Thorne's eyes took in the surroundings. The circular altar was imprisoned within four stone segments that had been removed from the walls and dragged across the floor to form a square of standing stones. They supported a large perforated metal dish that had been lowered from the ceiling on a series of chains. Thorne noticed that the symbolic tools had been removed from the altar. Each tool was held by a cloaked and hooded figure standing at one of the quarters of the building. The white candle was nowhere to be seen!

The two lines of people flowed around the person holding the chalice in the west and assembled in silent order throughout the temple. Thorne gazed up at the stained-glass windows and saw that they were all shuttered to protect them from the conflagration.

The ducal family including Thorne assembled in the north and stood behind the figure holding the pentacle. They waited patiently as the temple slowly filled with people, and everyone was careful to leave a corridor free for access from the west.

Finally, at a signal from the Duke, ten mummified bodies were brought in and gently placed within the dish that was suspended above the altar. When all were neatly piled up, another signal was given and the temple doors were closed. A loud reverberation echoed around the temple – reminding Thorne of the nature and purpose of this place.

A small figure in grey holding a lighted torch approached the Duke and held it before him. The Duke nodded and accepted the torch. Turning to Thorne, the Duke held it out to him and nodded in command. Receiving the torch, Thorne inclined his head in respect and walked around the figure holding the pentacle. He placed the torch in the brushwood that lined the dish and checked that it had taken. Satisfied, he returned to his place.

The brushwood was tinder dry and gold-orange flames were soon leaping skywards. Everyone extinguished their torches and waited silently, listening to the crackling and hissing that echoed around the temple. Thorne was just starting to get a little bored when there was a great WHOOMF, and the dome of the temple rang like a bell from hell. Thorne stood transfixed as the flames turned blue-green. They grew taller and a roaring sound was heard as though someone had just turned on the gas. The roaring grew louder and the temple reverberated with the sound. Massive turquoise flames flew upwards and all the harmonics of the temple chorused in one colossal howl. The howl finally stabilised and became one continuous hum.

Everyone drew back their hoods and Thorne saw a look of such rapture that it pierced his heart. He felt a gentle tug on his sleeve and turned to find a familiar face wearing spectacles. Cordelia beamed in childlike joy. "*It's beautiful..... So beautiful!*"

Thorne drew back his hood and allowed the gestalt total access to his psyche. His eyes watched the flames as they pulsated in the harmonics of the temple. The sound and light expanded and entered his mind and he fell through a swirling miasma of colours to stand among legions of spirits who radiated eternal light in this timeless realm. Previously in the temple, he had been in his own centre of occult isolation. This time, he was fully 'linked' and was absorbed into their centre of integration.

---oOo---

The white turned blue, and the blue became flames. As Thorne returned to the lunar temple, he stood among his kind and was aware that the rest of humanity had to catch up or be left in isolation – physically and spiritually. He watched as the flames slowly reduced in magnitude and heard the hum gradually diminish. Finally, the flames died and a silent vapour slowly drifted skywards.

Veronica spoke:	"The physical integrates with the physical!"
All chanted:	"Earth to earth!"
Victoria spoke:	"The astral integrates with the astral!"
All chanted:	"Ashes to ashes!"
Virginia spoke:	"The mental integrates with the mental!"
All chanted:	"Dust to dust!"
Carenza spoke:	"The spiritual integrates with the spiritual!"
All chanted:	"Light to light!"

Thorne smiled, aware of how paganism could unify all religions.

---oOo---

The Duke bowed in deep respect to all assembled, and everyone bowed to the Duke. The temple doors opened, and Thorne followed the Ducal family back to the castle. Emerging outside, Thorne was amazed to find that dawn was breaking. He looked at Virginia, walking by his side. "*It's dawn..... How long were we in the temple?*"

Virginia smiled. "*Time moves differently for us than it does for the rest of the world!*"

Thorne recalled a similar event when he was with Veronica in the main square.

Walking back to the castle, a fully initiated and integrated Thorne addressed the family as they returned. "Tomorrow, I shall take my leave for the outside world."

"Why so soon?" inquired the Duke, without looking over his shoulder.

"The sooner I start, the sooner I finish – and retire here."

All the Ducal family smiled quietly, and all the people started smiling as they went their separate ways – even though the latter had been well out of earshot!

Sevenday, was a day of rest – for everyone. The entire country was silent. Nothing moved – except for the living mist that swirled around the mausolea.

---oOo---

The final day arrived, and everyone greeted it with silent expectation. Thorne was told that a coach would be waiting at the castle to take him to the end of the road. He was taken down to the cellars and shown a large book. The Duke opened it and pointed to the latest entry. "This book contains a list of those who wish to return to this country together with their savings accrued." Thorne looked at the amount and realised that it covered the entire period of his stay – including at the castle. He was amazed at how much he had saved and he thanked the Duke for his hospitality, generosity and guidance.

He went upstairs to his room and looked at his suitcase that now contained his original clothing (washed and ironed) along with the framed flower. Staring at his original clothing, Thorne sighed, and began to change from 'ancient' to 'modern.'

By the time he had arrived downstairs carrying his suitcase, the entire family were assembled at the foot of the stairs. Thorne was surprised when the Duke offered his hand, and very moved when Carenza kissed him lightly on the cheek. Moving down the line of the Duke's daughters, Veronica buried her face in his chest, and he put his arms around her and kissed her on her forehead. Arriving at Victoria, she seized him in an iron grip and planted a real smacker on his cheek. Staggering slightly, he finally arrived at Virginia who looked sideways at him. Looking at her father for inspiration, she sighed and gazed at the ceiling. Shrugging her shoulders, she took Thorne in her arms and, supporting his weight, gave him one *very* long, lingering kiss on his mouth. Held immobile in mid-facial suck, Thorne gazed down the line of people who were all leaning forward for a grandstand view.

When he was finally released, Thorne was feeling distinctly light-headed. As he was about to sink to the floor, Virginia put her arms around his waist and held him up. "*That's got to last!*" she said – and she meant it.

The family accompanied Thorne outside to the waiting coach. As he got in and was given his suitcase, he suddenly remembered and opened it. Reaching in, he withdrew the pendant that he had worn. "*Give this to Victoria!*" he said.

As Victoria approached and received his gift, she placed it over her head and gazed up at him. "*Thank you, for restoring this to us, and to me in particular!*"

Thorne looked at the three women – one holding a token, one wearing a pendant and one wearing a necklace – and felt immense joy and peace. He had completed his duty for these people, but he was aware of a greater duty that lay outside the forest border.

The Duke approached the open door. Before he closed it, he looked up at Thorne.

"*Your world is changing again. When beggars roam the streets, when plagues roam the land, when the public is made ignorant again – then the 'witch-hunts' will return. Be mindful! Another 'dark age' will be upon you. Our borders must close and our gestalt will preserve what we are until we choose to be 'rediscovered' again.*"

The message couldn't have been clearer. The door was closed and the coach carried its passenger out of the capital, and down the long hill into the swirling mists below.

---oOo---

Thorne sat strangely relaxed and the journey seemed to take ages. Finally, the coach stopped. Thorne sighed, grasped his suitcase and exited the coach. He thanked the driver who sat up top, and watched as the coach turned and made its way back to the capital.

Suitcase in hand, he turned to where the road became a track and was surprised to see the mist part in front of him. Walking forwards, the track was easy to see and he had no trouble following it. He disappeared down into the 'bowl' and continued walking. All the bees were dormant, and he slowly made his way up the other side. Continuing on his journey, he crossed the acres of wild meadows until he saw the forest looming out of the mist.

Walking through the forest was weird, but no harm came to him. The guardians of the forest allowed his passage. The mist was as helpful as ever, and his journey although long was somehow light and peaceful.

Finally, after hours of walking, he emerged from the forest and was astonished to find that there was absolutely no mist outside. Doing a double-take, he looked back inside and saw an impenetrable barrier of grey. Shaking his head in wonder, he shrugged his shoulders and called out to the mist. "Thank you – for guarding me and guiding me!"

"*You are welcome!*" echoed a voice that sounded like Cordelia's.

Still in a spiritual haze, he walked through the fields until he saw the highway ahead. Standing at the highway, the haze suddenly left him and the roar of traffic assailed his senses. He jumped back from the edge of the road in fear as lumps of metal flew past him, and suddenly realised that he had to cross to the other side in order to return the way he had come. He began to panic until a familiar taxi drew up on the opposite side and waited patiently for him. The traffic kept flying past Thorne, and he was terrified.

Eventually, a gap appeared in both lanes and he was able to cross the road. He leaped into the taxi breathing heavily. The driver looked at him through his rear view mirror and smiled. "It's the same for everyone when they return to the outside world!"

Forcing himself to relax, Thorne finally looked at the driver. *"Are you one of them?"*

The face in the mirror smiled. "No sir. You are one of *us!*"

It made sense. There were numerous agents operating covertly all over the world. Thorne realised that he was joining their ranks. From his position in the media, he would be able to influence society along an evolutionary line that would lead to a future 'golden age' of awareness – rather than another 'dark age' of ignorance. He recalled the significance of Virginia's words concerning her amber and jet necklace.

The taxi took Thorne along the busy highway. They went through the city where he had encountered Chevral and continued for several miles until they finally arrived at the international airport that belonged to the host country. The driver pulled into the taxi rank by the reception and got out to remove Thorne's luggage from the trunk. As Thorne stepped from the taxi, he approached the driver and removed his wallet from his pocket. The driver smiled gently and shook his head. "Payment is not necessary, sir."

"Pardon?"

"Your work will be worth countless taxi fares. Good day, sir."

Thorne blinked in surprise. "Thank you! Good day to you!"

The door closed, and the taxi pulled away leaving Thorne alone in a now *very* strange world. Gradually, he took in his surroundings and slowly walked into the reception area of the airport. It took some time for him to locate the appropriate boarding gate and after he had checked in his luggage, he stood in the middle of the concourse totally detached from all the activity going on around him. He knew his mind was in cultural shock and that it had temporarily shut down in order to preserve its integrity. He accepted this knowledge calmly and began to understand how Chevral must have felt when he had to leave his people behind in order to defend their way of life to the outsiders.

Thorne smiled slightly as he realised that these people were *indeed* the outsiders. He could never feel the same about them again. Before his transformation, he had felt nothing but hate and contempt for these people. However, after his transformation, all he felt was a sadness beyond tears. His face must have shown something, because a security guard approached him. "Are you alright, sir?"

Thorne was startled out of his reverie. He nodded and smiled. "*I am - are they?*"

The guard grinned. "*Adjustment takes time.*" he said, and walked on.

Thorne stared after him, open mouthed.

---oOo---

Trying to find some kind of normality, Thorne decided to sit in the departure lounge and wait for the announcement of his flight. He sat and watched as countless people walked with great purpose towards personal futures that were anything but certain and wondered why he didn't go and do the same. He sat and watched as the storm clouds gathered over the outside world and watched it rain as only the 'temperate' autumnal monsoons *could* rain.

Now this *was* familiar!

Global warming was increasing in magnitude. In the high season, it was suffocatingly warm. In the low season, it was frighteningly stormy – and this was in the *temperate* zones! The tropical zones were under constant siege from hurricane-force storms that had obliterated nearly all the exotic flora and fauna. Tourism to the tropics was dead. All measurements of the carnage wreaked was undertaken by the 'met sats' that were placed in geostationary orbit around the world. There had been mass migration from the tropics towards the 'temperate' zones (north and south) and draconian laws had been ratified giving executive authority to the military to control immigration. Public debate had been silenced as it was finally accepted that issues on human rights were a luxury that *no-one* could afford. The survival of the *species* – not the culture – was at stake.

Thorne reviewed the recent history of his part of the world. He recalled his country joining the Common Market (eco) and watched as it had mutated into the European Econonmic Community (eco/pol); then the European Community (pol); then the European Union (**pol**). In the space of a generation, it had abandoned its economic foundation and had become purely political. Following this, the climate had altered which had given the EU elite the perfect excuse to 'batten down the hatches' and impose draconian laws to 'protect' its citizens from waves of encroaching migrants. Due to increasing public unrest backed by liberation groups, there was a growing revolution. The illusion of a 'democratic' socialist government vanished and a counter-revolutionary (soviet) elite took control. The EU was briefly renamed the European Soviet Union. Eventually, even *that* pretence was dropped and it became the Soviet Union. 'Moscow' had simply moved west.

Thorne gave a little smile as he knew that politics flourishes under a stable economy, but a stable economy can only flourish under a stable *ecology* – and it was the ecology of the world that was under threat. Sure enough, the Soviet Union was fragmenting as even the military (who were *also* human!) were rebelling along with the citizens.

Thorne reviewed his past life as a journalist who had taken evil pleasure in distorting the truth in order to maximise sales. He looked with new eyes at his world and knew that no distortion was necessary. Merely *reporting* the truth was depressing enough!

Thorne looked at the lost animals in their funny clothing who were still pretending to be something that they never were and wondered how he could possibly help them.

"*The Divine Plan is Being fulfilled.*"

Thorne jerked awake. "The Divine Plan is being fulfilled?"

"*The Divine Plan is Being fulfilled.*"

Thorne pondered aloud. "Emphasis on *Being*, not being." He slowly started to make sense of the message and nodded to himself. "Yes, the Divine Plan is being fulfilled – according to temporal law, but the Divine Plan is *Being* fulfilled – according to eternal law. Death is inevitable for the saint or sinner and everything passes away according to temporal law, but the Divine Plan is inevitable according to eternal law! *Accept the inevitable, and the inevitable will accept you!*"

Further musings were interrupted as a soft musical chime sounded and a sickly sweet voice announced the arrival of his flight.

Thorne groaned as he was reminded of the 'touchy-feely, holdy-handy, wipey-arsey' image of the 'Nanny State' that concealed 'Big Brother' .....

Then he grinned.

..... The Divine Plan was taking care of *that* too!

---oOo---

Following a nauseating flight, Thorne sighed with relief when the aircraft actually touched down on the tarmac and wasn't spread all over it. He followed the customary security protocols and eventually retrieved his luggage in the pleasant surprise that it wasn't in Dubai, and celebrated by hailing a taxi.

As he had arrived home late that evening, he unpacked and realised that he should turn in for the night in order to be fresh for work on Oneday – damn..... *Monday!*

Settling down in bed, Thorne switched off the light and closed his eyes. As he was drifting off with a contented smile on his face, a horrible realisation dawned on him and his eyes snapped open.

"*SHIT!*"

He had been given six month's leave on an 'exclusive' but he couldn't tell a soul about his experiences with these people!

"*OH..... SHIT..... SHIT..... SHIT!*"

The Editor-in-Chief would have his bollocks for billiards!

Chapter 20

Monday morning arrived with horrible speed and Thorne was dreading getting out of bed. He lay on his back staring at the ceiling whilst recalling a Latin quotation that the potentially doomed gladiators gave to their living 'God.'

"*Ave Caesarem! Morituri te salutant!*"

"Hail Caesar! The doomed salute you!"

It was *most* appropriate.

Fortified with accepting the inevitable, he prepared to meet his maker.

---oOo---

After navigating the rain-soaked streets, Thorne finally pulled into the staff car park. He gingerly removed his journalist's bag containing the dossier, locked his car and entered the reception foyer. The receptionist looked up and greeted him with her well practiced and well polished smile. "Well *hello* Mr Thorne! I'll inform the Chief that you're back safe and sound!"

"On my way up." smiled Thorne, thinking of the elevator to the top floor. As the elevator doors closed, he sank back against one of its walls and closed his eyes. "On my way up!" he groaned. "*On my way out! I'm going to be crucified!*"

The elevator slid to a smooth halt and its doors parted to reveal a long corridor. He got out and walked its length with as much dignity as he could muster towards a door at its terminus. Finally arriving at the door, he paused, took a deep breath, mouthed "Shit" one more time and knocked.

"Enter!" boomed a voice that could have come from the grave.

Thorne entered the room and closed the door behind him. The Editor-in-Chief was standing at the window surveying the weather. He had his back to Thorne. "Well?"

"Yes, thank you!" blurted out Thorne before realising that the Chief wasn't inquiring after his health.

There was a noticeable pause from the Chief. "Well?" he repeated with deliberate patience.

"I can't do it!" said Thorne flatly.

"Can't do *what?*"

"I *won't* do it!" said Thorne coldly.

"*Won't* do what?"

"*I won't sell those people down the river!*"

It went horribly quiet. Still with his back to Thorne, the Chief finally spoke. "Am I to understand that you've had six months *paid* leave with *no results?*"

Thinking of the people, Thorne answered coldly but calmly. "Yes."

"*You're a bloody liar!*"

"*If I am, it'll be the last time I'll lie for YOU!*"

The Chief slowly nodded. "The truth at last!" He turned to face Thorne. It wasn't the expression on the Chief's face that drew Thorne's attention, but rather the colourful tie that the Chief wore. It was bright blue with gold leaves! The Chief noted the direction of Thorne's gaze and the cold expression on his face softened to one of gentle amusement. "I see you are admiring my tie!"

Thorne looked up at the Chief's face in silence. The Chief nodded in confirmation. "Me too!"

Thorne found his voice. "What are we going to do?"

"What are *you* going to do?" inquired the Chief.

"May I sit down? I need time to think."

"Good idea!" agreed the Chief.

As Thorne sat down, the Chief walked to a drinks cabinet and poured two drinks from a bottle. Returning, he sat down and offered Thorne a glass, and grinned. "Mead?"

"Thank's Chief!" said Thorne gratefully.

They both sat back in their chairs and sipped thoughtfully before Thorne spoke. "I know what has to be done, but how can I do it without affecting my people?"

The Chief smiled at Thorne's involuntary use of "*my*" people.

Thorne looked pointedly at the man behind the large oak desk. "I would appreciate your assistance, sir."

The Chief laughed out loud. "*SIR - is it?*"

Seeing the look on Thorne's face, the Chief understood it all and nodded in sympathy. "I'm willing to bet that this is the first time you have *ever* asked for help. Correct?"

Thorne looked down at the glass of amber nectar in his hands. "Yes, sir."

"Your experiences have affected you deeply – haven't they?"

"Yes, sir."

The Chief nodded again. "Rest assured, David, the Divine Plan *is* being fulfilled. All you need to do is to ensure that the truth is reported daily *without distortion as to the relative whole.*"

Thorne frowned. "*The truth, the **whole** truth and nothing but the truth?*"

The Chief nodded "*The core principle of Justice **is** sound!*"

"Are we not falling into the age old trap of Trial by Media?"

"Not if we stick to the facts and show the public how to discriminate again."

"Wasn't discrimination outlawed by the State decades ago as being seditious?"

"Discrimination in itself is *not* a dirty word – only its misapplication is. The 'elite' consider themselves to be the only group worthy to exercise discrimination on their own behalf *and on behalf of the rest of society*. They have 'justified' this pseudo-intellectual philosophy by de-engineering society over several generations to 'prove' their case. Public libraries were closed decades ago. The internet is State controlled. The only 'libraries' that truly show how we have regressed – historically/culturally – are held for archival research and for future planning by the 'elite' themselves."

"What about the universities? They have libraries that are full of knowledge!"

"The 'elite' are aware that knowledge without discrimination proves futile - even regressive. For the masses; posessing a degree can still open doors to many jobs, but by and large, *that is it*. They may advance technology but they cannot evolve society. Only those who are of the 'elite,' have the capacity to do this. The State has decreed that degrees are for *everyone* - if they can afford them, but the price is decades of debt if your family is not one of the 'chosen.' Debt is actually sanctioned by the State as it keeps everyone in their place and only the children of 'elite' families can gain degrees that permit entry into professions of State influence." The Chief winked and smiled. "Remember the State motto: *A place for everyone - and everyone in their place!*"

"That's not the State motto!"

"It might as well be!"

Thorne snorted. "Debt is actually *sanctioned* by the State?"

"Of course! Debt has become part of our culture! The State has seen to that! How many advertisements from loan shark - sorry - *credit companies* are transmitted by the vid-link system every day? How many are printed in magazines and newspapers? How many are fronted by ostensibly 'respectable' glamorous personalities?"

Thorne chuckled as he could think of one *particularly* attractive and talented woman who was mentally blessed but morally cursed - like so many academics who appeared to be of the 'elite' but were merely its well-paid tools. Thorne let out a sigh and his face became serious. "How's the food situation?"

"The land is under siege from excessive people and excessive water. What farmland is left is subject to erosion via increasing storm activity – there is no forest buttress left to lock down the soil."

"Cholera? Typhoid? Dysentery?"

"Like the ocean, rising steadily. Drains and sewers are constantly backing up despite record numbers of applications for practical apprenticeships – *beyond the academic*!"

"So it's too late for the artisans to do anything?"

"Too little, too late – *that's the story of debate*!"

"Starvation? Cannibalism?"

"Just a matter of time."

Thorne looked at the Chief. "*What was the point in sending me to that commune*?"

The Chief smiled and shrugged his shoulders. "Why not, my friend?"

"It's not as though I can *do* anything for humanity – it's too late!"

"Maybe so; but we *still* have a newspaper to run."

"With respect, Chief, *aren't we all in denial*?"

"Didn't *our* people teach you anything?"

Thorne frowned in thought. He had learned and experienced much during his six month 'exclusive;' so much in fact, that he had trouble recalling anything salient.

The Chief prompted him. "How about quality of life over quantity of life?"

Thorne grunted. "I think I see where this is going. You want me to tell everyone that everything is okay despite all evidence pointing to the contrary? What happened to the truth, the whole truth and nothing but the truth?"

"The truth can only take you so far and then a higher principle takes over."

"You want me to instill *faith* within humanity – by telling them the whole *truth*?"

"Consider it your assignment. You are to be Assistant Editor – Special Projects!"

Thorne looked at the Editor-in-Chief in such disbelief that the Chief started laughing and added "I haven't lost my marbles – trust me; or rather – have *faith* in me!"

Thorne looked at his options and shrugged his shoulders. "You're the boss!" He finished his drink and rose to leave. "Thank's for the drink, Chief."

The Chief nodded. "Leave your dossier of our people with me for security."

"Gladly!" said Thorne, handing it over.

The Editor-in-Chief smiled gently at his co-conspiritor.

As Thorne walked towards the door, the Chief raised his voice in familiar quotation: "*When beggars roam the streets, when plagues roam the land, when the people are made ignorant again – then the 'witch-hunts' will return. Be mindful!*"

Thorne paused at the door. "*We've had beggars and ignorance for decades!*"

"But no plagues of consequence, until now. *Another 'dark age' is upon us!*"

"I agree – unless the whole truth is told. But how will that instill *faith*?

"Because they are desperate; and desperate people are willing to listen!"

"Surely the reverse is true? Desperate people are tradtionally irrational!"

"Only as long as there is a glimmer of hope. We must destroy *all* hope….."

"….. *and then they will listen to us?*"…..*Who the hell are we?*"

The Chief smiled gently. "Welcome to the elite, my friend."

---oOo---

Thorne found himself outside the Chief's office lying with his back against the door breathing heavily. Numbly he walked the full length of the corridor towards the elevator doors and summoned it. The doors parted immediately and he descended several floors to his own level and stepped out into the corridor that led to the general office. As he opened the door he was greeted with shouts of familiar voices which he barely heard. He went over to his own desk and sat down as his co-workers plied him with eager questions concerning his extended vacation. By now some of his old self had returned and his customary phrase of 'no comment' brought jeers of mock anger from the crowd.

As he was starting to get up to psychological speed with events, his former superior walked over from her office at the end of the room and stood waiting for the noise to subdue. As the 'crowd' dispersed to their duties, Amanda Carter motioned him to her office. Walking through the door marked Assistant Editor (General Reporting), she sat down and motioned Thorne to do likewise. Contrary to her profession, she was a woman of few words. She gave a thin smile. "Why you and not me?"

"You're an Assistant Editor - besides you wouldn't have enjoyed the experience."

"How do you know?"

"Believe me, you would *not* have enjoyed the experience!"

She looked into Thorne's face for a few seconds and – detecting no lie – grunted. "The Chief has informed me of your promotion. I'm sorry you're leaving our team."

Thorne smiled in mock affection. "*Like hell you are!*" he thought.

Ignoring his smile, she continued. "What pisses me off is that you report to *him!*"

Thorne shrugged his shoulders.

Her eyes glittered angrily. "What *really* pisses me off is that you're watching *me!*

"What can I say?" he said mildly.

"Where's your dossier anyway?"

Thorne pointed a finger skywards.

"*Don't I even get to see it?*"

"I guess you don't, Amanda."

"*This cloak and dagger stuff.....*"

"..... really pisses you off?" volunteered Thorne, helpfully.

"Are you a bloody Mason?"

He shook his head "Nope!"

"*Are you telling the truth?*"

Thorne's eyes lit up with an unholy light, and he leaned towards her. She edged back as he gave her an inhuman smile. "*Oh yes, Amanda! I always tell the truth!*"

---oOo---

Amanda Carter proved most eager to assist Thorne. She organised the transfer of his desk equipment and all his belongings to an isolated office some distance down the corridor with such efficiency that he had to admit that he was impressed. He toyed with the idea of asking her out as a reward but wisely decided not to tempt fate!

Hermetically sealed in his office from the outsiders, he sat back in the old armchair that had been provided and surveyed his surroundings. Alone, he began to relax and started to access the 'library' within. Before his mind, numerous chains of disparate impressions started to link up and presented him with coherent information that made absolute sense to his nature. The trick would be to *adapt* this information so as to benefit a society whose own nature was at such variance with his.

Thorne 'saw' that even if the entire human race perished – bereft of its physical forms, it would still *not* ascend collectively to divine grace. Its discarnate energies would be confined indefinitely on earth due to the 'envelope' of high intensity electromagnetic radiation that enclosed the planet. The earth's magnetosphere was yet another barrier to be overcome. Normally invisible to terrestrial senses, it lit up when there was a burst of ions from the sun and these charged particles of energy that created the solar winds were deflected by the earth's shields. Beautiful dancing curtains of light could be seen from the polar regions as energy collided with energy. Aurora Borealis in the north and Aurora Australis in the south.

Returning to earth, Thorne realised that the only way humanity would be able to leave its prison would be to evolve to a higher state of existence. In order to *keep* evolving, humanity needed more time, coherent force and cohesive form. Somehow,

Thorne had to engineer the survival of humanity so that it could continue to grow – *in prison.*

He nodded to himself as he realised the difference between the mystic and the occultist. They were the carrot and he was the stick. Both were necessary if society was to evolve enough to become divine – *again!*

There was a quiet knock on the door. Thorne looked up "Enter!"

The Chief poked his head around the door. "Are you done?" he smiled.

Thorne grinned. "For now, sir. What can I do for you?"

The Chief shrugged his shoulders. "Any questions?"

Thorne motioned him to sit. "The earth's magnetosphere?"

The Chief smiled. "This world is rare. Orbiting within the 'life zone' of an ideal sun; it has the ideal combination of gases to form water and for life to evolve. It has an ideal atmosphere to burn away most small meteors that may impact on the earth and destroy life. It also has Jupiter, a huge 'neighbour' whose gravity attracts most large meteors away. The earth's magnetosphere *and* its ozone layer collectively act as a shield of protection and prevention. They both protect incarnate life forms from premature degredation via radiation. They also prevent discarnate life forces from premature dispersal." The Chief grinned at Thorne. "Physically and mentally, we are tied to this world – God thinks of everything! *God is God!*"

Thorne pondered aloud. "What if all humanity left the earth?"

"From one question comes two answers. If they left before their *time,* they would disperse and God would be diminished. If they left after their *time,* God would be 'restored to his throne' as the quotation goes."

"So we will *never* leave in fleets of starships?"

"That *is* science fiction!" grinned the Chief.

"Why is there a discrepancy between the numbers of incarnate and discarnate?"

"The question is actually irrelevant since you are trying to compare two states that are fundamentally different. There will always be a *physical* limitation on the *quantity* of incarnate life forms since they take *time* to evolve and *space* to manifest. There are no *spiritual* limitations to the *quality* of discarnate life forces and, being *discarnate*, temporal and spatial dimensional laws simply do not apply."

Thorne slowly nodded. "So although they are *compatible*, they are not *comparable*?"

"Precisely. However, some of the discarnate are more sensitive and they are more 'adept' at absorbing and processing impressions and information when they are incarnate on earth. Their evolution is more rapid and they are charged with specific duties that extend beyond the scope of 'normal' evolution."

Thorne looked at the Chief. "Are you saying that we are those adepts?"

The Chief nodded. "Where we lead, the rest must eventually follow."

Thorne leaned back in his chair and closed his eyes as he recalled the names of the highest 'grades' of existence. "Ipsissimus, Magus and Magister?"

The Chief shook his head. "Not quite. Those are abstract states of awareness that are beyond the Abyss separating awareness from knowledge. The adepts function at a far lower level and are still subject to many human frailties although if an adept were to *re*-incarnate it would be as an Exempt Adept."

"What am I then?" inquired Thorne.

The Chief smiled. "There are other states of adeptship and they are divided into the functions of the Greater and Lesser Adepts."

Thorne grunted. "Let me guess my title – *Lesser* Adept?"

The Chief laughed. "Don't fall into the trap of regarding 'grades' in themselves as being important. Your *state* is important – not your grade; besides, there are four more 'grades' that are theoretically inferior to your own!"

At this revelation, Thorne gave a little mischievous grin.

The Chief just shook his head as he recalled the numerous pseudo-orders whose members spent their entire lives just spouting ritual and collecting useless titles. "Imagine the pocket-watch. Inside there are many cogs that make it work. A few cogs are relatively large and the rest are relatively small. They all have their place and purpose and must all function well for the greater good of the pocket-watch."

Thorne nodded. "Unfortunately, the pocket watch does not regard the small cogs as equal in value to the large cogs – reward is disproportionate. The small cogs are often subject to productivity evaluations and criticism. If they screw up they get dismissed. The large cogs are seldom subject to such stringent checks. If *they* screw up they get laterally promoted – or they receive a golden handshake!"

"True. Even after many centuries of so-called evolution and enlightenment, we *still* have the pyramid of feudalism (double standards) at the core of our society. Another pyramid is also reflected in the form of Maslow's Hierarchy of Needs."

Thorne frowned. "Self-Preservation to Self-Actualisation. Isn't that just a scale that goes from purely objective to purely subjective?"

The Chief grinned at Thorne. "In essence, yes. But nature is re-writing the rule book which will eventually eliminate both of these pyramids of human behaviour. Society is destabilising to the point of fragmentation. Virtually everyone is at base level. All we have to do is to destroy all hope of recovery otherwise the old pattern will simply lie dormant to re-emerge later and society will have learned nothing – *again!*"

Thorne looked at the Chief and then through him as his mentor contacted something very unusual – yet strangely reassuring. Its presence filled the room and all feelings of personal futility vanished as *this* gestalt brought through immeasurable power.

Thorne was awestruck at the magnitude. He looked at his mentor. "*Is this God?*"

"No. *This* gestalt represents the unconscious aspect of collective humanity that has been held in thrall by aeons of social and spiritual repression. The gestalt you joined with in the commune is the Lesser Initiator. *This* is the Greater Initiator. It is known by various names – The Divine Link, The Holy Ghost, The Holy Shekinah or Bride of God. It is *not* God. God is Ultimate Perfection. God is One and *eternal*. *This* is the multifaceted *reflection* of God and is merely *immortal*. We are *its* children – with as many personalities as the The Holy Ghost itself. *We must lose all our personalities if we are to become eternal and One with God.*"

Thorne lost all trace of personality. He spoke neutrally. "*A new law I give unto you.*"

The Chief noted the change in Thorne as the projection of his personality vanished to reveal his *true* nature. The Chief looked through his assistant and spoke to the world. "An old law *must* die so that a new law may live."

---oOo---

'Coincidentally,' the world descended deeper into chaos via unconscious democratic consensus. Power had finally come to the people. The 'children' had finally begun to see through all the lies and deceptions of the State and had left 'nanny' in her nursery and 'big brother' in his fortress. All that remained was for the people to 'lose' one more thing – their fear of death. All down the ages, humanity had been conditioned to fear anything that resulted in death. This was stupid; death came to all. Death was feared because it manifested in many ways that could be reduced to four basic causes: War, Plague, Famine and of course, Death. It was the duty of the occult elite to show humanity how to overcome a fear of something that ended all suffering – something that life had *never* done!

Chapter 21

Ten years later, like the proverbial 'time traveller,' David Thorne, Assistant Editor (Special Projects) returned to the present day and looked again at the small grey flower that was forever imprisoned behind its invisible barrier and was reminded of his people in their grey hooded cloaks of winter. He sighed at his ten year tenure and his time-sense made him glance at the clock on the wall. It was time to join the gathering of senior staff to mark the retirement of the editor-in-chief.

Thorne rose from his desk and left his office. He quietly locked his door and walked down the corridor towards the elevator. As the elevator doors closed behind him, he grunted briefly at the thought of the office 'party.' Parties didn't exist any more – the state of the world had seen to that. It was an office 'gathering'- an occasion to mark the retirement of someone held in high esteem. Thorne snorted at the thought of such a word as 'retirement.' Retirement to where? To do what? Witness the destruction of humanity? Some retirement that was!

The doors opened and he exited the elevator to stand in the long corridor that led past the boardroom on one side and the executive suites on the other to terminate at the office of the editor-in-chief. The gathering itself was being held in the boardroom and Thorne could just make out muted conversation. As he entered, he was given a glass of wine. He spied the Chief in conversation with two of his executive editors and turned away to gaze out of the window at the impending storms.

A moment later, he felt a presence at his shoulder and turned to see the Chief motion him out of the boardroom towards his office.

Alone in the office of his mentor, Thorne waited in respectful silence. The Chief sat down and motioned Thorne to do likewise. The Chief toyed with his glass and looked directly at Thorne. "Not much of a party, is it?"

Thorne smiled thinly and shook his head. "No."

"Have you heard the latest reports?"

Thorne raised his eyebrows in query.

"All Wars have ended. Man has submitted to Man. The 'First Horseman' is gone."

"But?" prompted Thorne.

"Plagues and Famines have escalated. Man is yet to submit to God."

"The Will to Live is still strong in many people – and of course, *all* criminals!"

The Chief nodded. "Criminals are the tools of the State." He smiled at Thorne and shrugged his shoulders in resignation. "Things will simply become worse."

"Nature will see to that." smiled Thorne. "With a little help from us!"

---oOo---

The Chief grunted. "How are our reporting teams handling the escalating crises?"

"Grimly professional. They all understand my instructions to report and not create. Few transgress. Those that do are quickly corrected before going to print."

"Good. How is the fabled Ms Carter performing?"

Thorne grinned. "Surprisingly well, considering the pressure she is under. I make no pretence to liking her but I have to admit to respecting her professionalism."

"Rottweilers are seldom loved – but they have their uses!" agreed the Chief.

---oOo---

Thorne was silent for a while and then he spoke. "How far must events deteriorate?"

"Until the subconscious aspect of humanity becomes fully conscious. When *that* happens humanity will be in a position to purify itself. In so doing, it will collectively begin to embrace its true nature – free from multiple personalities. Its name will no longer be 'legion' – all psychoses will end. We will become *One* – with God."

"How many bodies will die?"

"*All* bodies die. That is the natural order."

"My mistake. How many bodies will die as a result of *these* events?"

The Chief pursed his lips "The Black Death was far greater than the Great Plague."

"Collectively, these plagues and famines will eclipse the former – won't they?"

"Collective humanity has given its unconscious democratic assent….."

"….. and we direct the forces that humanity has unleashed." finished Thorne.

"By natural law – indeed we do."

Thorne was silent.

The Chief looked at Thorne with infinite compassion. "Few there are who – in the fullness of sanity – would stand in my shoes. My dear friend, be eternally grateful that your state is less 'exalted' than mine. When the time of my 'retirement' comes, I must have completely abreacted all karma that I incurred for *and* from my work. All my debts must be cancelled – if I am to have any chance of ascending."

Thorne understood. "Any final instructions, sir?"

"Events are fully in motion and cannot be deflected from their course. I have anticipated the onset of power failures and have installed several large generators. We also have a large stockpile of fuel to power the same. All electronic, electrical and mechanical systems will continue to function. This city is sited well above the maximum predicted ocean level. All you have to do is to maintain the impetus and everything will fall into place in a totally natural way."

Thorne nodded. "Even so, our systems will eventually fail and we will be plunged into darkness to face a new grim dawn – until we die. Wealth and status will mean nothing. Everyone will be reduced to the lowest level of poverty. Humanity will finally experience global equality – below 'Third World' level."

The Chief agreed. "That is why we are doing what must be done. For the first time on this world, no-one will be in a position to rule another. There will be no armies to organise. In effect, we are 'wiping the slate clean' so that humanity may start afresh and evolve along the true path that leads to Divine Union."

"What of *our* people? Will they survive to guide humanity?"

The Chief smiled. "*Our* people have mastered mutability."

"What's *that* supposed to mean?"

The Chief drained his glass and set it down on his desk. Easing himself back in his chair he placed his fingers together as if in prayer and gazed into the middle distance. "When humanity begins to embrace the next phase of its evolution, our people will begin to embrace theirs. They must do this in order to *continually* guide humanity forward. When your work here is done, you will return home – to our community."

Thorne frowned, only partially understanding. "Is there provision for a final exodus?"

"Yes. Our agents have guaranteed us a final flight home two calendar months from today. You have full executive authority to act on my behalf. My two associates will not interfere with your decisions. Stick to the plan and then head for the airport. If necessary, I'll hold the flight until you arrive – any questions?"

Thorne pursued his journalist's instinct. "*Our* people have mastered mutability?"

"Sharp as ever!" admitted the Chief. "Very well, my friend; I'll level with you." He paused and looked momentarily skywards as if seeking approval. Finally, he nodded to himself and looked straight at Thorne. "Humanity will *never* evolve as long as it is subject to the laws of the animal kingdom. As long as humanity is incarnate, it will *never* know God. We cannot continue as we are. The 'End of Days' is nearly here. Why do you think criminals are protected by the State? Why do criminals seldom target the judiciary, politicians, probationists or liberalists? Because they are aware of the truth. Evil is allowed to increase to convince everyone that we shouldn't be here in the first place. Evil is *in*structive as well as *de*structive. All the principal holy and sacred works state that Satan is subordinate to God! What does *that* tell you?"

Thorne paused to allow his thoughts to re-cognise "God gave us free will to live and to learn, but now we have to learn and to leave. We have strayed and played for long enough – maybe longer than we should. We must grow up and leave the playground. If we won't be guided by God, then we will be driven by Satan." Thorne paused as he realised that there was One Divine Force that manifested in this dimension as Duality. Following the 2nd Hermetic Principle, the mystics and the occultists had sprung forth.

The Chief smiled. "Celestially united in principle. Terrestrially divided in practice!"

Thorne understood and followed his occult training by wisely remaining silent.

---oOo---

The Chief looked at him. "Any further questions?"

Thorne lowered his eyes in respect. "None, sir."

The Chief extended his hand. "Goodbye, my friend. The plane will leave at noon."

Thorne shook his hand. "Two calendar months. Noon."

Thorne left his mentor alone in his office and walked past the murmuring boardroom towards the elevator doors.

---oOo---

Alone in his own office, Thorne sat in silence for a long time. Finally, he took a deep breath, rose from his battered armchair and headed for the general office. Work gave one an identity, and right now, he needed one.

Over the last few years, the atmosphere of the general office had changed from one of frantic activity to one of serious maturity. Gone forever was the party atmosphere and the times of frivolity. The nervous uncertainties of life had given way to an inhuman acceptance of death. Everyone had found a far greater purpose in their existence than they had ever dreamed possible. They lived to serve humanity - regardless of profit.

All over the world, pockets of plague and famine had grown to become regions. No country was spared - whatever its former status. Initially, there had been riots in the streets of all urban environs. Armed conflict between nations had changed to armed conflict within nations. Finally, even *that* had ended as the truth was broadcast to all who would hear it. The subliminal suggestion that there was *no hope* was starting to take effect. Increasing numbers of people began displaying a surreal detatchment to life. Instead of talking as individuals, they began listening as a collective. Ironically, this state would have been ideal for *firmly* establishing the European Soviet Union as *all* aspects of 'seditious' discrimination - constructive *and* destructive was dying.

Supervising the control of distributed information, Thorne realised with a slight smile that he was in a role that paralleled or parodied a political officer for a commissariat.

This 'Union' would be infinite - *God willing!*

Chapter 22

Thorne spent the remaining two months on auto pilot. Each day, he would arrive at work two hours before the day shift started and go over all the latest reports that were sent by his journalists worldwide. He deliberately cultivated this approach in order to maintain continuity from the previous day and also to psychologically reassure all the operational staff under his supervision. To her credit, Amanda Carter did the same so that both of them would meet in her office to go over the reports together and discuss the 'effect' on society that their 'cause' would have. Wisely, they had decided to omit any reports of cannibalism as this would cause global unrest. Ironically, social order is preserved by *not* openly stating the whole truth. It is on key issues like this that the administrators of policy, legality, divinity etc. diverge. All bureaucracies adhere to their truth to a different degree. Eventually, each bureaucracy considers their truth to be *the* truth. Each bureaucracy demands public trust in truth. Trust is inconsistent.

---oOo---

Thorne knew why his mentor had asked not for trust, but for *faith* in his works. Faith was spiritual and could not be distorted via material circumstances – unlike 'trust.' Trust was requested and required between people who wished to profiteer in some way from each other. Trust was conditional for a terrestrial practice of some kind. Faith, however, was an absolute and unconditional submission to a celestial principle. The celestial realm by its very nature would be free of evil so trust was inconceivable. The terrestrial world, however, contained persons and systems that were essentially corrupt and had their price – subject to negotiation. All were tainted. No exceptions.

Before the 'End of Days;' there had been a multitude of criminals in 'civilisation.' They had operated from a principle of perverted conviction (*convicts*), whereas the 'civilised' bureaucracies had no faith at all. Thus, there had *always* been countless converts to evil (illegal and 'legal') and it would remain so until humanity was in a position to *evolve* faith and transcended corporeal form. For the *in*struction of those who had evolved 'eyes' to see, all the principal holy and sacred works had stated that 'evil would turn upon itself.' As the 'End of Days' had grown closer, evil's chaotic lesser agents had turned upon evil's orderly greater agencies. Eventually, all evil would self-cancel and humanity in its current form would die out. Thorne pondered these revelations as he and Amanda formulated their latest plan for publication.

Following the total collapse of the world's economy, all issues of the Tribune were produced, published and distributed free of charge. Thorne raised a wry eyebrow as he realised that it had taken the manifest threat of annihilation to catalyse the desired mutability of humanity. Thankfully, his *own* people were ahead of the game! Of late, he had been wondering how they would be able to fulfil *their* part in the Divine Plan.

Each evening, when he sat alone in his office, he would think of his people and recall with infinite fondness the faces of those he had encountered. Everyone was beautiful, the country was peaceful. Why in God's name had the outside world taken so long to change? *"To little too late - that's the story of debate!"* he reminded himself. One evening, he was so immersed in his thoughts that he wasn't aware that Amanda Carter had opened the door to his office. She was staring at him in horrified fascination.

Thorne was sitting motionless in his chair, his face expressionless, his eyes staring into infinity. From those eyes, two rivers of tears flowed unchecked.

Quickly recovering her composure and displaying unusual sensitivity, Amanda Carter gently closed his door and quietly returned to her own office. Alone in her sanctuary, she finally allowed her mask to slip and surrendered herself to the agony and futility of her own human existence.

---oOo---

The following morning, everyone turned up for work as 'normal' and settled down to the psychological security of their jobs. No-one got paid, but no-one cared. To have purpose was enough. As the day wore on, Thorne and Amanda noticed that there were slightly fewer international reports coming in. Some countries had gone silent. They both exchanged glances and nodded in mutual understanding. Wisely, they refrained from mentioning this to their colleagues in the general office and 'business' continued as usual.

The next day, the reasurring routine continued as before but with fewer world reports. By now, some of the staff had begun to notice this and the section leaders had given a meaningful glance at Thorne - who shook his head in silent negation. All the leaders understood and had started to busy their staff with old news to maintain the quantity if not the quality. A thinning newspaper was not good news for anyone.

The weeks went by and the reports dwindled to such a degree that even the office cat would have noticed that there was something amiss. One morning, near to the end of of Thorne's tenure, the staff had sat down at their desks and were facing a now silent sea of computer terminals. They waited and waited. Finally, the section leaders got up and walked to the door of Amanda Carter. Their spokesman, a union convenor or 'father of the chapel' knocked on her door and entered. He looked at his manager and shrugged his broad shoulders in resignation. "That's it boss!"

Amanda Carter nodded in appreciation. "Thanks for everything, Don. Tell everyone to go home on indefinite leave with my blessing. I'll tell David."

Don's granite face softened. "Goodbye Amanda, God bless."

She smiled a rare and beautiful smile. "You too, Don."

The door closed and she was alone again.

She sat for several minutes. When she emerged from her office, the general office was deserted. She surveyed the vast room and slowly walked towards the nearest terminal. Smiling slightly, she threw the switch and the hissing screen went silent. She walked to the next and did the same. She continued along all the rows, killing screen after screen and the hydra hissing slowly diminished. Eventually, she arrived at the final screen. She gazed at it and slowly smiled. Blowing it a kiss, she ended its life. Amanda walked towards the door that led out to the main corridor. On the wall, there were a series of light switches. One by one, she killed those too. As she opened the door, she paused and turned to view her silent temple. "Goodbye, my children." she murmured and, closing the door on her profession, she went to inform Thorne.

Pausing at his door, she took a breath and then knocked loudly.

"Come in, Amanda." said a voice that sounded strangely alien.

"Creepy!" muttered Amanda as she entered his office.

Thorne motioned her to a chair and rose to open a familiar looking drinks cabinet that had been thoughtfully provided by his mentor. He poured two glasses of amber nectar from a decanter and offered one to Amanda before resuming his seat.

Cautiously, she sniffed it and looked faintly surprised. "Mead?"

Thorne smiled in fond memory. "A gift from the Chief."

Amanda opened her mouth to inform him of the exodus but Thorne raised a hand in negation. "No need, Amanda, I already know."

"You know this already? How?"

Thorne smiled a tired smile "Because it had to happen and you acted correctly."

"Am I so obvious, David?"

"Of late, everything is!" Thorne indicated the drink in her hand. "It's safe to drink."

Amanda eyed the glass of golden dancing light. "Safer than the water, anyway!"

Thorne chuckled indulgently for her benefit and raised his glass. "Your health."

She smiled in resignation and with a strange degree of fondness. "Yours too."

Together, they sipped their mead in an easy silence like two old friends.

When they had finished, Thorne poured her another, and another for himself.

Amanda raised her eyebrows. "Party time is it?"

"Party lights out – I'm killing the generators."

She smiled in mock playfulness. "Ooh! Can I come and play?"

"Bring the decanter, we'll do it together." he grinned.

Like two naughty schoolchildren, Thorne and Amanda went down to the basement to commit industrial anarchy. Sensibly, they chose the stairs since the elevators would be useless after shutdown. Amanda pocketed a torch and together, they began to walk downstairs towards the growing sound of generators in the distance. As they reached basement level, the temperature had become considerably warmer. They looked at each other and blew out their cheeks as much as from alchohol as from warmth. They then began to walk towards the humming giants that were providing life for the entire building since the failure of the power grids several weeks ago. Arriving between the two giants, Thorne and Amanda couldn't resist a drunken giggle when they saw that the plant engineer had painted a name on each of the monsters. Thorne refilled his and Amanda's glass. "Here's to Sodom and Gomorrah!" he pronounced solemnly.

"Sodom and Gomorrah!" added Amanda swaying slightly.

Thorne waved expansively. "Ladies first!"

Amanda eyed Thorne and then shrugged her shoulders. "To hell with feminism and political correctness – *sod 'em* in fact!" Her face beamed. "I'll take Sodom please!"

Thorne grinned. "I'll take Gomorrah."

They each stood by switchgear that was linked to each giant and exchanged glances.

"Goodbye Sodom." intoned Amanda throwing a switch.

"Goodby Gomorrah." stated Thorne doing likewise.

In the silence and darkness a little voice spoke. "Torch please, Ms Carter!"

He heard a muffled giggle and then felt two hands around his waist. Instantly sober, he quickly removed her hands as they had begun a journey into forbidden territory. "No, Amanda!"

He felt her body press against his and backed away.

"*I said no!*"

There was a pause; then a torch light flashed in his face.

"*For Christ's sake – lighten up Dave! It's the end of the bloody world!*"

Thorne's eyes winced in the harsh light and he shielded his eyes. "*I know!*"

Amanda sounded annoyed. "*If we've got to go, lets go with a bang – not a whimper!*"

Thorne's voice was cold. "And that's your problem!"

"*My* problem?"

"The problem that *all* modern feminist women have!"

"*What the hell's that suppost to mean?*"

"Why do think increasing numbers of men are turning off to women and are leaving them alone to fend for themselves? Why has the sperm count dropped to almost sterile levels, despite State sanctioned social engineering in the form of sperm banks? Why has homosexuality increased with every generation?"

"Because men lost the battle for supremacy! They cannot control women any more! They cannot compete against women! At nearly every level, they are inferior to women and they know it! Their bodies *certainly* know it – hence the sperm count! All they can do is to turn to each other for solace – hence the rise in homosexuality!"

"I agree." said Thorne, simply.

"You….. *agree*?" said Amanda, incredulously.

"I agree." confirmed Thorne. "Sensitive men seek love and co-operation. If they are unable to find a sensitive woman – and there are precious few indeed – they often feel compelled to seek it elsewhere. Invariably, they are forced to look to others of their kind for solace rather than risk embracing women who often prove to be demanding and demeaning. Only an aggressive or a vindictive man would seek lust, competition and domination over a woman."

"Wow!" said Amanda after a pause. "I didn't know you batted for the other side!"

"I don't." replied Thorne.

"What *are* you, then?"

"In essence, I am hetero*sensual*, but asexual."

"So you're happy to take a girl *halfway* to heaven and then you run? You bastard!"

"Mind games are wasted on me. Are you willing to listen to me, or not?"

Amanda paused and then grunted. "Okay David, I'm listening."

"Turn your spotlight off and let's sit on the floor."

There was an obliging 'click' and they were surrounded in a warm velvety darkness.

Thorne sat down next to Amanda and took a deep breath. "Many years ago, when I actually believed that human love was possible, I tried to find a woman who did *not* rely on me for lust or passion in order to be satisfied. I have always been convinced that any woman who relies on *me* for lust and passion in order to give *her* satisfaction is immature and lacking in self-confidence. There are so many of these 'independent' women who all too easily transfer their affections and attendant diseases from partner to partner like insatiable vampires. This is *not* love! I personally, have no concept of lust and cannot do 'quickies' in exotic positions. The 'thrill' of dynamic, gymnastic explosive passion has no meaning. Indeed, I regard passion as simply the release of tension that has built up between a couple who are actually *in*compatible. In sports parlance, I did marathons, not sprints, and I favoured artistic impression much more than technical merit. I am convinced that a healthy *mature* woman has the capacity to enjoy the pleasures of her own body and also has the confidence to openly express it. Such a woman is truly *beautiful* and she earns my admiration. I would have loved to have found such a magnificent woman because I could only *enhance* her personal satisfaction and not be under any psychological pressure to create it. A wise man should accept that he cannot compete successfully against a woman's fully released libido and should be content to support her intimately as *she* requires."

There was a long uncomfortable silence. Finally Amanda spoke. "Well, bugger me!"

"I'd rather not." replied Thorne, tapping 'Sodom' behind him.

In the darkness, the sounds of Amanda's sniggers mutated into cackles of laughter.

Thorne sulked – an expression completely lost in the darkness. "Bitch!"

The cackles became howls of mirth as Amanda totally lost control.

---oOo---

After what seemed like an eternity, the laughter started to diminish into chuckles and eventually became a merciful pause interspersed with the occasional giggle. Finally, there was a respectful silence.

Thorne rose with gentle dignity. "We're finished here, Amanda. Let's go home."

Amanda's voice sounded strange. "Please stay, David – for a while at least."

Somewhat puzzled, Thorne obligingly sat down again.

Amanda took a deep breath. "I don't want to die alone." She took another breath. "All my life, I've lived alone and kidded myself that I was independent and 'top dog' in my profession." She laughed bitterly. "Top dog my arse! Top *bitch* more like! Everyone referred to me as 'the rottweiler' and they were right! Sure, I got the results and I got them fast. I got promoted, but at what price? Plenty of money but no-one to love !" She snorted in self-disgust. "And from this day forward, I have no job, I have no identity and all the 'money' I made is now worthless since the market meltdown. *What the hell have I achieved?* I *have* nothing, I *am* nothing – and I'll die alone!"

"That is everyone's destiny." said Thorne, gently.

"Cheer me up, David. Lie to me a little!"

Thorne put his arm around Amanda and – pulling her towards him, he kissed her on the top of her head. "*I* love you, Amanda."

She snuggled up to him for warmth and comfort. "Lying bastard." she smiled.

Thorne's sincerity proved the folly of her words.

"David?"

"*David!*"

"*Dav….. ohh….. OHH….. Jeeesus!*"

---oOo---

Several hours later, Amanda lay in a happy soggy heap, snoring gently. Protectively, Thorne lay next to her and was pleased with the results. Making love without sex was far more intense and pleasurable. It brought out the highly creative artist in him and she proved a very willing canvas for his brush strokes. Idly, he wondered what would happen if he took his pleasure with her body whilst she was asleep. Instantaneously, his spiritual 'twin'informed him that, whilst making love was beautiful and spiritual, having sex was potentially regressive - and definitely not for him!

He felt her stir against his body and heard a deep yawn. "What time is it?" she asked.

Thorne gazed at the luminous dials of his watch. "Still light outside." he said.

There was a 'click' and a beam of light shone on the floor in the direction of the stairs. "Give me a moment to tidy myself, and I'll be with you."

Obediently, Thorne faced the direction of the stairs and waited for Amanda to finish rearranging her clothing. A minute later, he felt her hand slip into his and they both carefully retraced their steps towards the basement exit. Slowly, they mounted the stairs and eventually, they emerged into the main corridor at ground level. Hand in hand, they walked down the corridor and through the now-deserted main reception to stand outside.

Hand in hand, they surveyed the devastation around them as if for the first time. The streets were deserted, rubbish was strewn everywhere. Pages torn from a newspaper were blown across the road, empty cans rattled as they too were blown along by the gusts of wind that rose and fell. Countless bottles lay smashed on the pavement and scores of shop windows had been vandalised and looted many months before the final crackdown of governmental paramilitary forces. Anyone caught in the act of looting or vandalism was simply shot on sight. The forces had done their work with ruthless efficiency and had moved on to other areas. Those that remained stayed indoors with their supplies and quietly killed time, knowing with certainty that time would quietly kill them.

Thorne, Amanda and all their colleagues had done well in demotivating everyone's sense of survival into a surreal dreamlike detachment. Everyone was free to do what they liked as long as they did it quietly. Knowing that they had now joined the ranks of the futile, Thorne guided Amanda to his car that was parked outside the reception. They both carried automatic pistols for personal protection. These had been provided by the former editor-in-chief, who, because of his position as one who wielded influence in social engineering (media division), had been granted certain State liberties that had extended to his senior staff.

Amanda indicated her own vehicle. "I have my own transport."

Thorne opened the trunk of his car. "How many cans of fuel reserves?"

Amanda grunted. "Two."

Thorne indicated his own reserves. "Three."

Amanda nodded. "Together we have five cans – and six clips of ammunition."

Thorne smiled. "More than enough!"

"For what?"

"You live at the other side of town and I live at the outskirts – near the airport."

Amanda frowned. "So what?"

Thorne looked her directly in the face. "In three days time, precisely at noon, we need to be at the airport to board a final flight."

"Why? What's going on?"

Thorne grinned. "You always wanted to know about the place I visited, didn't you?"

Amanda's eyes widened. "You mean we're going *there*?"

Thorned nodded, pleased with her look of incredulity. "I suggest we combine our reserves and spend the remaining days at my place with a view to getting the hell out of here – *together*!"

"Agreed! First we have to swing by my place to pick up a few supplies and then it's your place!" Amanda walked to her car and opened its trunk to reveal two jerry cans of fuel. She returned to Thorne's car and dumped them in. Turning to her own car, she blew it a kiss and jumped into the passenger seat beside Thorne. As they pulled away, both their eyes were scanning the streets for any signs of trouble. Finaly, she relaxed and glanced at Thorne with a look of relief on her face and smiled. "It makes sense!"

Their journey through the city proved uneventful. Even so, the signs of devastation were everywhere. The few people they encountered quickly disappeared into gutted buildings with their ill-gotten gains. It was a ghost city. Only the desperate would brave the streets to acquire something of dubious value. All mains power was gone. Soon, the generators that powered the water purification and sewage sanitation plants would run out of fuel. The city hospital had been ransacked by gangs of drug addicts months ago. As they drove by the carnage, Amanda glanced at Thorne. "*This is the end, isn't it?*"

"Incarnate humanity has outlived its purpose and faces extinction. The life-force will reabsorb all required life-forms. It will go through a period of consolidation. In time, it will begin a new phase of expansion with new life-forms." Thorne's face clouded for a moment and then he slowly started to smile. "*Or not.*"

Amanda looked surprised. "*Or not?*"

Thorne smiled broadly. "*Not!*"

Amanda shivered. "You're creeping me out, what the hell do you mean?"

Thorne chuckled. "Remind me to tell you after you have met my people."

Strangely submissive, Amanda nodded. "Okay." After another half mile, they turned down a side street. "Here." she said.

After a brief check on the surrounding buildings, they entered the apartment block and began a trudge up the stairs as the elevators had expired long ago. Finally, they arrived at the door to Amanda's apartment. She let them both in and immediately began to sort out her supplies and clothing on the bed. "Grab some booze, it's the only safe stuff to drink!" she yelled as she shoved her essentials into a suitcase and slammed down the lid.

"Thanks Amanda, but I prefer to remain sober – at least until we arrive in haven."

Pausing, Amanda looked over her shoulder. "Did you say *heaven*?" she yelled.

Thorne stuck his head through the open doorway. "That comes after!" he said.

Ten minutes later, they were speeding away from her apartment back the way they had come. By now, it was growing dark and they were anxious to get out of the city centre to avoid any potential trouble. Although they were armed, neither felt secure enough to be stupid. They spent a good thirty minutes worrying if they were being followed, but the entire populace appeared to be shut up in their own buildings and occupied with their own thoughts.

By the time they arrived at Thorne's home, it was pitch black. Fortunately, his house was at the end of a small lane that was some distance from the main road. Amanda breathed a quiet sigh of relief. "Isolated and hidden. Still our best defence!"

"As is our destination." replied Thorne, carrying her suitcase indoors.

Amanda followed behind Thorne and gave her new 'home' a quick appraisal. It was the home of a confirmed bachellor. There was a place for everything and everything was in its place. The walls were off-white and simply decorated. The whole effect was to indicate that the owner strove for an order and a purity that was just beyond his natural capacity to attain. An 'almost-but-not-quite' kind of man. Amanda frowned; something was missing! But what? His personal collections were certainly described as eclectic and indicated a man of broad tastes, but also a man whose overall view on life was one of quests abandoned. It was as if a stranger had been marooned on this world and had tried to fit in to hide his origins – from others and from himself. Amanda nodded to herself. He needed the company of a woman who would help him connect with life (such as it was); who would show him what it was like to be fully human; who would be his 'eyes' and who would always be there to provide him with the warm safe haven of her body – with absolutely no demands on his 'performance.' Essentially, Amanda was a self-fulfilled woman, and she knew it. She could give him everything he needed without feeling short-changed in the process. Amanda allowed herself a little smile.

"I'm glad you like the place." said Thorne, neglecting to scan her before making such an assumption.

Amanda simply smiled and nodded, saying nothing.

Being mindful of the need for a prompt arrival at the airport in three days time, they unpacked only what they immediately needed. Everything else remained in two suitcases – 'his & hers.' As a newly established couple, they discussed ground rules and both agreed that they would sleep together after each romantic episode, but one would sleep in the spare room under normal conditions – guaranteeing genuine rest. As Thorne's guest, Amanda insisted on using the guest room for herself. Thorne was quietly impressed – feminism had certain advantages after all!

With a simple arrangement and few rules but clear ones, Thorne and Amanda quickly grew comfortable in each other's company and the three remaining days were spent in very pleasurable dawn and dusk indulgences.

Chapter 23

On the morning of their departure – after assisting Amanda in a particularly prolonged period of self-indulgence, they eventually surfaced and braved a cold shower together. Stepping outside, they dried each other and quickly got dressed as the wind picked up and the rain scythed down. Anticipating an increase in storm activity, many buildings had been upgraded, but structural integrity in some was at its limit. As Thorne and Amanda left the bathroom for the kitchen, there was a groan followed by a crash as a building collapsed nearby. They both froze. "*Shite!*" they exclaimed in unison.

After sharing a nervous breakfast of a can of (cold) beans and a can of (hot?) dogs, they were packed and ready within minutes. Before they left, Thorne spent a few moments looking at all the possessions he would be leaving behind and shaking his head in silent regret. He then walked back to Amanda and shrugged his shoulders in philosophical submission. "Sic transit gloria mundi!"

"The world's glories *are* transient." Amanda smiled.

Minutes later, they were heading for the airport leaving behind a 'civilised' world that was in its final death throes.

---oOo---

Their journey to the airport was mercifully uneventful. They passed a few abandoned cars whose lives had been prematurely terminated due to a shortage of fuel. Thorne and Amanda were very grateful that their former chief had shown such foresight.

As they entered the airport, their eyes were searching the terrain for any danger, but once again, their fears were unnecessary. The airport buildings had been gutted for supplies of food, alchohol, cigarettes and anything that desperate minds could regard as potentially having 'survival' value. The 'locusts' had stripped everything and had moved on in search of fresh pastures that were quickly vanishing.

Thorne and Amanda decided to park as near to the main runway as they could and just quietly sit it out – keeping their loaded automatics close by. Thorne gazed at his watch and looked across at Amanda. "One hour to go."

Waiting for that hour to pass proved to be the longest hour that they would ever experience. Several times one or the other would glance into the sky imagining that they had heard the sound of an approaching aircraft. Towards the end, Thorne and Amanda were becoming extremely nervous as the *torment of hope* played them false and false and false again. Finally, Amanda broke down – tears streaming down her face. Thorne put his arms around her and held her tightly.

They held each other for ages in a state of desperate devotion. They heard the wind picking up and growing in volume and still they held onto each other. They realised that they loved each other and that *even death itself* would never part them. The wind howled and shook their car. It rose in pitch to a deafening scream which finally made them look up from their embrace.

"Are you two going to sit and grope each other – or are you coming aboard?"

They both jumped at the sound of that familiar voice and quickly exited the car to find a private jet parked uncomfortably close, the engines lowering in pitch to a loud whine.

The Chief eyed the two vacant faces of his subordinates as they almost fell inside the aircraft. "Sorry for the slight delay, things on earth are getting really shitty now!"

Thorne and Amanda sat down and buckled in. Automatically, Thorne turned to the Chief for the latest news. The Chief read his mind and spoke first. "Really shitty! Earth's temperate zones are going under with typhoid and cholera. The sub-tropics have gone under with malaria and ebola-like plagues As the temperate zones become warmer, the malarial and necrotising plagues will follow. Dysentery is widespread. The *good* news is that the storms are destroying all locust migration from the tropics outwards!"

"That *is* good news!" remarked Thorne, dryly.

"Do you want the rest?" inquired the Chief.

"There's *more?*" exclaimed Thorne.

"For a long time, the earth will get warmer and wetter. Nearly all animals will die out. Only the insects will remain relatively intact. This world will become one vast malarial swamp." The Chief paused and looked at Thorne, who raised his eyebrows in further quiery. His mentor nodded in response and continued. "This, however, is not permament. Eventually, the world temperature will drop like a stone and it will enter another ice age. *Humanity flourished within an inter-glacial period.* Overall, this world is *cooling.* There have been ice ages before, there will be ice ages again."

Thorne looked at Amanda. They both looked at the Chief, who smiled at them like an indulgent father. "Global warming is true – from *one* level of vision. Global freezing is also true – from *another* level of vision. There is no *actual* conflict of opinions!"

Thorne nodded. "Time-frame reference is always relative to one's level of vision."

"Precisely!" agreed the Chief. "There is no *actual* paradox!"

Amanda finally found her voice. "*Who are you people?*"

The Chief looked at Amanda with a curious smile. "You have been working for us all these years – *and yet you do not know who we are?*"

Amanda frowned, her eyes blinking rapidly as her conscious intellect fought to accept what her sub-conscious intuition was telling her. She looked incredulous and shook her head in denial. "No! We've written for decades about the global conspiracies of the shadowy elite! We *can't* be part of it! *I* can't be part of it!" she looked helplessly at the Chief. "*I can't be!*"

"I do believe that your intellect has just caught up with your intuition."

Amanda looked back at Thorne, who merely nodded in confirmation.

Stunned by her own self-revelation, she gazed out of the window.

"Too late to jump!" grinned the Chief. "Enjoy the ride!"

---oOo---

For the next hour, Amanda sat in silence, her eyes closed, trying to make sense of her former job. Finally, emerging from her self imposed exile, she opened her eyes and addressed the cabin generally. "I thought women were the predators and men were just prey – or tools to be used to further the aims of women."

"Because it suited the State." said the Chief, gently. "Knowing the feminist ego, we had been closely watching as the State had – over the generations – been encouraging feminist women into areas of social and professional dominance over the masses. We knew that 'progressive' man was easily influenced by women and that 'traditional' man was virtually obsolete. We knew that a willing woman was easily manipulated as her ego blinded her to the truth. We watched as the State provided more and more for the needs of all those who felt aggrieved in order to convice them that they and the State actually shared common aims. The State controlled everyone via the egos of all who felt short-changed in life – *and <u>everyone</u> was made to feel short-changed!*"

Amanda looked into the middle distance as she quietly digested all that she had been told. Finally, her eyes refocussed. "Are we agents of the State – or something else?"

The Chief nodded approvingly. "We appear to be agents of social regulation. We are actually agents of spiritual evolution."

"What's that supposed to mean?"

"As long as humanity remains incarnate, we act as guards – enforcers – in order to preserve humanity in its current form. This has always been our duty to humanity. But, when humanity becomes discarnate, we act as guides – enhancers – in order to transform humanity into future force. This has always been our duty to divinity."

"So it is our divine destiny to become extinct?"

"From this current form – emphatically: *Yes!*"

Amanda pondered aloud. "Am I correct in assuming that the State is aware of 'us' in our current capacity as social enforcers?"

"Correct. We are the servants of the State."

Amanda frowned. "Am I also correct in assuming that the State is *not* aware of 'us' in our future capacity as spiritual enhancers?"

"Correct. We are the masters of the State."

Amanda did a double-take. "*So the servant is really the master?*"

"The paradox only appears as such – from *one* level of vision." The Chief closed his eyes. "Those who *command* always require support. Those who *create* – do not."

Thorne whispered in Amanda's ear. "The ultimate *creator* is God. Because God is the creator, God is alone – requiring no support whatsoever. Ergo: *God is One!*"

Amanda winced and shook her head as she tried – without success – to assimilate what her former colleagues were telling her. Searching for some kind of normality in an increasingly abnormal existence, she inquired how long the flight would take.

"About two more hours." came the reply.

Amanda sighed in resignation and let her eyes wander around the interior of the small passenger compartment. She blinked in surprise as her gaze fastened upon a little old man who was sitting in a seat in front of hers on the opposite side of the aisle. His lined face had the appearance of yellow parchment – which matched the saffron robes he wore underneath a dark red outer garment. He wore a necklace of alternating beads of amber and jet and his small sandaled feet didn't even touch the floor. Amanda felt a knot in her stomach and a chill ran down her spine. She had been aboard this small private jet for an hour already and she had never noticed him before! He must have sensed her gaze as he turned his face towards her and smiled gently. She frantically dug Thorne in the ribs with her elbow. "*Who the hell is he*?" she whispered to him.

It was the Chief's voice that spoke behind them. "If he's here, it's a good omen."

The words were barely out of the Chief's mouth when there was an announcement from the flight-deck. "We are approaching heavy storm clouds, please prepare for some turbulence."

Thorne and Amanda turned sour eyes on the Chief – who shrugged his shoulders apologetically. "I never said I was perfect!"

"Some turbulence!" stated Thorne.

"Good omen!" muttered Amanda.

The next two hours were spent in relative hell as the pilot of their aircraft fought the continual onslaught of the storm. Thorne had never liked 'funfairs' as he considered that the idea of being thrown around in all directions was certainly *not* fun! He and Amanda proved that they would have made excellent gunslingers as their vomit bags were drawn and ready for action before they themselves were aware of it. They soon learned to 'go with the flow' and were thus kept so occupied that they never had time to feel terror of the flight itself. Periodically, Thorne or Amanda would look up from the contents of their bag and their eyes would meet those of their strange 'companion' whose face held no trace of fear whatsoever. Unusually, the two hours seemed to fly by and they were vaguely aware that the pilot had announced that they were starting their descent towards the commune itself.

Ashen faced, Thorne and Amanda looked at each other, and then Thorne remembered that there was no actual runway at the commune. He mentioned this to Amanda.

"No bloody runway? How the hell are we going to land – in one piece?"

"The highway has been cleared of abandoned vehicles." said the Chief.

Amanda groaned at the thought of landing on an ordinary road.

Thorne remembered his taxi journey and felt relief. "The road is straight for miles."

Unimpressed, Amanda groaned and threw up again.

As the aircraft descended, the storm clouds gradually thinned out so that the highway came into view whilst they were still a few hundred feet from the ground. They both breathed a huge sigh of relief as the pilot informed them that landing would present no problems. Amanda risked a quick look across at the little man who was sitting on the other side of the central aisle. He merely grinned and gave her a wink. Amanda's gaze was drawn in the opposite direction out of her window to the land that was rising up to meet them. She had never been in an aircraft that had landed on a highway, and decided on balance that she would take *this* experience to the grave – if it was going to be her last!

There was a whine and a slight jolt as the landing gear extended followed by some slight buffeting as the spoilers extended to increase drag and reduce the airspeed. The ground quickly rose and the aircraft's nose lifted slightly to allow the rear wheels first contact. There was a jolt and a squeak as the tyres picked up ground speed. The nose lowered to allow the third wheel contact with the road and then there was a roar as the twin engines were thrown into reverse thrust and the air and disc brakes were applied to bring the jet to a controlled ground cruise.

As they cruised along the road, Thorne and Amanda finally relaxed and celebrated by throwing up in unison. When they had completely emptied their stomachs, they looked at each other and then across the aisle to a now vacant seat.

Their little 'friend' had disappeared.

"*A good omen.*" reminded the Chief.

Reverse thrust was cancelled and the aircraft simply cruised along the road for several hundred feet. Finally, the whine of the engines diminished and they slowed to a halt. As they gingely disembarked, Thorne recognised the narrow track that ran for several miles across the fields to terminate at the forested hill.

As their feet touched terra firma, Thorne and Amanda heaved a huge sigh of relief and turned to see their Chief and the pilot exit the jet with little apparent concern. The Chief noticed their gaze and beamed as he produced a small bottle and shook its contents playfully under their noses. "Pilot's Pills! Very effective for air sickness!"

Thorne and Amanda groaned and cast evil glances in his direction.

The Chief's face fell. "Oh dear!" Clearing his throat, he quickly took the lead along the track that led over the fields towards their final terrestrial destination. Thorne and Amanda walked in stony silence until the group had finally left the fields and climbed the hill to stand before the two huge oaks that fronted the great forest.

Pausing between the oaks, the Chief turned and gazed at his friends with a remarkable degree of fondness that made both Thorne and Amanda's restrained anger evaporate. Together, they journeyed through the ancient forest that still afforded them protection from the storm-level winds that raged outside. Noting the change, Amanda broke the silence to ask how it was possible for the forest to withstand such chaos as countless forests had succumbed over the years.

"There are several factors that when combined, form an almost impenetrable barrier to such events. Firsly, the forest is ancient, its roots go deep. Secondly, the soil has been impacted over the centuries, it has never been distrubed. Thirdly, all the trees support each other by growing closely together and intertwining branches and roots into one solid mass. A solid forest buttress securing heavily impacted soil cannot succumb to storms alone!" The Chief paused and turned to face them – his hands cupped together as if in prayer. "The ovoid shape of the forest acts to deflect the wind around it. What little wind penetrates dissipates within the first few hundred feet of the forest wall. This forest has grown in this shape because the prevailing winds have removed all deviations that would run contrary to the forces of nature!"

Amanda looked to Thorne for clarification of this last point. "The Chief is saying that this forest has remained this way for many centuries because no other shape or form is possible. *It has evolved itself into the ideal pattern for self-preservation.*"

Amanda pondered aloud. "So forces *antagonistic* to forms actually cause those forms to evolve into the pattern that is ideal for optimum survival!"

Chapter Twenty-three

Thorne and the Chief nodded in unison. "Out of evil....."

"..... comes good!" finished Amanda.

"Any air-borne plagues are likewise deflected." added the Chief with a smile.

"Infectious plagues, *yes*. Contagious plagues, *no*." reminded Thorne gently.

"True!" sighed the Chief. "But time is *still* on our side – for a while!"

The group continued on their journey for a while before Thorne addressed the Chief. "There *is* a way for infectious plagues to affect the commune."

"How's that?" inquired the Chief.

"The underground streams for the wells and the river that flows through the country."

"The underground streams flow through miles of rock that acts as a filtration system. In times of plague, the water is always boiled before drinking. The river is more of a problem. In the ancient past, the mills near the river were abandoned and all the grain was ground in domestic querns in the kitchens of every house. All the fields that were by the river were avoided and allowed to grow fallow. The bridge was the only area that brought the people close to the river. As protection from the vapours, the entire bridge was boxed in and canvassed. Those that crossed always covered their faces."

Thorne grunted and nodded in satisfaction. As they arrived at the border post with its familiar striped pole, Thorne stopped and frowned as he realised that it was the winter season – the hut was *visible*, as was the path from the beginning. *Where was the mist?*

"Chief." said Thorne, uncertainly.

Noting the change of tone in Thorne's voice, the Chief paused to look at his assistant. "What is it my friend?"

"We have walked a mile through the forest and it is the winter season. We shouldn't even be able to get *this* far! *Where is the protective barrier of mist?*

The Chief nodded sadly. "Communal protection is no longer required. Our gestalt is concentrating its energies in other areas."

Thorne frowned. "Such as?"

"Such as our little companion in the aircraft. He was manifested to reassure us."

"*That was our gestalt?*"

"An *aspect*, yes. Our little friend was a manifested thought form - a tulpa."

"A tulpa?"

"Tulpas are quite well known to Tibetan mystics. They exist as exemplars, they serve a semi-divine purpose before being reabsorbed into the collective. Tulpas can also be created magically by individual magicians. However, these latter creations invariably degenerate into unholy entities."

"Oh Christ!" muttered Amanda.

The Chief smiled gently at Amanda. "Do not be afraid, my dear. He was generated by the collective - not conjured by an individual."

Amanda managed a weak smile.

Thorne looked across the clearing towards the wooden hut that had held the beginning of such fond memories. There was no guardian. No Tyler to symbolically protect the sanctuary of the sacred commune from the profane. The profane were finally running out of ritualistic games to play. They faced extinction – as all incarnate species do.

As they ducked under the striped pole and deeper into the forest, Thorne took hold of Amanda's shaking hand. He nodded in silent confirmation. The commune would be their final terrestrial destination.

Chapter 24

The rest of their journey passed uneventfully. They walked between the two huge expanses of meadow, down through the hives where all was silent (the bees being in winter shutdown mode) and up the other side where, in the distance, a familiar landau was waiting for them. As they approached, a thin somber figure in green dismounted from above and beckoned them into the coach. "Thank you, Garfield." said the Chief as he followed the rest of the group into the passenger compartment.

All four of the group sat silently as the landau trundled along the lane until the coach approached the bridge at mid-point. As they passed over the bridge, they noticed that it was *not* boxed in. Each of the passengers looked at the others and all shared the same thought. No attempt had been made to protect the commune. Emulating their river, the commune would – this time – simply 'go with the flow' of events.

They passed over the bridge and continued along the lane between the two rows of mausolea and started the long gentle climb towards the capital. No-one was on duty inside the archway. They progressed down 'Main Street,' across 'Market Square' and along 'Castle Street' towards the castle itself. As they were trundling along, Amanda began to take in the fact that *all* the people were dressed in Georgian costume. She gazed vacantly at Thorne. "I thought it was just the *coachman* who dressed like this!"

The coach passed under the gatehouse and halted outside the front door of the castle. As the Chief was the last person in, he was the first person out and after assisting Amanda with her dismounting, he led them towards the castle door where he swung once on the great brass knocker.

A great boom echoed inside the castle and the door was quickly opened by Veronica who ushered them inside. Thorne and Amanda were surprised to see a large number of foreign visitors standing in the hall. It looked like an international ambassadorial convention. Noting their reaction, the Chief informed them that all these people had been like themselves – former agents of the elite. They had been carrying out similar duties in their own countries to prepare their own people for the exodus.

Thorne and Amanda were introduced to the various dignitaries and their eyes beheld an array of national costumes. From European slacks to Arabian kaftans, from Asian robes to Oriental smocks – a panoply of cultures was on display. People from all over the world – men and women – had created a common destiny that would give *everyone* their ultimate dream – a *permament* end to suffering. Finally, there would be equality and peace for everyone – *forever*.

In order for this to happen, humanity was being forced to confront and to embrace the one aspect of life that it dreaded the most. A force that daily demonstrated its love for humanity by removing all pain and giving peace to the chosen recipient. A force that – despite its gentle nature – was hated and feared by virtually everyone. Its name was Death.

Death released all from the torments of 'Life' – which actually represented prolonged spiritual death whilst incarcerated within an incarnate prison. The supreme irony was that humanity longed for the fruits of Death whilst dreading the bearer of those fruits!

Thorne bore this in mind as he and Amanda engaged with his 'Fratres et Sorores.'

Over the next hour, Thorne and Amanda engaged with scores of people all of whom radiated a strange surreal peace. Despite exoteric differences of colour, culture and costume; *eso*terically, they were One when linked with their gestalt – and it showed. As they conversed, flickers of turquoise flame danced above their heads. Amanda gazed open mouthed at what she was witnessing. Every so often, she would look up to see if there was a tongue of celestial fire above her own head – there wasn't.

Finally, everyone's attention was diverted as the Duke, Carenza, Victoria and Virginia descended the stairs. Veronica walked across the room and joined them. The Duke and the senior members of his family waited for all the general conversation to end. As silence descended, the Duke addressed the gathered assembly. "Within this room, all agents of our gestalt are now assembled. We are One – with *our* gestalt, but those outside have yet to join with *their* gestalt and the two unite as the Holy Ghost!" The Duke smiled and all assembled reflected his smile. "Events are unfolding as they should. They cannot be reversed or deflected. We have about one month to prepare for the exodus. However, being mindful of the fact that all of us have been taught to be cautious; I plan for ourselves to ascend within two weeks time. Our severance will liberate our gestalt to unite with its larger 'twin' outside. Once this is done, the reconstructed Holy Ghost will provide heaven – sorry – *haven* for all liberated souls. As the Holy Ghost, we can then elect to either leave this world immediately and search for another to begin a new cycle of evolution, or we can wait for a while and watch this world as it becomes uninhabitable and mutates through various stages until it finally joins with the sun. Even as the Holy Ghost, we still need to complete the final stage of our evolution before we are allowed to return home to *heaven* and to God – The Eternal Source of Perfection!"

"Divine Willing!" the collective murmured.

"Divine Willing!" the Ducal family replied.

On this parting note, the formality broke and everyone resumed their conversation. Thorne watched as the Duke approached his 'twin' and smiled as Amanda's face betrayed her surprise at the similarity between the two men. The Duke grinned as he immediately read Amanda's thoughts and quoted aloud: "As above....."

"..... so below – *but after another manner!*" finished Thorne.

"Tweedledum and Tweedledee, more like!" muttered Amanda under her breath.

Thorne cringed, but the Duke beamed. "Good analogy! *I like this one!*"

"This one has a name." said Amanda, seeing Thorne in the Duke's face.

"I'm sure you do. Please come with me and meet my three daughters."

Amanda looked blankly at Thorne as she was gently propelled away.

"That was too close for comfort!" said the Chief's voice in Thorne's ear.

Thorne paused and then smiled. "She has no chance with my other self!"

---oOo---

Over the next few hours, Thorne and Amanda began to adjust to the atmosphere and to the excellent cuisine that had been placed on numerous sideboards along both sides of the hall. Initially, they had both been a little reticent since their stomachs were still not quite up to working capacity, and the idea of throwing up in the middle of a party did not appeal to them at all. Even so, towards the end, they had managed to do *some* justice to the festivities and were somewhat relieved when they were finally reunited to be guided uptairs to the room that Thorne had occupied many years ago. The Duke smiled knowingly as he opened the door to reveal a familiar four poster bed with *two* pillows, side by side. He nodded to Thorne and Amanda. "With your permission, I will bid you both good night. Breakfast will be at your convenience. Everything has been prepared in advance. Please be at liberty to do as you wish – until the exodus."

Thorne nodded and was about to bid the Duke good night when Amanda interjected. "Thank you for everything. Good night, your Grace."

The Duke paused in mid-turn and looked back with a smile. "Good night, Amanda."

As the Duke departed, Thorne looked at Amanda – who had an odd smile on her face. He nudged her in the ribs. "*After another manner!*"

"After another man? Er......" she teased, and shrieked as he threw her onto the bed.

---oOo---

The following morning, Thorne showed Amanda how to prepare and they both spent a long time in the bath at the end of the corridor playing in soapy state. By the time they had dressed and had gone downstairs for breakfast, the Ducal family were about their tasks. Fortunately for them, Virginia was available and she brought them bacon and eggs followed by toast and honey and a large pot of mint tea. Thorne correctly guessed that the 'outsider's fare' was in deference to Amanda's sensibilities. He was informed that the Ducal family had breakfasted early in order to assist with serving all the dignitaries that had stayed in the castle. When Thorne gently inquired how Giles and Clive would fare with any surplus guests staying at the inn, Virginia looked very sad and told him that two years ago, Clive had come into the parlour one morning to find Giles lying on the floor. His little friend's heart had finally given out. Everyone was aware of the event and they had stayed away out of respect as they all knew that Clive would quickly follow. Later that day, they opened the front door to find Clive lying next to his friend with one arm protectively over his shoulder. They were both placed together in one of the niches in the catacombs. Their names were added to the list of names that were carved on the wall of the mausoleum above. Virginia looked intensely at Thorne and Amanda. She smiled. "*No more pain, only eternal peace.*"

Thorne understood. He nodded and looked at Amanda. "*For those who love.*"

Amanda was silent as she tried to assimilate the significance of those words.

Thorne kissed Amanda. "*Everyone dies alone. Love re-unites us.*"

Virginia leaned over and kissed Amanda. "*Remember.*"

Amanda found herself looking at Virginia.

Virginia just smiled and walked away.

After they had breakfasted, Thorne decided to acclimatise Amanda by taking her directly to the Solstice Temple. He judged correctly that one such as she would be able to absorb the full impact of their purpose. Privately, he had been amazed that she had not become hysterical when the tulpa had materialised in their aircraft. He sensed that its manifestation for their 'reasurrance' was *not* its primary function. The gestalt was already re-conditioning her by eliminating her personality – to reveal her as she truly was. Then, and *only* then, would she be free to fulfil her divine destiny.

They exited the castle and strolled down 'Castle Street' towards 'Market Square' and turned east to traverse its length. Amanda looked at the stone obelisk. "No clocks?"

Thorne shook his head. "Time means nothing to us. We follow the seasons."

Amanda cast another look and noted its shadow on the stone floor. "Of course."

They continued their way along the square until the open space closed in and ran down between two rows of houses to finally emerge into another *square* square! Thorne raised his hand and pointed towards the far side where a large domed building sat in silent expectation of events. "Mors Januar Vitae – Death is the Gate of Life!"

Amanda nodded. "The End and the Beginning." She smiled. "Far nobler than lying in one's own excrement whilst the body slowly rots before finally shutting down." She gazed at Thorne. "Suicide, even Euthanasia, has its place in a civilised society."

"True." agreed Thorne. "But the State does all it can to to dissuade people from this course because it demonstrates free thinking which opposes all forms of control over the masses. Under *this* culture, it is difficult to subdue a nation for the purposes of manipulation and exploitation. A nation that has Absolute Faith is blessed indeed!"

"*God is Great*! Quad Erat Demonstrandum!"

Thorne looked at Amanda and his eyes shone with love. "Let me show you inside."

Together they walked under the pillared portico where the two huge doors were both ajar. Amanda gasped as she saw the interior and even Thorne was surprised. Before them the huge round stone altar stood underneath a colossal metal dish whose sides had been extended to accommodate far more corpses than ten. Supporting the dish, three giant stone pillars surrounded the altar reminiscent of an enclosed Stonehenge.

Thorne's eyes had grown used to the gloom and he saw that there were now three huge alcoves in the temple walls. The temple builders had thought of everything!

They slowly walked underneath the perforated dish and emerged facing the east wall. The third alcove revealed a set of symbols that had been carved into it at the building of the temple. A circle containing a triangle containing a celestial eye. They smiled as a voice spoke to them. "*The circle represents Protection. The triangle represents Manifestation. The celestial eye represents Divinity. These symbols have been used to Protect those who would Manifest any aspect of the Divine. In turn, they would be guarded and guided by the manifesting gestalt or Holy Ghost, to evolve towards God.*"

Amanda's eyes had also become accustomed to the darkness beyond the light of the open doors and she was checking the orientation of the temple against its layout. She turned to Thorne. "I thought all pagan temples were oriented north/

south with focus in the north. Here, the emphasis is east/west reflecting Christo/Islamic values!"

"*Nothing is as it appears.*" said a voice that reflected the emanations of the gestalt.

They both turned to find a woman in the prime of life dressed in black with a white shawl and a pair of spectacles perched on her nose.

"Cordelia!" beamed Thorne, totally taken by surprise. He turned to Amanda. "This young lady saved my life!"

Cordelia blushed shyly. "Not possible. I only postponed your death – nothing more."

Anxious to avoid her further embarrasement, Thorne asked her what she had meant concerning the temple.

Being valued for her mind, Cordelia visibly perked up. "Traditionally, pagan temples *were* oriented north/south with the north dominant, whereas Christo/Islamic temples are oriented east/west with the east dominant. Our temple reflects our faith in that the *north* represents lunar darkness alluding to knowledge that is occult, hidden or secret. Our temple also reflects our faith in that the *east* represents the direction from which solar waves of light emanated westwards carying new religions. Many centuries ago, paganism was eclipsed by Christianity – a foreign import from the east. The western pagans received the 'smile' of the friend (the kiss), and let them in. Once established, they received the 'frown' of the ruler (the scourge), and were subdued. Centuries later, the west was eclipsed by Islam – a foreign import from the east. They received the 'smile' of the friend (the kiss), and let them in. Once established, they received the 'frown' of the ruler (the scourge), and were subdued. But, these apparent 'evils' are part of the Divine Plan. As our forest was shaped into the ideal form for survival by forces that seemed antagonistic, so humanity has been shaped into the ideal force by forms that seemed antagonistic! The first (Christo) wave taught us how to love 'Man.' The second (Islamic) wave taught us how to love God. Humanity has always been pagan at heart, but we receive Divine Emanations that 'chastise' us into higher states of awareness – *whether we like it or not.*

Amanda nodded. "Between emanations, we 'spare the rod and spoil the child' – thus requiring *another* emanation for correction." She smiled thinly. "Cause and Effect."

"Precisely! Since humanity *finally* learned how to love God, incarnation serves no further purpose – hence the exodus."

"What will happen here?" inquired Amanda, gesturing around the temple.

"The fire from scores of corpses will be so large it will melt the lead plug that crowns the dome. When that happens, a venturi effect will cause the flames to fly out of the dome skywards, gradually removing the air from the temple. Prior to rarification, we will have ascended to our spiritual realm. Do not fear rarification or confuse it with decompression or asphyxiation. There is no suffering. On this world, the fire in the temple will increase in temperature. Our temple will fulfil its final function – that of becoming a charnel-house."

Chapter 25

Thorne and Amanda spent the final two weeks exploring the contours of the land during the day and the contours of each other during the night. Towards the end of the fortnight – as Amanda stretched and relaxed after one of her nocturnal labours, she raised herself on one elbow and looked into Thorne's face. "Our time has nearly run out. Don't you fancy having just *one* go at 'drilling for oil' before we lose out bodies forever?"

Thorne groaned inwardly, but as her best friend, he knew he should communicate as fully as he could. He smiled gently at the love and concern that showed on her face. "My love for you goes far beyond mere lust. I know that you are totally self-fulfilled and do not actually need sex – least of all from a man! I live for *your* pleasuring and that gives me all the satisfaction that I need." He gazed at her body with admiration. "The well requires no 'drilling' – the oil gushes forth with gay abandon!"

Amanda actually blushed and looked away. "You are the only man who has *not* found that intimidating. My former partners all dropped me when they saw that I could 'outgun' them. For years, I've hated men because I thought I was a freak."

Thorne shook his head in disbelief. "Intimidated? Incredible! I've always dreamed of finding a woman like you. Attractive, healthy, vigourous – and above all, *honest*!"

Amanda looked back at him – a puzzled look on her face. "Honest? Please explain."

Thorne nodded emphatically. "Over the generations, men have evolved a distrust of women who are so adept at falsification, manipulation and intimidation. But, to find a woman who – by demonstrable evidence – cannot *fake* an orgasm certainly earns *my* admiration, *my* trust, and – over time – my *love*!" Thorne grinned. "*Who needs sex?*"

Amanda put her head on one side and looked quizzically at him. "*You're serious*!"

"Absolutely." Thorne became purposeful. "Shall I play with your body again?"

Amanda slowly smiled and snuggled down under the sheets. "Is all day, okay?"

"All day, is truly *my* pleasure!" replied Thorne, as he happily went prospecting.

---oOo---

Fully indulging each other's needs, they spent the last few days in a ocean of bliss.

---oOo---

On the morning of the last day, they awoke and prepared for the communal ascension. As required, they uni-formed themselves in the traditional hooded cloaks of grey and descended the stairs for their final breakfast of porridge with honey.

Arriving promptly for their final day, they were met by the entire Ducal family. As before, Veronica (the 'Maiden') was cloaked in dark green, Victoria (the 'Mother') wore dark red and Virginia (the 'Crone') was swathed in black. Sitting at the head and foot of the table respectively, both the Duke and Carenza were cloaked in dark purple reflecting Unity in Force/ Duality in Form. Also sitting at the table, cloaked in grey, two young men sat in silent expectation. The secret commune was finally about to fulfil its function for the world.

As Thorne and Amanda sat down, the Duke informed them that everyone would eat and drink lightly in order to begin the loosening of their automatic reliance on their bodies. They were also informed that all the non-assimilated (residents) had already passed beyond form and were waiting in summerland for the arrival of the nationals who would begin the process of their unification with the restored and unified gestalt.

Thorne looked at the Duke. "How will this assist the ascendancy of *all* humanity?"

"It won't!" replied the Duke. "The elite are elite for a reason. They are the ones that will ascend and *remain* discarnate. Those of a lesser nature will be held in stasis until another world is discovered whereupon they will have to reincarnate in other forms to begin again the process of evolution. Those of a lower nature will *not* ascend at all!"

"What happens to the latter?" inquired Amanda, uncomfortably aware that she was the only one whose aura had not been visible at all – let alone been turquoise-blue!

The Duke smiled knowingly at her. "You are safe because of your genuine love and compassion for my 'twin.' Those whose nature is based on fear and hate will die in *both* senses of the word. Their bodies will die of course, but their spirits will remain earthbound as ghosts until the earth joins the sun in final conflagration." The Duke noted Amanda's expression and continued. "This 'global warming' will eventually cease and the world will plunge into another ice-age. There will be several more of these episodes whereby the ghosts may incarnate in lower forms of evolving animal life, but they will never ascend to our state nor enter our realm. In the end, the final global warming will become a global *burning* – hell on earth as it *becomes* the sun." The Duke smiled pleasantly as he offered the pot around the table. "Mint anyone?"

Amanda felt immense relief that she would share 'haven' with Thorne, but felt chilled at the prospect that there was, indeed, a hell. "What happens after aeons of burning for those trapped in the sun?"

"They will float isolated in darkness until the end of time. When time ends, it will begin to reverse and all that still exists in the universe will begin to un-create until it passes beyond the point of its own creation. When that happens, *it never will have existed.* God's clean-up is perfect – *and absolute!*"

Amanda nodded awestruck. "*God is God!*"

"Precisely!" smiled the Duke.

---oOo---

When they had all finished their final breakfast, they all rose and began their final journey from the castle to the solstice temple. The journey from the castle to the gatehouse was an informal one and it afforded Thorne the opportunity to thank the Duke for enabling Amanda to in-form herself as to the nature and purpose of God.

"Due to us being incarcerated in physical forms, it is sometimes necessary for one aspect of divinity to remind another aspect of its true nature and purpose via occult communication popularly referred to as subliminal influence. Amanda is informing herself via her own in-tuition. This is an example of '*a posteriori*' programming."

As the group emerged from under the portcullis, Thorne experienced a sense of déjà vu as he saw that the entire route to the temple lay between two rows of grey-robed nationals and agents. The Duke and his wife led the family in procession for the last time. As before, the two lines of people closed in behind them as they walked slowly along a route that had become so familiar to Thorne. Eventually, they emerged into the square square and the pillared portico of the temple loomed into view. Reaching the temple, they walked under the portico and went inside.

As Amanda's eyes took in the view of the tripodal pillars supporting the huge dish, she saw scores and scores of mummified corpses piled inside and the significance of the event finally dawned on her. As the citizens were beginning to file inside, she turned a horrified face towards the love of her life and shook her head, her eyes pleading for his understanding and his forgiveness. "*I can't do it! God forgive me, I can't do it!*"

Thorne turned to reassure her but his 'twin' interrupted. "*Let her go!*" said the Duke.

As everyone filed in and took their place, one grey-robed figure fought the flow of the river and left the temple to stand alone outside. Amanda now knew the real meaning of the phrase 'outsider.' She watched everyone else go inside and the two great doors slowly closed. As they met, there was one loud boom followed by two clangs as bolts were drawn across the doors barring entry to all whom God had 'marked' as profane.

Inside the temple, the three daughters of the Duke each took their places by the pillars that supported the great dish. In the north-west, Veronica stood with her back against her pillar symbolising Virtue. In the south-west, Victoria stood with her back against her pillar symbolising Valour. In the east, Virginia stood proud with her back against her pillar symbolising Victory. Thorne noticed that the four tools that had symbolised the four terrestrial elements were now absent. He felt a chill as he saw that the tool of the missing (celestial) element – the candle – was now present, lit, and securely held in the hands of his 'twin' – the Duke.

His 'twin' spoke to all assembled. "As there are many spokes on the wheel that lead from the outer rim to the inner hub, so there are many paths that lead from the outer world to the inner realm. Each path appears different and separate from its neighbour when seen from the rim, but all paths start to blur as they converge on the hub. At the hub all paths terminate at the one mystic goal. *All become One.*"

"*All become One!*" everyone chanted.

The Duke himself, slowly climbed the ladder that led to the massive perforated dish. In his hand he held the one candle that would light the pyre of corpses. Arriving at the top, he carefully lit the pyre of brushwood that would start a reaction that would herald the end of their terrestrial existence and the beginning of their celestial return.

---oOo---

Standing alone outside the temple, weeping in despair and loneliness, Amanda heard the words of the Duke and then silence. All the residents had committed suicide via the 'top shelf' herbs of the herbalist and the doctor. The bodies of the residents were all lying peacefully on their beds in a state of simple dignity – in very marked contrast to those in the outside world.

Amanda stood alone wanting to die but not knowing how. Her induction incomplete, she knew her future but the knowledge terrified her. The Abyss of Doubt assailed her soul and – in pure terror, it cried out for divine aid.

She felt the wind blow gently on her face and wiped away the tears that blinded her eyes. She looked towards the temple praying that the doors would open and that her love would walk outside to meet her and tell her that everything was going to be fine. But the doors remained shut and the little man guarding them would not open them for her. *What little man?* She jerked awake as she realised that there was a 'familiar' spirit in the guise of a Buddhist monk sitting in a lotus position who had been hidden in the shadow of the portico. Knowing him – or rather *it* to be benevolent, she slowly walked towards this, this – *creature*, this – *tulpa.*

Standing only a few feet away, she was startled when its eyes opened and a mildly reproachful voice came into her mind. *"Please do not regard me as a creature."*

Hearing its 'voice' for the first time, Amanda could only stand and stare – all thoughts of loss and fear forgotten. "You speak!" was all Amanda could say.

The tulpa shook its head in negation. *"You hear."* the voice replied.

Amanda tried to voice her fears and her needs but was struck dumb.

The tulpa smiled gently. *"Now we are equal. We cannot speak, we can only hear."*

"Christ!" thought Amanda. *"He can read my thoughts!"*

Chapter Twenty-five

"*Thank you for accepting this form – but I am not Christ.*"

Amanda was instantly confused, but the tulpa just smiled. "*Sit with me for a while.*"

Feeling like an actor in a play that has suddenly become surreal, Amanda dumbly complied and prayed that he could understand her and help her face her fears of life – and of death.

Being unable to speak, all Amanda could do was to gaze desperately into the monk's face and pray that he could understand – as she had never felt so helpless or hopeless in all her life.

The monk nodded and smiled. He started fiddling with the amber and jet beads that hung around his neck. The action distracted Amanda and she found herself absorbed in the significance of those beads.

"*They symbolise many things. For me, they symbolise the hypocrisy of life that the outside world relies upon. Under the pretext of human rights, the rich countries only defended the human rights of those countries that could offer payment. Payment in gold – either yellow or black. Tibet could not offer gold nor oil. To western eyes, Tibet had nothing to offer of any financial value and so China continued without opposition from those who wielded authority. In the end, it took ordinary citizens to begin a momentum that culminated in the release of Tibet from China – momentum that was initialised by a torch of hope that was carried across the world for another purpose. But when two practices carrying the same principle coincide, then anything is possible.*"

"*How can that help me?*"

"*Apart from a few monasteries high in the mountains of Nepal and Tibet, you will be the only survivor on a dead world. Even* *those monasteries will eventually fall as famine reaches the highlands. Death is inevitable. <u>Love forms your 'link' to the hidden realm. Ask for death and you will live</u>.*"

"*No pain! Please God, no pain!*"

"*Death brings peace, not pain.*"

Amanda looked into the eyes of the monk and saw no deception - he offered release.

"*Release me from this torment!*"

The old man smiled and Death touched Amanda. Everything went blank, and when her vision cleared, she was witnessing the events that were happening in the temple.

The pyre was well alight, the flames a hissing hue of gold-orange that twisted like a set of hydra's coils. Everyone was clearly still alive and the children smiled without any trace of fear. Amanda watched and waited for something else to happen. She didn't have to wait long, there was a terrific WHOOMF, and the dome of the temple rang like a bell from hell. She saw Thorne smile - *he'd seen this before!* All were transfixed as the flames turned blue-green. They grew taller and a roaring sound was heard as though someone had just turned on the gas. The roaring grew louder and the temple reverberated with the sound. Massive turquoise flames flew upwards and all the harmonics of the temple chorused in one colossal howl. The howl finally stabilised and became one continuous hum. Everyone was apparently used to this and it was obvious to Amanda that they were waiting for something else to happen.

She saw the turquoise flames grow taller until they reached the lead plug that sealed the dome. The lead plug began to melt and soon a silver rain began to fall onto the corpses until there was a huge burst of flame as the seal was opened. This triggered a venturi effect and a tornado of blue fire roared skywards. The humming of the temple changed tone and became a howl of triumph. Amanda looked at the people and saw that their eyes had changed colour. They glittered silver and silver tears began to run down their faces as auras of turquoise fire surrounded their bodies. One by one, they began to fall like snowflakes. More and more sank to the floor their faces all wearing an expression of sublime peace. Eventually, everyone had fallen to rest together and still the flames grew. The fallen bodies began to smoulder. Soon, all the bodies were smoking heavily and began to melt. Gentle faces darkened and charred like dolls in a furnace until no-one was recognisable. Ascension by rarification was a very civilised form of exodus.

Amanda entered the turquoise flames and was taken slowly up through the roof of the dome where she viewed the plan of the temple from on high. She saw through the dome to the great circle that was supported by the triangle of pillars. In the centre of the dish, an aura of turquoise flames blazed that surrounded a silver eye. The gestalt was commencing its final unification with its unconscious greater self. Soon, all that was hidden – *occult* – would become Universal Awareness forever.

Amanda had seen enough. She needed to leave this dead and dying world and found herself standing amidst legions of spirits who radiated eternal light in this timeless realm. She heard a voice though no voice had spoken. "*All are One.*"

"*Gestalt*" they all echoed.

---oOo---

Epilogue

As predicted, the world became one vast malarial swamp. The mammals and avians had a particularly hard time of it. The reptiles and amphibians suffered too. Only the insects were relatively undisturbed – for them it was pretty much business as usual. Occasionally, out of the filth, blue-green flames would emerge and dance aimlessly around. Occasionally too, these aimless flames would grow, take vague form and move ghostlike over the swamps as though searching for life-forms to inhabit and perhaps evolve until they could enter the 'havenly' realm in order to raise their hell.

The gestalt (holy ghost) would observe them dispassionately from its realm until the following ice-age. After that, it would leave to seed another world and observe a new generation of generations. In so doing, it would continue to travel the universe like a glorious magellanic cloud cyclically refining and redefining itself until it had attained perfection. It would then be summoned to return to heaven and remain with God as its universe was being un-created. At point zero of un-creation, the multi dimensions of space and time (constituting the Abyss) would close and seal shut – thus perfecting the Cabala.

Afterword

Assuming that you have read this work, I truly hope that you have developed at least one quality that all governmental 'elitists' would desperately prevent you from acquiring. They have given this word so many negative connotations that everyone is convinced that it is a 'dirty' word - a word of sedition. This word is 'Discrimination.'

What does the word 'Discrimination' mean to you? What does it evoke within you?

Feelings of *fear* because of what others might think of you?

Feelings of *hate* because of what you might think of others?

Nearly everyone is ruled by the State via fear and hate - and this is the 'control' word.

Society's Salvation, however, lies within the Good Book.

It is not the Bible, nor the Qur'an, nor the Torah, nor the Dharma, not the Gita. It is not in any Holy Book. It is simply the *Dictionary*. Please study this Common Work. It shows the true meaning of words thus highlighting all that is profound and profane.

Governments think long-term. When honest citizens are forced via circumstances of legalised *in*justice to take action that results in their imprisonment and are soon freed by the donations of some obscure 'anonymous benefactor,' the government is merely playing one of its cards of damage limitation. This diffuses public anger thus keeping the citizens quiescent for future manipulation and exploitation. Individual criminals are of little concern to the State as they invariably target the masses – not the 'elite.' However, when the citizens en masse begin to rise up as one against the government, then the State is forced to act in self-preservation. It admits anyone from any culture under a policy of Diversification. Diversification prevents *unification* of the masses *as one* against the State. It also serves to create a large gene pool for future eugenics programmes – note the sperm banks created for *our* (?) convenience.

Governments also think relatively. They accept the occasional loss of 'pennies' if it keeps society quiescent. They know all too well that in the long-term they are saving 'pounds' and are maintaining control by keeping their perceived 'inferiors' ignorant. How many media promotions subliminally emphasise that 'dumb' is cool?

On the other hand, governmental policies may be the key to our future survival. If we adopt the matriarchal 'hive' culture of the insects and forgo the patriarchal predatory culture of the animal kingdom, humanity may well continue in its incarnate form for generations to come. Remember, it is the *insects* who will survive in the long-term!

Regards, John George Odd

Glossary

Avatar (Divine Exemplar)
Avatar Exemplars are of the highest order. They
manifest in pivotal moments of humanity's history in
order to cause change to occur in conformance with
the Will of God.

Cabala (Kabala, Qabala etc.)
A Judaic system of interlinked levels of awareness
whose states of automatic emanation are experienced
by traversing paths of systematic progression.

Conceptive Thought (Intuitive – what it is by what it is)
Automatic conclusion reached without temporal
deduction.

Deductive Thought (Intellectual – what it is by what it isn't)
Systematic conclusion reached using temporal
deduction.

Empathic (Psychism)
A shared creative awareness between evolving
intelligencies.

Empiricism (Philosophical)
    Exponents – Locke, Berkeley and Hume.
    Forerunner – Aristotle.

Esoteric (Illuministic – the study of the Cause)
    The study of the invisible realm and its effects on
    the visible world by identifying subliminal truths via
    arcane practices.

Exoteric (Academic – the study of the Effect)
    The study of the visible world and its effects on
    the visible world – resulting in the re-affirmation of
    established truths.

Gestalt (exoteric definition)
    An organised whole that is perceived as greater than
    the sum of its parts. (Oxford English Dictionary)

Gestalt (esoteric explanation)
    A unified collective discarnate intelligence that is
    gradually created over time from the minds of an
    ordered society. It mirrors that society and can
    eventually become self-aware. It is the conceptual
    source of the Holy Ghost/Divine Link.

Mage (Occult)
    One who has turned theory into practice. A
    transmitter.

Mystic (Sage)
    One who is linked to a gestalt and has semi-divine
    vision.

Occultist (Theorist)
    One who studies the hidden realm via arcane texts.

Psychism (Empathic)
> A shared creative awareness between evolving
> intelligencies.

Psychism (Vampiric)
> A draining of life forces between devolving
> intelligences or a form of Shunamitism as exemplified
> by King David with his favourite concubine Abeshag,
> the Shunamite girl.

Qlippoth ('Shells')
> The remnants of ancient primitive gestalts that are
> still partly active. No longer conducive to an evolving
> society. Avoid!

Rationalism (Philosophical)
> Exponents – Descartes, Spinoza and Leibniz.
> Forerunner – Plato.

Rosicrucianism (Celestial Principle – the Force)
> The evolutionary path for Man to ultimately unite with
> God.

Rosicrucianism (Terrestrial Practice – the Forms)
> The name used by several terrestrial orders who
> propagate the celestial principle with varying degrees
> of success.

Sage (Mystic)
> One who is linked to a gestalt and has semi-divine
> vision.

Stone Taping
> A somewhat archaic term used to explain the
> 'recording' of images or impressions received by
> psychic researchers when they are within an area
> of, or in contact with, space or form occupied by a
> gestalt.

Tulpa (mystical origin and magical origin)
Refer to Character Symbolism – Assimilated Nationals
(Cardinal)

Witchcraft (Hereditary, Gardnerian, Alexandrian, Dianic,
Celtic, Saxon.)
The craft of the wise involving healing (herbal
and psychic), the study of natural forces (Gaea
philosophy), celebrating the seasons (ritual) and
protection/projection via spellcraft.

Commentary

Rosicrucian Cabalistic States of Awareness ('Grades')

Ipsissimus (10 = 01) 'Release' for Eternity (Transcendence)
  The tenth Rosicrucian grade equating to Kether
  (Judaism) or Anatta (Buddhism) or Brahman
  Abstraction (Hinduism).
  It is the culmination of the Mystic* pillar (Cabalism).
  (Cardinal/Not-being/Abstraction/Regeneration/Anti-
  Stasis).

Magus (09 = 02) 'Change' for the Future (Universal Wisdom)
  The ninth Rosicrucian grade equating to Hokma
  (Judaism) or Anicca (Buddhism) or Shivan
  Transformation (Hinduism).
  It is the culmination of the Orphic* pillar (Cabalism).
  (Mutable/Becoming/Externalising/Transformation/
  Fission).

Magister (08 = 03) 'Sorrow' for the Past (Universal Empathy)
  The eighth Rosicrucian grade equating to Bina
  (Judaism) or Dukka (Buddhism) or Vishnan
  Preservation (Hinduism).

It is the culmination of the Hermetic* pillar
(Cabalism).
(Fixed/Being/Internalising/Assimilation/Fusion).

The three supernal states above tend to blend into each other
and can be regarded in the following way. The Magus and
the Magister are two sides of the same coin of the Ipsissimus
which is Universality.

Magus ('Sunlit' Yang of Ipsissimus – mirror's Islam)
    Tarot magician's right arm raised to the celestial
    realm
    Project Divinity for Humanitiy's sake (Guide)
    Divinity is essential for the Plan (Wise)
    Change Expressed (for Love of God)
    Aspirant conditioned for Becoming
    Sees the future (what Will be)
    Magical Extension (Catalysis)
    Prioritising Divinity
    Progressive Participator
    Chaos Theories
    Philosophical
    Fission
    Mutable

Magister ('Shaded' Yin of Ipsissimus – mirror's Christ)
    Tarot magician's left arm lowered to the terrestrial
    world
    Protect Humanity for Divinity's sake (Guard)
    Humanity are essential to the Plan (Kind)
    Sorrow Impressed (for Love of Man)
    Candidate conditioned for Being
    Sees the past (what was Lost)
    Mystical Intention (Analysis)
    Prioritising Humanity

Orthodox Observer
Order Theories
Psychological
Fusion
Fixed

Definitions of the middle and lower 'grades' vary according to the interpretations of the various pseudo-orders. Ideally, there should be a smooth transition from the functions of those 'grades' listed below to the functions of the three supernal states defined above. It must be emphasised that *the smoother the transition, the purer the order*!

Adeptus Exemptus	(07 = 04)
Adeptus Majoris	(06 = 05)
Adeptus Minoris	(05 = 06)
Philosophus	(04 = 07)
Practicus	(03 = 08)
Theoricus	(02 = 09)
Zelator	(01 = 10)

*Cabalistic/Masonic 'Pillars' of Wisdom, Beauty & Strength.

Mystic Pillar (Spiritual Unity – Neutrality)
The path of Faith via Emanation. For 'Avatar Exemplars.'

Orphic Pillar (Mental Duality – Positive)
The path of Truth via Experience. For 'Pagan Artists.'

Hermetic Pillar (Mental Duality – Negative)
The path of Truth via Education. For 'Occult Scientists.'

Character Symbolism

THORNE

David Thorne symbolises **The Fool** in the lowest terrestrial sense. He goes through life searching for a partner, purpose and plan. He is restless and initially unfulfilled. His apparently arrogant and pushy manner conceals a lonely and frustrated soul that is trapped within several layers of prisons – his mind, his body and his world. Because of this, he is spiritually blind and emotionally isolated. His nature is ideally suited to his profession – but, ironically; the more successful he is, the more unfulfilled he is. Because of his tenacious drive and willpower, he also symbolises **The Chariot**. As Thorne encounters each of the 'people' he is inducted with that corresponding aspect of the gestalt, but the twin sphinxes of his nature bear constant watching!

CHEVRAL

Chevral symbolises **Justice** and is responsible for the protection of the exoteric aspect of the 'hidden' community. Being linked to the gestalt, he is fully aware of the nature and purpose of Thorne. As a result, he simply allows Thorne to fall into his own trap. Although he is a lawyer and a diplomat, he uses those skills only in accordance with the Divine Plan, and *not* merely for the arrogant and evil joy of manipulating others!

TYLER

Tyler symbolises the **Caution** of the Outer Guard as used in Masonic Lodges. He is on guard to deter all civilised minds from profaning the commune *before their time*. Unfortunately, the influence of his office precludes him from being able to deter any criminal mind. This alludes to the fundamental truth that evil cannot be neutralised by Human Rights which is really Diplomatic Appeasement. It can only be defeated by Natural Justice – referred to as *the country's real defence*. It also means that evil cannot be defeated by 'legal justice' of the liberal political elite, but only by natural justice of the people. Like the bees, the 'workers of the world must unite' if they are to be heard via national referendum.

MYCROFT

Mycroft symbolises **Fortitude**. He is the twin of Maxwell (symbolising temperance). He is pure of heart, gentle in conduct, long suffering and patient. He is attractive to many ladies and admired by many gentlemen. He is the proverbial 'gentle giant.'

BRADLEY

Bradley symbolises **Humility**. He is the twin of Bentley who symbolises creativity.

GILES & CLIVE

Giles and his 'twin' Clive are semi-nationals. Collectively they symbolise **Harmony**.

VERONICA (Beauty)

The youngest of three sisters and daughter of the Duke. Very empathic with compassionate qualities that give her awareness of the human heart. Constant exposure to children has imprinted her with a need for a partner who embodies a father-figure image for her to admire. She needs a 'parent' and symbolises **Virtue**. She wears green which symbolises freedom and is the classic wiccan 'Maiden.'

VICTORIA (Strength)

The middle of three sisters and daughter of the Duke. Very emotional with passionate qualities that puts the fear of God in most human hearts. Constant exposure to the dying has imprinted her with a need for a partner who embodies qualities of patience and passion. She needs a 'partner' and symbolises **Valour**. She wears red which symbolises thraldom and is the classic wiccan 'Mother.'

VIRGINIA (Wisdom)

The eldest of three sisters and daughter of the Duke. Very experienced with dispassionate qualities that give her awareness of the human race. Constant exposure to nature has imprinted her with a need to pass on her experiences to all who are willing to learn from her. She needs a 'purpose' and symbolises **Victory**. She wears black which symbolises wisdom and is the classic wiccan 'Crone.'

STRAKER

Straker symbolises **The Hierophant** and is responsible for the protection of the esoteric aspect of the 'hidden' community. He is also responsible for realigning potentially good souls who have begun to show signs of wandering from the path.

'DUSTY'

'Dusty' the miller symbolises **The Hermit** as he 'lives and labours in isolation.' As master to Thorne's mystical chela/occult apprentice, he stands aside to allow Thorne to experience this aspect as part of his spiritual training – to 'labour in darkness.'

STEDMAN & SPELMAN

Stedman and his twin Spelman symbolise **The Sun** and **The Moon** respectively. As they are symbolically indistinguishable from each other, they love to play tricks on the unwary. They work as do the fabled identical twin guardians of identical twin passages that lead from a sealed underground chamber. The seeker needs to escape his thraldom and notices words on a wall stating that one passage leads to liberation and the other passage leads to annihilation, and that one guardian always shows truly and the other guardian always shows falsely. He can ask only one question but both guardians are indistinguishable. To escape, what question does he ask – regardless of the guardian? *The answer alludes to the very nature of the human condition itself!*

QUELLER

Queller symbolises **The Star** as his profession represents (to Thorne) a simpler, purer age of communicative journalism. In ages past, the light shone brightly before clouds of corruption obscured its clarity.

MAXWELL

Maxwell symbolises **Temperance**. He is the twin of Mycroft (symbolising fortitude). Never subtle, he loves working with heavy tools and hammers away contentedly in order to refine or redefine metal. Tempering is the process of refining and purifying for fitness of purpose. The phrase 'fit for purpose' is used commonly and carelessly in the outside world in conjunction with Quality Systems (BS, EN, ISO and TQ).

CORDELIA

Cordelia symbolises **The Lovers**. She is in love with love itself and is self-fulfilling. Her eyesight is poor inferring that pure love is blind. She wears black symbolising an avoidance of normal social customs – even of her own culture. She is apprenticed to Lucinda who watches over her. She specialises in pharmacology and herbalism.

LUCINDA

Lucinda symbolises **The Magician**. She studies occultism and works magic. She is also gifted in surgical and medical techniques and has taught these skills to another of her apprentices – Victoria. Lucinda wears black symbolising an avoidance of normal social customs – even of her own culture. As an *occultist*, she has a view of humanity that is – rather ironically – similar to Thorne!

AGATHA

Agatha symbolises **Death**. It is a gentle, dignified and peaceful death. It is a death well earned and a relief to all. It is peace everlasting; eternal rest. It is the ultimate reward for a life well lived. It is also transformation and liberation. We go home.

BENTLEY

Bentley symbolises **Creativity**. He is the twin of Bradley who symbolises humility.

THE DUKE

The Duke symbolises **The Fool** in the highest celestial sense. As such, he always wears appropriately garish clothing and 'serves' to catalyse 'change' within all who encounter him. He also equates to **The Emperor** as he is responsible for the welfare of all his people. It is mentioned that he is physically similar to Thorne. This alludes to the universal truth that the final destination of the seeker is to meet himself. To see through a *mirror* darkly, *and then face to face*. This also follows the second hermetic principle of "as above, so below – but after another manner." He is, and is not he!

CARENZA

Carenza symbolises **Devotion**. As the *living* wife of the Duke, she also symbolises **The Empress** of **The World**.

CLARISSA

Clarissa symbolises **Devotion**. As the '*dead*' wife of the Duke, she also symbolises **The Priestess** of **The Wheel**.

THE GESTALT / HOLY GHOST / DIVINE LINK

Holds the Cabalistic forces of **The Hanged** and **Judgement** symbolising **Submission** and **Resurrection**.

THE OUTSIDE WORLD

Holds the Qlippothic forces of **The Devil** and **The Tower** symbolising **Temptation** and **Annihilation**.

---oOo---

SEGREGATED RESIDENTS (Fixed)

Representing retired stagnant material success. They are segregated from the gestalt by personal choice and collectively symbolise the decadence within any society.

ASSIMILATED RESIDENTS (Mutable)

They respond to the gestalt and convey that response by art in its various expressions.

ASSIMILATED NATIONALS (Cardinal)

They currently exist as incarnate mortals in total symbiosis with their created gestalt. Over time, they will eventually cease to incarnate but their *essence* will remain within their 'holy ghost' and they will continue to manifest as exemplar tulpas or self-aware thought forms in order to guide all compatible souls home. These exemplar tulpas function in a similar way to avatar exemplars but are of an inferior order. The former emanate from the Holy Ghost and the latter emanate from God Itself. As their name suggests, *exemplar* tulpas are beneficent. They only 'die' as such when their specific function is ended. They are then reabsorbed into the gestalt from whence they came in the same way that the 'angels' are reabsorbed into God. (2nd Hermetic Principle)

It must be stressed that a magically *conjured* tulpa is an extension of a magician's will and invariably degenerates into an unholy entity. This example serves to illustrate the fundamental difference between *mystical* origin and *magical* origin. Once again, the 2nd Hermetic Principle of – "as above, so below but after another manner" – applies.

---oOo---

THORNE (As The Proverbial Outsider)

Thorne experiences each major arcana card (facet of the gestalt) as from a *random* shuffle (as would any person seeking a reading). A random presentation catalyses assimilation and evolution whereas a systematic presentation does not. This is a subtle but significant difference between Art (conceptive) and Science (deductive). This is *why* tarot cards are shuffled before a reading. The seeker is told to select only a few cards, and the tarot reader gives a reading from a relatively limited scope with a view to giving the seeker the confidence to make a few key changes to his/her life. Within *this* work, the entire deck of the major arcana is 'shuffled' and placed before the seeker (Thorne). Thorne represents *any* outsider. Like any outsider, he is affected by all terrestrial influences that are represented by the minor arcana ('life'). In order to evolve, he must embrace all aspects of the major arcana (the gestalt). Also like any outsider, Thorne contains certain latent qualities that have been pre-programmed into his psyche prior to his birth. In philosophical *rationalism* this pre-programming is referred to as '*a priori.*' This is 'void' within academic philosophical *empiricism*.

Alchemically speaking, in ancient times, the marriage of the black tincture (Science) with the white tincture (Art) should have begotten the red quintessence (Illuminism). Instead, all it begat was a grey tincture (Philosophy). The letter without the spirit or the form without the force.